A Being Darkly Wise

A NOVEL OF SURVIVAL

BY

JOHN ATCHESON

Copyright © 2012, John Atcheson

ISBN-10: 0985071214
EAN-13: 9780985071219

BOOK ONE:

A BEING DARKLY WISE

Plac'd on this isthmus of a middle state,
A being darkly wise, and rudely great:
With too much knowledge for the Sceptic side,
With too much weakness for the Stoic's pride,
He hangs between, in doubt to act or rest;
In doubt to deem himself a God or Beast ...

Alexander Pope, "An Essay on Man," Epistle I

PART ONE:

LESSONS FROM THE LAST SHAMAN

When Saya brought the beasts to heel, he saved some of their wildness, some of their wisdom, some of their cunning. He gave the wildness to the Bear, the wisdom to the Wolf, the cunning to Man. It is the Shaman's curse to have all three.

Lynx: One of the Last of the Dunne-za

CHAPTER 1

The ad was circled in bold red magic marker. Pete Andersen read it over and over while he waited for his morning coffee.

> *Learn survival skills in the majestic peaks of British Columbia's Eaglenest Mountains – one of the last remaining wild areas left. Month-long trial taught by an expert in all facets of wilderness. Not for the faint hearted.*

Then there was a number with a local area code, followed by: *Ask for Jake*. Pete flipped to the front page. *The City News*. One of those free rags that appear in most cities of any size. When Lenny showed up with his coffee, Pete asked, "When did you start carrying this fishwrap?"

"Oh that? Some Hollywood-lookin' dude left it there." He finished pouring the coffee, then said, "Spooky guy. When I got to the shop this morning he was standin' out front in the freezin' cold in his shirt sleeves lookin' like he was in the Bahamas. Came in, had a cup of coffee, asked a lot of questions, then left that paper right where you sit."

Pete studied the ad. He ran his finger across the last line as if he were reading Braille and mumbled, "Not for the faint hearted."

"What'd you say?"

He looked up, surprised, not realizing that he'd spoken out loud, then smiled. "Nothing. I'll have the usual."

"How about some jalapeño home fries with that oatmeal this mornin'?"

"Just the usual."

Lenny sighed, "Whole grain toast, no butter; one oatmeal, plain; half a banana; and a large orange juice comin' up." He headed for the counter, calling back over his shoulder, "How was the run this mornin'?"

"Pretty good. Ten miles in just over an hour."

"Smokin'."

"It's the oatmeal."

Lenny laughed and slipped behind the counter. The grill hissed to life and the aroma of onions, bacon, and sage sausage mingled with the coffee, and Pete felt a stab of hunger, sharpened by his run around Hains Point, over to the monuments, down the Mall and past the Capitol in the frigid pre-dawn chill. As usual, he had the little café to himself this early. He soaked up the warmth and savored the forbidden scents while he waited for his oatmeal and organized his day over at the EPA. First thing up was a meet and greet with the newly appointed administrator – Dan Keller. Have to remember to re-read that bio on Keller before going up, he thought.

He shoved the calendar back into his briefcase, wrapped his hands around the hot coffee and held it to his lips, letting the rising heat drive the sting out of his cheeks and hands. He read the ad again ...*One of the last remaining wild areas ... Eaglenest Mountains.* Did he know them? He visualized a map of British Columbia. *Nope, never heard of them.* Finally, he shoved the newspaper aside and pulled a file marked "Signature" from his briefcase and began to plow through a batch of memos. He signed most of them, a few he edited and put in a different folder to be re-written.

Behind the counter, Lenny started singing a Neville Brothers' version of *Bird on a Wire,* an old Leonard Cohen tune, as he set the grill sizzling and steaming anew with an assortment of onions and peppers and fried potatoes, while he waited for Pete's toast to pop. When it did, he delivered Pete's usual, and asked with a wink, "You sure you don't want a side of bacon or sausage with that oatmeal this mornin'?"

"Better watch it, Slim. I'll tell your doctor what kind of junk you've been eating."

Lenny laughed. "Long as you don't tell my old lady. You all set?"

"I'm good. Thanks." He ate slowly as he continued to work his way through the stack of memos, draft regulations, white papers, legal briefs – the stream of cellulose and ink that passed for progress at the EPA these days. When he was about halfway through, he slid them across the table and picked up the newspaper and stared at the ad again. *Not for the faint-hearted.*

He checked his watch. "Hey Lenny. Can I get the check?"

"Not too hungry this mornin'?"

"Guess not."

"You know Pete, wouldn't hurt you none to eat something besides oatmeal once in a while."

"That other stuff'll kill you."

"Better'n dyin' from boredom."

Pete looked at the remains of his breakfast: half-eaten toast, dry; plain oatmeal, now a congealed lump squatting in the center of the bowl; then contemplated the stack of folders. Pretty much the same stuff as yesterday and every other day; different words, same old equivocations. "Yeah. You're probably right." He took out enough money to cover the bill and leave a generous tip and laid it on top of the check. "Tell you what. Give me the *huevos rancheros* tomorrow. With extra jalapenos on the home fries."

"Whoa. Walkin' on the wild side?"

"Think I just saw my epitaph. 'Middle-aged man drowns in oatmeal. Heart in top condition'."

Lenny laughed and pocketed his tip. "Save the whales, Pete. Save them whales."

Pete organized the piles of paper and slipped them into his briefcase. It had been a long time since he'd saved any whales, he thought. Too damn long. He started toward the door, hesitated, then turned back and scooped up the copy of the *City News*. Lenny saw him and said, "What do you want with that?"

"There's an ad I want to check out ..."

"I saw it." Something in Lenny's voice made Pete stop.

"What? Aren't you always telling me I need to spice up my life?"

Lenny was quiet for a minute. He seemed to be weighing what to say next. He looked down and said, "You and me's friends, wouldn't you say?"

It occurred to Pete he'd had breakfast at Lenny's every morning in the six months since he and Elizabeth had separated, and lunch, too, on most days. Outside of Karen Flannigan and his staff, he'd seen as much of Lenny as anyone. He'd found himself talking to the old guy in those early mornings, and listening, and he'd come to like him, and trust him. "Yeah. We're friends."

Lenny stared straight into Pete's eyes. "Good. I'm tellin' you this as a friend, then. Don't be messin' with this Jake fella."

"Why?"

"He asked too many questions. Nosed around in other people's business. Includin' yours. Normally, I send a guy like that out the door knowin' nothin' more than what he knew comin' in an' he don't even notice it. But this guy? Other way around. Smooth as a squid in a barrel of soap. Felt like he picked my pocket. Far as I'm concerned, you want to spice up your life, you stick with jalapenos and forget about this guy an' his death trip."

CHAPTER 2

Outside Lenny's it was dark and the air was still frigid, but the eastern horizon was starting to glow, giving Pete the hope that the anemic February sun would finally show itself. The last week had been gloomy, and the plowed remains of the season's only snowfall had hung around too long, picking up the city's endless supply of grey-black grit and soot along the roads and sidewalks. Snow, Pete thought, was a lot like life. It starts out clean and white, and the longer it lasts, the dirtier and uglier it gets.

Enough of that, he told himself and returned to reviewing his day as he headed across the street. First up was Keller's meet and greet with the agency's top managers. He'll probably want to make it some kind of rah-rah meeting. Impress us with their commitment to protecting the environment and fighting global warming. But words are cheap, Pete thought. Be interesting to see what happens when scientific reality and politics collide.

Once inside, he showered and changed at the health center, then took the elevator to the suite that housed the agency's policy office and read with satisfaction the nameplate outside his suite: Peter Andersen, Acting Assistant Administrator for Policy. Now that the White House had their man in place, he'd get bounced back down to office director – the highest level a non-political federal civil servant could aspire to – and Dan Keller would appoint some minion with political aspirations to take his job. Still, office director wasn't bad for a guy just turning forty.

Jan was already at her desk right outside his office. The world's most effective gatekeeper. Not that he needed one these days. "Morning,

Pete. Your calendar's on your desk. Administrator at 9:00, conference call with the regions at 2:00. Pretty light other than that. Oh, yeah. Your wife's lawyer called. The papers are ready for your signature."

Pete felt as if he'd been punched in the stomach, but did his best to hide it. "Ask him to mail them to me. We're OK to take staff with us to the meeting?"

"Principals only."

"OK. Call Karen and see if she wants to go up together."

"Will do. You'll want those papers sent to your new place?"

"Yes. Please."

"I'll need that address. And when do I get to see this bachelor pad?"

Pete paused. Was she flirting with him? No. Probably wishful thinking, he decided. "I'll throw a party when they replace me."

"Can't wait," she said, grimacing.

"Hold all calls. And no one gets in except Karen, OK?"

Pete closed the door behind him and took out Dan Keller's bio. First in his class at Yale Law School. Clerked for the Supreme Court's Chief Justice. Eight years on the Hill rising to majority staff director for the Senate Judiciary Committee. General Counsel for one of the largest corporations in the country. Governor of Montana. On the board of directors for several Fortune 500 companies. Major contributor to the campaign. Smart, politically ambitious, collector of powerful friends. But not exactly a greenie.

On the plus side, he'd been an active outdoorsman for most of his life. Raised in Montana, he was an avid hunter and fly-fisher, and he'd ascended several major peaks in the Andes and the Himalayas, as well as Kilimanjaro and McKinley. All this at forty-three.

Mt. McKinley. Pete looked up at a set of photographs on his wall from the trip he and Elizabeth had taken to Denali early in their marriage. The two of them smiling back at the camera, standing in front of a braided stream bed, its various tributaries filled with terraced gravels, McKinley looming up behind them. Beside that, another of a grizzly mother shooing her cubs over a ridge, not twenty yards from where they'd stood. He remembered the jolt of adrenalin they'd felt when they'd encountered her, and how they'd relaxed once she'd disappeared. But the sow had come back over the crest, raised her immense bulk upright, and stared at them for several minutes, wagging her snout back and forth straining to catch their scent, a long cord of thick, mucus-laden spittle swaying from her massive maw as she'd cocked her head, trying to decide if they were a threat. He and Elizabeth stood stock still, her hand squeezing his so hard her nails punctured his skin, but he'd clenched his teeth and stayed silent until the grizzly dropped onto all fours and padded back over the hill. Much later, he showed her his wounded hand and they'd tried to laugh about it as they huddled together in their small tent and listened to wolves howl somewhere very near their camp site in a remote corner of the park.

To the right of the Denali pictures were a series of Elizabeth and him bouncing off the froth of class VI rapids on the Colorado River, and below those were four panoramic views of fields of wildflowers, their scarlets, indigoes, yellows, whites and greens set against the jagged granite peaks and summer snowpack near Carson Pass in the high Sierras.

He looked back at the young couple in the Denali picture – how old, twenty-eight or so? The man staring back at him seemed so full of hope and promise that he felt as if he had to hide from his steady gaze. "What happened to you?" he asked the young Pete.

"Shit. I'm a walking Prozac commercial," he mumbled. "Nuff of this." He began removing the pictures of him and Elizabeth, studying each in turn before placing them in a neat pile on the small conference table in his office. When he was done, he returned to his desk, glanced down and found the ad in the *City News* staring up at him from his desk top. Not for the faint-hearted? We'll just see about that. He dialed the number. After a few rings, someone picked up and said, "Jake Christianson."

"Uh ... I'm calling ..."

"You're calling about the ad."

"Yes."

"Tell me about yourself." The voice sounded like an idling chain saw – or maybe like something that would come from a burning bush.

"My name is Pete Andersen. I'm ...uh ...I'm the Acting Assistant Administrator for Policy ... at the ...uh ..."

"Environmental Protection Agency," Jake finished for him.

"Yes." As soon as he'd said it, Pete wished he could rewind and start the conversation over again. He'd never been one of those people who tossed around titles or anything and the whole idea of responding to an ad in the *City News* was starting to seem preposterous. Besides, Lenny's warning was still fresh in his mind.

"So. You interested in the survival course?"

"I'm not sure. Maybe."

"Maybe is it, Peter? You'd rather sit around in some faceless bureaucracy, editing memos that don't say anything for people who won't actually do what needs to be done?"

Pete's hackles went up, but he answered in a reasonable voice. "There'll be some room to do a little good. There always is."

"A little good, Peter? Think that'll get us where we need to go?"

"That's the way it works. You take what you can get."

"And if it's not enough?"

"You press the envelope a bit."

"Spoken like a good soldier."

Pete shifted in his seat. The conversation was beginning to feel like an inquisition. "You running a survival course or a therapy session?"

"I'm giving you a shot at getting your life back. A shot at redemption."

Pete shivered. Get my life back? Redemption? What the fuck? Too weird. The whole thing was just too weird. Lenny had been right. "Look, Mr. Christianson I'm sorry to have bothered you. Think I'll have to take a pass."

"Call me Jake. You remember when you were young, Peter, and your head was filled with dreams?" The man's words were starting to feel like medical probes, peering beneath his skin and uncovering long dormant diseases, and Pete wanted to hang up, but as Jake continued, something in the rumbling timbre of the man's voice held him on the line. "You get to a certain age, and you don't do something, all those dreams start to die, one by one."

Pete looked at the stack of pictures on his table. The one of Elizabeth and him at Denali was on top, still smiling back at the camera, frozen in a decade when she'd still believed in dreams. So had he, back then. Finally, he said, "That's what dreams do. They die."

"They don't have to. You can be more than the sum of your fears and failures. And you can do more than a little good. But you'll have to climb out of that fur-lined coffin you call a job, first. Come by All Souls Church tonight if you're interested. Seven o'clock."

CHAPTER 3

Pete stood at the window and stared down at the street. A thick cloud cover had moved in, obliterating the prospect of a sunny day and now a cold rain tapped at the glass, forming rivulets and flowing down the window pane, turning the street below into a kind of animated black and white Cezanne. While he watched the scene fracture and reassemble before him, he contemplated Jake's comment: *You'd rather sit around in some faceless bureaucracy, editing memos that don't say anything for people who won't actually do what needs to be done?* Shit. What did he know about how the system worked? You take what you can get, and when the time is right, you go for a bit more. It's all you can do. It's all anyone can do.

He'd been using these words to anesthetize himself for eight years. More, if he were honest. And they'd worked. But now, with that young Pete smiling up at him from the table, he heard Jake's chainsaw voice: *Think that'll get us where we need to go?* and the words lost their power to deceive. He watched the raindrops drizzle down the window, and felt as if his life was draining down with them, while he marked time in his ... fur-lined coffin.

And the thing was, the awful truth he was running from was this: it wasn't going to change much, even with the new guys. Congress danced to K-Street's tune, and nothing could happen without Congress, no matter how well-intentioned the administration might be. To get real change, someone would have to tell the American people they didn't have a divine right to blindly consume everything in sight, trashing the climate in the process. That kind of honesty? ... well, the system wouldn't tolerate it. So, we'll get a better brand of rhetoric, and maybe a little more action, but at the end of the day, it'll be the same ol' Washington two-step.

And what am I prepared to do? *A little good.*

When had it happened? When had he stopped trying? Or caring? A fur-lined coffin? Yeah. That's about it. He looked around at the accumulation of fifteen years of stuff – files; awards; pictures; the leather easy chair in the corner he and Karen had liberated from the General Counsel's office after working late one night. They'd slid it down the hall and slipped it into his office, laughing hysterically. Oddly enough, it was the thing he valued most. The rest of the stuff felt like a betrayal to that young Pete who stared up at him now from the table with trusting eyes. Somewhere along the line, he'd become the head architect of the Potemkin Village – in charge of incremental footholds in the face of an onslaught of insults, designed to create the illusion of progress. Pissing into the wind, his father would have said.

You don't do something, all those dreams start to die, one by one. Yeah. Well, fuck you, buddy. Welcome to the real world.

The phone rang, and he grabbed it, glad for the distraction.

"Peter?" It was his soon-to-be ex, Elizabeth, and she was spoiling for a fight. She was using that high-pitched nasal voice with the edge to it. "Quit stalling and sign the goddam papers."

"What's your hurry?"

"I'm getting married ... to Howard."

"You're marrying your divorce attorney? Are you sure that's ..."

But Elizabeth continued talking over him, "... And furthermore, I'm pregnant." There was triumph in her voice, but there was an equal measure of blame, too, and the unspoken part of that sentence – it's your fault I had to resort to this – sounded louder to Pete than the rest.

Yet he was surprised to find that he was happy for her, and he said, "I'm glad for you ..."

But she didn't hear him. She couldn't stop herself now, a decade of anger and frustration was boiling over and she wanted to hurt him the way she'd been hurt "...And another thing, Peter, I always hated all that environmental crap and those god-awful wilderness trips ..."

"I know. That's why I took you on them," he said.

There was a long silence, then she said, "Just sign the goddam papers," and hung up. It seemed impossible to believe that those two young people staring up at him from the picture on his table were the same people on that phone call. Certainly he'd stopped loving her a long time ago. And she him. It wasn't her fault. All she'd wanted was what everyone wanted – a life. Children.

They'd talked about kids early on. Being a father had seemed possible, then. Sometimes he'd imagined a little girl; someone who would beguile him into sharing all manner of feminine mysteries – fake tea parties, dolls, frilly dresses, magical ponies and unicorns. Or maybe she'd be a tomgirl who'd wear a Yankee's cap and share his love of sports.

But mostly he'd imagined a son.

Imagined standing out in the yard with him on one of those brilliant October days, brittle brown leaves hissing across the lawn in a crisp breeze. Imagined showing him how to hold a football and throw a perfect spiral, letting it slide latterly off his fingertips as he released it. Imagined teaching him how to track and lead his receiver; how to place the short balls low and away so no defender could get them; how to heave the long balls – those touch passes that drifted down from heaven like some gift from the gods – right where the receiver could put his body between the defender and the ball, right where he could run under it without missing a step.

And someday, this boy, his boy, would grow up and hear the drums on a Saturday afternoon; feel the adrenaline course through his veins while he waited for the game to start; know the sound of the crowd cheering as he led the team onto the field ... that thrumming, drumming cacophony of adulation that made you feel, for that single moment, like you could do no wrong. The way he'd once known it.

He'd show the boy these things, just as he'd shown them to his little brother, Gus.

His brother had been a natural. He'd have been better than me, Pete thought. He had the arm, but he also had that fearlessness that made a quarterback something wild and dangerous. Pete had been the ultimate mechanic, picking the safe receiver, playing the percentage play, moving the team methodically down the field. But Gus? Gus would have changed the play at the line of scrimmage and thrown the bomb at the most improbable time – and he would have completed it. He would have made coaches cry and shortened their lives by decades, but he would have won games.

Would have. But never got to. Not after that night. That night that had carved a line bisecting Pete's life like a surgeon's scalpel, with all that was simple, certain and true on one side, and all that was murky, uncertain – and yes, frightening – on the other.

He imagined that with care and treatment, he'd put that night behind him, but after he was married it began to grow in stature and the more it grew, the more fatherhood seemed something to be put off until ... later. "When?" Elizabeth had asked with increasing desperation as the years crept toward a decade. At some point, later had become never. "Why not?" she'd asked. He'd tried to tell her about that little girl or boy – never to be born now – about how he mourned their loss as much as he'd mourned Gus. Wanted her to know he wished he could be different, more like that guy who'd wanted to share fake tea with his little girl. But he couldn't be, and in the end, Elizabeth couldn't be bothered with his doubts and his explanations. She wanted what she wanted. Finally, she'd quit asking.

There was a knock on his door and Karen poked her head in. "We're on with the new guy," she said.

"C'mon in, and say something funny. I'm having a Prozac moment."

"It's all that oatmeal."

"That's not funny."

"Exactly."

"You and Lenny. Well I got news for you. It's strictly jalapeños and hot sauce for me from here on out."

She walked in and sat at the small conference table, crossing her legs. Typically, she'd managed to dress in a way that made her appear business-like, yet distracting. A wool suit, a silk blouse revealing a camisole beneath, her skirt just a bit shorter than the usual, riding up over her knees and exposing her thighs. He always wondered whether she knew the effect she had on him when she sat like that. For the most part, when she did, he concentrated on making eye contact, but sometimes he'd discover himself staring at her legs. She usually noticed, and it seemed to him he detected the slightest smile on her face when she did.

Karen said something, but he didn't hear her. He was looking at the *City News*, reading the ad again. He looked up and said, "Hey. You busy tonight?"

"Well, Brad Pitt called, but I told him I had to do my hair."

He tossed the paper onto the conference table in front of her. She picked it up, scanned the page, then turned it over and examined the masthead. "What am I supposed to do with this?"

"Check out the ads."

"You want me to call the personals in the City News? Let's see, *Homeless person seeks lady with good income – looks and age not important. Must love Sterno.*"

He laughed, then came over and pointed to Jake's ad. He caught her scent as he stood over her, and watched her breathing, the hollow between her collar bones rising and falling while she read it. She looked up, "Please tell me you're not considering going on this thing."

"Not sure. I'm going to a meeting about it tonight. Why don't you come with me?"

"You're out of your mind."

"Dinner on me afterward?"

"In that case, you've got a deal."

CHAPTER 4

At five minutes to seven, Pete found himself in a classroom at All Souls, hunched up in a too-small desk feeling something like the first day of high school. Beneath humming fluorescent lights, amidst the smell of chalk mingled with cheap floor wax, he experienced the same buzz, the same sense of the unknown, of possibility, of impending adventure he'd carried with him into school each year. And the same undercurrent of dread.

As he looked over the group of twenty or so, Karen leaned across the aisle and whispered, "Let's just go get dinner. I mean, why would anyone with a credit card need to learn survival skills for god's sake?"

"Why? To find the meaning of life, of course."

"Oh. Didn't I tell you? Found it yesterday. In Neiman Marcus."

"You mean Needless Markup?"

"Funny man. Seriously, Pete. Let's get out of here."

"You can go."

"Who's going to keep you from signing up and getting yourself killed ..." Karen stopped in mid-sentence and said, "Is *that* the instructor?"

Pete followed her gaze and saw a man leaning against the blackboard. He had intense blue eyes, a sun-worn face, and thick black hair that hung to his shoulders. He seemed excessively angular, as if he'd been chiseled from a block of granite by a beginning art student. His face would have been dominated by his large forehead and heavy brows, but for the intensity of his eyes, and the hawk-like way his nose and chin reached out from under them. His neck was long and thin and his Adam's apple jutted out in sharp relief. His shoulders were too broad for the rest of him, as if the student had sculpted him from two different models. Ichabod Crane on steroids, Pete thought.

He'd simply appeared, as if he'd always been there, and now he waited calmly for the class to quiet down. Even though it was frigid outside, he wore only a plaid wool shirt, jeans and a pair of ancient hiking boots. It was impossible to tell his age, Pete decided. He could have been a well-preserved forty to fifty, or a well-worn thirty-something.

He scanned the classroom, appraising each of them in turn. When he'd completed his evaluation, he stepped forward and said, "My name is Jake Christianson. If you're not here for the wilderness survival course, now's your chance to escape." He waited a moment, but no one left.

"OK. Good. First things first: How many of you have done any survival training?" Pete put up his hand along with a few others. Jake took careful inventory then he turned and wrote on the blackboard in large, neat letters: LIMITED FOOD; SURVIVAL TRAINING; ADVANCED SURVIVAL TRAINING. When he was done, he crossed them out with broad, bold strokes. "What we'll be doing is *not* any of these. They're traditional – and responsible – programs. They all last about a week, they all pack in some food, and the companies that run them have lawyers who write up contracts about liability and responsibility.

"I'm going to make it simpler for you. We're going to one of the most remote areas left in North America. There's only one way in, and one way out, and that's by plane. We take in no food and precious little in the way of stuff. We stay for a month. Why a month? Because you can starve to death in three weeks. So, you *are* risking your life. It's your choice.

"I'll pick twelve of you. If you're not one of the chosen ones, or if you decide this trip isn't for you, I'll help you find something more in line with your abilities or interests. Those of you lucky enough to be chosen will be among the last of your kind to taste true wilderness, and it *will* transform you. But it will not come easy."

He looked over the group again, reading the response. "If any of you decide you want out, now's the time. No fault, no foul. I'll give you the names of outfits with lawyers."

Pete glanced around the room while Jake gave them time to consider what he'd said. After hesitating, a middle-aged man with a slight paunch stood up, said to no one in particular, "Who needs this?" and started out.

Jake frowned as he watched the man approach the door, then said, "Thom."

The man hesitated, then turned back. "Yeah?"

The two locked eyes for what seemed a long time until Jake finally said, "You do."

Thom nodded automatically and slumped back to his desk and sat down. Pete studied him. He was staring at his desk and massaging his temples rhythmically. After a moment he looked up and glanced around the class. For an instant, he and Pete locked eyes, and Pete felt as if the guy was issuing a silent appeal, but the moment passed as Jake started talking again.

"Now, about my credentials. I spent three years in the Navy as a SEAL. I took every survival course they offered. Here's what I learned. If you carry enough shit on your back and you use your wits you can survive until you're rescued or until you find your way out. That wasn't what I was after. I wanted to know how to live in the wild, not how to escape from it.

"When I got out I took survival courses and read everything I could get my hands on about the wilderness. I learned the techniques and the technologies of survival. How to climb; how to use a watch as a compass; how to use the stars, the sun and the moon to find my way out; how to find water and make fire; where to find food; even how to flake a knife and arrowheads out of stone. I thought I was ready. But I hadn't learned the most important lesson.

"You see, I went out there filled with notions about finding myself. About experiencing the sublime, about triumphing over nature …" as he spoke, his voice lowered to just above a whisper, and then he was quiet, as he stared out the window.

A young, broad-shouldered lady Pete had noticed earlier spoke up, "That's beautiful … that's exactly why I'm …"

"That's BULLSHIT." Jake's voice came at her like a physical force, and she recoiled as if from a blow. Pete felt it, too. There was raw power in it. While she struggled to regain her composure, Jake continued to talk, his voice quieter, almost soothing, and he walked toward her as he spoke, his eyes fixed on her alone. He sat on the edge of her desk, and said, "Sarah, isn't it?" The girl nodded. "I'm sorry if I frightened you, Sarah, but it's romantic notions like those that get people killed. They nearly killed me. And I don't plan on losing you." He smiled down at her, and she smiled back, restored.

Karen leaned over and whispered to Pete, "I think we got trouble here." He didn't answer, and when he turned to her, she was staring at him with a look he couldn't decipher. Concern? Perhaps. But more. She gave him a quick covering smile then broke off her gaze.

Jake was up now, circling the classroom. "Here's the truth: Nature is both sublime and mean. And when she is sublime, she is ..." Jake paused, smiled beatifically, shrugged, then went on, "but when she is mean she can wound you to the core of your soul, and leave you blubbering and cringing in abject terror, totally impotent in the face of forces far more powerful than you can even imagine. And in the end, that's what she teaches you. The meanness and the sublimeness of nature are one and the same." He paused a minute and searched the classroom, eying each of them intently, gauging their reactions.

"And what of you, *homo sapiens sapiens?* What about man the double wise?" He almost spat the phrase out. "You are both the most powerful force on Earth, and the most fragile. Wouldn't you agree, Mr. EPA?"

Pete realized with a start that Jake was staring straight at him. But how could he know that he was the one who called from EPA? He searched for something witty and sophisticated to say, couldn't think of anything, then searched for the profound, and failed at that, too. Finally, he had an inspiration. "Yeah, I'd agree. Our strength lies in the fact that we are the only force on Earth capable of destroying ourselves, our weakness is that we seem hell-bent on doing it."

"Well said, Mr. EPA." Jake seemed delighted. "Well said."

Jake's approval washed over Pete like a benediction, and he indulged himself in its affirmation, until one of those small internal alarms sounded – off-key and dissonant. Why was he performing like a trained seal for this guy? Why was he scraping for his crumbs of approval? But when Jake began to speak again, his voice at once mesmerizing and reassuring, the dissonance passed.

"Now, for my real credential."

He picked up the sheaf of certificates that lay on the back table and held them aloft. "None of these qualifies me – or anyone else – to take you out into the kind of wilderness we'll be living in." He tossed them down and stalked back to the front of the classroom. "After getting all that paper, I decided to live for a year in the most remote place I could find, with nothing more than my wits. To take Mr. Thoreau's test: *To meet nature on her terms, head on, and triumph.*

"I searched for the wildest place I could find, and this is what I came up with." He pointed at an empty expanse that filled the better part of the northern portion of a large map of British Columbia. It was hung on the blackboard with masking tape, its edges were well-worn, the corners dog-eared, and a lot of hand-drawn lines crisscrossed it. The area Jake pointed to was outlined in thick red marker, forming an oval trending north by northwest, with two parks located roughly in the center.

"This is the single largest stretch of true wilderness forest left in North America. It straddles the continental divide and measures more than four hundred miles one way, three hundred the other. And there is nothing in between. And everything," he said, gazing at the map reverently. "In five, maybe ten, years, most of it will be gone."

A tinny voice – vaguely familiar – interrupted from the back, "Aren't you exaggerating a bit? Surely the park areas won't be cut down." Pete turned and recognized the ruddy face of Eunice McGrath, an unpleasant woman he'd worked with in her capacity of chief of staff on the Senate Environment and Public Works Committee. Karen had dubbed her Unnice McGrath.

Jake studied her a moment, then said, "I don't exaggerate, Ms. McGrath. The weapons you wield against my forests are far worse than a chain saw or an ax. The planet's a web. Everything is connected. Change one thing, and the rest changes too. And you're changing the climate. It's warming up there, and the balsams, pines and spruces are weakening as a result. An army of tiny insects – the mountain pine beetle and the spruce bark beetle – is spreading north as it warms and eating the boreals alive. Right now, it's a race between you with your axes and chain saws, and the mandibles of these beetles to see which one gets the last trees standing. If it were just your axes, Eunice, I ... we ... could stop it. But it's gone beyond that. Comprende?" he asked.

Pete knew McGrath was not one to fold in an argument. Her face had reddened as Jake lectured her, something Pete had seen before when she was preparing to rake some unsuspecting cabinet member or assistant secretary over the coals on budget numbers. Pete sat back and waited for a withering rebuttal. It never came. Jake stared at her and she seemed to shrink into her seat. "Understand?" he asked again.

McGrath, her face still ruddy, said simply, "Yes," her voice barely audible.

He turned to the map and stared at it, then he turned back to the class. "Seven years ago, I found a man in Smithers willing to fly me in and drop me off. I left on May first. I did pretty well until about October. Then a run-in with a grizzly left me injured." Here Jake stopped, unbuttoned his shirt, and pulled it off his shoulder, revealing a series of long shiny scars that started atop his shoulder and ran down across his chest. Pete noted that his assessment of Jake's condition was inadequate; he seemed to be cast from steel, not sculpted from granite. He also noticed that Jake wore a rawhide necklace strung with four grizzly claws, each the size of a knife blade.

Jake replaced his shirt and continued, "Nothing that'd kill me directly, but out there, there's a small margin of error. I wasn't able to hunt or forage much for a couple of weeks and I lost a lot of weight and got weak. And the wilderness is no place for the weak. I won't go into details, but by late December I was desperate. I knew I had to get out, but I was in no shape to get over the mountains, so I started thinking about the possibility of death. I'd been struggling to reach the AlCan Highway following the Toodoggone River. I didn't see any game, and the nuts, seeds and pine cones had been picked clean by the marmots and squirrels – it was already a miserable winter. All I'd eaten for weeks was an occasional fish, but in the cold, I wasn't getting enough fat and calories to keep me going."

"So here I was, with all this training, about to die. And I would have, but for an old warrior from the Dunne-za tribe. He found me staggering around, half-frozen and half-starved. Or I guess I should say I found him. I can't be sure, but it might even have been Christmas Day. It turned out he'd retreated to the mountains from the Peace River area to die in solitude. He'd been calmly sitting on a rock for two days, waiting for Death, while I'd been running headlong from it.

"I told him my story. He smiled, then said in broken English, 'Now I know why Death has not come. With one so stupid as you roaming around, He has easier pickings.'

"I asked if he had any food. 'It is all around you,' he said.

"I grew angry and shouted at him. Something like, 'I've taken every survival course there is. I'd know if there were some goddamned food around.' He smiled again, a big toothless grin this time, stood up and walked down the slope. He gestured at me to follow him. He headed toward a rocky area on the south-facing side of the mountain, studying the ground as he went. When we reached the rocks, he stooped, examining the cracks and crevasses carefully. After going over the area for a few moments he spotted a tuft of fur, and grunted. He lowered himself carefully, made some noises, and reached into a burrow, jamming his arm in up to his shoulder. He felt around for a moment, pulled out a wad of seeds and nuts and laid them out on a patch of snow, then reached in and pulled out some more. I gobbled them down. While I ate, he wandered off. In about an hour, he returned with a good-sized hare, skinned and dressed. He sat down, prepared a fire and twenty minutes later I had a full belly for the first time in months.

"As Lynx watched me eat, he repeated 'survival courses' and laughed. A little ruefully, I think. Then he said to no one in particular, 'But why a white man? Why not one of the Real People?' Lynx waited, seemed satisfied, then told me his story.

"His people had taken to the ways of the whites, and his knowledge – the skills of the hunter and the collected wisdom of his ancestors – had fallen into disuse. And, as it had been foretold, the world of Dunne-za, the Real People, was passing away. So he'd come out to join the ancient ones. But he took my appearance as a sign that Saya, the First Man, who the Dunne-za believe tamed the terrible beasts and made them into the animals of today, wanted him to live yet a little longer – at least long enough to pass on his knowledge. He believed I'd been chosen by Saya to be his student. And so, for two and a half years I lived with the Dunne-za, and learned the ways of the hunters, and the magic of their people."

An attractive coffee-colored woman Pete recognized as Clio Corbette – the lead attorney for one of the country's largest environmental organizations, asked, "What do you mean, magic?" She pulled one of her curls out and let it snap back as she waited for an answer.

"The Dunne-za believe that each person has their own magic. Beginning in adolescence they go on quests where it is revealed to them. In a sense, they believe we're all Shamans. Or they used to."

"You can't believe that ... that ... superstition, can you?" she asked.

Jake walked to the window, fingering one of the grizzly claws on his necklace. He stood there for what seemed a long time, then he spoke, his voice quiet, so that once again Pete had to strain to hear. "I'm a scientist by training. Astrophysics. Until I met Lynx, I might have called their beliefs superstition, too. But not now. I learned things. Things you have no way of talking about ... and I have no way of explaining ... and yet, these are things we've always known."

He walked back up to the front of the class and stood with his back to the group, facing the map and said, "I suppose, in some ways, you could say I was born on the day I met Lynx." His voice trailed off, and Jake stood there as if he'd forgotten the class entirely. The silence stretched on, and a few people began to fidget. Pete looked over the group, and caught the eye of an older guy who was sitting one aisle over. He looked like a runner, thin and sinewy, and he had thick, bushy eyebrows that dominated his face. He smiled, and arched his right eyebrow. Pretty weird, he seemed to be saying. Pete smiled back and nodded.

Abruptly, Jake spun around and spoke, his voice once again strong, "Anyway, it was there I learned the ultimate survival technique – you survive by becoming a part of nature, not by standing outside it. Not by trying to triumph over it. And so while I have my certificates from the various courses I've taken back there for you to inspect, none of them truly qualifies me to take you into the wilderness. My time with the Dunne-za and with the Shaman-hunter Lynx, does.

"Let's wrap it up for tonight. We leave on May first. Between now and then, if you're among the chosen, you'll have to be prepared to meet here once a week, and there will be homework." Thom, the heavy-set guy who'd tried to walk out earlier, groaned.

"Why homework? Because in a hunter-gatherer society, the average kid spends an equivalent of five hours a day in nature's classroom understanding how to live. By the time he or she is fifteen, they can move about in it with nothing more than a small pouch and a stone knife and survive indefinitely. The best we can do is to carry sixty pounds of gear on our backs and lumber across it for two weeks. They live *in* it. We pass *through* it. When you finish this course, you will be able to walk with them."

He looked around the room again and said, "Most of you will have to get in shape. This won't be a picnic. I want you to read *Outdoor Survival Skills* by Olson and *How to Stay Alive in the Woods* by Angier. They've got a few good ideas in them, and they're an adequate introduction to survival literature. Pay special attention to the discussions on first aid, and staying warm. We'll be going over that next week. I'd like those of you who are chosen to be prepared to tell me a bit about yourselves; why you came here, and what you hope to get out of it. You will also need to schedule physicals."

Jake was already at the door, when Clio stopped him with a question. "What's the fee?"

"There is no fee for those of you chosen, Clio. Just airfare. And you'll have to buy carbon offsets for the flight. See you next week."

At that, Jake spun on his heel and walked quickly out of the room.

CHAPTER 5

"Well that was weird," Karen said, as they approached the car.

"Why do you say that?"

"Oh, I don't know. How about a Cornell *summa-cum laude* physicist, cum Navy SEAL shaman survivalist? Anything in that combo strike you as a bit out of the ordinary?"

"Yeah. When you put it that way."

"And I don't know whether you noticed it or not, but throw out the creeps and weirdoes and that group looked like a who's who of Washington's environmental power players."

"Yeah. So?"

"Well, it's not exactly a list of those most likely to answer an ad in the *City News*. Can you see Un-nice McGrath volunteering to go on a wilderness trip?"

"You're gonna slip up and call her that to her face one day."

"I hope so."

Once they were in the car, Karen fiddled with the radio, and as she flipped through the channels, she leaned toward him, her hair cascading over the side of her face, and he caught the scent of her perfume. He recognized it as the same one she'd worn that night in the parking lot when he'd held her ... OK, stop, he told himself ... no sense going there. Too soon. After a few minutes she gave up and said, "When did *All Things Considered* stop considering all things?" then turned the radio off and stared out her window.

He edged the car through the ever-present traffic down Calvert Street and Rock Creek Parkway. When he'd accomplished the merge he said, "So, I take it you don't think much of Jake?"

"Are you kidding? He's a nut case."

"I kind of liked what he had to say."

"Oh, pulleez. All that shit about Shamans. And other ways of knowing things? That's so not you. And what about the way he talked to that poor girl?"

"The one with the shoulders?"

"Yeah. Sarah, I think."

"He was a little rough on her ..."

"Rough? He practically took her head off."

"Look, what he's proposing to do is serious business. He'd be irresponsible not to be straight with us. Besides, she ended up feeling OK."

"Yeah. After Rasputin worked his magic on her."

"Why are you so down on him?"

"Why aren't you?"

"OK. He's a bit eccentric. But he knows his stuff. Did you see those certificates on the back table? The guy's a Norman Rockwell painting come to life."

"Yeah. But what about the shaman bit?"

"Who do you want to learn wilderness survival from? The Dunne-za or some college kid on summer vacation?"

"How about neither? Isn't that an option?" When he didn't answer, she shifted in her seat to face him, and said, "You're gonna go on this thing, aren't you?"

"Yeah. If he chooses me."

"That's another thing. Chosen ones. Who talks like that?"

"He does. It's his trip."

"Why do you need him? If you're so determined to kill yourself, why not go up to Denali again for a week or two?"

Pete struggled to figure out how to answer her. The truth was, he didn't really know. It had something to do with that night when Gus died – and what Jake had said about dreams; it was as if the man had known; as if he'd promised him he would find answers out there. Maybe even redemption, whatever that might look like. But how could he explain any of this to her, when he couldn't explain it to himself?

Finally, he said, "I'm not sure I can explain."

"Do me a favor. At least Google him."

"OK."

"Promise?"

"OK. OK. I said I would."

When they arrived at the restaurant Pete had picked out it was closed, and Karen offered to fix something quick at her place. Although he'd been there several times over the years, this would be the first time they'd be alone there together. Now as she sat next to him in the dark, Pete found himself remembering that time –what? Three years ago? – when they'd stood in a summer rain in a parking lot outside the Channel Inn and shared intense bourbon-flavored kisses, unwilling or unable to stop until, finally, they'd broken off and discovered themselves in an empty parking lot, their clothes soaked through to their skin. They stood a few inches apart, clutching each other by the forearms and searching each other's eyes for a sign of how they got to this place and what to do next, while they tried to regain control of their breathing.

It was supposed to have been a simple goodbye peck; a vaguely European gesture of affection, as each prepared to climb into their respective car and go to their separate homes, but it had exploded into something else. A mistake, they both agreed; one they'd run from since, one they'd chalked up to the drinks and the joy of celebrating a rare victory in court that day over several petroleum companies represented by a bevy of Harvard attorneys. A real David and Goliath story, bound to make you feel heady and invulnerable. Besides, they'd been working night and day for months, side by side. Of course that kind of thing happened, they'd told themselves. Didn't mean a thing. And so they'd filed it away, and they'd not spoken about it since.

But to Pete, they'd been the kind of kisses that couldn't be put away. Long afterward he'd recalled them, usually late at night as Elizabeth lay sleeping beside him in a cocoon of anger. Sometimes they'd even appear as he and Elizabeth made love.

Now, as they maneuvered the twists of Rock Creek Parkway on their way to her house, he studied her out of the corner of his eye – auburn hair, cobalt eyes and an athlete's grace – the excitement of that moment rumbling up inside him. He tried not to make too much of it, but there was no getting around it. He was a single man now, and there was a chemistry between them that had been smoldering for three years.

Being alone together at her place was bound to ignite it. He thought of those kisses they'd shared, then allowed himself to imagine holding her ...

"Did I tell you I met someone?" She said.

Pete laughed.

"You find that funny?"

"No. I was laughing at myself."

"Maybe you *should* go on that trip," she said, then she slipped a CD mix she'd made for him into the radio – chick rock he'd called it, although he secretly loved it. It opened with a DixieChicks cover of an old Fleetwood Mac tune, and then slipped into Dido's version of *Best Day of My Life.* They listened silently while Pete made his way out of Georgetown, along the Potomac and past the Watergate and the Kennedy Center – the river's dark water shimmering an other-worldly orange from the street lights that lined the drive – finally, merging onto Independence Avenue and continuing past the monuments.

"So tell me about him," Pete said, turning down the CD.

"Oh. My new boy?"

"Yeah."

"Not much to tell. I met him at the gym. He's tall, dark and handsome, but I don't think he's a rocket scientist. Some kind of beltway bandit. Works mostly with the Defense Department."

"Great. A muscle bound arms dealer with a low IQ. Just what the world needs."

"He's straight, he's not married, he's not divorced, and he doesn't have kids. No baggage. Aren't you the one who's always telling me to get back out there?"

"Yeah, but ..."

"But nothing. That's what's out there."

"I'm sure you and Rockman will be very happy."

"Shut up."

When they arrived at Karen's, a small row house on the Hill, she handed him a bottle of Kendall-Jackson Chardonnay and asked him to uncork it and start a fire, then headed back to the kitchen. "Does a blue cheese and mushroom omelet sound edible?" she called out, but set to work without waiting for a response. Pete prepared the fire, then surveyed her living room. Since he'd last been there, she'd painted – it was now a very warm apricot – installed a new mantle over the fireplace, and laid a slate hearth in front of it. Typical Karen. Always a project, always changing something. The one constant was the picture of her and her Dad aboard their sailboat. It was still hanging above the mantle. It always will be, he thought. He checked to see if the fire caught, then examined the picture. She's about sixteen and her hair is whipping in the wind, obscuring her face slightly. She's leaning into her father, and they're both staring at the camera, their expression telling anyone who cares to see, that there is nowhere else either of them would rather be. The Golden Gate is a grainy shadow in the distant background. Pete smiled at the pair then said, "Good luck, Rockman."

"You gonna give me some wine, or not?" she called.

"Coming up." Preparations were well underway when he entered the kitchen. It smelled incredible. Garlic, onion, jalapeño, butter, blue cheese, basil and the earthy aroma of sourdough rolls filled the small room.

She accepted the wine from him and took a generous swallow. "God, I needed that." She took another sip and put down the glass. "Would you do the salad?" she said, nodding at a head of Romaine, some heirloom tomatoes, a mess of Portobello mushrooms and a Vidalia onion. He set to work, the act of cooking with her at once familiar and intimate, as if they'd done it a hundred times before. As if nothing would be more natural than for them to eat this dinner, then go up the narrow staircase together to her bedroom and make love.

While he chopped and diced, she sautéed the veggies, humming along with a soft jazz tune he didn't recognize and swaying in place. She sounded almost like a cat purring, and her movements had a kind of feline grace. After a moment, she transferred the veggies into a second pan where the eggs were nearly done, then added the cheese and folded a thin layer of egg over the mixture. After a minute, she flipped the omelet over, and said, "Perfect," and resumed swaying to the music. Pete was standing right behind her, captivated as he watched the back pockets of her jeans trace a slow figure-eight in front of him and he imagined his hands slipping around her waist as he joined in her dance. Yes, now or never.

"What did you think of the living room?" she asked, when she'd centered the omelet.

He collected himself. "Love it. Did you do the mantle yourself?"

She nodded, "And the hearth."

"You're amazing."

"And don't you forget it." She turned to face him, her back against the counter. They were just a foot apart, and she was beaming as she looked up into his eyes.

An awkward silence descended as she stood there, waiting. Now, he thought. Kiss her now. But he didn't. The smile froze on her face, no longer radiating, but rather appearing as if it wanted to hide or retreat. Finally, she looked away. "I ... I think it's ready," she said.

He touched her arm. "Karen?"

She turned back toward the stove hiding her eyes. Adjusting the heat she said, "Would you get the plates ..."

"I just want you to know ..."

"They're in the cabinet to the right of the sink," she said quickly.

Reaching across her, Pete took out two plates, put them down, then stood back, his arms drooping at his sides as he watched her dish out dinner with a quick, almost martial precision. They were at the table in minutes. Dating's not going to be as easy as I remembered it, he thought. They ate in silence, the two candle flames making their shadows dance along the walls behind them. When the CD stopped playing all he could hear was the ticking of the pendulum clock from the living room.

But by the time they'd finished eating, things seemed at least close to normal, and they'd even sang Jimmy Buffet tunes as they'd done the dishes, managing a few great moments of harmony helped along by more wine. Pete started to feel awkward again when they were done cleaning up and he plotted a graceful exit. "Look, it's been a long day and ... uh ... I think ... I think I'll just be heading home."

"Not so fast. There's something you have to do first." She fetched her laptop from her case and started it up. "Google," she said.

"Later."

"You promised."

"Yeah. But not tonight."

Karen had been tapping out on the keyboard. "Here," she patted the couch next to her, "It's coming up." He sat down beside her, not at all sure how close to sit, or what she expected of him. He knew exactly what he wanted to do, yet he felt as if acting on it would be the equivalent of attempting to pick up stemware with a catcher's mitt. Had she rejected him earlier, or he her? Or maybe it was neither. And maybe it doesn't matter. Maybe I just go for it.

"Jesus," she said, "Look at all these hits."

He leaned a little closer to her and studied the screen as she scrolled down. There were articles by Jake, articles about Jake. Page after page. It seemed he was something of a celebrity in the Northwest, if not a legend. "An Environmentalist of a Different Stripe," read one article from the *Vancouver Sun*. "From Out of the Mists" announced another in the *Prince George Free Press*. "Dunne-za Traditions Live On," declared *The Peace River Block Daily News*. "Mystery Man Single Handedly Stops Logging" screamed the *Omineca Express*.

As they scanned the various articles on Jake, Pete pieced together a story of a man who started a simple survival training course, and parlayed it into a successful business aimed at building teams and coalitions among the rich, the powerful and the politically connected in the Northwest. The steady rise in his influence and his fortunes was told by the names and positions of those who provided testimonials about his expeditions. Newspaper editors, reporters, broadcast journalists. Corporate CEOs and CFOs. Foundation executive directors. Even the mayor of Portland and a senator from Washington State. And in the articles, he found that those who went came back transformed, and full of praise for Jake and their experience in the wilderness.

Except some didn't come back at all, as a *Seattle Times* story detailed. Karen clicked on it and they read the headline, "Grizzly Kills Two." He scanned the lead paragraph.

> *Two prominent Seattle residents were mauled to death by a grizzly on Tuesday. William Kent, CFO for Synsystems, Inc. and Jerome Calvin, Executive Director of the Northwest Pacific Foundation, died*

as a result of the attacks. The two were part of an extreme wilderness survival trip run by nationally recognized expert, Jake Christianson. A third man survived when Christianson confronted the bear, armed only with a stone knife ...

"See," she said triumphantly.

"See what? It says he was a hero."

"People died. You'd think he'd mention that."

"He did. He said we'd be risking our lives; that it was our choice."

"That's not the same, and you know it."

They argued about it for a few minutes, then Pete got up to leave. When he was at the door he said, "If he picks me, I'm going. Period."

"Then you're an idiot." She slammed the door.

CHAPTER 6

Over the next week he worked with Karen on a climate change strategy Keller, the new administrator, had asked for, and Pete thought things were almost back to normal between them. Karen didn't mention Jake or the trip until Wednesday morning, when she asked if he was going to class that night. When Pete said yes, she surprised him by announcing, "Then I'm going with you."

When they entered the classroom Jake hadn't arrived yet, and Pete chose a seat on the far side of the room about halfway back. Karen settled in beside him in the next aisle then leaned over and said, "It's not too late to split."

Pete smiled and shook his head. Then he surveyed the room. It looked like Jake had done a little pruning. The collection of tattooed and pierced that had shown up the first week were not in evidence, but the rest had come back. The two congressional staffers – Eunice McGrath and Joan DuMont – were locked in discussion, McGrath's high-pitched voice dominating, while Joan nodded in agreement, her graceful neck extending out from a turtleneck sweater. Clio Corbett and Sarah, the young, broad-shouldered woman Jake had so intimidated, were laughing at something the sinewy older guy with the eyebrows had said, and the middle aged man with the paunch – *Thom? Yeah, that was it* – who'd tried to escape, looked around, appearing bored.

As he continued his scan, Pete was surprised to see Ruth Shaw, a reporter with *The Post* he'd known for years. She was dressed in a white blouse, grey pleated slacks and a blue blazer, wore no make-up, but as usual she managed to look both austere and attractive. She'd taken a seat in the back of the room in the aisle closest to the door, separating herself from the rest of the class. Before she caught Pete looking at her, she'd been studying them all as if from a distance. When she noticed Pete, she gave him a barely detectable nod then looked down.

Karen followed his gaze and said, "Well, if it isn't your little friend, Ruthy."

Before he could answer, Jake appeared and called the class to order. "OK. Let's get started. We've got a lot to cover, and not much time to do it. But first I'd like to learn a bit about each of you to help me decide who's going. Let's go around the room and tell each other why we're here, and what we hope to get out of this. Pete, you want to start?"

Uncharacteristically, Pete hadn't thought through how he'd answer this question, and he realized that if he didn't come up with a satisfactory explanation right now, he would, in all probability, not get to go. With the sense that the clock was running out, he started. "I've spent most of my life working to protect the environment, but not enough experiencing it. And the thing is, it's not working. I can feel it slipping away. I know that in my lifetime, we will consume the last wild places ..." Pete stopped for a minute. He was getting choked up. This is good, he thought.

"So what?" Jake asked.

Pete wasn't sure he'd heard right. "So what?" he asked, puzzled.

"Yeah. So what if it's slipping away? What difference does it make?"

"Because ... because ... I have to save it."

"You, Peter? Why you?"

"I meant we. We have to save it."

"Why do you care? Why should we?"

The answer should have been obvious, but he was stunned to find that it wasn't. He flipped through the reasons he usually gave – the human economy needs natural capital to keep going; ecosystem services can be monetized at more than $60 trillion a year – yada, yada, yada. All those rational arguments that put a price on nature and enabled him to speak about it in terms that Washington valued, but somehow, he knew Jake would deem them trivial. Again, he felt the clock ticking down, and so he spoke without thinking, "Because if there's anything sacred in this world, it resides in places like Spatsizi. And if we destroy them, it would be like burning down our cathedrals." The words, coming from some long-neglected place within, surprised him, and he checked to see Jake's response. He was smiling broadly.

"Very good, Peter." Jake clamped a ham-sized hand over Pete's shoulder and stared at him the way a proud father might.

Pete's own father hadn't been one to dispense much in the way of approval, and Jake's gesture touched him. Every eye was on the two now, and the silence dragged on, the only sound the gentle hum of the air vent. Suddenly, it seemed loud. Breaking his silence, Jake said, "Yes. That's exactly it. If you are to rediscover whatever shred of the divine that remains within you, you'll find it out there." Abruptly, Jake straightened up and walked to the front of the classroom snapping the spell. He turned to the young lady he'd jumped on last week, "How about you, Sarah?"

"I...I'm afraid you've already dismissed my reason," she said, sweeping her long blond hair back from her face. Pete studied her. She was tall and broad-shouldered, but despite her size and obvious strength, she was essentially feminine and quite attractive. Karen had dubbed her the Valkyrie after the first class.

"Ah, yes. Sarah Tillington, seeking the sublime?" The girl nodded. "No, Sarah, that's exactly what a young lady your age should be doing. But it's not a particularly popular notion these days. So why do you think you'll find it out there?"

"I grew up in Potomac. I lived in what I guess you'd call an estate. I had my own horse at twelve, a BMW at sixteen, a trust fund at twenty-one and a Princeton degree at twenty-two. I got an athletic scholarship for swimming even though my family is very wealthy. Except for the swimming, it was all handed to me. And yet it's the swimming that I valued the most. I guess I wanted to get that feeling back. To have to strive for something again."

Jake held her gaze as she spoke. When she finished, he said, "If you're chosen, you'll certainly get your chance for that." He backpedaled up the aisle to the front of the class, looking around at the students as he went. He ended up in front of Eunice McGrath. He stood there for a moment, smiling at her. Pete noticed that Eunice squirmed a bit under his scrutiny but to his surprise, she was obviously enjoying Jake's attention. "And how about you, Eunice? What brings you here?"

Struggling to make her thin voice carry, she said, "Basically, my committee chairman told me I had to go."

"Senator Werener, right?"

Eunice nodded, and Jake continued. "OK, are you sorry you're here?"

"Not if I get to keep my job."

"Well, that's one reason for wanting to come." Jake squatted on the balls of his feet in the aisle beside her desk, and looked into her eyes. "But I'd like to see about getting a little more enthusiasm – maybe even a little passion – into your decision, eh?"

Eunice blushed, and said, "It's just really not my thing."

"I promise you, if you're chosen, you'll remember the time we spend out there as the most exciting in your life, for as long as you live."

Eunice said something back, but Pete didn't hear it, because Karen leaned over and whispered, "Which might be a matter of days."

Jake jerked around, the way a wolf might at the snap of a twig in a darkened forest. He studied Karen for just a moment, then stood and turned across the aisle to where Joan DuMont was sitting. "And you, Ms. DuMont?"

"Well, you know Congressman Conners, I believe?"

Jake nodded. "Of course. He accompanied me on one of these sessions." He paused and looked at Pete for a split second and then continued, "Two years ago, I believe?"

"Yes. And he's been quite a fan of yours ever since. When I saw your ad, I asked him about it, and he said I'd be crazy not to go. Said it would change my life."

"And do you want to change your life, Joan?"

She stretched her long neck, looked down at the desk, and said quietly, "Yes."

Spoken with conviction, Pete thought. He'd known her through work and he'd given testimony before the committee she staffed. They'd even jogged together a few times during lunch on the Mall. Pete had found her intensely guarded, but he'd sensed a well of sadness there. Still, he was surprised that she'd allow any of her private pain to show in such an open forum.

But, of course, that's it, he realized. That's the thing about Jake – when he talks to you, everything else disappears. It was like staring at the sun. He could have made a complete ass of himself in his own interview with Jake, and he wouldn't even have noticed. Had he, he wondered? No. In fact, he'd probably come closer to articulating why he cared so much about the environment than he had in years. But for the few moments they spoke, the rest of the class had melted into the walls.

"Well, maybe you'll get the chance. And if you do, you'll come back closer to the Joan you'd like to be."

DuMont nodded, while still staring down at the desk.

"And now, old timer, what about you? What do you hope to get out of this?" Jake asked as he approached a wiry older man with the bushy eyebrows. Pete recognized him as the guy he'd shared a skeptical glance with in the first class when Jake had gone silent in front of the map of British Columbia.

He looked up at Jake, a twinkle in his eye and said, "I thought I'd have one last fling before being sent to the rest home," then laughed. His voice sounded like the crunch of footsteps on a gravel stream bed.

Jake laughed with him, and waited for him to go on.

"Ben Fisk. I'm sixty-two years old. I recently retired. I lost my wife of thirty-eight years last fall. I've always been active. I feel like if I stop moving, I'll die."

"Sounds to me like you're trying to run away from things, Ben."

"I don't run away from things. I run toward them. And the thing I'm running toward now is my grandchildren's future."

Jake nodded, smiling again in that subtle way. "And what makes you think you could keep up with us, old man?" he asked.

"I finished my third triathalon last month. My guess is people will have a hard time keeping up with me – including you, young man."

Jake laughed. "We just might get to see about that."

Jake backed up the aisle to the person in front of Ben. It was a big quiet guy who'd escaped Pete's notice until that moment. Odd how someone so huge could be nearly invisible. "What about you? Tell us why you should go."

He looked up, surprised, but collected himself. "Jim Colliers. I'm a former SEAL like yourself – I'm a contractor with Blackguard, now."

Jake waited a moment for him to go on, but he said nothing more. "So what's a mercenary doing in DC, Jim?" he asked.

"I'm between assignments."

"And what brings you here?"

After several seconds he said, "I don't know. Peace? Meaning? A way to make sense out of all ... this."

"*This*? You're going to have to give me a little more than that."

He shifted his massive body a bit. "I spent two years in a place where I saw a lot of stuff a man shouldn't have to see. Did some things ..." He stopped, rubbed his eyes then went on, "And after making that kind of sacrifice, I get back here and see ... *panem et circenses.*"

Jake smiled and repeated, "Bread and Circuses. I know what you mean. I feel some of Juvenal's disdain myself. At all *this*. But why do you want to go?"

Jim looked down, then gathered himself and started up again, "I grew up hiking the high Sierras. I guess I want to go because I find peace there, ya know? I mean, it's like ...when I get above tree line, things start to make sense again." His voice trailed off.

"OK. Why should I take you?"

"Beg your pardon?"

"Why should I take you?"

"I'm not so good with people, but I love the mountains. I understand them. And I am the most disciplined and dedicated person you will ever know. I'm a man who will do whatever needs to be done, Sir."

"Call me Jake. I guess we can't ask for much more than that, Jim. You're a candidate."

He walked over to the reporter, Ruth Shaw, and said, "Ruth here is a reporter with The Post on the environmental beat. I expect she thinks there's a story here. Maybe even a book. Something in the Rachel Carson vein. Do I have that about right, Ruth?"

She smiled. "I noticed you've had a kind of love-hate relationship with the press."

"As in they love me but I hate them?" he said.

"Something like that. I might write an article or two if I go. But I've got personal reasons, too."

"And what might they be?"

"They'd be personal."

The words hung there in the growing silence as the two looked at each other. Finally, she said, "As for a book? I doubt there'd be enough to fill a book."

"Oh, if you're chosen, you'll be able to fill several volumes with what you learn." Jake backpedaled up the aisle to the reluctant portly guy who'd tried to escape in the first class, "And speaking of books, Mr. Thomas Kline. My guess is you see a couple of novels and another movie or two in this?" Pete realized then where he'd heard the name. Kline had written two blockbusters about fifteen to twenty years back. Both had been eco-thrillers, and both had been made into movies. And then he'd simply disappeared.

"Until you called, I was thinkin' more in terms of a Caribbean cruise. Truth is, I'm stuck. Haven't been able to write anything since *On the Edge of Planet Earth*. As you said, this just might give me a jump start. But I gotta tell you, I'd rather try the sun and rum cure."

"Seems to me you've tried that one a time or two."

Jake turned to Clio Corbet, the senior environmental attorney at the Institute for Sustainable Development. Clio was in her early thirties and her entire face was dominated by the densest, curliest brown hair Pete had ever seen. "How about you Clio?" Jake asked.

She uncoiled one of her curls, let it snap back, and then said, "Well, you remember Peter's reason? That the natural world's slipping away, and we don't seem to understand how to stop it? That's why I'm here, too. I want to see it before it's gone, and I hope by being out there, I can figure out how to convince others why it matters. And I guess, ultimately, I want to save some of it for my two boys. I would hate for them to live in a world where nature was dead. And besides, I think it'll be a gas."

"And how old are your boys?"

"Seven and twelve. Going on twenty-one."

"Very good, Clio. Lynx used to say we don't inherit the world from our fathers, we borrow it from our children."

He turned to an African American of about thirty-five, who was one of the new faces in the class. "What about you, Bill?"

"Bill Markham. I'm the president and CEO of the New Ecology Foundation, the largest environmental endowment ..."

Jake interrupted him, "Bill. We're leaving titles and affiliations behind on this trip. We want to know why you're here."

Bill looked confused a moment then regrouped, "Because you called me."

Jake, smiling, interrupted again, "You could have said no."

"Well, you're a very persuasive man, Jake."

"But ultimately, you're a man who makes up his own mind."

"Yeah. I guess it was your point that if I'm going to manage the biggest environmental fund in the world, I'd better know something about the environment first hand. And growing up in Harlem didn't give me much opportunity to do that. So here I am."

"Great." Jake walked over to another new face in the class, Rita Woodson. Pete knew of her – anyone in the environmental community did. She was one of the pre-eminent lobbyists on K Street, and she'd single-handedly dismantled most of the Clean Air Act in the last eight years. He was surprised at how young she was. Maybe forty. She was slim, her hair was a suspect blond, and when she spoke, her raspy voice suggested a pack-a-day habit.

"I'm a bit like Bill," Rita said. "I'm here because you called me, Jake. And if you're going to ask me why I said yes, I'd have to say it's because for the past fifteen years, I've been living on caffeine, nicotine, and bullshit. I guess it's time for me to take a long look at where I'm going. Besides, any place with no crackberries, no cell phone reception, and no goddam fax machines is starting to look pretty good. Especially if there's seven men along," she added in a respectable May West imitation.

Jake went to the front of the classroom and looked the group over. "I'll make up my mind this week. I'll be calling each of you to let you know if you're among the chosen." He turned to the backboard and wrote *First-Aid* and beneath it, *Hypothermia*.

Karen called out to his back, "Last week you said you'd take twelve. Why?"

Without turning, Jake said, "Twelve is a number that works. Twelve disciples. Twelve jurors. Twelve. No more, no less."

"But you only interviewed eleven," Karen said.

"There is another who will accompany us."

"Can I take the class?"

"I'm sorry, Miss, but the class is only for those chosen."

"What are you gonna do if someone drops out?"

"Nobody will drop out."

"One of your chosen could get sick or have a heart attack. What then?"

Jake turned and looked the class over and Pete thought he saw a moment's doubt. "What exactly are you proposing?"

"Let me take the classes. I'll be your reserves. If one of these guys can't go, I will."

"And why you?"

"Obviously you're looking for people with influence. Well, I'm acting General Counsel at EPA, I'm fit, I've backpacked in the wilderness, and I can do anything I set my mind to."

He turned around and stared at the map, his back to the class for several moments as he studied it. Finally, he turned and said, "I'll consider it." Then he smiled at her and added, "But be careful what you wish for, Ms. Flannery."

Something cold – even savage – in Jake's smile made Pete shudder, but when he resumed his lecture, it disappeared like the echo of a silent scream.

CHAPTER 7

The next morning, Pete arrived at Lenny's with two copies of the climate plan Keller had requested. "Give me something that passes the straight-face test with the greenies, but doesn't scare the shit out of the corporations," Keller had said. Pete and Karen had been working on it steadily over the week and Pete had spent the previous day filling the presentation with charts, graphs, trends and formulas outlining the science behind global warming and the consequences of ignoring it.

When Lenny brought his coffee, he said, "So you're goin' on this damn fool trip with Mr. Rasputin."

"You've been talking to Karen."

"Could be."

"It'll be fine."

"You be walkin' around with bears and shit carryin' nothin' but a stick. How's that gonna be fine?"

"I know what I'm doing."

"You're playin' checkers and this Jake guy's playin' chess." Pete started to respond, but Lenny raised his hand and said, "I had my say. You gonna do what you gonna do. I can see that." He shuffled back to the kitchen and started working the grill, but he didn't sing.

Before Pete was halfway through with his coffee, Karen burst in and slipped into the seat opposite him. "Rasputin called me last night. Said I could attend the classes."

"Me too. Apparently I've been chosen."

She didn't say anything, pretending to study the menu for several moments. Finally she reached over, put her hand on his and said, "We have to talk."

There was a kind of pleading in her eyes, uncharacteristic for Karen. Pete's chest tightened, remembering that moment in the kitchen. He felt her hand on his, warm against the chill he'd picked up on his run. Her simple touch was as sensual as a caress, and it sparked a desire he wanted to deny. He looked up at her and she immediately lowered her eyes. She seemed surprised and a little embarrassed to see she was holding his hand. Should he man-up? Tell her how he felt? But instead, he fished the briefing out of his backpack with his free hand and said, "Let's get started. Last chance to save the world before the politicians take over."

She let go his hand and after a moment, said, "OK. But we talk afterwards."

He nodded, and said, "Let's do a dry run. You be Keller." He could still feel the warmth from her hand, and when their fingers touched as he handed her a copy of the presentation, he lingered before releasing it. They were looking at each other, and he could see she wasn't ready to move on. "Set your watch," he said with more conviction than he felt.

She did, then looked at the briefing he'd handed her. "I wouldn't give him this. He'll read ahead, and we'll lose him."

"This is just for you. I've got it loaded on my laptop. We'll run through it one slide at a time with Keller." Pete began to spin out the science underlying global warming, "We've got a window of two years or less to act, and act decisively. After that we pass some tipping points and get locked into devastating and irreversible warming that will make the Earth a different planet ..."

Karen interrupted him. "He's not going to give a shit about the Earth. And he's going to make up his mind in the first few minutes, so you'd better put the economics and the politics right up front."

Pete had learned to trust Karen's read on people. The press, the politicians and the public acted as if global warming were some variable in a cost-benefit calculation, not an existential choice about the future of humanity. Keller wouldn't be any different. "You're right."

Pete started again, going straight to the strategy – outlining a stringent cap and trade plan that would drastically cut US emissions, with a number of innovative financial schemes that kept costs near neutral. He summarized with, "So the US would actually gain jobs, make money, enhance national security, reduce the trade deficit, clean up the air and fight global warming with this legislation. Internationally the US goes from global environmental pariah to respected leader."

Karen smiled. "Good. Drop the pariah, but good. We've covered all the usual objections."

Pete nodded, but before he could go on, she said, "He won't go for it."

"He's got to."

"No, he doesn't," she said.

"Yeah he does. The White House wants it. Besides, if he doesn't come up with something real, he can kiss all his political ambitions goodbye. And he knows it."

"Keller's not going to make this decision, Pete. Neither is the White House. Congress and the coal and oil lobbyists on K Street will. It'll die in the Senate. It takes sixty votes to pass a bill, sixty-seven to approve a treaty. You think we're going to get that kind of support?"

"It gives us time to transition ..."

"Why would they want to transition? They're making record profits selling an increasingly scarce commodity," Karen said. "The longer we wait, the more they make." She picked up a fork and twisted it in her hands, then laid it down. "You ever get the feeling we're in the middle of a Kabuki dance?"

"I prefer to think of myself as the chief architect of the Potemkin village."

She smiled and said, "We've been holding on for eight years, waiting for the good guys, and now they're here, I'm not sure there's enough of a difference."

"All we can do is try."

"Yeah. I guess."

"Besides, if we get him something he likes, he's giving me the month of May off."

"And you'll use it to go up there with Rasputin?"

"Yeah."

Karen looked out the window. He noticed she was chewing her lower lip and her eyes glistened. *There would be no avoiding the talk.* "Go ahead and say it."

She shook her head. She looked down at her coffee cup, and played absently with the presentation Pete had given her. Reaching across the table, she took his hand again and held it for a long time. Finally, she gathered herself and after a moment said, "I'm afraid of this ...this thing you're doing."

"So am I. That's why I've got to do it."

"But why?" she asked.

As he sat there facing her, her hand warm in his, he thought again of that instant last week in her kitchen, when she'd looked up at him expectantly and he'd let the moment evaporate in self-doubt. How could he tell her how Gus's death had hounded him for decades, now, and that somehow this trip held out the promise that he could purge something in him – something rancid and shameful, and until he did, he wasn't worth being with? He couldn't. So he squeezed her hand and said, "Nothing's going to happen to me. I promise. And when I come back, Ms. Flannigan, I'm going to bowl you over like you've never been bowled over."

She took her hand away and said, "You already have."

CHAPTER 8

When they arrived in the lounge in front of Keller's office, Gail looked up and smiled. "He was asking me about the Duluth Lab this morning, Pete. That got anything to do with you?"

He leaned over and whispered, "Well, after this we'll either be on our way there or we'll be your new boss's best buddies."

She laughed and dialed up the intercom, "Your eight o'clock with Pete Andersen and Karen Flannigan, Sir."

She listened for a moment, frowned, and then hung up. "He says Pete only."

"Pig," Karen said.

"Tell him Karen has to be there. She helped develop it ..."

Gail looked worried and shook her head. "He's not big on negotiation."

Karen put her hand on Pete's arm. "Go ahead."

"You sure?"

"Yeah. If he likes it, tell him I'm the brains in this outfit." Pete smiled, and she continued, "You know what this means don't you?"

Pete shrugged.

"It means he doesn't want witnesses. It means a sell-out." She left. He knew she was right. But as he gathered up his laptop and walked in, he realized it meant something else: Keller thought he was the weak one – the guy who could be counted on to play the old Washington game – go along to get along. Taking a deep breath, he started in, determined to prove him wrong.

Gail stopped him at the door and whispered, "Remember, he likes to be called Mr. Administrator or sir."

Pete rolled his eyes. *Sir. Just like dear old Dad.* He took a deep breath and plunged in, saying, "Morning, Dan."

Keller had managed to get on the phone already, and he waived Pete to the couch in the corner. Pete expected the phone bit. Making people wait was just another way of showing you who the big dog was. Nothing more than ersatz electronic piss on a tree, marking borders and showing rank. Pete looked around the office. Keller had done some re-decorating. The conference table was gone, replaced with a couch, a love seat, and several heavily upholstered wing back chairs arranged around a large, circular rosewood coffee table. There was a new curtain on the window running along the east wall, and the overhead lighting had been replaced by strategically placed floor lamps, so that the area looked darker, more intimate. Pete knew nothing about furniture, but he had the sense that he'd just walked into an upscale model home – the kind of place Elizabeth would have loved. He spotted some additions to Keller's ego wall: four pictures of him standing atop mountains. He went over and studied them. Aconcagua, Everest, Kilimanjaro, and McKinley. Nothing but a peak bagger, Pete thought.

He returned to the couch, set up his laptop and prepared his pitch, struggling to hear Keller's conversation, but he couldn't make out anything from where he sat until Keller concluded his call, saying, "OK. We've got an understanding. Just remember, I'm going to be calling you collect in about three years." Plotting his career while the world goes to hell, Pete thought. Keller hung up and turned to Pete, "Morning, Pete." He walked over to the pictures and said, "You noticed my peaks. I plan on doing the Seven Summits before I'm fifty. Got Everest, McKinley, Kilimanjaro and Aconcagua so far. He admired the pictures for a moment then said, "Well, let's get to it. I'm anxious to see what you've come up with."

Pete gave the pitch following the script he and Karen had worked out. Keller listened attentively, and began to nod affirmatively about mid-way through, and by its end, he was beaming.

"I knew you'd do it. Brilliant stuff, Pete. Brilliant."

"Thanks. Karen deserves a lot of the credit." As Keller pumped his hand, Pete was looking forward to telling her just how wrong she'd been.

Keller rounded his desk, sat down and picked up the phone. "Gail, see if you can get me the VP's office."

"Yes sir."

Keller leaned back in his chair, a smug smile stuck on his face. "Course we'll have to push your schedule back a decade or so, and drop those fuel standards to thirty-five mpg."

Pete felt as if he'd been punched in the solar plexus. "We can't do that..."

"Your deadlines won't fly, Pete."

"But sir, we can't stay over 350 parts per million or we'll ..."

"Relax, it'll only be a decade or so."

"Sir, we're flat out of time. We're already risking sea levels ..."

"Spare me the ecobabble, Anderson."

"But you said you were concerned about the cost – you said you were concerned about jobs. Well, this takes care of all that."

"It's not that simple."

"What's not simple? We choose to bake our children in an atmospheric oven, or we don't."

"That's enough, Andersen." He took a deep breath, collecting himself then continued, "Politics is the art of the possible. We've got to take what we can get. Understand?"

For a moment, Pete didn't know what to say. Had Keller been right? Was he the weak one? Then he heard Jake's question, *A little good, Peter? Think that'll get us where we need to go?* His mouth went dry, and he tried to steel the courage to press Keller harder. He had to speak up now, or carry around yet another failure for the rest of his life. He stood up and leaned across the desk. "And what happens when the possible isn't good enough, *Mr. Administrator?*" Pete said, skirting the edge of mocking Keller and humoring him.

Keller stood up and leaned into Pete, their faces a couple of feet apart. Pete could feel him exhale, his breath picking up speed and force like a locomotive. For a moment he thought he was going to explode, but then he turned and went to the window and looked out at the scene below him for a long minute. When he spoke again, his voice was calm. "You don't succeed in this town by pissing off the people with the checkbook."

Pete reached into his briefcase and thumbed through the papers he'd brought along. There was the latest data on droughts, spreading diseases, increasing floods, rising sea levels, exploding forest fires, mass extinctions, killer heat waves, record hurricanes, melting glaciers, and disappearing polar ice caps. What it said was that all the stuff that wasn't supposed to be happening for fifty years was happening already. He thought about pulling them out, but didn't. Instead, he said, "With all due respect, even a few more years of business as usual and we'll hit a tipping point. And if that happens all hell is gonna break loose and the politics will shift pretty quick. People will be looking for someone to blame."

Keller said, "They won't blame me. I'll be the man with a plan. Your plan."

"I've got some polls you might be interested in ..."

"Save 'em Pete. It's real easy to tell a pollster you're against global warming. Especially if nobody's asking you to actually *do* anything." Keller called Pete over to the window. Pete hesitated a moment, then went and stood beside him. Keller pointed to the scene below. "What do you see?" he asked.

A light mist was falling, obscuring the view below. Pete felt as if he were a step behind, and he struggled to see whatever it was that Keller saw. The only things to stand out were people scurrying along the sidewalks toward the restaurants, umbrellas raised. "I see people."

"Look again."

He did, but nothing stood out. "What am I supposed to see?"

Keller smiled, sweeping his arm grandly over the panorama below, ending at the street. "Traffic, Petey-boy. And every other vehicle an SUV. A pound of carbon dioxide per mile each."

"It's more like two."

"Whatever. And look at the people. Cellphones, Blackberries, smartphones. Energy, everywhere you look. The point is, Petey boy, no one gets elected or stays in office by telling them they can't have their toys."

"But that's just it. We don't have to do without. We could power the gizmos with renewable energy and use plug-in hybrids and get the equivalent of more than a hundred miles per gallon even with those pig-mobiles. Or with a better battery, we could use EVs and run our cars on renewable energy."

"All in good time. All in good time."

"Dammit. We don't have time." Pete immediately cringed. He avoided Keller's eyes, watching the cars and SUVs pass by like a mutant parade; he searched for a pedestrian that wasn't on a cell phone or using a crackberry, but couldn't find one. When he looked up, Keller was staring at him, his look menacing, but Pete took one more stab. "Sir, if we don't act ... it becomes irrevocable ..."

Gail knocked on the door and walked in. "I have the Vice President's office on the line, sir."

"Good, put them through." He sat back behind his desk. "You've done well, Pete, but you're skating around the edge of what I'm willing to take from a subordinate. Clear?"

Pete answered, "Yes sir, I understand." He felt as if he were shriveling and his stomach churned with shame. In an attempt to salvage a little self-respect he said, "Let me ask you something."

"Make it quick."

"Whatever happened to leadership?"

"Leadership? Why, we sold it to the highest bidder, Petey-boy. Now, it's all about polls, spin doctors, political strategists, corporate campaign contributions, Superpacs and K-Street power brokers. You may not like it, but that's the way it is. At the end of the day, if you want to win in politics, you have to play the game." Keller's smile dissolved, and he stood up and leaned toward Pete, "This is great stuff, but you're gonna have to get with the program. Understand?"

"Yes, sir. I understand."

"Good. And Andersen?"

Pete choked out another, "Yes sir?" then looked down again.

"Don't cross me ..." Before Keller could finish, Gail rang the VP's office through. "Gotta take this. We'll talk later."

"Yes sir."

Gail came in and escorted him out, whispering, "So are you the new director at Duluth?"

"Assistant in charge of counting fish scales, I think."

"Sorry. Didn't go too well?"

"You could say that."

"Karen called. She's waiting in your office."

"Great." *Now I get the 'I-told-you-so's'*. As he walked the halls back to his office, he felt as if he were shrinking. Keller's condescending *Petey-boy*, played over and over again, and he heard himself saying *Yes sir*, and *I understand, sir* his voice growing increasingly childlike with each repetition. He thought of his father and how the man had simply retreated into a sphinx-like stoicism after Gus died. *Do you understand, sir? There was nothing I could have done. Nothing*. It was what the shrink suggested he say – air it out. Settle it once and for all. But how do you have it out with a stone? Yeah, his father had said: *I understand, son. I know there was nothing you could do ...* but they were just words. And from that night forward, Pete remained imprisoned in a world of silent, loveless blame, each glance saying *it should have been you*. Nobody's fault. Everyone understood. But no one did. Least of all his father.

By the time he got to his office, he'd managed to quiet the old ghosts, and when he told Karen how it went, there were no I-told-you-so's. Instead, she put her arms around him and whispered that she was sorry, told him it was worth a try, said all the right things. He was still furious at himself for caving in so easily, but as he wrapped his arms around her and felt her body against his, felt the curve of her waist, and felt her breathing quicken to match his, the anger and self-loathing melted into desire. He leaned back to kiss her but said, "I folded like an accordion at a polka festival, Karen. It's what I do best. You should know this about me, before ... before ..."

But he didn't finish. She put her fingers over his lips and said, "I don't know why you're beating yourself up. There was nothing you could do." And then they were kissing, and it was as if those kisses in the parking lot had never extinguished. As if they'd lingered there on their lips, smoldering coals waiting to be ignited, and now the dance of their lips – at first light and teasing and then deep and hungering – set them ablaze. He felt his hands run down her sides, over the sweet swell of her hips, down under the hem of her skirt, then up her legs and across her hips and around her buttocks. She was rocking against him, now, and their bodies moved together in that scripted primal dance of desire, soft moans escaping from her lips as they kissed. He said the single word *Karen* over and over again, whispered as if in prayer, while his hands began to remove her clothes. She helped him, and for one last moment, they looked at each other, knowing that there was nothing either of them could do to stop this, no matter how insane. He ran over and locked his door, as she slid her hose and panties down and pulled her skirt up over her hips. They made love for what seemed an eternity, and several times she bit her lips, trying to hold back the joy, and finally he exploded into her, and they held each other, motionless as their breathing slowly returned to normal.

After a while Karen leaned back, and laughed. "Wow. I can't believe we did that," and she scurried quickly to get her panties on, button her blouse and tidy up her skirt.

Pete smiled, feeling a deeper sense of satisfaction and ... peace? Yes, that was it, peace – than he'd felt in decades. He wanted to tell her everything. "Karen ... I ...this trip ..." he stammered.

She kissed him quickly and said, "Go. Go on your trip, if you have to. But come back to me. Promise you'll come back to me."

"I promise."

CHAPTER 9

When Pete and Karen arrived at class the next Wednesday night, there was Keller sitting right up front. He smiled and nodded as they passed by, and they nodded back. Pete looked around and saw that the class now stood at an even dozen, plus Karen.

When they were seated, Karen leaned over to Pete and whispered, "Why did you invite *him*?"

"I didn't."

"What's he doing here, then?"

"I don't know. Ask Jake."

"Jesus, with this much testosterone in one place, the whole room is likely to explode."

Pete nodded, "Yeah, there's certainly a full load between those two."

Karen looked at him, arching an eyebrow, "I was including you in that equation."

Pete looked innocent, "Me?" he said.

"Don't pull that shit on me, testosterone breath."

Once again Jake had managed to slip into the classroom unnoticed, and he clapped his hands before Pete answered. The room immediately quieted. "All right, let's get started. We'll finish up the introductions and get to tonight's lesson, the rule of threes. As you can see we are twelve. Thirteen, including Ms. Flannigan. Dan, would you tell us a bit about why you're here?"

Keller embarked on a long review of his resume, and it took Jake three tries to get him off it. He used a skillful blend of force and acquiescence, and ultimately a brutal confrontation of wills, but he left a graceful exit for Keller – one the man just barely took. In the end Keller summed up his presence by saying he was here because he was one of the most powerful men in the environmental community, and he was destined for even bigger stuff. Pete passed glances with Karen. The testosterone was flowing already.

"Great. I want to thank each of you for your candor and your willingness to share yourselves with the rest of us. OK. We're a little behind schedule, but it was important to get the right group." Jake looked out over the class, "And I'm very pleased at how it's shaped up. Now let's see if I can teach you enough to get you back alive." He turned to the blackboard and wrote in big letters: THE RULE OF THREES, underlining it. As he wrote he spoke out loud, "A human being can survive: "Three minutes without air; Three hours without shelter; Three days without water; Three weeks without food."

Then he turned around and looking directly at Ruth, he said, "And according to some, three months without love." Pete noted that the reporter actually blushed – something he'd not expected from her. Jake continued, "One point of clarification: shelter. We're going to be out in May, so this three hours doesn't apply to us. Right?"

The class stared mutely back. Finally, Keller answered.

"As I understand it, we'll be above fifty-five degrees latitude, and around four to five thousand feet in altitude most of the time, right?"

"Right," Jake answered. There was a note of encouragement in his voice.

Keller continued, "We might have a little more than three hours, but it can still get cold up there and if you get wet, hypothermia is definitely an issue."

"Right again. Good. The bottom line is that this simple set of rules tells you everything you need to know to set priorities out there. It should tell you civilized folk one other very important thing. Anyone want to take a stab at what that might be?"

Again, the class stared in silence. Jake said, "Come on, people. Try!" He waited a moment and said, "Let's get one thing straight right now. You people are all used to being on top ... to being the one in the know, the one who doesn't make mistakes. In this class, the only one who fails is the one who doesn't try. Now give me an answer. Any answer."

Pete thought he knew what Jake was looking for, "It tells us how estranged we are from the Earth." He caught Keller rolling his eyes at the edge of his peripheral vision.

"Bingo. Bang on. An aboriginal child wouldn't have to be told these things. To him they are assumed ... a part of his or her background knowledge. Known in the same way your kids know you flip on the thermostat for warmth, turn the faucet for water, go to the grocery store for food. Peter's right, in my opinion, but I was trying to show something else with this question. I was trying to illustrate the greatest survival tool we have." He walked to the front of the class, spun around, then thundered, "*Innovation.* Adaptation. Informed risk taking. And by that I mean the tendency toward informed *action.* The bottom line here? There was no right answer, and the only wrong answer was no answer. In wilderness, innovation and action are your greatest gifts. Think, act, adapt, then do it all again."

Pete watched Jake warm to the subject. He came alive. A perpetual font of energy and action moving around the class, his voice rising, his body moving rhythmically, his fists and fingers punctuating the air, his face moving from the contorted pain of a frost bite victim, to the pleasure of a man by a warm fire. He was, Pete realized, much like a revivalist preacher. And he was good. Pete watched as the class smiled with him, frowned with him, hunkered down as he described a freak bone-chilling blizzard he'd encountered one July on Mystery Mountain, then watched them spread out in relief as Jake described the luxuriant heat of the sun that had greeted him as he emerged, safe, from a cave he'd shared with a wolf for six tense hours. Pete glanced over the class. Ruth, Rita, even Karen were watching Jake, rapt. Pete could even feel himself succumbing to the spell Jake wove as he continued his sermon.

"Look at you. The best of you has less than half the speed of a deer, a quarter the strength of a cougar. There isn't a predator in the forest that can't outrun you. And yet you reign apparently supreme. Why? Because you can think. Because you can innovate. If you use your brain, you can find water in a desert, and warmth in a tundra. And you can survive anything. Over the next few weeks, I will be telling you how to build shelters, get water, and find food. But first I want to put things in a context. And it's one you civilized folk might have some trouble comprehending.

"After sex, what's the number one preoccupation of US citizens?" Again, he was greeted by silence. Pete saw an edge of anger in Jake, and he heard it in his voice, contained, but there, and it was powerful. "Come on. Only the passive die. Eunice, how about it?"

Eunice looked startled. "I'm sure I don't know."

"Come on. You want to be a politician? Then you're going to have to know these things."

Her face brightened, "Health care?"

Jake's face contorted, a mass of contempt. "NO," he thundered. Eunice flinched and her eyes narrowed to slits as an angry flush began to creep up her neck. "God. We really do have to get you people out of Washington."

Definitely a mistake, Pete thought. She's too insecure to take this shit. And too powerful to have to. Pete looked around and was suddenly struck by the caliber – or was it status – present in this class. Karen was right. There was enough ego in here to explode, and Jake had just lit the first match. But as Pete waited, Jake began the process of putting it out. He walked over to Eunice's desk, stood directly in front of it, placed his hands on its edge, then bent down so that their faces were just inches apart. He was barely audible when he spoke. "Trust me, Eunice. Take this journey with me, learn what nature has to teach you, and you'll have the kind of wisdom and power that sets you apart from the others. Isn't that why you're here? Isn't that what you long for?" He stared at her and Eunice stared back. Finally, she nodded, and then looked down at her notebook, while she rolled her pencil between her fingers.

Jake straightened up and backed up the aisle, still looking at Eunice. When he reached the front of the room he scanned the class then re-sumed speaking in his preacher's voice. "OK. If you want to know what's going on in this country just look at the Tabloids and the maga-zine covers. And I don't mean *Atlantic Monthly* or *The New Republic*. I mean *Cosmo, Men's Health, Reader's Digest.* The number one thing on America's mind is losing weight. And that means most of you are locked in a constant battle to cut calories. I've got good news for you. Out there it's the other way around."

He walked to the center of the room and pulled his shirt up over his stomach, revealing rippling rows of rock hard abs and he slammed his fist against them. "Out there, everything you do is about conserving calories and storing fat. You want to stay warm because cold saps calories. And what are calories?" He turned, looking for an answer from the class.

Pete answered, "They're a measure of heat energy. A calorie is actually a kilocalorie ..."

"Exactly. A calorie is a measurement of the most basic metabolic requirement for life. *And that means your entire society is choking on overabundance.* You have a surfeit of life. Now think about this a minute. Work with me here. Because it's very important that you understand just how bizarre this is. I don't want anyone dieting once we get out there. I want you all to be fat-grubbing, calorie-hoarding, food-sucking machines. I want your every decision – whether to move or stay put; whether to cut wood or build a shelter; whether to go after venison or fish – to be centered on how it effects your ability to conserve or add to your energy stores. And that's calories. Fat is good. Not *being* fat, but eating it. It's got close to twice the calories of protein or carbs. You won't have a problem with weight out there."

Jake walked to the front of the class and let what he'd said settle. Pete looked around to see how folks were reacting. He caught Ben's eye and they shared a smile. Before he could complete his scan, Jake started up again.

"Shelter. This is our most important module, but it's deceptively easy. Faced with a survival situation the first thing you want to do is find or make shelter. Could I have the lights, please?" Jake walked down the center aisle to a projector and flicked it on. As he did, Keller's cell phone went off and he answered it, rising to step into the hall. Jake said, "In a survival situation, even a few minutes can be the difference between life and death. Discipline and courtesy, please." Pete could see Keller bristle under the mild rebuke, but he ended the call abruptly and sat down.

Jake started immediately. "The first thing you need to figure out is where to put your shelter. Any suggestions?"

Pete was about to answer when he saw Karen's hand shoot up. Jake looked around the class, but she was the only volunteer, "Go ahead, Karen," he said.

"You want to locate about a third of the way up on a south-facing slope."

"Good. Anyone want to tell us why?"

Karen answered immediately. "Because cold air sinks into the valleys and you have to worry about floods. A south-facing hill or cliff will hold heat from the day for several hours into the night. You don't want to go too high, because then you get wind and it gets colder as you approach the top."

"Bang on. Did she leave anything out?" The class was quiet, and Karen looked about apprehensively. Pete had never seen her so eager to please. "Come on people. There is a very subtle difference between life and death out there."

Pete spoke up, "If you can, you want to be near a spring or stream. You don't want to be climbing up and down for water, because you'll end up burning calories needlessly. Also, if you can put your shelter in a depression or on the leeward side of a rock, you'll break the wind. You need good drainage. You can either find it or build it. Finally, if you can locate on a dark patch or near a dark rock, it will radiate more heat for a longer time."

"Good. Good. This man is going to make it out there. It's all about energy. It's all about calories. They can come from outside, or you can burn your own. If you burn more of your own than you get from the outside, you're going to die. If you get more from the outside than you burn, you're going to live. Plain and simple. Shelters help you conserve your own. But there's a few more things worth mentioning. Any guesses?"

"This isn't a guess, just a fact," Keller said. "You want to stay below tree line, or you become a human lightening rod."

"Good, Dan," Jake said, ignoring the arrogance in his answer. "You want to be below tree line, but not necessarily under a tree. If you can't be below tree line, you want to make sure you're not the highest point on the slope. And I would also pick out a level place. That seems obvious, but I've spent my share of nights at some god-awful slant, not willing to move because I was half asleep and not willing to get up and build a shelter somewhere else in the middle of the night.

"So let's review. You want comfort, you want a south facing site about a third of the way up a slope with good drainage, you want access to water and fire wood, protection from the wind, maximum radiating heat, and you don't want to be a lightening rod. Pretty simple.

"Now, one more thing. Check for bear signs before you locate your site. If you see any, move on. Period. Grizzly scat is pretty easy to identify. Basically, it's the biggest pile of shit you'll see. It can range from looking like dog feces, to looking like a splatter of black stuff with seeds and berries in it. You should also look for fur in the bark of trees, torn open logs, claw marks – especially on dead trees – and ripped or bent over saplings."

As he spoke, he flashed a series of slides on a screen upfront, starting with scat, moving on to tracks. On one of the slides, there was a human shoe placed inside of a grizzly print; it almost looked small within the huge paw, and five four-inch claws extended well beyond the shoe and the track. "Just for reference, that's a size thirteen shoe." The last slide was an extreme close-up of a grizzly, its tiny black eyes exploding with rage, its teeth looming in the foreground like peaks in a scarlet-tipped mountain range, so close to the photographer that the entire frame was filled with black eyes and snarling, blood-tipped teeth.

Jake moved to the front of the room, flipped on the lights, then turned to face the class. "I used to think there was nothing in the world I needed to fear. I know better, now. Ursus arctos horriblus. Lynx, my Dunne-za teacher, believed it is the one creature that Saya could not tame. It is his world out there. He owns it. He moves through it as a monarch, in confidence, with a complete disdain of all other creatures. Out there, we are guests, and he is the host. And he can be a very ornery one. Bears. Be aware of them. Know where they are. Avoid them."

"We'll bring guns, right?" asked Thom.

"No. We'll be armed only with the knowledge we learn in this class and we'll bring only the clothes on our backs, and a space blanket and some twine. And I'll have a radio. That's it."

The room fell silent. Pete searched the faces of his classmates. Eunice McGrath was gazing around anxiously, her pale skin turning blotchy again at the neck. A long way from congressional committees, Pete thought. Clio took a few curls between her fingers, pulled them out and let them snap back. She was smiling. The rest of the class wore a collective look of dread. Even Ben, and the mercenary: *What's his name? Jim? Yeah, Jim.*

Pete felt that fear, too. It was not simply the bear that scared them; it was the realization, perhaps for the first time, of what they were proposing to do. They were heading into a world that had shaped every fiber of their being, every strand of their DNA, yet it was as alien to them as the surface of the moon.

Thom finally broke the silence, "You're crazy."

Jake laughed. "We all are, Thom. We all are." Then he began to stalk between the rows, talking in that way of his. "But think of this, Thom. You will have done what few on this continent have done for eons. Something that has made you who you are – that has sculpted you as surely as Michelangelo did David. Something almost no one can do any more. And in doing it, you will take the Grizzly's power, his dignity, his wisdom, his godliness for your own. You will carry it back with you. You will know that you can transcend any challenge. Overcome any obstacle. You will walk with the Grizzly, and you will have his courage, his nobility, his pride. You will have mined those qualities from that wilderness just as surely as your people will go in and cut down that magnificent forest and carve out the Earth's bowels in search of her riches. You will know nature and you will touch her soul in the moment before you have destroyed it. And it will transform you."

"Now for shelters. You've all read the assigned reading I presume? I'm going to show you some I've used to supplement our assignment. We'll go from simple to complex. For you guys in the class, chances are this is a review. If you built forts as a kid, you know a bit about shelters."

"We didn't do a lot of that in Harlem, Jake," Bill said. The class laughed.

Jake, smiling slightly, walked over to Bill and laid his hand on his shoulder and said, "Well, in West Virginia, we did a heck of a lot of it, only we didn't call them forts, we called them home." There was more laughter, and Pete marveled at how easily Jake had pulled them back from the abyss.

The rest of the class passed quickly. Using a projector, Jake showed several kinds of shelters with step-by-step illustrations explaining how to build each of them. Their reading assignment had covered most – lean-tos, wigwams, dugouts, firebeds – and Pete had even built several at one time or another. He knew from a previous survival course how to water proof by choosing the right material, layering from bottom to top so that there were no pockets or catches for rainwater and setting the slope of the walls at the correct angle to encourage drainage; how to insulate by building double walls with moss and dry leaves between them; how to assure the right ventilation; and how to use the natural lay of the land in constructing one.

When Jake finished, he turned on the lights and walked to the front. "OK. Rule of threes. Why shelter?"

"To stay warm," Ruth answered.

"Right. Save those calories. And how do we lose heat?"

No one answered.

"You're gonna have to do better than this, people. Come on, re-peat after me: Conduction, convection, radiation, respiration, and perspiration."

The class repeated it in desultory tones, and Jake smacked a desk near him. "Again, with a little feeling this time," he thundered. "This was in your reading." The class repeated it again, louder. Jake seemed satisfied. "If you keep these rules in mind, you'll make the right choices. The temptation for you people is to build a McMansion – even out there. I once watched a guy near starvation adding embel-lishments to his hut, trying to make it a little better than everyone else's while a herd of caribou passed within a mile of camp." He let that sink in, the said, "OK. We're out of time. Here's your homework. Read *Bear Attacks: Their Causes and Avoidance* by Stephen Herrero of the University of Calgary. It's the best book by far on how to keep from ending up as bear food. As the good professor points out, though, there is no foolproof way to prevent an attack. But if you follow his advice, you'll increase your odds out there. The best way of avoiding an attack is to avoid bears. Herrero tells you how to do that, and what to do if you can't."

"Will we be tested on any of this?" Rita asked.

"I suppose you could say there'll be a final exam."

"How will it be graded?"

"There'll be no grades."

"But if there's no grades, how will we know whether we passed or not?"

"If you're still alive at the end of the month, you passed." Jake shot her a smile, and Pete tried to decipher its meaning, but Jake continued, leaving it hanging there like an unanswered question. "Here's the rest of your assignment. I want you to construct one of these shelters." The class groaned and Jake held up his hand, "And I want you do it with nothing but a knife. Bring a picture – a slide – of it in to the next class. And don't cut down any live trees. See you next week."

"Jake?" Clio called out as the class began to mill out.

"Yes Clio?"

"How did you get that picture of the grizzly without getting killed?"

"I didn't. That film came from a camera I recovered when I was investigating a mauling for the BC Provincial Parks. Not too far from where we're going. It was still wrapped around the poor bastard's wrist when I found it. A couple of hundred yards from the rest of his body."

CHAPTER 10

As Pete and Karen left the class, Ben approached them and invited them to dinner. They tried to beg off at first. Their desire for each other was an appetite far stronger than food. Yet Ben was so persistent and engaging, that they ultimately agreed.

As the three of them entered the hall, Ruth, reporter's notebook in hand, approached Pete. "I'm so glad you're going on this safari."

Karen muttered loud enough for Pete to hear, "Of course you are."

Ruth licked the tip of her pen, and said, "I hear the administration is coming out with a big announcement on global warming next week. Know anything about it?" Pete had dealt with her over the years on various stories, and to the extent Ruth had friends, he suspected he was one. She'd even helped him find the houseboat he was living on since he'd separated from Elizabeth.

"We were just going to grab a late dinner. Why don't you join us?" Ben asked. "We'll talk there." She accepted immediately.

Ben took them to Cashion's, a short walk from All Souls. Along the way, Pete and Ben talked running, and then Ben bragged about his grandchildren. Pete took an immediate liking to him, but he had the sense there was more to him than a kindly grandfather who ran triathlons. When they arrived at Cashion's, it was closing, but the maitre d' recognized Ben and escorted them to a large corner table and a waiter hustled over immediately and called him by name. Ben said, "Let's start with the 2003 Switchback Ridge Cabernet, William."

As soon as the waiter left, Ruth turned to Pete and said, "So, what's up?"

"Why don't you ask Keller?"

"I did. He wouldn't comment. Told me the White House was scheduling a press conference soon."

"Yeah. Next Tuesday. In California."

She took out her pad and flipped it open, then switched on a small tape recorder. "What else do you know?" she asked, trying to sound casual.

He weighed his options. She would offer him anonymity, and promise not to name him as her source in anything she wrote. And in the past, she'd been good as her word. But he and Karen were the only ones outside the politicos to know anything about the plan and the delays Keller had shoved into it. If it leaked, Keller would know who did it, and he'd be merciless. If he were lucky, he'd spend the rest of his days in Duluth, counting fish scales. Better to be prudent, he thought. Besides, Keller was probably right. Congress wouldn't pass anything as stringent as what was needed, anyway. "It's a good plan," Pete said.

Ruth looked skeptical, and Pete started to speak, but hesitated. She closed her pad and turned off her tape recorder and said, "I'm surprised to hear you say that. From what I hear it's a preemptive capitulation to the dark side."

"We're doing all we can."

"Really? A few details have leaked out, and I gotta say, Pete, I'm not impressed."

"You know how this town works. We've got to deal with congress, and they've got to deal with the K-Street crowd. We take what we can get."

Pete felt Ben staring at him, and when he looked over, the older guy appeared disappointed. He thought briefly of his father, then turned to Karen. She was looking down, avoiding his eyes. He recalled Keller's warning: *you get on board, hear?* and swallowed hard. He was about to punt again, make some lame comment and change the subject, when he thought of the long walk back to his office last week, Keller's mocking voice braying, *Petey boy,* his own impotent reply, *Yes sir,* and then his father's lie, *I understand, son ... there was nothing you could do ...* remembered Karen's fingers on his lips as she'd said the same thing ... *nothing you could do.* Could be my epitaph, he thought. *Here lies Petey boy. There was nothing he could do.*

Then he recalled that phone conversation he'd had with Jake – was it three weeks or three years ago? *You can be more than the sum of your fears ... and your failures ... and you can do more than a little good. But you'll have to climb out of that fur-lined coffin you call a job, first.* He could feel Ruth's eyes on him waiting for a reply.

"So you think it's a good plan?" Ruth repeated, but Pete barely heard her.

Prudent. He turned the word over in his mind and it looked like an emotional oil slick, spreading out over the surface of his soul, disguising all manner of foulness beneath its rainbow shimmer. He thought of his testimony to Jake: *If there's anything sacred in this world, it resides in places like Spatsizi ... if we destroy them, it would be like burning down our cathedrals.* And it occurred to him that for most of his career, he'd been cranking out rules and policies covering the toxin of the month, while all around him these cathedrals were vanishing one after another until now only a handful remained. And would he once again watch mutely while Keller allowed the rest of them to be consumed in a global man-made holocaust? He knew what he had to do. But he was afraid. Simple as that. The same fear he'd felt twenty-four years ago. The same fear that had scripted his life ever since. And as he stared into the candle at the center of the table he saw Gus's tear soaked face, ghostly white and swollen from the blows, staring back at him from that knife-edged night. Blaming or pleading, Pete wondered for the thousandth time.

And then, he knows it's coming. Feels it, as he had once before. Knows he can't stop it. In the middle of the restaurant that night rolls in on him like a black tide, swallowing Ruth and Ben and Karen and ... *he's back in that alley, a sixteen-year-old boy, and he's afraid – no, beyond fear– as he listens to the thuds of four guys working Gus over. Thuds, and then the groans. Then the thuds again, then finally, Gus's voice begging them to stop. More thuds, and Gus's protests fade – like water disappearing down a drain. Pete wants to help him, but there are three guys holding him, one on each arm, the other behind him, crushing Pete's windpipe with his forearm and jerking his head back. He feels sharp steel pressing against his back. The guy's beer-tinged breath wafts across Pete's face. Later, he will realize that he didn't even try to get away; didn't even yell.*

After a while, one of the guys holding him says to the four who've been beating and kicking Gus, "Stop – you're gonna kill him," and they step back. They stare down at Gus as if they're seeing him for the first time, and they're surprised that he's just lying there. One of them utters a single word, "Shit," and then the seven retreat through the alley like a dark mist, leaving Pete trembling, and Gus's inert form lying on the ground. Pete crouches by his side and calls his name, but there's no answer. When he pulls his brother's head up, it feels like dead weight, and when he checks his neck he feels no pulse. He places his mouth over Gus's anyway and begins CPR; breath, compress, breath. Over and over again – breath, compress, breath – until he's bathed in sweat, until the traffic beyond the alley thins out and finally stops altogether. Breath, compress, breath as if the sheer act of repeating it will erase what's happened. He doesn't know how long he's been at it, but Gus's lips have turned clammy, and when he presses his chest, it feels inert and stiff. Sometime after midnight, Pete stops and places an index finger on Gus's neck. Cold. Dead. The tears that have been streaming down his cheeks, have soaked Gus's face and shirt, and he says to the corpse, "Why couldn't you just shut up. Why'd you have to mouth off?" But Gus lies on the ground, silent, his eyes forever frozen in a mute plea for help. Or blame.

He felt a hand on his arm, and looked up. Karen was staring at him, "You OK?" Turning, he noticed Ben and Ruth eying him uneasily. Something warm and sticky was trickling down his hand, and when he looked at it, he saw that the wine glass he had been holding was shattered, and noticed a thin pool of blood forming in the soft spongy flesh between his thumb and forefinger. Karen handed him a napkin, and he daubed it off and inspected the cut. Not too bad. Ben gripped his shoulder. "You want to go outside. Get some fresh air?" he asked.

"No. I'm ... I'm fine. I could use another glass, I guess." He tried to tidy up the table with his napkin, but it was stained with the wine. This must be what an epileptic feels like after a seizure, he thought. It had only happened once before, and never since the hospital. The others were still staring at him. He had to get away. Releasing himself from Ben's grip, he said, "I'm going to the rest room to clean up."

Thankfully, the men's room was empty, and he splashed water across his face, trying put that night back where it belonged. He was starting to feel better, but the past had one more scab to pick, and he heard that long-dead phrase floating out from the kitchen in hushed tones. *He didn't even try, Ellen. He just let them beat ...* " and then the voice choked and his father couldn't continue. Pete slipped into the stall and sat on the toilet. Tears were streaming down his cheeks, and through clenched teeth he said over and over again, "What was I supposed to do, sir?" at some point it morphed into, "What was I supposed to do, you son-of-a-bitch?"

He'd been in the stall for a long time when he heard a knock on the bathroom door, and Karen's voice drifted in, "Pete? You OK?"

He checked his eyes, wiped down his cheeks and called out, "Fine. Be right out." He removed the damp paper towel he'd been pressing against the wound and inspected it. The bleeding had stopped. As he passed by the mirror, the reflection staring back at him was a little red-eyed. He studied the eyes, wiped his cheeks again, then muttered, "coward." After blowing his nose, he stepped out. The tears had been cathartic, and he felt oddly light. Karen was leaning against the wall, her face shrouded in shadow but even in silhouette he thought she looked incredible. Before she could say anything, he said, "I never did like that 2003 Switchback Ridge. More of a MD 20-20 man myself."

Karen laughed, but said, "Not funny, Pete. Not funny."

He studied her, letting his gaze linger on her eyes, which even in the shadows still radiated sea blue. Next he moved to her lips. The lower one was sticking out slightly the way it did when she was worried or concentrating. It felt infinitely good to see her.

"You sure you're OK?" she asked.

"Yeah ... but there are some things we need to talk about."

"Are we OK?"

He nodded, then smiled and she looked relieved. "Look, I'm going to tell Ruth everything. And I'm giving her a copy of our original proposal."

"Keller will kill us."

"I can set it up so you're insulated."

They'd entered into the dining area now, and Karen took his hand and examined the cut in the light. She dropped it, then looked him in the eye and smiled. "Fuck him. Count me in."

Yet another reason to love you, he thought.

When they got back to the table, Pete said, "OK. You got your story." Ruth turned on the tape and flipped her pad open.

Ben slapped Pete on the back and smiled, "All *right*."

Ruth scribbled notes furiously as he and Karen spoke. They gave quotes, named names and arranged to get her background interviews from the best scientists in and out of government, as well as the original legislative proposal he'd given Keller. Pete summed up, "We're about to hit some tipping points that will take us straight to hell on Earth. I'm talking a third of the world turned into desert, and more than half subject to crippling droughts. Dead oceans. Sea levels rising by twenty or more feet. Seventy percent of all species extinct. Diseases, starvation, and mass flooding on a biblical scale. Mega-storms, rampant wildfires, killer-heat waves off the charts – and we'll be permanently locked into this future in less than four years if we go with Keller's targets. Hell, some scientists think we already are."

When Ruth looked up from her pad, Ben said, "Now listen young lady, I don't to want see one of those he-said, she-said stories."

"We have to be balanced," she answered.

"This isn't about balance anymore than the shape of the Earth is. It's about facts. You guys keep trotting out the three climatologists that the coal and oil boys put on payroll and pretending there's a scientific controversy ... Christ, you even quote Michael Crichton. Science isn't a goddamn popularity contest, or an opinion poll. The stuff Pete's outlined has already started."

"Tell him how it works Pete. I don't write the headlines, I don't place the articles and I get orders just like everyone."

Ben's eyebrows clamped down over his eyes like storm clouds and he leaned forward, "Look. Pete and Karen are sticking their necks out here. And because you guys have been more interested in manufacturing a false controversy for the last two decades than in doing your job, we're about out of time. You need to kick ass and take names, young lady. The public's gotta know we're down by six, it's fourth and goal with two seconds on the clock ..."

Ruth was staring at Ben blankly, and Pete said, "He means, it's the bottom of the ninth with two outs, a full count, bases loaded and we're down by three..." Ruth turned from Ben to Pete, her expression going from blank to openly perplexed.

Ben watched her reaction, then caught Pete's grin and guffawed. The rest of the table erupted with him. Pete put a hand on Ben's forearm, "She's one of the good guys."

Ruth smiled and said, "I've been trying to get The Post to take this seriously for a decade, but you're right. They're hung up on reporting the controversy. But I've got a few ideas that just might let me write the article I want." She turned to Pete, "Can you tie the funding for the usual suspects to the fossil guys?"

"There's a lot in the public record, but I'm sure there's even more they're hiding."

Ben interrupted. "I can get it. Friend of mine owns one of the nation's best investigative companies. If it exists, he'll find it."

Karen looked at Pete, then turned to Ben. "Have him check out Jake, while you're at it."

"Already have."

"What's he found?"

"So far, he's everything he claims to be." Ben twisted one of his eyebrows a moment and said, "And maybe a whole lot more."

Before Karen could pursue this, Ruth took a deep breath and said, "No matter how careful I am, your fingerprints are going to be all over this. I did a story on Keller. You need to know, he plays for keeps. If he comes after you – and he will – it won't be pretty."

"Yeah," Pete said, looking at Karen. She nodded, and he repeated, "Yeah. We know."

CHAPTER 11

The following Tuesday evening Pete and Karen watched from his houseboat as Keller and the President stood in Point Reyes National Forest backed by virgin Douglass firs and unveiled the climate strategy. The announcement garnered full coverage on the cable and network news, and as expected, Keller had rolled back deadlines and weakened the mileage standards.

When the press conference was over, Ruth called and described how The Post would cover the story. The paper would run a banner head-line which read, *Administration Announces Climate Plan.* Beneath this headline, there would be two stories. One was a simple summary of the announcement and what it contained, written by the Post's White House correspondent, appearing in the upper right hand side of A-1. Ruth's would appear on the upper left, and it would be labeled "analysis."

Ruth read her head line: *"Experts Skeptical of Climate Proposal. And here's the subhead, K-Street Wins Again?"* Then she read the first paragraph: *"EPA's Administrator ignored the advice of the Agency's top scientists, attorneys, and policy experts, and imposed substantial de-lays in greenhouse gas reductions. A range of outside experts on en-ergy, climate science and economics have said the administration's plan calls for too little, too late, and will lead to a costly global catastrophe. Sources within the administration said they were forced to roll back deadlines in order to get Congressional support. Others suggested they were influenced by the fossil fuel industry and their K-Street lobbyists ...* ya da ya da ya da. *An anonymous source close to EPA's Administrator said it was largely an issue of politics and laid the blame directly on Dan Keller. ...*let's see ... yeah, here ... *Copies of the original legislation* *obtained by the Post contained a far more aggressive set of actions and deadlines...*"

When she hung up, Karen said, "We're so screwed."

Pete poured two glasses of Champagne and said, "Let's jump off that bridge when we come to it." He tried to ignore the nagging voice within, telling him that he had to tell Karen about Gus, about his long black night that followed it – the hospital; the breakdown; the electro-shock therapy. Would she still love him if she knew? Could she? But then she put her glass down and kissed him, and he forgot about everything but the waves of passion that swept over him, sweet, but undeniable, and they made love and fell asleep in each others arms.

The next morning, as they read the Post with satisfaction, both of their cell phones got calls from Keller, but they ignored him. The anger in the messages he left was corrosive. He would be returning from California by commercial flight for most of the rest of the day so they managed to avoid him, until that evening when they pulled up to All Souls. He was standing in the parking lot waiting. As soon as he saw Pete's car, he ran along side it and stood by the door as they pulled to a stop. "Guess he read the paper," Karen said.

"Do you think?" Then he took the door handle and said, "No sense in both of us getting fired. You try and get past him ..."

"No. I'm not gonna back off from this asshole."

Keller began banging on Pete's window. Pete opened the door and stepped out and Keller immediately attacked him. "Goddam you, Andersen. You're history. Do you understand me? History. Nobody fucks Dan Keller. Nobody." He turned on Karen, "And you. I thought you had better sense. Why didn't you stop him?"

"She didn't know. It was my idea."

Keller turned on Pete, eyes bugging and mouth literally frothing, spittle ejecting as he roared, "What'd I tell you about being a team player, huh? What'd I say?"

"Something about taking what you can get, as I remember ..."

"No. That is *not* what I said. I said I wanted you on board." Keller was screaming now, backing Pete against the car with the force of his anger. "And you just fucked yourself. Because I *will* fire you. Do you here me? I don't care how hard it is. And I'll make sure you never work in this town again. You're history. You crossed the wrong man you son-of-bitch."

Keller was working himself up to new levels of rage, when a voice intervened from behind. "That's enough, Dan." It was Jake.

Keller turned on him. "Stay the fuck out of this. It's none of your business."

"Are you forgetting our talk? It can play out the way we discussed. Or not."

Keller hesitated. To Pete, he seemed suspended between his rage and something else – something in what Jake had just said. Turning a beacon of hate to Pete, he said, "He screwed me. Nobody gets away with that. Nobody."

"He did you a favor."

"Fuck off."

"How far do you think your ambitions will get without their support?" Jake said gesturing toward the class. Keller didn't say anything. He'd continued to stare at Pete while Jake talked, but now as the silence stretched out he rubbed his eyes then squeezed the bridge of his nose between his thumb and forefinger. When he finally looked up and resumed his glowering, Jake continued, "Pete's going. He's got a part in this. He's been chosen, just like you."

Keller continued to glare at Pete, but after a few moments he glanced over his shoulder at Jake. When he turned back, Pete saw doubt forming around Keller's eyes. After one more glance, Keller said, "It's him or me, Christianson. Take your choice."

Jake clutched Keller's shoulder and spun him around. As they stood there, Jake seemed to rise up before them like a storm cloud boiling heavenward in a time-lapse movie. Keller had been about to say something, but stopped. Jake paused, suspended above them, and Pete cringed, thinking he was about to strike. But Jake's eyes were boring straight into Keller, and he still gripped his shoulder. Without looking away, Jake said, "Would you two excuse us a moment?" It wasn't a real question. It was a command, a quiet monotone, but sharp as obsidian. They left immediately.

Now, as they headed toward class, Karen clutched Pete's arm. "What the hell was that?" she asked.

"I don't know."

"Is ... is ... Keller in danger?"

"I don't know." Then he paused and asked, "Should I go back there?"

"No." Karen pulled him into the class.

Pete let her lead him, the coppery taste of cowardice rising up from his gut and burning his throat as he took his seat and waited. It felt as if the rest of the class were staring at him and he thought he could feel their scorn. From somewhere, his father's voice echoed: *He didn't even try, Ellen ...* and he knew he had to go back out. Something bad was going to happen. Maybe it already had. Not again, he thought. Not this time. He choked down the fear-bile and tried to will himself to get up. His legs felt weak, and he was having difficulty making them move. As he sat there cursing himself, Jake walked in with Keller in tow. He brought him straight over to Pete, and without saying anything, Keller stuck out his hand.

Pete watched Keller's hand tremble, but he was unable to take it. He looked up into his face. It was pale, almost chalky, and his eyes were flat and emotionless. Jake turned and said to Pete, "Go ahead. Take it." Pete nodded, and as he took Keller's hand, he thought he knew what made it tremble.

The moment they shook hands, Jake's demeanor changed. He seemed to shrink back to a normal size, and he threw an arm around Keller's shoulder and steered him toward a seat on the other side of the classroom. Karen placed a hand on Pete's arm and whispered, "What just happened here?"

"I don't know. But I don't think it was good."

"No shit."

Ben caught Pete's eye and raised his eyebrows in question, but Pete shrugged his shoulders. Before they could do much more, Jake went right to work.

"Sorry for the delay. We were just engaged in a little conflict resolution out there." He stared over their heads at the back of the class for a moment, then said. "Look, let's get this out right now. We will have disagreements. Once we're out there, we're likely to have more, and they'll be more intense. And that's as it should be. There's a lot at stake and some of it may be a matter of life and death. I'll try to let you settle things yourselves, but if you can't, at some point, I'll break in. And if you have a disagreement with me, then god help you." He laughed, and the class laughed with him. Everyone except Karen and Dan, Pete noted.

"Let's get started. We have a lot to go over tonight and we're way behind, so I'm going to be throwing stuff at you pretty quickly. Pay attention. Do the homework; practice the skills we go over. Do it with care. Because there will be a final exam. It'll take place out there, pass fail. Right Rita?" He smiled at her and she nodded, crossing her legs and leaning back in her chair obviously enjoying his attention.

"Alright, here's what we've got tonight. First, Herrero's take on bears, then a quick review on your experience building shelters, then a section on water. You're lucky. Water is usually a big deal, but where we're going, we won't have any trouble. I'll go over purification, and we'll learn how to build a solar still. Not because I think you'll need one, but because I think they're an elegant little piece of technology. With one of these babies, you can get water in the middle of the Kalahari Desert. And even if you've got plenty of water, you can use a solar still to purify it without fire. All you need is a sheet of plastic and a little ingenuity. "OK, who wants to give us the bottom line on bears according to Herrero?"

Jim raised his hand, and Jake nodded toward him. "It comes down to three things. Keep a clean camp. Don't surprise them. And don't act like prey if you see one."

Jake and the class waited for more, but Jim was obviously through. "You're a man of few words, aren't you?" Jim, his huge weight-trained frame jammed into the seat, simply nodded without saying anything further. "Well, they're the right words. I'm not going to go over the first two points except to tell you an old saying you'll hear woodsmen use from time to time: 'A pine needle fell in the forest. The deer heard it. The eagle saw it. The bear smelled it.' These suckers can smell. Under the right conditions, they can smell a salmon cooking at well over three miles. If you leave food, toothpaste, deodorant, smelly socks – whatever – lying around, a bear will smell it and he will come check it out. To him, modern humans moving through the forest are the equivalent of a supermarket on wheels. Keep a clean camp. Hang your food. Don't camp where you've cleaned fish or gutted an elk. Move on. 'Nough said." Jake paused, taking off his grizzly claw necklace and holding it above his head. "I'm going to pass this around while we talk bears. Feel how sharp the claws are. Imagine them attached to a half a ton of pissed off muscle and bone. These guys are serious business." He handed it to Rita, who was sitting in the front seat nearest the door.

Jake then reviewed the book's main points. Never surprise a bear: make noise when you're in bear country; know which way the wind is blowing; keep a lookout for sign like scat, striated tree bark, torn saplings. Know the difference between a grizzly and a black bear. Know the difference between a bear behaving defensively and one that's behaving like a predator. Know how to back away; know how and when to stand your ground; if you're charged, know when to fight back and when to play dead. He used a series of slides to illustrate his points. "But above all, never run." Jake said as he finished.

"Why not?" Thom asked.

"Two reasons. First, a bear can run as fast as a horse –thirty-five miles an hour. Second, a lot of times a bear will do a bluff charge. He'll stop, or veer off. If you duck, drop, or run, you may turn a false charge into a real one."

"And if it's real? If he does hit you?" Eunice asked.

"Drop, cover the back of your neck, tuck your head between your legs, and kiss your ass goodbye," Ben said. The class laughed.

Jake shut off the projector and walked to the front of the class and flipped on the lights. The fluorescent bulbs blinked and hummed to life and Pete found that he was holding Jake's necklace. Four pale knife-sized claws, each one sufficient to rip out a man's guts in less time than it takes to figure out a bear's motivation, Pete thought. He shuddered when he realized how close Elizabeth and he had come to seeing these attached to the business end of a grizzly paw.

Rita raised her hand, and asked a question Pete thought must be on everyone's mind. "OK. Let's get real, here. They can weigh as much as half a ton. They run as fast as a horse. They've been known to literally crush a car just to get at a picnic basket. How do you find the courage to stand your ground when you're getting charged by an animal like that?"

"You get it like you get most things out there. From places inside you that you didn't know were there."

"Yeah, right. Like anyone could really stand in the face of a charging bear," Thom said, derisively.

Pete watched Jake turn and walk toward Thom, feeling the force of his displeasure as a wave blasting over the class. He reached Thom's desk and hovered over him for a moment then spoke, quietly. "I have. Several times." Jake straightened up and faced the class. "Lynx says a charge is a mark of honor. It is a test from Saya, and if you're found worthy, Saya makes the bear turn."

"Tell us about your attack," Rita asked. "Did you fight or play dead?"

"I've done both."

"How about the one where you got those scars?"

"Not much to tell, really. I was cresting a peak near Kitchener Lake in late October at about five thousand feet. I didn't expect to see any bears. Figured most would be denned up by that time. But as I came over the ridge I surprised a huge male – I'd say he went nine hundred, maybe even a thousand pounds. He was gorging on a young elk. We weren't more than twenty-five yards apart when I first saw him. Unfortunately, he saw me at the same time. He charged immediately." Jake rubbed his shoulder unconsciously, and went on, "I stood my ground and spoke softly, but it only took a few seconds for him to reach me. He pulled up at the last second, and I thought I was going to get lucky. He stood there, towering over me, breathing in my face, elk blood dripping out of his mouth, fury in his eyes. Every part of me wanted to break and run. We held that pose for ... I don't know ... it must have been less than twenty seconds, tops. But to me, it seemed like hours and I could feel his hot breath on me the whole time. And I could smell him, a mixture of musk and death – a male bear has a smell you can't forget – reeking, foul – the smell of the devil. Just when I thought he might break off, he swatted me – the way you or I might swat at a fly, and I was knocked back about ten feet. I took advantage of the hill and rolled several yards further, hoping to put some distance between me and him without running."

Jake was quiet again for a moment, and Pete could see that as he recounted the story, the man was transfixed – not by fear, but in some other way Pete couldn't identify. Jake continued, "I lay there, belly down, my shoulder aching already, but feeling very lucky to be alive. But I heard him snarl and snort, and then he began to shuffle down the hill toward me. As I lay there, hearing him come for me, I understood, for the first time in my life, the meaning of the word terror. When he reached me, he stopped, flicked me over on my back as if I were a rag, then sniffed at the wounds on my shoulder and chest. He sat beside me, leaning over, his face in mine, and I could feel his breath on me. Hot, acrid, and I thought the mixture of smell and fear would make me retch. I struggled to stay motionless, but I could feel the nausea overtaking me. I clenched my teeth and I began to convulse as I felt the vomit rise, but I choked it back down, swallowing it. This was all happening inside. From the outside, I managed to remain motionless. Finally, he left me and shuffled off to his kill."

The class was still – not simply quiet, but stone frozen still, as Jake, mesmerized, stared off to a mountain somewhere in British Columbia where death still stalked. Pete waited for Jake to snap out of his reverie, but the man continued to look past them into that place only he could see. As the silence dragged on, Pete caught Ben's eyes, and the older guy raised his eyebrows and waggled them like warning flags.

After a long moment Jake started to come back, but to Pete it looked as if this story with its simple and intimate connection between life and death and terror had taken hold of him. With effort, Jake went on, but his voice was strangely disembodied, his demeanor trance-like.

"Anyway, I puked my guts out there on the side of the hill, not twenty-five yards from the bear and listened to him gnawing and tearing flesh, thanking the gods that it wasn't mine. When I finished throwing up, I got up and backed down the hill. That bear and I stared at each other until his eyes were just twin black beads, barely visible. When I was finally out of sight, I began to run, and I didn't stop running for nearly an hour, and by that time my coat and shirt were soaked in blood and I was lightheaded. But you know, in some ways I've never felt more alive in my life, before or since."

Jake walked to the front of the class and seemed to snap himself fully back by force of will. "We've got a lot to do. Let's get those slides up. Sarah, you go first."

After the class ended, Keller approached Pete in the parking lot. "I want to talk to you."

"Go ahead," Pete said, his guard up. Keller looked around nervously, but didn't say anything. Pete waited as the man's eyes searched the area over his shoulder. After the silence dragged out, Pete said, "What happened back there?"

"That son-of-a-bitch outmaneuvered me." Keller looked around the parking lot once more, and then said, "I can't get out of going on this fucking trip. And I'm going to have to get along with you. But I warn you, nobody – not you or that yokel – gets away with blackmailing Dan Keller. If I get my chance out there ..." Keller stopped.

"If you get your chance, what?"

Keller shook his head a bit then looked Pete in the eye. The old Keller – the man in charge – was back. "Forget all that. You've got a choice, Anderson. Me, or that simple savage."

"Jesus, Keller. Not everything's about power ... we have to be a team ..."

Keller grabbed Pete, his fingers digging through the soft flesh of his inner arm, pressing into the bone. "After what I just saw, I can tell you this is all about power. You want to come back alive, you better think seriously about who you side with." With that, he let go of Pete's arm and started off, but he stopped and turned and said, "You don't want me as an enemy, Andersen. Hear?"

"Yeah. I hear." Pete watched him stalk off toward his Mercedes. His arm was throbbing where Keller had gripped it, and he massaged it absently as he watched him go. Typical Keller, Pete thought. It all comes down to street rules. Picking sides and having it out, mano y mano.

"You OK?" Karen said.

"Yeah. Fine." He went over and took her arm.

"So I'd say Jake is blackmailing him," Pete said. "Wonder what he's got?"

"That's easy. Keller's got a zipper problem."

"What makes you say that?"

"He's only been around EPA for a couple of weeks and he's already come on to several women – including me. And there was nothing subtle about it."

"Asshole. I oughta ..."

"I handled it. You've got more important things to worry about."

"Like what?"

"Like in the last month you've signed up for a death march, ruined your career, and made a very serious enemy. Have I missed anything?"

"No. That about does it."

"Remind me to find a new mentor," Karen said.

"Hey, I thought you were the mentor."

"Well, that explains our career paths."

Pete didn't respond. He was trying to remember the exact wording Keller had used as he held his arm. After a few minutes, Karen asked, "What is it?"

"I wouldn't swear to it, but I think Keller just threatened to kill me. And maybe Jake, too."

"I thought that was the bears' job."

CHAPTER 12

Karen and Pete had arranged to meet Ben at Cashions again. The short walk passed in silence with Pete pondering Jake's little trance. There'd been something unsettling about it, but he'd been unable to figure out what it was.

When they arrived, there was a line and Ben was nowhere in sight. Pete approached the hostess to inquire about him, but as soon as she saw him she said, "Mr. Andersen?"

Pete nodded, and she immediately escorted them to the same table they'd occupied last week. He was there, surrounded by Clio, Sarah, Ruth, and Bill Markham. They were all laughing, but Bill's drowned out the others – it was deep, melodious, yet cottony smooth. As Pete and Karen approached, Ben spotted them and shouted out, "Hey. Over here. I hope you don't mind. I took the liberty of inviting some of the others."

Pete did mind. He'd wanted to talk to Ben about Jake's behavior in class. He slid in beside Ruth, who'd exchanged her Lois Lane uniform for jeans and a sweater. He'd forgotten how attractive she could be. Her eyes were dark, almost black, and she looked vaguely Celtic, with short hair cut in no-maintenance bangs. As soon as he sat down, she held out her hand and they exchanged a fist bump. "Hey, we kicked butt today."

"Yeah we did. It was a great piece."

"You still got a job?"

"So far."

She leaned past him and said to Karen, "How about you?"

"Pete took all the arrows."

Returning her glance to Pete she said, "He did, did he? Well isn't he the gentleman." She laughed, then patted him on the back, "I saw Keller go after you in the parking lot. Bad?"

"Could have been. But Jake stepped in ..."

"Yeah. I saw that, too."

Sarah, who'd been listening in said, "Great article, Ruth. I'd have led with something on the sublimity of nature, though." They all laughed, but Sarah turned serious for a moment and continued, "Somehow, it wasn't so bad. When he jumped on me, I mean."

"Yeah. There's certainly something about our guy, Jake" Clio said. "I got a friend in Seattle who told me he's a pretty controversial fellow out there."

"Why?" Bill Markham asked.

"For one thing, he seems to be taking Seattle's best and brightest – CEOs, foundation presidents, politicians – on trips like ours and they come back sounding like Rachel Carson on steroids. Scares the shit out of stockholders, but the greenies love it."

"Did your friend mention that some of them don't come back at all?" Karen said.

"What do you mean?" Clio asked.

"A couple of people died."

"Died? How?" Sarah and Bill said in unison.

"Bear attack," Karen answered. "And a third one got mauled." The table fell silent. Before anyone recovered enough to speak the waitress brought their drinks and took their orders.

"How do you know that?" Bill Markham asked when she left.

"I Googled him."

Ruth cut in, "So did I. He also stepped in front of the bear. If he hadn't been there, more people would have died."

"And if they hadn't gone with him, no one would have," Karen said.

"Karen's convinced Jake's dangerous," Pete said.

"Why?" Clio asked.

"Did you see him and Keller out there in the parking lot?"

Bill nodded, "I watched them come in. Reminded me of an old African saying. When Elephants dance, the ants get out of the way."

Pete cut in. "Yeah, that whole conflict – whatever it is – could give us trouble. Keller's going, but he's pissed." Pete looked around, then said, "But there's something else that makes Jake a dangerous man."

Bill Markham said, "And what would that be?"

Pete struggled to put his finger on the feeling he'd had as he'd watched Jake speak about death. He was quiet for some time, and he noticed Ben giving him a worried look, so he began, "I don't quite know how to put this, but when he was talking about the bear attack, I had the sense that he was relishing the whole thing..." Again, he paused, trying to put into words what he'd seen in Jake as he'd talked about the attack.

He'd almost tuned out the group at the table when he heard Ben say, "What is it, Pete?" His voice sounded gentle.

Pete cleared his head and started again. "Well ... I think for Jake, this whole thing is all about confronting death. Literally."

"Bullshit."

"Let's hear him out, Ruth," Clio said.

As Pete struggled for the words, he recalled an essay Jake had written. One he'd read several times. "There's an essay Jake wrote online that lays all this out. Catchy title: *Armani, Our Money: The Twin Horsemen of the New Apocalypse.* You all oughta read it."

"Give us the Cliff Notes," Clio said.

"OK. For starters, here's how he described our civilization: "...a world of plastic, silicon, asphalt and marshaled electrons hurtling down silica lines and across space, clicking switches in an endless set of meaningless binomial questions – yes or no? – off or on? – 01 or 00? A world capable of asking the irrelevant several billions of times a second, while the real terror, the issue of the survival of a million species and maybe the human race and the planet goes unasked, unseen, obscured by detritus, the flotsam and jetsam of a flawed civilization built on the sands of empty coveted brands, rather than the bedrock of what's real and enduring and sustainable."

"What the fuck does that mean?" Rita asked.

Pete shrugged, "It means we kill things wholesale, yet we never confront the reality of death. Twenty thousand acres of rainforest a day, twenty-seven thousand species a year and rising – we all know the litany. But we don't really know it. A tract of five-thousand-square-foot trophy homes goes up and an entire forest dies. But it happens 'out there'; we don't see it. And it's not just the natural world. We hide our own deaths. When people get old or sick, we hustle them off to hospitals or hospices to die, then we make them look as lifelike as we can, and then we plant them in the ground as quickly as we can. Sure, we know it up here," Pete pointed to his head, "But not down here."

He gathered himself and continued. "Jake doesn't just want to show us the last of a great wilderness. He wants us to experience a world where we confront things –where we see the consequences of those five-thousand-square-foot McMansions – where we put our lives on the line and we not only know it, but we feel it. He wants us to know death."

"And what possible reason would he have for that?" Ruth asked.

"Because it's the only way we can really know life."

The table had gone quiet, and they stared at Pete. Finally, Bill Markham said, "Figures. As soon as the black man has a shot at buying one of those big 'ol McMansions, it's no longer cool to have one."

Pete laughed. "Yeah. Sorry 'bout that, Bill."

"Seriously. What exactly are you driving at, Pete?"

"OK. Look. Every living system is in decline, but what do we hear on the news? The GDP. The Dow Jones. The NASDQ Index. We monitor our economy on a daily basis, but we haven't got a clue as to how healthy the Earth is. All the bullshit we spend our lives chasing after, the stuff we call wealth? Out there it's irrelevant. Out there, it's the stuff that's in you that makes the difference. Out there, every act has a consequence, and you see it immediately. There's a purity; an intimate connection between what we sow and what we reap.

"I think Jake wants to take us out there because there, we aren't the top predator – the grizzly is. He thinks being in its world will do for us, what it did for him. When he was talking about that bear, there was a peace, a clarity in him. I know you guys saw it, too. It's a test, and if you pass, great. You're a little bit wiser for it, and Saya smiles. But if you don't ... Well, that's what makes Jake a dangerous man."

They were all quiet for a long time, when Ruth spoke, "All great men are dangerous. Maybe that's just what we need right now."

"That sounds right sitting here in this restaurant, surrounded by good food and good people. But I'm starting to wonder what it will sound like up in that wilderness, say about midnight sometime in the third week."

Bill responded, "I know who I'm *not* sitting next to if that starts happenin'."

"A little too heavy on the doom and gloom for you, Bill?"

"You're a walking Zanax advertisement ..."

Pete laughed. "Yeah. Maybe sometimes I think too much." He raised his glass, " OK, then. To good food, good people and better times."

CHAPTER 13

The next week Jake stood before the class and he seethed with scarcely contained anger. After scanning the class with X-ray intensity, he said, "Someone forgot to return my necklace after last week's class. Whoever has it, leave it on the desk, no questions asked." But then he gathered himself and launched into his lecture, and for the rest of that class and over the next several weeks, he seemed anything but dangerous to Pete. He proved to be patient, charming, and he worked to build their confidence and their knowledge as the deadline for departing approached.

Keller pretty much left Pete alone at work, so he focused on getting ready. He upped his miles on the morning training runs and spent most of the rest of his time studying the increasingly demanding literature that Jake assigned, or practicing the skills he insisted they master.

Keller continued to come to class, and Pete would often catch him glowering at Jake. He was cordial, and even charming to all the others, and Pete thought there might be a romance budding between him and Rita Woodson.

Karen had become even more distrustful of the whole venture, and of Jake. Several times she urged Pete not to go, but he was set on his course. In late April, after the second to last class, the usual group dined at Cashion's, Karen asked Ben, "Has your PI friend finished his investigation of Jake?"

"He said he had a few lingering questions. But I'm satisfied."

"Can I talk to him?"

"Yeah. But give him a couple of weeks. He just had a heart attack and a triple bypass." He scrawled a number on a napkin and gave it to her.

By the end of April prior to the last class, Pete felt ready. He thought the rest of them did too. Gone was the tentativeness and fear that had dominated the early classes. Jake had done a good job of preparing them; they would leave armed with an intimate knowledge of the wilderness and the confidence that knowledge spawned.

The last Wednesday in April found Pete sitting in the same desk he'd sat in nine weeks before. He was waiting for class to start, but Jake stood in front fumbling with a set of notes – something Pete had never seen him do before. The class buzzed with excitement. Finally, Jake put the notes down and started.

"Let's take a closer look at where we're going," Jake said, moving to the map of British Columbia at the front of the room. "Come on up here." They filed up then huddled around the map and studied it as Jake traced a route with his finger. "We will be dropped by plane on Kitchener Lake in the Tatlatui Provincial Park Wilderness Area just south of the Continental divide."

"My God, there's nothing around for a million miles," Ruth said. Several others murmured in agreement.

Jake smiled and stepped back. "On the contrary, everything is right there." He let that sink in for a moment. Pete scanned the group. Joan, Eunice, and Thom looked stunned. He couldn't believe they hadn't looked at the map. He'd been over the whole area a hundred times on Google.

Jake stepped back up and continued. "OK, if the game's good, we'll stay around Kitchener; if it's scarce, we'll head west and camp hard by the headwaters of the Spatsizi River. After a month, we'll hike out to Cold Fish Lake where we'll be picked up and flown to Vancouver. Thirty days in all. Enough time to starve to death." Jake backed away from the map and let the class study the area he'd just described. "This is god's country. Literally. The earth is pretty much as he left it. This is where Lynx came to die. You could say this is where I was born."

Keller pointed to the Tatlatui Park and the Spatsizi Plateau Wilderness Area, "Hell, these are nothing but parks..."

Up to now, Jake had ignored Keller's comments. But this time, he simply laughed at him. "These aren't the kinds of parks you're used to. This is the center of the Northern Cordillera Forest – an area about the size of Colorado, with just three villages of any size, and three useable roads. These Parks get a total of five hundred visitors in an entire year – about what your Shenandoah Park gets in a slow winter morning. Most of them are fishermen. They come in the summer and fall and they take float planes directly to one of the big lakes. No, Dan. These aren't like any parks you're familiar with. They're more remote than Everest. We won't see a soul out there. Because there isn't anyone. There's no ranger on site. It'll be just us, the wolves, the grizzly, moose, some caribou, mountain goat, and stone sheep."

Again, Pete studied the group as they looked at the map, and each expression told a story.

By now Pete had divided the class into groups. The two Hill staffers, Eunice McGrath and Joan DuMont were at the bottom of the list with Thom, the novelist. Pete came to believe they were here, not because they wanted to be, but because Jake wanted them to. They'd been lax in studying and with the exception of Joan, they were in the worst shape physically. Next came Bill, Ruth and Rita. Rita had quit smoking, and she'd been hitting the gym religiously, and Bill had trimmed down, and he was studying hard, but like the other two he was just too essentially urban to pick up the information Jake was doling out. All three seemed to almost be studying a foreign culture, too alien to comprehend in nine short weeks. Keller was a special case. He was fit enough, and he understood survival from his mountain training, but the tension between him and Jake persisted, and it was anyone's guess how much knowledge he'd picked up. Then there were Ben, Sarah, and Clio. All were experienced campers in excellent physical shape, and all had applied themselves. He would have put Karen in the latter group, had she been going. She'd studied harder than any of them, and she was fit.

Finally, there was Jim. He was an extraordinary physical specimen – possibly stronger than Jake, and his SEAL training prepared him as well as anyone. But he didn't fit, somehow. He sat in the back and kept to himself, but several times Pete had caught him scanning the class through narrowed eyes as if he were taking the measure of each of them. In the last few weeks Pete came to believe Jim had singled him out and increasingly felt the man's raptor-like gaze boring into his back. When he turned, Jim would glance away casually. An enigma, but something more, too.

For most of the rest of the class, Jake shot questions out and in the main, people responded sharply and correctly. When there were about ten minutes left, he walked to the front and stood in silence for a time. Finally, he began. "I know many of you – maybe all of you – are afraid. You should be. What we are about to do is virtually unprecedented for people from your culture. We will step back more than ten thousand years into the Stone Age – to a time when nature and nature alone was your reality. To a time when she provided all the delights – and all the terrors. It will be a journey of the mind and the soul, as well as the body. You will be transformed."

Jake laughed, "Transformation. It's become just another commodity in your culture. Bought and sold. But real change takes more than popping a pill or spewing a mantra or swallowing some swamis' pseudo-science. It's won by effort, sacrifice, work, commitment. It's won by facing the things you believe – no, you *know* – you can't face and prevailing anyway. That's all I can promise you. Challenges unlike any you've ever faced and the opportunity to overcome them. And that's why when I say you will not come back the same person, it's true. It's true, but it won't be easy."

"Now there is something else. I've debated whether to tell you this, and I've concluded you have a right to know. I've led other trips of this kind. They have not been without incident or controversy. On one of them I lost two men to a grizzly. I tell you this, because I want you to know that the dangers you face out there are real. But I believe that is precisely what you lack in modern society – real danger, real risk."

"Well, speaking for me, I've done just fine without it ..."

"Really Thom? Isn't danger – fear– what sold your first two novels? Isn't that why your movies were such a success?"

"The point is, you *need* danger in your lives. It is the crucible in which you were formed. It's as much a part of you as hunger, sex, and pleasure. The need of it is hardwired into your DNA. It's been with you and your hominid ancestors ever since you appeared on this planet. It's made up of three hundred and sixty-five million nights huddled in dark caves, listening to the howls and growls of animals swifter and stronger than you. Listening to the roar of winds slamming into your meager shelters, watching the skies anxiously for storms and the streams for floods. That's how it was until the last few hundred years. Now, you've come to believe you've conquered nature. Or at least fought her to a draw. But having fought nature to a standstill, you miss danger. You court it. You even try to manufacture it.

"You've seen the commercials. 'We live in a fast paced world, where the difference between success and failure is measured in seconds'; or 'It's a dog-eat-dog world out there'; or 'When it absolutely positively has to be there'. But of course, none of it really matters. It's all man-made. It's all artificial."

Keller interrupted. "Bullshit. Are you saying our crises aren't real?"

The class cringed as one, but again, Jake merely laughed at him. "That's exactly what I'm saying. And it's a fact. Nothing really happens if you don't get 'it' there. Nobody eats a dog or gets eaten by one. Up there you may be faced with both situations."

"You're looking skeptical, Dan. Let's take a quick poll." He turned to the class. "How many of you have busted your ass before going on vacation to get all those urgent things done, only to return weeks later to find the same shit facing you. Stuff you thought absolutely positively had to be done." Most of the class raised their hands. "Still a few skeptics, I see. Dan, Ben, Ruth, maybe one of you can tell me why every labor saving device your civilization makes immediately turns into an urgency machine? Computers? Gotta make it perfect, gotta get it on-line first. Gotta, gotta, gotta. Jets? Air travel? You get there faster, so you can do more, right? But would Lincoln have been able to write the Gettysburg address on a fifteen-minute helicopter ride to the battlefield?

"Copy machines? Get everyone a copy and get it to them all at once. You end up with less and less leisure, even as you make more and more labor saving devices. Why? I think it's because you want it that way. I think it's because you're trying to replace the real danger you evolved in – the danger that has defined you and shaped you – with this ersatz bullshit urgency in your so-called work.

"Look. The average hunter gatherer spends five hours a day providing for his or her basic needs. You spend nine. And what do you do with the leisure you have? Buy books or go to movies that scare the shit out of you. Why? Because you need it; you crave it."

Ben interrupted. "Jake, I disagree. There were times when if I didn't act, and act fast, everything I'd built would have been in jeopardy."

Jake turned to the class, "Most of you don't know this, but Ben's built two companies and sold both – at a profit in the nines, as they like to say on the Street. But tell me, Ben. You'd have lost a lot of money. But would you have survived?"

"Well, yeah."

Jake pointed to the oval on the map, "You're going to face choices out there you won't survive if you don't act, act fast, and act right. We all are. And that makes all the difference."

Bill Markham caught Pete's eye, and nodded. Pete thought he must have been recalling his doom and gloom speech from a few weeks back. He returned the smile, then studied the rest of his classmates. Each of them was staring up at Jake, their faces etched in apprehension. Except Thom and Keller. Thom looked bored. Keller wore an expression of contempt. He could see that Jake was taking this all in, too.

"But don't worry. You're ready," he said quickly.

CHAPTER 14

After the last class, the group decided to skip dinner. They would see each other the next day and everyday thereafter for thirty plus days, and there were goodbyes to be said, affairs to be brought in order, and, as Thom put it to Pete, "Funeral arrangements to be made."

As usual, Pete gave Karen a ride home. When they arrived, he turned the engine off, and sat in silence, until it started to feel awkward, like a first date gone bad. Several times he started to say something, but there wasn't anything he could think to say that wouldn't sound lame. "Well, I'd better get going. I have an early start tomorrow."

Karen put her hand on his arm, and said, "You're not getting away that easy. Besides, I have something for you."

She fumbled with the locks, and once inside, she went straight to the mantle piece and picked up a small package, neatly wrapped and tied up with a red ribbon, and handed it to him.

"Open it," she said.

He pulled the ribbon off to the side and carefully unwrapped the paper, revealing a small box. Inside there was a silver medallion, affixed to a raw hide string. It was oval, about the size of a quarter, and two figures embraced in the center. There was some writing beneath the figures, and Pete struggled to read the small print. "It says, *Together in heaven*. My father gave it to my mother for their tenth anniversary, and when she knew she was dying, she gave it to me ... it always made me feel like she was still with me, somehow."

"But I can't take this ..."

She put her index finger to his lips, silencing him. "It's a loan," she managed to choke out. "You can give it back to me when you get back ..." at this, she began to sob silently, and Pete took her in his arms. After she quieted, he kissed her.

It was a kiss that had no end. When, much later, their lips parted and he leaned back to catch his breath, they were in her bed. Their clothes trailed out the bedroom, into the hall, down the narrow staircase to the mantle piece. He didn't know if an hour or a week had passed. He lay on her bed, spent, Karen next to him, her body glistening in the dim light from the hall. They talked and made love for the rest of the night.

She shared stories of her childhood, growing up in Santa Cruz, the privileged daughter of doting parents. She talked about her father – a successful venture capitalist who'd essentially retired after Karen's mother died suddenly from pancreatic cancer. She'd been just thirteen when it happened and at first, she'd described to Pete how it felt as if she'd been thrown into a pit too deep for the sun to penetrate. But her father was there every morning to wake her and serve her breakfast; he was there every afternoon when she got home from school; and he tucked her and her brother into bed every night. This man who had stood astride the financial markets like some latter day Colossus, who had more friends in higher places than almost anyone in Silicon Valley, had simply dropped out and become a house dad.

On weekends, when other girls her age were haunting malls and coveting the latest new thing, she'd be out with her father on his Pegasus 55 slicing across Monterey Bay with the ship tilted at forty five degrees and the keel straining to free itself from the water, always on the edge of tolerances, and she'd watch him, his eyes looking far off towards places she couldn't see, as she cleated lines and kept the luff from the sails, taking foam and spray full in the face, her cheeks stinging wet in the wind.

Sometimes, he'd take some of his friends, and they'd spend the night on the Bay, and she'd fall asleep to the clink of ice in whiskey glasses, the sound of poker chips and bravado, male laughter, and later, long after she should have fallen asleep, she'd hear from her berth, the talk of the women they'd known. When she got older, she'd join in the card games, and in this way she came to know men the way few women did. Still later, her father would bring a date out with them, and Karen would take delight in making her feel inadequate, either in the sailing, or in the cards. Her father never said anything, but when she was nearly seventeen, he suggested that it was time she start dating, and Karen knew he was right. She'd spent the next eighteen years trying to find someone who would love her as much as her father had, and measure up to him at the same time. She'd found many who would love her, but very few who could compare to him. "And only one who both loved me, and could stand outside his shadow," she said as she toyed with the hairs on Pete's chest.

For his part, he'd talked mostly of the times before Gus's death. He told her about the camping trips he and Gus had taken in the Ramapo Mountains in Jersey. Not mountains really, he realized now. More like hills. But to a pair of boys they were as wild as the Himalayas, and at night you could frighten yourself with the snarls and growls of bobcat – sounding more like a stray cougar than any bobcat, particularly as the fire died and the moon crept behind a cloud bank and the trees moved in on you.

He told her what it was like for a young boy on the edge of adolescence, to run rustling though the dry leaves on a fall day so clear and sharp it might snap, on your way to the high school football game, the drums and brass throbbing, striking some nascent primeval chord and setting it thrumming with a longing to stand atop the hill and roar challenges at one and all. He told her of his junior varsity career, and later, of the season when he got to answer that longing, and emerged as the starting varsity quarterback and the star pitcher on the baseball team in his senior year, after a year hiatus. And then he told her about that missing year, and why he'd not been able to play.

As dawn broke, and they lay in each others arms, he told her about Gus's death. About his own cowardice; about the long night that came after, a night from which Pete slowly surfaced, a night that ultimately ended in jolt of electricity designed to scramble his synapses and enable him to start over. Then he told her about his father's retreat into silence, about the phrase uttered in the kitchen that still haunted him. Told her the only certain thing he knew was that Gus had called out, and he'd not answered that call.

He told her these things expecting she would turn from him, the way his father had, his eyes averted or full of numbness and blame. But

Karen didn't do that. She'd put her arms around him and said, "It wasn't your fault. They would have killed you."

"Maybe some things are worse than death." And then he told her about Elizabeth, and the two children who would never be borne now; how he knew he could never trust himself to be a Father. "I let him die, Karen. There's nothing that will ever erase that. Nothing."

And then she held him, and he felt her tears dripping onto his shoulder, and he let his tears come, too, and they remained in each others' arms until the sun streamed in and it was time to go.

On the ride over, she tried one last time to talk him out of going, but Pete stopped her. When she dropped him off at All Souls, she said, "I'll meet you in Vancouver on June 2. We'll go sailing."

"I'll be there."

"Promise?"

"Promise." He kissed her a long lingering kiss, designed to last the month, and watched her climb into her car and drive off. Just before she was out of sight, he touched the medallion, and said quietly, "I love you," then stepped forward to join the others.

PART TWO:

THE WOLVES DID COME

When Saya tamed the beasts, he left two free of Man; the Grizzly, to keep him from hubris and to teach him humility; and the Wolf, to watch over him, and teach him to love that which he must ultimately take, so that he might not take too much.

Lynx, One of the Last of the Dunne-za

CHAPTER 15

Twenty-four hours later, Pete was soaring over an endless expanse of trackless wilderness in a De Haviland Twin Otter piloted by a transplanted Haitian named Bob Duquoin. Now, two and a half hours out of Smithers, they banked east and passed over a spine of snow-capped summits. The land was dotted with lakes, bogs, and rivers, with vast stands of spruce, grading up slope into krumholtz and alpine willow, which finally gave way to granite-grey summits covered with snow. To the west, the mountains took on the blood-red hue characteristic of the Spatsizi Wilderness Preserve. There was no sign of humanity anywhere.

Jake gestured ahead, and Duquoin descended and eased the plane between two snow-capped peaks. As they dropped down a bit more, they inched past a huge granite face on their right, and a long narrow lake, its axis running east-west, came into view. It was surrounded by snow-capped mountains, and ice still covered the western end. Jake pointed to a spit of land to the northwest, and Duquoin passed over the lake, inspecting it for drift wood or other obstructions, then circled back and set up for his landing.

The plane dropped quickly, and Duquoin touched down on the east end. Pete checked his watch – a little after two. The noise intensified as they taxied toward the small peninsula. Throttling back, Duquoin beached the Otter on some soft ground on the south side of it. When he came to a stop, he shut down the engines, plunging them instantly into an ear-splitting silence.

No one said anything for what seemed several minutes. They just looked about in awe. Finally Jake spoke. "This is it, ladies and gentlemen. This is what we have been training for. Welcome to my world."

Pete looked around. The lake was surrounded by a wall of snow-capped mountains and to the east and north, the snow covered the ground in patches right down to the water's edge. The air seemed colder than he expected, and he zipped up his windbreaker against the chill. Jake stood up. "What are you waiting for? Get out there." He looked about with satisfaction, then turned back to the group, "Thom. What's the first thing you need to do?"

"Find a way back, home, Drill Sergeant." They all laughed, including Jake.

"This *is* your home, Thom. It's always been your home. You've just forgotten it." He stepped down onto the pontoon, then leaped onto the shore and quickly rounded up some branches to make a crude bridge. Balancing himself on a couple of rocks, he helped the others out, one by one. Everyone but Eunice managed to make it without getting wet. When they were all on shore, he hollered to Duquoin, "June 1st. Cold Spring Lake at the Tommy Walker Cabins."

Duquoin waved and hollered back, "I'll be there. Be safe ... and good luck, Bro'," then he revved the engines up and taxied out toward the middle of the lake, orienting his plane eastward for takeoff. Pete stood on the shore with the rest of them and watched the plane accelerate down the lake, ascend, and disappear around a peak. He listened as the racket from the DeHaviland faded away, like a dying breeze, until it simply wasn't there any longer.

Before Pete could drink in the place, Jake mounted a rock by the shoreline and called them around. "Listen up. I'm going to scout around the area, and then there's something I've got to do. This is your home now, so start getting it in shape. With this many people you should be able to live pretty well if you're smart and you share the labor. While I'm gone, put some shelters together, and get a fire going. You might want to try catching some fish. There's monster Lake Char in here, and you might get some Dolly Varden, and Arctic Grayling. Remember, this is bear country so take the proper precautions." With that, he hopped down and started to jog up the slope.

"Where are you going?" Eunice called after him, but Jake was already too far away to hear her tinny voice.

Rita hollered, "Hey. You can't just leave us here."

He'd disappeared into the forest, but his answer resonated across the distance, "I'll be back. Meantime, Pete's in charge." And then he was gone, leaving the twelve to stare at one another in disbelief.

Pete looked the group over. The last thing he wanted was to be in charge. Ben stood by his side. Sarah, Bill, Clio, and Ruth were in a clutch, awaiting instruction. He could count on them, although Bill and Ruth both looked like they were craving a latte, and Rita, who was off to the side seemed to be having smartphone withdrawal. She was playing absently with a small rectangular piece of pine bark she'd found. Eunice, her skin flushing, was muttering disapprovals to Joan who nodded, her long neck punctuating each complaint. Keller had walked up the slope a bit, and stood off by himself, studying the group. Jim was leaning against a spruce, his huge frame bigger than the trunk of the tree, regarding Pete sullenly. Thom was still at the shoreline, gazing at the spot in the sky where the plane had disappeared. *Not exactly the A-team,* he thought.

He did a quick inventory of what needed to be done, and who best could do it. OK. Rule of threes: Three minutes without air, three hours without shelter, three days without water, three weeks without food. And three months without love, he thought. Caressing the medallion Karen had given him, he wondered how the hell he'd ended up here with this crew, and with Jake. And what the hell Jake was up to, leaving us here on our own, not ten minutes into the trip? Karen was right. This is insane.

But we're here now, he thought. Might as well survive. "Ben. You and Sarah start setting up some lean-to's and a fire ring up on that knoll." Ben gave a mock salute, and the two headed off.

"Clio. See that stream coming in?" He pointed to a stream that entered the lake where the small peninsula met the mainland about a quarter mile east of where they stood.

"Yeah."

"Take Joan and Ruth and set up one of those Indian fish snares across it." Clio looked back quizzically. "It was in our third class, I think. Kind of like a net, remember? You put a series of stakes in a v-shape with the 'v' facing downstream and weave in webbing made from saplings. I think I saw some willow ..."

"OK, Kimosabe, I remember, now."

"When you're done, give Ben a hand. And keep your eye out down there."

"Thom, Bill?"

They stepped forward and Thom said, "Yeah, boss?"

"Gather some fire wood and then start a fire."

"OK if I use these?" He fished a package of matches from his pocket.

Pete smiled, remembering the confrontation between Thom and Jake back at the airport. He'd forced Thom to pitch a carton of cigarettes and his lighter. It seemed so long ago. "Absolutely."

"Jim, you and Rita scout the area east and north of here for anything edible. Pine nuts, stuff like that. And pick out some saplings for spears."

"Jesus. A pansy-ass bureaucrat giving orders." Jim growled. "What's next? You gonna hand out merit badges?" There was an almost palpable hostility in his voice, Pete noticed with a shiver. Great, he thought. Keller's threatened to kill me, and the biggest guy on the expedition hates me. He struggled to think of a way to defuse Jim's hostility without a confrontation, but couldn't come up with anything.

Before it had a chance to turn ugly, Rita stepped up to Jim, and slipped her arm beneath his. "Relax, big boy, and I'll make it worth your while," she said, vamping as usual. Pete could have kissed her.

"I'll scope out things to the west and north," he said, relieved. "Oh, and keep an eye out for bear sign while you're out there. You both know what to look for?"

Jim gave him an annoyed look, but Rita answered, "Scat, prints, scraped bark, torn saplings, dens."

"OK, Good. When you're satisfied, come on back and give Ben a hand."

"We might be a little late," Rita said to Ben as she tightened her hold on Jim's arm and ushered him towards the east end of the clearing. Everyone laughed except Jim and Keller.

Pete had deliberately avoided giving any orders to Keller, fearing the response he'd just gotten from Jim. But Keller surprised him and said, "I'll go with them." Chasing K-street, Pete thought.

He turned to Eunice who was still looking a bit scared, "You can come with me."

He took her and headed west. He intended on hiking up the shoreline a ways and then striking north toward a cliff face he'd seen from the plane. It had looked to be a couple of mile's walk up a steep mountain face, but it was high enough to allow him to examine the entire area. Then he'd come back east a ways and head towards camp, checking for signs of bear and anything edible along the way.

Now, as he hiked up the slope he noticed that Eunice was struggling to keep up. He was used to outpacing people, but even at that, he could see that she was in pitiful shape. After ten minutes, she'd been forced to stop and bend over to catch her breath, and they were less than half way to the cliff. Baggage, he thought. Nothing but baggage. Can't imagine why Jake chose her.

It took longer than he'd intended, but they came to the clearing above the cliff and found themselves on a small open plateau with the lake and the valley below and in front of them, and a thick forest of spruce and lodgepole pine surrounding them on three sides. Pete surveyed the area below while Eunice gulped down air beside him. When he was satisfied that he'd catalogued key details such as streams, peaks and mountain passes and formulated a mental map of the area, he checked to see if Eunice was ready, then headed back down to the join the others. They walked in silence, and Pete scanned the area for sign. He saw a pile of scat and some wolverine tracks, but little else, and no edibles to speak of. As they neared the camp, Eunice said, "I have to pee." She looked miserable, and for a moment he felt sorry for her.

"I'll walk ahead," he said. "Will you be OK?" She nodded, hesitantly, and he started down. A few minutes out, he heard her scream, and he raced back to find her staring at the ground, while her hands worked her ruddy face. When she saw him approach, she said, "Don't you *ever* leave me alone out here again."

"What's the matter?"

"I heard something."

"It's just your imagination."

"Then what is *that?*" She pointed to a print in the soft ground at her feet. It'd been left by a good sized wolf, Pete noted, and he cursed himself for missing it. But when he bent down to examine it, touching the sides gently, he thought he detected some warmth in the heel pad. In any case, the fact that the moisture was just starting to weep back into the depressions confirmed that there was a good chance he hadn't missed it. The wolf may have passed between them. He studied the tracks, beginning where the animal had intersected their trail, then walking a few yards down slope. He studied the wolf's foot placement, recalling Jake's lessons on tracking. What he saw made the hair on the back of his neck rise. From the gait, it looked like the animal had been stalking Eunice. Pete traced the trail a few yards further down slope to be sure. No mistake. The animal, coming up slope toward Eunice, had dropped its rear foot directly into the print of the front paw – something trackers called direct register, or perfect walking. Pumas were known to do this as a matter of course, foxes, too. But wolves generally used it only when stalking prey. Pete walked the trail back up slope to where Eunice stood, and then went several yards further. Somewhere very near where they stood, the animal had slipped back into a standard diagonal gate – it hadn't run away, but at least it had stopped stalking.

"What is it?" Eunice hissed.

"Shhh. Keep quiet." He continued to trace the tracks up slope from her, scanning the area ahead to see if he could spot the animal before it retreated from view. After several passes, he saw out of the corner of his eye, what looked like a pair golden embers glowing in the shadows of a spruce tree not fifty yards away. When he focused on the spot, a silver grey wolf appeared. It was sitting on its haunches and staring down at them, nearly invisible in the dappled light that filtered through the spruce. If it hadn't been for the eyes he would have missed it. As Pete expected from the depth and size of the prints – they were more than five inches long – he was a big fellow, probably weighing in close to one hundred and twenty five pounds.

At that moment Clio scampered up, "Everyone OK?" she asked. "I heard a scream."

"Look," Eunice said, pointing at the print.

Clio examined the print. "It's a wolf ..." she ventured.

"But is it dangerous?" Eunice asked

"Nah. He won't bother us," Clio answered. "Wolves won't attack people, right Pete?"

"There's been a couple of instances but nothing real serious," he said, still looking at the wolf above them. But we might have just come close to changing that, he thought. "Come on. Let's go give Ben a hand." The two headed toward camp, and Pete followed, feeling the wolf's eyes boring into his back as he went.

CHAPTER 16

Karen called in sick after dropping Pete off. She was trying to focus on a brief due the next morning, but she found herself wandering around her townhouse, picking up a piece of mail, staring at it for a moment without reading it, then tossing it down, and foraging for another. She tried going through her email, but couldn't stick with it either. After a while, she gave up, made some coffee, and allowed herself to be consumed with memories of the last few weeks; the touching, the talking, the lovemaking, the lingering intimacy of bodies and souls. For the next two hours, she sipped at her coffee while she retrieved pieces of their time together, turning them over and examining them, not quite trusting that the whole thing could have happened the way she was remembering it, but knowing it had. She could still feel the echoes of the night before in her limbs and muscles – warm, relaxed almost to the point of being liquefied, yet potent, like a satiated lioness.

She knew Pete needed to go on this trip. Somehow, he'd convinced himself that being out there would wipe his slate clean. Not that he'd been guilty of anything. There was nothing he could have done to save Gus. Nothing. But men, she knew, are funny creatures. Curious mixtures of strength and vulnerability, and in this, Pete was no different.

She loved knowing this about him. Loved learning his secrets, and sharing hers with him. For three years she'd been intrigued with him – drawn by his passion for what they did, a passion leavened by a sense of fun and a healthy cynicism for the bureaucracy they operated in – and by his brilliance and quiet confidence. Long before she admitted that she was in love with him, she'd find herself making excuses to work together. Sometimes in the evenings, she'd replay the times they'd spent together, remembering a look, a laugh, a touch. Mornings, she began checking her calendar before getting dressed to see if she would be seeing him, and choosing her best outfits for those days when she would. And yet, now she knew beneath the veneer he presented to the world, he'd been carrying around this baggage for decades. And it made her love him even more.

Yeah, funny creatures. Well, if this trip helped him sort it out it would be worth it.

But maybe Pete hadn't convinced himself to go, she thought. Maybe Jake convinced him. God knows he'd made each of his chosen group believe they could purge their secret shames, escape their darkest fears or realize their most cherished ambitions in the purity of the wilds. Even Ben. By the end, she'd almost wanted to go herself. They all seemed to have some angle Jake exploited – ambition, redemption, escape. And Jake had used that to select them in some way. Of that she was sure. All of them except Jim. She'd been unable to figure him out. It was almost as if he'd invited himself.

And even if Pete thought he'd find answers out there, the trip bothered her. Jake bothered her. Coming out of nowhere. Ads in the City News. Selected phone calls. The way he'd winnowed down the class to his chosen twelve, no more, no less. His whole save-the-world bit. Messianic. She'd learned to trust her feelings over the years, and she decided to get to know a little more about this Jake guy, starting with the PI Ben had mentioned. She rummaged around in her purse and found the number. What had Ben said? Give him time to mend. She flipped back to their discussion and figured it had been close to a couple of weeks ago. Two weeks. That'll have to do. Three hours difference to Seattle, so ... let's see, it's seven o'clock out there. Too early? Tough. She dialed the number.

"Barnett residence." It was a woman with a Spanish accent.

"Chas Barnett, please."

"I'll have to take a message."

"Wait. Please. Tell him Ben Fisk suggested I call."

The woman hesitated, then said, "Jus' a moment, I will tell him."

After a few minutes a man came on and said, "Can I help you?" His voice sounded surprisingly strong.

"I'm sorry to bother you. My name's Karen Flannigan. I believe Ben Fisk said I'd be calling?" She stopped, not sure what to say next.

"Yeah. About that Jake character, right?"

"Yes. I'm in need of a little reassurance, Mr. Barnett."

"Call me Chas. Go on."

"Well, a man I care about went on this trip with Ben. And I can't shake the feeling that he's in danger." She'd almost said, *the man I love.* Amazing she thought.

"If he's with Ben, he is."

The comment landed like a blow. "But Ben said you found Jake to be OK. He said he checked out with you."

"Oh, he did. As far as the numbers go. But danger is sort of the point of this trip, isn't it?"

"I suppose. But what do you mean, as far as the numbers go?"

"There's at least two levels to a background screening. There's the numbers, then there's the man behind the numbers. What he says he is, versus who he is. Ben asked me to check and see if Jake was what he claimed to be. And he is. Age, birth date, birth place, military service, high school and college degrees, grades, addresses, all that stuff was pretty much as Jake claimed. He was even being a bit modest. If he hadn't gone into the Navy, he probably would have ended up as a starting linebacker in the pros. Or he could have been a world class physicist. CalTech, MIT and Princeton were in a bidding war to get him into their graduate programs," he added.

"So he's OK?"

"As I said, I found Jake to be everything he said he was and more." Chas was quiet for a moment. "There were a few loose ends that bothered me, though. I was going to check them out when my ticker went."

"Like what?"

"I'm not sure it's appropriate to get into that."

"Appropriate? You let these people put their lives in the hands of a man you had doubts about. That sound appropriate to you?"

"Calm down Miss. Ben Fisk is my best friend. If I hadn't just had my chest ripped open and my heart stopped while they played roto-rooter with it, you can be sure I would've followed up by now. Even though Ben didn't ask me to."

Chas was quiet after that, and Karen listened to his breathing, now sounding a bit raspy. What the hell am I doing she wondered? I'm going to kill this poor bastard if I don't get a grip. "I'm sorry. I'm usually not so ..." Karen stopped, and then began to cry softly into the phone, hating herself for doing it. Such a cliché, the helpless damsel. Covering the mouthpiece, she collected herself, "I'm sorry. I shouldn't have bothered you with this so soon. I'm sure they'll be fine ... Thank you for your time. I hope you feel better." She hung up and let herself have a good cry, and decided it would be the last tear she shed over this. She would figure out a way to do something. Anything. No standing idly on the widow's walk with tear-stained cheeks for me, she told herself. In the meantime, she'd stay busy. Just as she was managing to pull herself together, the phone rang.

She recognized Chas' voice immediately. "What are you so worried about?" he asked.

Karen thought a minute. "It's Jake."

"What about him?"

"I think you'd have to have met him to understand."

Chas didn't say anything for a while, and Karen was beginning to think the line had gone dead when he said, "Tell you what, I'll have one of my investigators pin down those loose ends."

"Thank you. But I wish you'd tell me what you mean by loose ends."

She heard Chas sigh on the other end of the phone, and waited. Finally he said, "You get a feeling in this business after a while. You examine the details of a person's life and a little alarm goes off. Look at this guy. Physics major, 4.0 average. Football star, eligible for the NFL draft. And what does he do? Joins the Navy as an enlisted man. That sound right to you?"

"No."

"Me neither. Then there were a few major gaps in his timeline. And he seems never to have used credit in his life, and he's never been sick as near as I can tell. Oh, and then there was the witness."

"The witness?"

"The one who survived the bear attack. This guy was the thing that really made my alarm go off."

"Why?"

"He was a tenured college professor, engaged to be married, an environmentalist, political aspirations. That whole bit. But after the trip, he all but vanished. When I finally tracked him down, he was hiding out in some remote research center in the San Juan Islands and refused to talk to me. He seemed ... I don't know ... terrified."

"I don't like the sound of this."

"Neither did I." Chas was quiet for a moment, "But look. Sometimes there's a good explanation for these things. I don't want you worrying because I've got an overactive imagination."

"Disappearing witnesses aren't an overactive imagination. Especially if they're terrified."

"Let's not panic. I expect the Doc's gonna clear me for limited work in couple of weeks. When he does, I'll get to the bottom of things with this witness. In the meantime, I'll have one of my guys do that follow up work. I'll call you with anything I learn."

"I don't know if I can wait that long."

"They're all grown ups. And Ben is as good a judge of character as there is. In the end, we have to trust their judgment. They went into this with their eyes open."

"I wonder. Now that they're gone, I'm not sure they had a choice. Jake's a snake oil salesman. And a damn good one. He almost had me wanting to go."

"Nobody makes Ben Fisk do anything he doesn't want to do."

"You don't know Jake."

"No." Chas was quiet again, and Karen listened for his breathing. Finally he said, "But after this conversation, I'm going to get to know him. Real quick. Meanwhile, try to relax. Jake's highly thought of around here – practically a legend."

"Yeah? Like Sleepy Hollow?"

CHAPTER 17

Pete stood out on the edge of the peninsula and looked back with satisfaction. Smoke curled up from a fire flanked by four snug lean-tos, closed on three sides, but open to the fire. A stack of wood sufficient for the night and the next morning lay nearby. Clio sat by the fire cutting a spear from a birch sapling, using a crudely knapped piece of chert Pete had flaked to a sharp edge. Jim was hardening the tip of another in the flames. Earlier, Pete had inspected the fish trap, and several good-sized fish – Greyling and even a couple of Lake Char – were pinned against the stakes and webbing by the current. They'd have enough to eat for now. Later he'd have a look for some arrowroot or maybe cattail shoots near the shore. Both were rich in vitamins, and they'd provide fiber. He sorted through the list of edible plants they'd studied, trying to find other sources, but came up blank, except for some miner's lettuce and a kind of edible lichen, both of which he'd seen growing in abundance along the slope northeast of the camp. Early spring was a tough time in nature, he knew. The nuts and seeds were mostly gone, and the fruits and berries weren't out yet.

Pete took one more look down the lake. The sun was getting low; in less than an hour it would set behind the mountains. Already, the light was shifting to that green-gold glow that forests take on just before sunset, and the day was pausing as a stillness descended.

This was one of his favorite things about real wilderness. The complete absence of man-made sounds. To Pete, it seemed as if he lived within a din that was impossible to get away from. The hum of a copy machine; the annoying chirp of the proliferating cell phone; traffic; horns; beepers; sirens; radios; a babble of voices, shouts, and hollers.

Every where he went it followed him. But not here. Here, he would know the world as it was before civilization had rendered nature mute. He closed his eyes and listened. A jay screamed at them from his left, a breeze hissed through the forest behind him, carrying the faint odor of pine to his nose. He heard footsteps approaching and turned to see who it was.

Ben strolled down to his side. "Beautiful isn't it?"

"God, Ben. I feel like I've waited my whole life for this, you know?"

"Yeah. I feel it, too. It's like I've come home."

They were quiet for a while, watching, listening, feeling. After a while Ben said, "He's been gone a long time. Think something could've happened to him?"

"Who knows? Worst case? He got eaten by a bear or something and we're on our own."

"Should we send out a search party?"

"No. He'll be back. He's probably messing with us."

"Do we have the radio?"

"I think it's with him."

"Great." Ben looked at the sun and then back at the others. "It's going to be dark soon. The natives'll get really restless."

Pete checked the camp. They seemed content. Jim, Rita and Keller were going off to the fish trap to spear some dinner, and Clio and Sarah were layering more branches on the lean-tos as the evening's chill came on. The rest sat around the fire. He checked the sun; fifteen minutes till dark, he thought. Then they'll start freaking out. He sat down on a flat rock and watched the lake turn to glass as evening came. Ben sat opposite him. "Karen's meeting me in Vancouver when we get back," Pete said.

Ben nodded. "Good. She's a keeper."

"Yeah ... but I'm not sure it's the right time for me to be getting serious with anyone."

"If I were you, I'd worry a whole lot less about the right time, and a whole lot more about the right girl."

"It's so soon after my divorce and ... there's some stuff I need to figure out."

Ben frowned, turning his big eyebrows into exclamation marks. "Let me ask you something."

"Shoot."

"How many truly happy marriages do you think there are?"

Pete thought of his own failed marriage, his parent's marriage, his friends' marriages, and then recalled the statement his marriage counselor made early in their sessions. "The issue isn't happiness. The issue is, can you make it work?" Most could best be described as functional. He came up with only one. "Some," he answered.

"Damn few," Ben replied. "You ever looked around at commuters? People charge off to work like their tails are on fire, but most come home dragging their butts. And when they get home they invent things to do to keep from spending time together. The less imaginative go for lawn care. You ever wondered about that?" Pete shook his head. "You've got grown men spending most of their weekends in their yards. Hell, some of them the better part of every minute they're home. And the wives are just as happy to let them. Why? Do they really hate dandelions that much? Hell, no. They just don't want to be stuck in that house facing each other.

"But me? I had dandelions. Yard was covered with them. Because I loved my wife. Thought the sun set and rose around her. It was like that from the first time we met. She could light up a room just by walking in. Everybody who knew her was better for it – me most of all. She was a real partner, too. Everything we did in business, we did together."

"I guess that's what we all want. But you're right. Damn few get it."

"Ahhh. You would have loved her, Pete. Strong. Good. Fun. And passionate. God she was passionate. About everything. And I tell you, I look at you and Karen and I see me and Louise when we were young."

"Yeah. But it's complicated."

"It always is. But here's the deal, young man. The only thing you need to ask yourself, is would you and Karen have dandelions in your yard. Me? I think you'd have a yard full of them ... if you could just trust what you feel."

Trust myself, he thought. Wouldn't that be nice. He looked over at the mountains across the lake. Shadows had crept up the peaks, and the valleys between them were slipping into the night. The ranges looked purple now in the twilight and although the south-facing campsite they'd chosen would get sun for another few minutes, Pete knew that in the mountains, darkness would come quick when it came. He tried to gauge the time, and decided it was after eight.

"Mind if I ask you something?" Ben asked.

"Go ahead."

"What happened with your marriage?"

Pete sighed heavily, "The short version? She wanted kids and I didn't."

"Really? You don't strike me as someone who doesn't want kids."

Pete rubbed his eyes, bringing his hand down over his chin. This was going places it shouldn't. "It's more complicated than that. I wasn't ready ... and I guess she got tired of waiting. Can't blame her."

"Everything's complicated with you." Ben checked the campsite then said, "If people waited until they were ready the human race would've died out eons ago. But the way it works is, you have 'em then you learn."

"What if you learn you shouldn't have any? Then what?"

Be studied him a long time. "We don't know each other very well, but I'm a good judge of character. I'd say any kid would be lucky to have you as a father. Thing I'd like to know, what makes you think he wouldn't?"

"We better get up to camp."

"Why is this so hard for you to talk about, cowboy?"

Pete shrugged. The last crescent of sun slipped behind the mountain across the lake, and the air took an immediate chill. He watched as evening stained the wispy clouds salmon and he let the colors shrink westward and deepen to blood-red while he contemplated what to say. A part of him wanted to tell Ben everything, but another part wanted to end this conversation now. He split the difference. "I had a little brother. Great kid. He had everything. Charm. Looks. Brains. A phenomenal athlete." He watched the darkness closing in for a minute, recalling Gus, then continued. "He had this way about him. When he walked into a room, it just got better. And when he grinned at you, you smiled back. You couldn't help it." Pete felt himself smiling now, despite the memories; smiling at the thousand times Gus had made him laugh, or changed the trajectory of a shitty day, or simply made him feel more alive, merely by his presence. Then he came to that night and he frowned. "He died right in front of me. I let it happen."

Ben looked as if he'd been struck, then he quickly turned to hide his expression.

"Yeah," Pete said, "That's usually a conversation stopper."

As Pete watched, Ben's expression shifted from shock to compassion. Better than most, Pete thought. Finally, Ben said, "I'm sorry, Pete. That was a bit more than I was expecting."

"Usually is."

"What happened, exactly?"

"We got jumped. He got beat to death. I didn't stop it."

"There's got to be more to it than that."

"There were seven of them. Three held me. The other four beat Gus."

"Why'd they jump you?"

"I think they were gangbangers of some kind. One of them bumped into Gus and he said something to the guy ... Something like watch where you're going asshole. It escalated after that, but Gus wouldn't back off. I finally pulled him away. But they followed us, and caught us in an alley and ..." Pete didn't finish.

After a while, Ben said, "Nobody could stop seven people."

"Yeah. That's what I keep telling myself. But I could have tried." Across the lake, a fish jumped, and he watched the concentric rings of opalescence expanding over the black water. "My father took it pretty hard. Gus was his favorite. I think he started dying from that day on, and he pretty much blamed me."

"Did you ever get some help on this?"

"Oh yeah. I went into a deep depression afterwards. Places so damn dark I thought I'd never see light again. Spent some time in the hospital. Finally got blasted out of it with electro-shock therapy."

"How about your father? Did he get help?"

"The shrink wanted us to do family therapy. Said I'd never be able to put it behind me until I confronted my father." It was nearly dark now, and Pete paused. He could just make out Ben's face searching his through the gloom.

"Did you?"

"My father wasn't the type to talk about feelings. He came to the hospital once, but after a few minutes he said, *I don't see the point ... is any of this going to bring Gus back?* The shrink said, *This isn't about*

Gus, it's about Pete. My father said, *He can take care of himself. It's what he does best.*

Ben stared out at the Lake for a full minute. Finally he said, "You can't spend the rest of your life running from this. Or blaming yourself ..."

"Then who do you suggest I blame?"

"How about Gus."

"He was just a kid. And I didn't prevent it. How do I stop running from that?"

"That's a mighty heavy burden to be carryin' around by yourself. Might want to talk about it a bit more before we leave, eh?"

"Thanks. But I seem to do better when I let this dog lie."

"Dogs like this don't lie down for long ..." Ben's usually strong voice trailed off. "I'm going to guess this had something to do with why you crushed your wine glass that night."

Pete nodded, then looked behind him. The shadows were climbing rapidly up the mountain, and but for the fire, their little campsite was already obscured in shadow. An argument of some kind was breaking out. "We'd better go see what's up." They stretched as they stood, then they walked up the slope to the campsite. When they arrived, they found Rita and Eunice holding a twenty pound char on a spit over the fire. Fish guts were strewn on the ground not far from them, and Clio was fuming.

Pete looked around at them in disbelief. "What the hell are you doing?"

Thom was looking down, avoiding his gaze. Clio, looking disgusted, said, "I tried to stop them, but they wouldn't listen."

Eunice interrupted. "Well, if it isn't the self-appointed leader of the pack," she replied. "Through contemplating your navel?"

"Jesus Christ. Get this shit cleaned up. And get that fish out of here. Now."

Rita looked confused. "But ... Dan and Jim said it would be OK."

"Are you trying to get us all killed?"

"Don't be such a wimp." Jim answered.

"Little Petey's scared," Keller said.

Pete stood there, the smell of char wafting out from their campsite, a silent signal to every bear within miles, and felt fear – but not of bears. He was hearing those thugs again, seeing them close in like a pack of jackals, feeling his guts turning to ice. Again.

CHAPTER 18

The voice fired out of the forest and struck like lightning, "And you should be, too, Keller." Jake's figure seemed to coalesce as he stepped into the orange glow of the fire, and his words reverberated like a thunder clap rumbling up a valley. "Now do as he said. Clean this shit up. Get it all. Burn the soil. And set up a cooking fire down by the stream."

For a long moment, Keller and Jake stood facing each other, the flickering fire making their faces alternately disappear and reappear in an eerie orange-tinted glow. When Jake finally broke the silence, his voice was quiet, but each word sliced the air like tempered steel, "Do you want to live, Keller?"

"Fuck you, Christianson. I'm not afraid."

Pete watched Jake's fists clench and open and clench, and he waited for the inevitable fight. But Jake took in a giant breath, exhaled, then smiled. "Well I am. So humor me, please. Clean up this mess. Help him out, Jim. Pete, you and Clio get a fire going down by the stream and finish cooking up this Char. Start smoking the rest. You're lucky. Food's not always going to be so easy to come by."

The moment passed, and Jake inspected the four lean-to's and complimented them on their craftsmanship. Pete watched Keller and Jim. They went through the motions, but without any sense of urgency.

Twenty minutes later, they all sat a quarter mile off down by the stream bed, waiting for the fish to finish cooking. Clio had cut two large filets with the piece of chert Pete had sharpened and they hung suspended about a foot above the fire on spits made from green willow. The skin was blackened, and fat began to drip off the filets into the fire, hissing, and sending up an aroma that made Pete's mouth fill with saliva. He suddenly realized how hungry he was. It had been only twelve hours since he'd eaten breakfast in Smithers, but it felt like he'd already passed his three weeks. "That thing ready yet, Clio?" he asked.

She pulled a hunk off gingerly, and tasted it. "Yeah. Damn, this is good." She placed it on a rock near the fire and took the stone blade and started cutting thick strips from its flank and laying them out on the rock. "Dig in," she urged. 'Careful. It's hot." The group gathered around, jockeying for position, and one-by-one they grabbed a slab and retreated to a spot around the fire and started gorging themselves on the rich meat. You could almost see the hunger enveloping them, Pete thought. No one talked until the smaller filet was gone ... better than a pound of meat a piece.

While they were eating, a pack of wolves began howling north of the camp, somewhere near the cliff face Pete and Eunice had climbed to earlier. When he'd eaten his fill, Pete recounted the story about the wolf, revealing for the first time that it had been watching him the whole time he'd tracked it. Eunice asked Jake, "What do you think he was doing?"

"I think he was laughing at us," Jake said. "I expect he finds us very entertaining."

Thom leaned back and unleashed an enormous burp. "Hell, this survival stuff is a piece of cake," he said, his chin and hands shiny with the heavy fish oil natural to cold water fish like char. Pete thought somewhere that wolf must be laughing again. Still, they had done well. Except for that incident up at the lean-to's. He glanced over at Keller. He was talking to Rita, but he looked bored, like an A-lister stuck at a D-list party.

When everyone was finished, Jake had them wash up and led them up to the camp, leaving Clio and Pete to smoke the remaining filet.

The place seemed wilder and darker after they left. Clio stoked the fire and she and Pete put green wood on it, and strung line above it. Next, Clio cut the remaining filet into slim strips and Pete proceeded to hang them about three feet above the fire, in the thick of the billowing smoke.

This would be a tricky time – they had to stay and feed the fire while the fish cured, but it was like an open-house invitation to every critter in the forest. Pete stared into the infinity of darkness that surrounded them, and struggled to penetrate it. He listened intently, but the stream gurgled and rushed over the rocks. Suddenly it sounded loud.

They were quiet for some time after that, listening to howling wolves, the stream, and the wind shushing through the branches above. They tended the fire and turned the fish periodically, but mostly, they tried to see through the frightening murk into the darkness that surrounded them. After a several minutes, it became obvious that the wolves were on the move, as their howls drifted off into the wind.

The smell of the fish as it smoked above the fire seemed like a silent alarm to Pete, and he was acutely aware that they were faced with the prospect of defending their catch against an animal capable of swatting them aside with about as much effort as he and Clio might expend on a hamster.

As he sat there guarding their cache, Pete thought about how fragile we were as a species – all of our evolutionary eggs in one basket: intelligence, reason. Sitting here in the middle of a black night, more than two hundred miles from the nearest gun or car or house or highway, he wondered what good his reason would do against a grizzly.

He started to share his thoughts with Clio, but she stopped him after the third sentence and said, "Does this lecture come with tranqs?"

He was stunned, then angry, then finally amused. "Bet you'd never guess my nickname was the Professor in grade school."

"No shit?" Then she looked serious and said, "I love you, man. Truly I do. You're what we used to call a righteous dude. But you've got to lighten up. You start thinkin' too much out here, you'll go mad."

"Yeah. And if I don't, we'll die."

"Maybe. But I'm gonna die smilin'."

After some time, Clio reached up and took a hunk of fish and examined it. "Should be ready in a few more minutes," she said. "So, how long before Keller and Jake come to blows?" she asked.

"I think that'll sort out. They're just pissing on trees and figuring out who the Alpha is."

"Still, it could be trouble."

"Well, I'm not gonna get all hung up worryin' about it."

Clio looked startled, then smiled. "OK. Sarcasm, right?"

Pete laughed. "Yeah." He reached up and tore off a strip of the fish. "How do we know if this is done?"

"I think it's supposed to get dry and leathery. Here let me see." Pete handed it to her and she felt it, then held it up to the firelight. "Looks pretty good." She took a taste, then made a face. "Jesus. This stuff is foul."

Pete tasted it. It had an almost petroleum tinge to it. He took another taste, and then he knew. Pine. Spruce. "It's this wood. Tastes like pitch." He swallowed the bit of fish, choking it down. A dozen pounds of this stuff. Still, they couldn't just throw it away. "Nothing to be done about it. Let's hang it up out of reach."

"Alright. But I'll tell you one thing. I'm sure as hell not going to fight a bear over this shit."

They made their way up to camp, and just before they turned in, Clio said, "Pete?"

"Yeah?"

"You keep thinkin', I'll supply the tranqs." She smiled, "You did good today. A lot of us were pretty scared there when it looked like Jake was gone."

"It ain't over yet."

Ben and Bill had left a space in one of the lean-tos for Pete, but he wasn't ready to sleep yet. He stoked the fire one last time and stared into it for a while before slipping into the lean-to. The ground was hard, but smooth. Normally, Pete could sleep anywhere, anytime. Even in the midst of his divorce after a harrowing argument, he'd drop off as soon as he hit the pillow. But tonight he was having trouble. He'd felt so prepared back in Washington. Now, out here, he was beginning to know how much he didn't know. And it was a lot. But most of all, he wasn't sure anymore why he was out here. Cathedrals. It had made sense back there. But out here, he was cold, dirty, itchy, and Keller was already screwing things up. He thought of Karen, and he fished the medallion out from under his shirt. He couldn't see it, but he felt the figures embrace with his finger tips, then kissed it. After a while he dropped off into a deep sleep and dreamed strange dreams of wolves.

CHAPTER 19

The next morning, Karen found herself standing in front of Lenny's at six thirty. Unable to sleep, she'd taken a long run along the mall and around the tidal basin, and over to the Arial Rios building. As she'd come down 12th Street, the sun was just kissing the tops of the buildings, and the streets were dark and quiet, the sidewalks mostly empty. Only a few grim-faced pedestrians were out, type A's trussed up in their Windsors and rushing toward their appointed heart attacks, Karen thought. Could have been me just a few years ago ... but for Pete.

Although the morning held the promise of warmth and the first really hot day of the year, it was still cool down on the street, and she'd decided to stop at Lenny's as much to avoid the empty office as anything. The door was still locked when she arrived and she saw him rummaging about inside behind the grill. When he spotted her, his face lit up and he hustled over to unlock the door. "Good to see you. I was just thinking how quiet it is in here without Pete," he said as he let her in. "Got kinda used to him stoppin' by 'bout this time an keepin' me company."

"I couldn't sleep." It was all she could think to say.

Lenny guided her to a table, "You're missing him, too huh?" Karen nodded. "Something besides coffee this mornin'?"

"Just whole wheat toast and some OJ."

"You're as bad as him."

He delivered the coffee then went back to the grill and continued his morning ritual, singing a good version of Percy Sledge's "When a Man Loves a Woman." Karen had been wrestling with demons all night, and she'd hoped the run and a breakfast at Lenny's would distract her, but the lyrics only made her feel Pete's absence that much more. Best friend, and now lover. He had been from the first time they'd met, but he'd been off limits and she'd kept her distance with strategically timed cynical banter, and a focus on business. She'd even managed to keep her feelings from herself, until that smart-assed therapist had called her on her whole careful construct of denying, not just him, but all thoughts of love and happily ever after with anyone. That stuff was a fantasy for other people, she'd said in her appointed hours, for several weeks on end. Nothing real about it. After about month and a half, the therapist had stopped one of these lectures and said, "You're in love with him, do you know that?" Karen denied it with such force that they both knew it had to be true. And then she'd had the nerve to be right again a few weeks later, when she said, "Have you considered that the reason you picked Pete is because he's not available ... Is it possible you're only willing to want what you can't have, because if you can't have him, you can't lose him, like you did your parents." Of course, Karen had no choice but to quit therapy after that. Too bad. 'Cause it would have been fun to tell the woman that she'd been wrong. Now she had Pete and she wanted him all the more. Somehow, he'd broken down those walls and let her trust again – not with a battering ram, but bit-by-bit, the only way anyone could have. The problem was, now that he was gone, she was in fact, terrified she'd lose him. Maybe feeling nothing was better after all, she thought.

"You OK, Karen?" Lenny was at her side, with the toast and OJ.

"Fine, thank you Lenny."

"You're scared for him, aren't you?"

Karen had spent the night reciting all the reasons he'd be OK and convincing herself she wasn't worried, but Lenny's comment cut through them all. She blinked back some of the moisture gathering in her eyes, then said, "Yeah. I am."

"You want to talk 'bout it?"

"No. I'm fine."

"You're a long way from fine, Karen." He sat down across from her and said, "Who else you got to talk to 'bout this but Lenny? No one. Right?"

She nodded again.

"I may not be edjumacated, but I ain't stupid. An' for a man with a big mouth, I can be a pretty good listener."

She surprised herself by taking him up on it. She launched into an abbreviated version of what she'd been thinking: about her therapist's barbs; about her conversation with the PI and the gaps he'd found in Jake's life; and finally, about how terrified she was, now that just when she'd let herself love someone, he might be in danger. Lenny listened closely, asking a few questions here and there, getting up once to tend to the grill, and refill her coffee.

When she was through, he said, "I don't know 'bout all that psycho-babble, but what I *do* know is this guy *is* trouble. An' I told Pete exactly that. Would he listen? No. But there ain't no two ways about it. This Jake fella's got more sides than the Pentagon, and just as many secrets. I seen it in him first and only time I set eyes on him. The other thing I know is this: there's one person for everyone on Earth. Most times, seems like they don't find each other. You and Pete's lucky. You did. Even when you were acting like a couple porcupines doing the tango, I knew you'd get together. So, if you're worried about him, you best do something. Anything'd be better 'n sitting around here making yourself crazy."

"But what can I do?"

"Go help that Chas fella. Be his legs. Get to the bottom of things. And if things are like I think they are, you go on up there, wherever it is Pete's at, and bring him back."

"I can't. There's my job ..."

"How many jobs are there?"

"What do you mean?"

"I mean there ain't but one Pete. There's lots of jobs. You figure it out. You love him, you got to do something."

"But I can't go traipsing around the wilderness by myself."

"You got a bad case of the cant's. Just start with that Chas fellow. An' if you do need to go out there an' get him, you had the same classes Pete had."

"But that's just books and lectures."

"You go on and do something, Karen. Otherwise you're gonna wake up and figure out you're right where that therapist lady said you was."

At first, Karen was angry, but the more she thought about it, the more she realized he was right. Hiding out back here in Washington was just a cop out. Besides, she'd go crazy sitting around for a month just waiting and wondering. As for the job? She'd banked two months worth of vacation. And if they didn't let her go, she'd quit ... it was long past time anyway. They hadn't been able to work on anything meaningful for eight years now, and prospects were only slightly better. Yeah, she had to *do* something. For the price of toast, coffee, and OJ, she'd gotten an hour of the best therapy she'd ever had. She got up, and hugged him, feeling his big round belly like a barrel between them. "Thank you," she said softly.

"Pete's my friend. So are you. Now you go on and get him."

CHAPTER 20

Morning came with a shock. Pete was balled up tight against the cold, and the sun streamed in bright, but weak. He checked the sky. Seven, maybe seven-thirty. Clio was already up, coaxing a fire from the coals. He tried to uncoil, and felt the stiffness in his joints. He was dirty, his head itched, and he felt as if he had a two-inch crust in his mouth. "Jesus. I need some coffee and some orange juice. And some tooth paste. And a shower."

Clio glanced over at him between puffs on the fire. She looked almost as good as ever. Her brown hair was a wild tangle of curls but apart from a streak of dirt on one cheek, she could have been back home with mirrors, showers, and makeup. "Boy do you look like shit," she said.

"Thanks. I must look better than I feel."

"Sleep OK?"

"Yeah. You?"

"Pretty good," she said, "Except those damn wolves started up again in the middle of the night."

One-by one they got up and gathered around the fire. Pete watched as two distinct groups formed. Keller, Rita, Joan and Eunice huddled together on one side of the fire. Thom, Ben, and Sarah joined Pete and Clio on the other side. The split wasn't surprising. Pretty much a microcosm of Washington. Special interests and power politics vs. idealists and other credulous believers of one sort or another. K Street vs. DuPont Circle. Bill and Jim kept to themselves, joining neither group.

Forty years old and hundreds of miles from civilization and we're still playing fucking high school games, Pete thought. Ruth was the one

Pete couldn't figure out. She'd been trying to maintain a certain aloofness, maybe a journalistic integrity, but it was obvious that she was becoming increasingly enamored with Jake. He kept her nearby – they were plainly attracted to each other, but so far as Pete knew, nothing had happened between them. The closer she got with Jake, the more withdrawn she'd become. It bothered Pete that she was so distant. When he did try to approach her, she appeared nervous and anxious around him. Only Ben seemed able to make her smile.

When they were all up and assembled, Jake appeared. He offered no explanation of where he'd been, or what he'd been up to the night before.

Rita said, "What's for breakfast?"

Jake looked at her and smiled. "Well, we could order out, but it might take a while."

She answered with a single word, "Fuck."

"Or we could bag a caribou and have steak."

"We've got fish," Pete said.

Jake laughed, "Yeah. And you cured it with spruce. Pretty tasty?" Pete shook his head, and Jake said, "We need rawhide and skins and guts to carry stuff. Water. Fire. Even your fish. And some of you are going to need warmer clothing." He looked the group over and selected Pete, Jim, Sarah, Bill and Ben to accompany him.

Keller immediately said, "I'm going, too."

"No. You're not."

Keller started to protest, but Jake cut him off. "We do things my way, out here. If you don't like it, there's the door." He pointed to the snow-capped mountains west of the Lake. "Cold Fish is about a hundred and fifty miles northwest of here. And you'll have to cross the continental divide to get there." Pete looked at the mountains marching westward, and shivered. While Keller considered his options, Jake turned quickly to Sarah and said, "And as for you, Ms. Tillington, which'll it be? Driver or hunter?"

"Hunter."

"You sure? Wood caribou can weigh the better part of three hundred pounds."

"I'm sure."

"So be it." He turned to Jim, who was holding one of the two spears they'd made and said, "Give the lady the spear." He picked up the other one and turned to Pete, Bill, Jim, and Ben. "Come here." He squatted down and swept the pine needles clear of the dirt and drew a crude map with the point of the spear, and laid out the plan. "You guys'll be the drivers. Follow the stream over that rise." He pointed to a break in the mountains north of the camp. "It heads west behind that range and crosses a meadow – maybe two miles in. You'll find a small herd of caribou grazing there. Keep downwind," he stopped and sniffed, "that's east – until you get around behind them. There's a stand of willow across the stream. Use it for cover and spread out in a line. Sarah and I will be in the woods on this side of the stream valley. When you're in place, signal me. I'll key off of you, Pete. When I want you to start driving them, I'll do this – here he made the call of a raven, indistinguishable from the real thing. When you hear that, come out hollering. Once you start, stay close enough together that they don't try to get through you. Twenty yards is about right. Pete, Ben, you take the flanks. Don't let them get around you, no matter what.

"Now, when they get near the woods they'll be a little nervous, and try to bolt so close in as you drive them. Sarah and I will do the rest. Oh, and watch the wolves. They're denned up northwest of here and there's some new cubs. They might be a little skittish."

He turned to Sarah. "When the caribou near the forest we'll attack from the side. Don't ... I repeat, don't try to take one head on. I'll pick out the animal. Follow my lead. The best place to put the spear is right behind the shoulder just about half way down." He examined the point of his spear. "It'll take a lot of force to penetrate their hide. The tendency when you first try to kill is to be gentle. Don't. It's a violent act, there's no way around it. Ready? Questions?"

There were none. "OK, let's do it."

Ben and Pete took off at a trot, heading toward the point east of the peninsula they were on. Jim and Bill followed. They climbed to the top of the rise, passing a series of small waterfalls formed where the stream cascaded down the steep slope. Once they'd crested the last fall, they saw the meadow Jake had mentioned about a half mile west. Pete turned them and picked up the pace a bit. It felt incredible to be out here running, not only through the forest, but through time, on their way to a Neolithic hunt, exercising the one physical advantage humans have – the ability to outdistance almost any other animal. On his longer training runs, Pete would imagine he was on just such a mission; a predator chasing its prey. It made the twenty or so miles he covered seem trivial.

As they broke into the meadow, he saw them. About six woodland caribou and a few calves grazing in the grass by the stream maybe a half a mile west. Pete stopped, ducked down, and gestured to the others, pointing first to the caribou, then toward the stand of willow just northwest of where they stood. If they made for it, they could get across the stream valley and behind the caribou without being seen. He noticed that Bill was breathing hard, and decided to rest the group before they tried crossing the meadow and herding the animals. "We'll rest here a minute." he whispered.

They nodded back, and Ben mouthed, "Yes chief," and he and Bill laughed silently. Pete gave them the finger. Jim was ignoring them all and suddenly he broke for the willows, running in a semi-crouch.

"Shit," Pete whispered. "What's that boy's problem?"

"Don't know, but he's carryin' a shitload of anger," Bill said.

"You OK to go on?" Pete asked.

"Fine."

"We better catch up, then."

They ran, crouched over, across the streambed to the willows, where Jim waited. "We have to do this together," Pete said.

"Then keep up," Jim answered.

"Listen asshole. I could run you into the ground. And so could Ben. We have to do this as a team or it's not gonna work. Clear?"

Jim shrugged, avoiding Pete's stare.

Ben said, "You want to eat?"

Jim nodded his head reluctantly.

"Then stick to the plan," he said.

Pete reviewed their roles. "OK. We spread out behind them on this side of the stream. No more than fifteen yards or so between yourself and the next man. I'll lead, Jim and Bill take the center, Ben, you take the flank." They nodded. "Good. No talking from here on. Stay in sight of the person in front of you. Move on your toes and watch for dry leaves and twigs. If you see their heads go up, freeze. Ready?" they nodded again and Pete said, "Let's go."

He took off through the stand of trees. It felt good to be out in front, alone, and his heart began racing, not from exertion, but from something far more primitive, a mixture of fear and excitement and strength, creating within him a focus he'd never felt before. Fierce in its intensity, fatal in its design. His feet flew across rocks, clumps of sedge and roots as effortlessly as on a cinder track, and all the while his eyes were fixed on his prey, attuned to every nuance of their consciousness. He noted how the calves moved with their mothers. He recorded the flick of an ear, the twitch of an eye, the slightest imperfection in each one's stride or posture or coat. Darting through the trees and brush, he instinctively evaluated each animal, sifting through these cues and a million others, sorting, reading, ranking, until one animal – an older cow – stood out as if lit by some celestial source, and he fixed his sights on her and her alone, saying yes, this is the one; this is our gift. As he dashed along amongst the willows, a prehistoric calm enveloped him, and he sensed the world as if in a tunnel containing nothing but him and his chosen quarry.

Suddenly, on the edge of his tunnel, he saw the cow nearest them raise her head, sniff the air, and hold her head back on arched neck, still as a sculpture. He froze, and signaled the others to do the same. Glancing over his shoulder, he saw that Jim stood motionless about twenty five yards to the south. The others must have gotten the signal, because the willows were silent. He waited, studying the young cow's eyes. They were deep and brown and seemed haunted by a constant fear – or was it vigilance? She searched the area, scanning it with her nose and ears, as much as her eyes, which Pete knew were notoriously bad. Capable only of seeing black and white, and not discriminating enough to pick out a still predator from the background, deer and caribou nevertheless survived, and escaped more often than not. They did it on the strength of extraordinary hearing and smell. The wind was coming from the west, Pete noted, so she wouldn't register them until they got a little further up the valley. She finished her scan, and went back to feeding. Pete let her eat for a moment before giving the signal to continue.

He was even with the last of the caribou now. Another twenty or so yards and he'd be far enough to keep them from skirting around his flank. He moved west, consumed still with that total focus; acute, aware, alert, alive. When he was far enough past the herd, he settled in behind some brush, and waited.

It was perhaps because of his heightened sense of awareness that he turned and saw it. Because later, he would realize that he felt it first. It was sitting up on a knoll just behind him and to his right, maybe fifteen yards into the woods. The same yellow eyes boring into his back again. The wolf sat on its haunches, and watched. Studying me as prey, Pete wondered? But no, when their eyes met, it was the exchange of equals, not a predator stalking prey. It was, Pete thought later, one of the most beautiful creatures he'd ever beheld. Its eyes were framed by a lush, almost metallic silver-grey coat, making their golden color glow against the darker background of forest and fur. And there flowed from those eyes, a wisdom and a sadness – a sadness that he would soon come to know. It was the sadness of the predator who has become one with that which he must take. Who knows that it must kill its prey with care, for in taking it, it also takes from its own potential to be. In each triumph, a death; in each victory a defeat; predator and prey sharing equally in both. But there was something else in the exchange, too. Something else he would come to know. It was the ruthlessness that enabled the wolf to kill despite this knowledge, despite this wisdom. Not malevolence, but a kind of fierce joy in playing its part.

Reluctantly, Pete took his eyes off of the wolf and returned them to the caribou. Across the clearing he saw Jake and Sarah waiting, ready. He checked Jim, who gave a thumbs up. Pete repeated the gesture to Jake. It was time. Jake raised his hand to his mouth, and the cry of a Raven pierced the air. Pete shot out into the clearing whooping, shouting, tearing at the surprised beasts who stared in shocked disbelief at this strange creature. Jim, Bill and Ben were charging out at twenty yard intervals to his left, and the caribou, alarmed now, sprinted for the forest, splashing across the small stream that bisected the valley, toward the wood and the waiting hunters. It was just a hundred or so yards to the edge, and the animals closed on it quickly. Pete was sprinting now, his breath leaving a trail of white puffs behind him. At the last moment the caribou veered away from the wall of trees in front of them, just as Jake said they would, and Pete raced to his right to intercept them, his arms pulling air, his feet churning dirt. By picking his angle carefully, and running as he'd never run before he just managed to turn them, but they still would not enter the forest, heading east instead, parallel to the trees so that in about forty yards they would pass the spot where Sarah and Jake waited at the edge of the forest. As Bill and Ben raced to stay out in front and keep them from bolting back across the stream, Pete watched in awe at the creature's movements. What he beheld was liquid grace, their bodies coiling and arching in astoundingly powerful leaps, each leap sending them soaring above the ground, eating up distance effortlessly. Here was true beauty, and Pete was mesmerized.

It was the sound that snapped him out of it. He heard it as they passed Jake. At first he thought it might have been the wolf, but then he saw Jake leap from the forest, spear raised, mouth open, issuing an otherworldly cry, a shriek really, chilling every living thing in the valley. He thought he heard the wolf answer, but he couldn't be sure. Jake appeared to cover the ground between himself and the caribou instantly and he cut off one of the creatures within seconds. It was the same older cow Pete had singled out. As she wheeled to avoid Jake, he plunged the spear into her side, and continued to push until it was buried deep into the caribou's shoulder. After lurching a few steps forward, she went down, still skewered on the spear. She fought to get up, but using the spear, Jake held her down while he continued to push, until his hand pressed hard against the animal's smooth flank.

Pete, who was close now, could plainly see Jake's face as he was plunging the spear in. He would remember it forever. His lips were pulled back, showing his teeth, and his eyes seemed lit from some dark glow within. It was the face of madness, of savagery. The caribou continued to struggle – her own wildness, her own desperation – showing in her eyes, as the life faded from them. Jake gave one more shout, then pulled the spear out and jammed it in again, sending the life shivering out of the animal in a mass of blood as the spear pierced her heart. She quivered a few times then lay motionless, dead.

Jake leaned over her, his face against the butt of the spear, as still as the animal. He remained like that, hunkered over the caribou in silence.

Pete watched, saying nothing. From the other side of the carcass Sarah stared, whether in awe or terror Pete couldn't tell. Finally, Jake lifted his face, but he seemed unaware of Pete or the others, who were running toward them now.

His hand was covered with blood, and a streak of red ran across his cheek where he'd leaned it against the blood-drenched spear. His foot rested on the animal's side, and he was hunched over the spear, his breath coming in great heaves. He seemed almost to be praying. His face no longer wore a mask of savagery. Or perhaps this other visage was the mask. Pete could not say. Finally, he slipped the spear out of the carcass. It made a slight sucking sound as it came.

CHAPTER 21

Karen stood on the street in front of the PI's house and checked the address. It was a large corner residence set on a hill in a decidedly upscale Seattle neighborhood with a view of Puget Sound and the Olympic Mountains beyond it. She'd been expecting something a little less grand; maybe a Chandleresque walk up in a rundown section of town. She knocked on the door, and it was answered nearly immediately by a well- tanned, silver-haired man in his mid 50's. He was trim, and dressed in expensive but casual clothes.

"You must be Karen." He stuck out his hand, "Chas Barnett. Come in. Come in." He continued, "I'm having dinner out on the deck. Can I offer you anything?"

"I'm fine, thanks."

"You can't tell me you're all filled up on airline food."

Karen smiled. For a guy recovering from a quadruple bypass, he exuded energy and confidence and she immediately trusted him. "I don't want to be a bother."

"Nonsense." Chas turned and called toward the kitchen, "Maria?"

"Si, Mr. Barnett?"

"Can you rustle up another dinner?"

Marie came around the corner to inspect the guest, giving Karen a disapproving glance after a cursory examination. Then she turned to Chas and said, "You need to rest." A matron with an unruly charge, Karen thought.

Chas just smiled at her, and nodded, then turned back to Karen. "So, you're a friend of Ben's?"

"I've only known him for three months. But yes. I'd say we're friends."

"He's easy to know and impossible not to like. A good man. Smart, too. Made two fortunes and got out at just the right time. Building a business is the fun part. Runnin' it is a pain in the ass. Heart attack makes you think about things like that, you know?"

"Yeah. Jake said the only thing that can get us thinking about life is death."

Barnett nodded again. "Quite the philosopher," he said, "Among many other things."

He escorted her through his living room and dining room to the back of the house. The furniture was an exquisite collection, all early oak pieces of Shaker design. They passed through double French doors onto a sunny back deck with a view of the snow-capped Olympians across the sound.

"They're out this evening. Doesn't happen too much."

Karen walked to the edge of the deck and stared. "This is something, for a ..." She stopped, not knowing how to complete the sentence.

"For a private eye?" Barnett finished it for her.

Karen smiled, "Sorry. I'm afraid I've listened to one too many Guy Noir episodes."

Barnett laughed. "We're not all Sam Spade clones. Take my wife and I. We have ten investigators on staff – each bills out at better than $250 an hour, plus expenses. Hell, my computer specialists bill at more than twice that. About half my business comes from corporate accounts, another third from private security accounts with corporate executives and we have affiliates in seven countries. Thank god my wife was in the business with me, or I'd have been screwed." He tapped his chest. "Between taking care of me and trying to keep all the balls in the air, poor girl's been working sixteen hours a day."

When they were seated at a large round glass and wrought iron table, Maria appeared with a carafe of red wine, two glasses and another place setting. After pouring their wine and setting Karen's place, she handed Chas Barnett a cup containing three pills. He took them from her reluctantly and put them on the table. Maria frowned then said, in a no nonsense voice, "Mrs. Barnett said I was to watch you take them."

He took the cup, mumbling, "Witch doctors," and downed the pills. "Stay healthy, Karen. 'Course, you never know. Look at me. I jogged, ate well, had the right genes. Then wham. You never know. But enough about me. I must say, I was surprised when you said you were coming out here. How long will you be in Seattle?"

"As long as it takes."

"As long as what takes?"

"Getting to the bottom of Jake."

Chas laughed, caught himself. "I'm sorry Ms. Flannigan ..."

"Karen."

"OK. I'm sorry, Karen. You're welcome, of course. In fact, Rose and I would like you to stay with us while you're here. But what exactly do you propose to do."

"How about the witness? I could talk to him."

Chas put his glass down and looked across the table. It was the first time since she arrived that Karen saw him without a smile. She felt his gaze, penetrating, and it became uncomfortable, as if she were watching someone read her diary. Finally, he seemed satisfied, and said, "You get right to the point, don't you?"

"Pete's in danger up there. I know it."

"Well, the good professor's got lockjaw. He's scared and he's hiding and he won't talk to anyone."

"There must be something I can do to help."

"Why are you so sure they're in danger?"

"I told you. I don't trust Jake."

He waited while Maria delivered a couple of smoked salmon salads. On a whim, Karen asked for some hot sauce. She caught Chas and Maria sharing a look and shrugged her shoulders. "I seem to have developed a craving for spicy foods," she said.

Chas took a generous swallow of his wine. "After your call the other day, I asked one of my men to chase down some of those blank periods in our man Jake's history. He was supposed to get back to me by COB today. Let's enjoy dinner, then I'll check and see whether he's come up with anything." Chas began eating, but noticed Karen wasn't joining in. "More wine?" Karen shook her head, and he topped his own glass to the brim. "It's my only vice left." He raised it, took another sip. Karen watched him, without touching her dinner. He put his glass down and said, "You're not going to eat until I check my computer are you?"

Karen smiled and shook her head.

"Alright. You win." He got up, and moving with the stiffness of the recently bed-ridden, left the room, and returned a few minutes later with a laptop. He started it up, and Karen waited impatiently as he went through a seemingly endless set of codes and passwords before saying, "It's here." He began reading, nodding now and then, while he munched on his salad. When he came to the end of the report, he said, "Jesus."

"What?"

"Do you know where they went?"

"Tatlatui. Then to Spatsizi."

"Can you find them?"

She shrugged. "It's a big area. Why?"

"I don't like what I'm seeing here."

"What is it?"

"Seems Jake spent some time in a State Institution up in British Columbia."

"Prison?"

"No. What we used to call an insane asylum."

"Oh my god. What for?"

"Can't tell, for sure. But it was court-ordered. Just after his stint with Lynx. My guys are checking it out."

"I would never have figured Jake for a nutcase."

"No. Me neither. It doesn't fit. Still, people get hospitalized for all kinds of reasons. Some good, some bad."

"When will you know more?"

"Hard to say. They tend to lock this stuff up pretty tight."

Chas slid the laptop over to Karen and said, "You still interested in taking a crack at getting that witness to talk?"

CHAPTER 22

They spent the next few days down at the fish camp turning the caribou into the products they'd need to survive and making an assortment of utensils and tools. Clio and Sarah scraped the hide clean, stretched it on a birch frame, then cured it by rubbing the animal's brains into it until it glistened. Keller and Ben stripped the meat neatly off the bones, putting aside the best steaks to be eaten first, and smoking the rest in a makeshift yurt in a fire of green birch and alder. Jake carefully removed and cleaned the stomachs and intestines to serve as containers, and then he and Pete worked the bones and antlers to make needles, knives and arrowheads. Jake removed the tendons from the animal's legs to use as string, and soaked them in the stream. Thom and Jim and Rita discarded the viscera and kept the fires going, and Bill, Eunice and Joan worked up at the sleeping camp fortifying the shelters and trying to improve the bedding.

Two days after the hunt, in the late afternoon, they took a break and ate the last of the prime pieces of caribou steak cooked on a spit over the fire. As usual, Pete was exhausted by this time of day, and famished and he decided that the caribou was about the best meal he'd ever eaten. He looked around with satisfaction. The area had been transformed – smoke curled from the yurt smokehouse Thom and Bill had built, filling the air with rich odors. Eunice was wearing a knee-length coat made from the caribou's hide and sewed water-tight with double stitching using bone needles and sinew, and a series of bone tools lay on the ground to his left. He'd already lost track of time – at least clock time. Time was now measured in the fullness of his belly, the quality of the light, and the degree of fatigue he felt in his bones and muscles. And although he ached all over, and his scalp itched incessantly, he also felt a growing sense of competence – even worthiness – from what they'd accomplished. The link between work and payoff, so elusive back in Washington, was now immediate and tangible.

He turned to Clio. "This beats the shit out of the senior staff meeting."

She laughed. "You had them, too?"

"Hell, yeah. Monday mornings and Friday afternoons, whether there was something to say or not."

"Us too," Joan said. "Friday afternoons, like clockwork."

"We had a weekly Friday afternoon crisis, instead. Happened everywhere I worked, without fail," Bill said.

"Oh yeah, Clio said, "We had a Friday crisis, too, after staff meetings. Made for more dramatic stuff, you see. Vic would conclude the meeting saying, 'Clio, Hank, I'd like you two to stay behind. Something urgent has come up.' It was all oh so important."

"Same here," Joan said. "Every Friday the Senator would thunder in with some critical issue."

"Jesus. I thought we were the only ones who had to go through that shit." Pete said.

"It's all about the weekend ego charge." Thom noted.

"And just what is that?" Sarah asked.

"It's simple really. These guys – or girls – are the supreme commander at work. They make the 'big' decisions," Thom made air quotes with his hands as he said big. "People scurry at their every whim. But when they go home, their wives ask them to take out the trash, and their daughter asks them to *please* stay out of the TV room while her friends are over, because," here Thom's voice raised an octave, "'Daddy, you're *such* a geek.' Takes a lot of importance to get through that with your ego fully inflated."

Here Pete interrupted, "God, yes. That explains it. That is so very EPA. You should see my Boss. Some of the so-called crises he's dredged up on a Friday were laughable ..."

Pete stopped short. Keller sat across the fire, staring at him.

"You know what Andersen? That's something you won't have to worry about when we get back."

"What are you going to do, Dan? Fire me for failing to contribute to your overdeveloped sense of self-importance."

Keller pitched the remains of his meat aside, stood up, his jaws clamping, his fists balled up at his sides and stalked over to Pete and loomed over him. "Get up, Andersen."

Pete felt all eyes on him, and he felt the other thing, too. The fear, reaching out from the past and grabbing him, even here, at the end of the world. It paralyzed him, and he sat mutely, his eyes downcast, wrestling with a shadow-shrouded doubt he knew now he'd never escape if he didn't just trust himself and stand up.

As Pete began to get up and face Keller, Jake moved quickly between them. "Alright. Back off Keller." Keller ignored him and tried to reach past Jake to grab Pete, but Jake pushed him back. "I said, back off. We have too much to do to be fighting each other." Keller withdrew slowly to the other side of the fire, and Pete felt his eyes bore into him, filled with hate.

After dinner, Pete retreated to the rock on the end of the peninsula to watch the sun go down, his mind filled with thoughts of what he should have done. He should have decked Keller. He should have stood up and pushed Jake aside. His face burned with shame, but in truth, Keller was just the most recent in a long line of shoulda's. And so he sat there, tracing the line back and inevitably he came to his brother, Gus, and to the words he could not escape ... *He didn't even try, Ellen.*

Taking in sunsets had become a habit with him from his days at college. He counted on the time to gather his thoughts, to regroup when necessary, to drink in the beauty and joy when possible. And to escape.

The weather took on a predictable pattern that would hold for most of the time they were there. The sun appeared in the mornings and evenings, with the rest of the day alternating between brilliant blue skies and a heavy overcast, as if the gods were battling for control, but with a few exceptions they never had a real rain. Even beneath leaden skies, it was still the most spectacular place he'd ever seen. Now, as the evening sun peaked out beneath the clouds, mists began to rise from the ice and snow patches across the lake, meandering their way through the forest, steaming up valleys, twisting around the peaks and disappearing in sunlit pink grapefruit colored vapor clouds directly above the crests. Grey rock and dirt, white snow, green forest, and blue waters all bathed now in that golden-pink hue from the fading sun, the colors further filtered through the rising mists, created a scene almost like a Turner painting, surreal, but true, an ideal of what should be. As he sat there, taking this in, the confrontation with Keller slipped into the background, if not quite gone, muted into irrelevance by the fact of so much perfection.

"Incredible isn't it?" It was Jake.

"Yeah. Hard to believe it's real."

"Odd that *this* seems less real than buildings and traffic and cities."

"Yeah. Odd." Pete was hoping that Jake would leave him alone. He needed to think, or maybe just to sit here and feel.

"I'm going to a place Lynx considered sacred. I'd like you to come with me."

There was something about the invitation that bothered him, and he thought about trying to beg off, but he knew that wouldn't go over well. He gave it a shot anyway, "I don't suppose this is optional, is it?"

Jake smiled. "No. But take a few more minutes here." He sat down on a rock nearby and was silent, drinking in the view.

Pete loved this time of day. Even in the city or suburbs, the light changed things quickly, creating a new scene every few minutes, each turning the mundane into the extraordinary – and out here, in the absence of the mundane, the effect was astonishing. It took only a moment to forget Jake, and lose himself in it again, so that he was surprised when Jake cleared his throat sometime later, as the last rays of the sun poked through the V formed by the two mountains at the west end of the Lake. When the sun disappeared, Jake said, "It's time. We better get going."

Pete stood up, trying to tamp down his growing sense of anxiety.

CHAPTER 23

The familiar tang of sea spray and salt wind hit Karen as soon as she stepped out onto the foredeck. She was on the evening ferry heading across Puget Sound on her way to the University of Washington's Friday Harbor Laboratories on San Juan Island to talk to the elusive Professor Dawkins. The other passengers were hunkered down inside the cabin, swilling coffee and cinnamon buns, hiding from the weather, but Karen had headed straight out to the bow as soon as they left the dock to take the full brunt of the harsh salt-soaked winds. Right now, they were making about ten knots through some heavy swells, directly into a headwind.

As they churned towards Friday Harbor, she thought of Pete, now sliding into the stone age with a guy who just possibly might be mad as a hatter, and she shuddered. She tried to peer northward but the wind kicked up and the salted sea-spray hit her full in the face, stinging her lips and eyes. It reminded her of those days with her father on the Pegasus, when they would find themselves alone, tacking through winds that kept other ships in dock, froth and spray coming at her so thick that the line between air and water blurred, the ship rocketing through the cold dark waters of Monterey Bay at dizzying speeds, and how, as she released the boom and the sails snapped around billowing, they would heel precariously as each tack was completed. When they got into dock on such days, others would chide her father for taking risks with his daughter aboard, but he would wink, and say while looking at her, "The degree of risk is inversely proportional to the skill of the sailor, right Kit?"

But Karen knew it was dangerous. That was the point. It was what he had to do in order to stay home with her and her brother. It was the fix that enabled him to keep out of the financial markets and the meeting rooms; to help wean him from rolling the die on an adrenalin-stoked million dollar deal, and it was, to her, a small price to pay for his presence. Her brother quit going on "Dad's death wishes" when he reached sixteen, but Karen continued to until she went off to school, and even afterward, she'd go out with him whenever she was home until the day he died. Besides, she trusted him implicitly. "What would you do now, Dad?" she said aloud as she stood on the deck of the ferry, staring northward, trying to divine Pete's fate through dusk, mist, spray and miles. But she knew. He wouldn't be out here on a ferry chasing ghosts. He'd be on a float plane, headed for Kitchener.

After docking, she found her way to the Labs about a mile from the center of town, and located Dawkin's place – the only mobile home at the laboratory site, something Chas had discovered on-line. Mozart drifted out through the closed door. Eine Kleine Nachtmusik. A good sign, she thought. She pasted on a smile and knocked.

Now that she was here, she was nervous about meeting him. She waited as Mozart played on, and she wondered whether she should knock again. Part of her was relieved that he wasn't answering. Dawkins was obviously a loon – the look on the kid's face back at the reception center had been as good as truth serum, when she said she was looking for Professor Dawkin's mobile home. "Why?" it asked silently, "would you even consider seeing *him*?" He'd also stared at her boobs, and uncharacteristically, she'd felt self-conscious. Kids, she thought. Still, it was usually her legs that drew attention. But then her blouse *was* tighter. They all seemed to be these days – bras too.

She was about to knock again when she heard the sound of footsteps coming and braced herself. As the door opened, she was struck by the face that greeted her as if by a blow. The man at the door had long dark hair, and a beard to match, both unkempt and wild. He was thin to the point of gauntness. A strand of oily hair hung down across the middle of his face. His eyes were the eyes of a street person – haunted, suspicious, vulnerable, and they darted back and forth, never resting on one point, always roving, searching. His clothes had that second hand look, the jeans lose and ill fitting, the shirt tattered and unbuttoned, worn over a white t-shirt, now yellow with too many washings.

"Dr. Dawkins?"

"You alone?" he asked, his eyes still searching beyond her.

"Yes," she answered.

"Were you followed?"

"Not unless they're invisible."

"What do you want?"

"I'd like to ask you a few questions."

" 'Bout what?"

"About Jake Christenson."

His face blackened, and she was just able to shove her foot in the door as Dawkins attempted to slam it shut. The edge cut into her instep, but the thick soles of her running shoes took most of the force. She cried out anyway, and leaned heavily against the door. "My foot," she said, sounding as pathetic as possible.

Dawkins immediately opened the door and took her hand. "You OK? God I'm so sorry ..." He guided her into the kitchen, shuffling beside her, then gestured to a bench behind a fold down table. It was covered with newspapers, a box of Coco-Puffs, and a bowl of half-eaten cereal, the soggy remains resembling a tepid brown brew. He knelt down before her, still apologizing. Karen's opinion of Dawkins shifted immediately, as he sat before her. Beneath the fear, his eyes had the same sad expression as a Basset Hound, and he was obviously distressed to have caused her pain. He seemed more pathetic now than scary. "Here, let me take a look at it." He said as he took her foot and rested it on his thigh. His touch was gentle, but she withdrew her foot immediately, and stood up, testing it with her weight.

"I'm fine."

"How'd you find me?"

"Easy enough – you're still listed in the University's Directory."

Dawkins flinched at that, then he began to tidy up, removing the bowl, piling the newspapers in a recycling box, and putting the cereal in a cupboard. Then he took a damp rag and wiped off the table. When he was satisfied, he asked, "You a reporter?"

"No."

"Cop?"

"No."

"Why're you here, then?"

"I just stopped by for a bowl of Coco-Puffs."

Dawkins laughed, briefly, caught himself and put his guard back up. But a smile lingered behind, like an echo. She was astounded at the change it made in him. He seemed softer, saner. "You should smile more. It suits you."

"Yes. I should." He said it mechanically, and as soon as he'd said it, he took on the same haunted look he'd had when he'd answered the door. Yet he seemed pleased that she'd paid him a compliment. "OK. You're not a reporter. Then why do you want to know about Jake Christianson?"

"Someone I care about is on an expedition with him. And I'm worried about him. I thought if I got a little more information about what happened out there I might feel better."

Dawkins sat down, stroked his beard, then pushed a damp crumb around the table top with his forefinger. She waited, but he kept his eyes fixed on the table. Mozart was reaching the fourth and final movement, and the music picked up, but Dawkins continued to stare at the table and coax the crumb back and forth. Finally, when it was clear Dawkins wasn't going to say anything, Karen said, "My father loved Eine Kleine Nachtmusik. It was his favorite piece." Dawkins raised his head from the table and studied Karen, struggling to look her in the eye. It seemed difficult for him.

After several moments, he stood up and looked out the door. The sun was setting through the mist, and a small breeze was picking up. "Can you walk?" he asked.

"Yes. I'm fine, really."

"Then let's get out of here."

"What about Jake?"

"I'll tell you about my experience. But it won't make you feel better." He pointed to the dock in front of the Fernald Lab, a long building facing the harbor, "Let's sit there. It should be quiet."

Karen began walking, but when she'd crossed University drive, she realized she'd left him behind. She waited for him beneath a street light. Dawkins shuffled across the street with the gate of an old man, but Karen judged him to be about forty. As he reached her, she said "I'm sorry."

"Don't worry, it's the medicine. Makes me a little unsteady."

She walked slowly after that, and offered him her arm for support. He took it gratefully. "Maybe you should stop taking it for a while. See what happens," she said.

"I know what happens," he said. They walked along in silence after that.

When they arrived at the dock, Dawkins seemed to relax for the first time. They sat down, and let their legs dangle off the edge and looked at the town across the harbor. There was a light breeze, and the masts of sailboats bobbed in the distance. The smell of creosote from the dock mingled with the fertile odors of the sea, briny and organic, and the shrill calls of gulls and terns pierced the air as they settled for the night. There is something universal about ports, Karen thought. It could have been the Monterey Marina. An old tune, one her father used to hum on mornings as they prepped the ship, came to mind – Otis Reading, Sittin' on the Dock of the Bay.

"I come here often," Dawkins said. Then he turned to her, "My doctor doesn't want me talking about this stuff, yet. He says it will dredge up old memories ... and the voices."

Looking at this poor sick man, Karen suddenly felt as if she'd made a terrible mistake. "I'm sorry. Perhaps I shouldn't have come."

"No. It's OK. You're a nice lady, I think. I can see it in your smile. And you made me laugh. It's not ... I don't do that very often, these days."

She put a hand on his arm. Studying him in the fading sun, she had the sense that he'd been hollowed out, or that he was little more than a walking wound, yet she could see the remains of the former Professor Dawkins – the one Chas had outlined to her from his bio on the net, and her heart ached for this poor, childlike creature who'd replaced him. "Look, Dr. Dawkins ..."

"Ed. Call me Ed."

"Ed. Maybe your doctor is right."

Dawkins smiled, "No. He's not. I don't hear the voices, but I still believe in them – even with this damn medicine. I just make him think I don't believe in them. The school says I can teach again, when he says I'm OK and I want to teach again. Very much. So I tell him that I understand that they weren't real. But I will never actually believe that."

"You do research still?"

"Some. It's one of the only things that brings me peace. I can get lost in it. That and the writing. But I want to teach."

"Can you tell me about the voices?"

"You won't tell the doctor? If I tell you about them, you won't tell?"

"No. I promise."

"Not too much to say, except he put them in me."

"Who?"

"Jake."

"But the others – he didn't do that to them?"

"I think he did."

"But they seem OK."

"Some didn't fight him. They weren't strong enough. Or he wasn't asking them to do anything they didn't want to do."

"What do you mean?"

"Just things is all. He could kind of take you over. He talked about rooting out the beasts inside us. If you didn't agree with him, he made you hear things ... and see them. I don't see them any more. And I think that means I'm getting better. Pretty soon I may be able to call Susan."

"Susan?"

"My fiancé. At least she used to be."

Karen didn't know what to say. She sat there listening to him talk through his devils. As he spoke, her eyes misted. Chas had tracked down Susan Palmer and Karen had called her before coming out. She remembered Palmer's final statement: 'The man I loved doesn't exist anymore. He's dead.'

Dawkins saw the welling in her eyes and said, quietly, "Don't be upset. I'm told that none of this is real. Perhaps someday I'll believe it. And if it's not real, your friend has nothing to worry about."

They had dinner together, and her company seemed to make Dawkins feel better. He relaxed and told her some about his life – honor student, social and environmental activist, popular teacher, avid cross country skier, brilliant academic career as one of the few who could bridge science and policy; he talked about his engagement to Dr. Susan Palmer. He spoke about it all as if it had been someone else, as if he were talking about another man he'd known years ago, a man he'd admired and liked. Karen found herself telling him about Pete, her job, and her fears. It was easy to share with him, with those eyes, deep wells of sorrow and empathy. By the end of dinner, a degree of emotion had crept back into Dawkins' voice, and he even appeared more animated, his hands moving about as he spoke, and his eyes holding her gaze rather than scanning the area around them.

After dinner, Karen walked him back to his trailer. On the way, she asked, "Can you talk about the bear attack?"

His arm stiffened, and for a long while, he said nothing. When he finally did, he spoke in the same monotone he had when she first arrived. "It was him," he said.

"Him?"

"Jake. He made the bear appear."

Karen didn't know what to say. He might be a kind, sweet man, but he was daft. Clearly. "But the others said he fought the bear off," she pressed.

"They would, wouldn't they," He said. "But then, they all drank the Kool-aid."

"And you didn't?"

"No. And that's when the troubles started."

"The voices?" she asked. Dawkins nodded.

They continued walking in silence, and as Karen tried to think of something soothing to say, Dawkins continued, "I wish I could tell you something to make you feel better, but if he's with Jake, your friend's in danger."

Karen merely nodded, and continued to let him hold her arm as he sidled, crab-like across the street and past the cottages towards his trailer. When they arrived, she hugged him and thanked him for his help. To her shock, Dawkins held her tightly, and didn't let go. She didn't have the sense that she was being groped; his embrace was more child-like than erotic. She held on until he stopped. Finally, he leaned back and looked at her.

"Thank you," he said. "That's the first time anyone's hugged me in a long time. People mostly avoid me." He said it in that same monotone, but his eyes revealed the pain his voice could not convey.

"People will hold you again, Ed. I know they will." And she turned, leaving him standing there watching her go. As she headed for the town, she felt a deep sadness for him. Whatever had happened to this man, it was more than any trip to the wilderness could have done. More than Jake could have done.

CHAPTER 24

Pete followed Jake through the camp, up the slope behind the peninsula, then west toward where he'd encountered the wolf on that first day. When they'd passed through the camp, Pete felt Keller's eyes burning into his back.

Once into the forest, Jake moved quickly, and to his surprise Pete soon found himself breathing deeply despite his marathon training. Jake talked as he went, and Pete could see no sign that the climb or the altitude had any effect on him. "This is the last Eden, Peter. The last place where man is not, and therefore the last place where he can become what he was meant to be."

The talk of Eden and sacred places bothered Pete, and he decided to confront Jake on it. "I'm not a Luddite. I don't believe we can go back to Eden."

"Then why are you here?"

"I told you in class."

"Ah, yes. Saving cathedrals. Tell me, Peter, does still it seem so clear to you now? Out here?"

"Never clearer."

"Still so sure? Good. But the journey is just beginning." He walked on into the twilight and when he came to a knoll where Pete and Ben had sat the night before, he stopped a moment, inspecting the ground. "Did you have a nice chat with Ben?"

"Yes," Pete answered, astounded at Jake's ability to read signs.

"He's a good man. A very pure man, I think."

"Yeah. He's become a friend."

They continued past the knoll and headed well north and west of the area they'd hunted earlier in the day, striking up a steep slope. Pete was just barely keeping up with him, yet Jake was scanning the ground as he went, drinking in data. Pete waited while Jake bent down to examine some print he'd spotted, and he noted that Jake smiled to himself, when he stood back up. They continued up the slope for some time, until they reached the tree line, then Jake scaled a rocky bluff and sat down cross legged, while Pete scrambled up beside him. As Pete sat on the cliff face catching his breath, the wolves began to call each other from the valley far below.

"Wolves," Jake said, smiling.

"Yes, we heard them the first night. And one stalked Eunice. The same one watched me on the hunt."

"And did he scare you Peter?"

"Not especially."

"You're an odd mixture of cowardice and courage." He said it matter of factly, with no judgment or malice, but it hit Peter with a physical force. Before he could say anything, Jake continued, "You were right not to confront Keller, Peter."

"Yeah? Then how come I feel so shitty."

"Suppose you'd decked him. Would it have changed anything?"

"Maybe I wouldn't feel like such a fucking wimp."

"We both know you're not a wimp."

"Do we?"

"Close your eyes. Listen with me for a minute."

Pete started to protest, but Jake put up his hand, closed his eyes, and sat sphinx-like, in silence. After a moment, Pete followed suit. At first he heard nothing, but then there was the ubiquitous cry of a raven off to the east. From somewhere down slope a creature – perhaps a ground squirrel – rustled around in the dry leaves and litter on the forest floor, sounding like a rattle. A breeze rose up from the lake hissing as it brushed through the spruce boughs below.

"Did it ever occur to you that if the Earth cried out, it would be with the absence of sound?" Jake asked.

"Crying out in silence?"

"Exactly so. And she is crying out, Peter. I've listened as one-by-one the voices of the rain forests were extinguished. I've heard her cries in the stillness of the savannahs. I've heard her in the muted deserts. And

I've listened to the sterile pounding of waves on a birdless shore." Jake looked out over the mountains before them, now faint indigo shadows in the dusk. "I've watched you, Peter. Sitting by the lake, listening. I think you hear the silent cries of Gaia, too. Your redemption lies in answering her pleas."

"My redemption?"

"Yes. Redemption. We've both heard cries silenced before, haven't we?"

Shocked, Pete stared through the darkness trying to read Jake's face. But he couldn't see anything other than his eyes. He tried to think, tried to fathom how this man could know. And for the first time, Pete's vague worries about Jake coalesced on a tangible reality. He did know. And if he knew, he was way more than a simple survival trainer. But who could he tell? Ben? What could he tell him? Fighting fear, he spoke to the eyes before him. "Let's not play games. If you've got something on your mind, say it."

"I don't play games. I'll tell you what's on my mind. Your girl-friend's been right all along."

"What do you mean?"

"Her little theory that I'm preparing you all to save the world."

"How did you know about that?"

"Ruth and I have become quite close. She tells me everything." Jake stood up, "Come, let's walk a little." He started up the hill again, his long strides eating up yards at a time, and Pete struggled to follow.

"Is saving the world such a bad thing, Peter?"

"Depends on how you plan on going about it."

"Does it, I wonder?" Jake pointed to the peak. "Let's take the summit," he said then struck off at a punishing pace.

Pete looked up. It seemed an insane distance to try to cover this late at night in the cold and dark, and besides he was hungry and tired, but Jake was already disappearing up the slope so he followed. By pushing himself to his aerobic limit he was just able to keep Jake in sight, although he was losing ground as they climbed. He lowered his head and focused on the footing, and did what he always did when his body screamed at him to stop – negotiated one more step, and then another, and another, until he'd covered the distance. When he was halfway up, he was forced to pause to catch his breath and he caught a glimpse of Jake's shadowy figure high on the face of the mountain, clambering up catlike, using his hands and arms as much as his feet to propel him over rocks and debris that Pete would have gone around. He was just below the crest, and Pete mumbled, "Shit," and took off. By the time he reached the top, he was covered in a film of sweat, even though the air felt thin and dry and cold. He could just make out the form of Jake, sitting cross-legged by an old fire ring, coaxing a fire to life as he waited. Pete made a mental note to apologize to Eunice, then settled down across from him and caught his breath. His training paid off, and he recovered quickly. When he was able to speak without panting, he said, "So now that you've got us all here, what are you planning to do? It's not like you can turn Keller and his buddies into ecofreaks."

"But that's precisely what I'm going to do."

Pete laughed. "You're insane, Jake. Keller could give a shit about ..."

Pete felt a big hand clamp down hard on his shoulder, and then Jake's voice came out of the dark, "You, of all people, should know better than to toss around a word like that." Jake's fingers dug into the hollow of Pete's shoulder but after a moment he released the vice grip. "Now, I have no illusions about Keller's ideals, but I can be very persuasive. Besides, my guess is, like anyone with political ambitions, Keller can be bought and I can line up a lot of campaign money for him if he's willing to carry our water."

Pete tried to ignore the ache in his shoulder and the warning bell it was setting off. "Why Keller?"

"He heads up EPA. He's ambitious. He wants to be President. And he's got a lot of support from the people who decide these things."

"Well, you're not gonna get anywhere with Keller. He's owned by the Corporations."

"They all are. But maybe before we're through out here, I'll own a piece of him, too."

"Never happen."

"Then I'll have to make sure he doesn't get elected."

More alarms. Karen was right. A certified megalomaniac. Too bad, Pete thought. He'd begun to let himself believe that somehow Jake could make things right. But which things? His own private redemption? Saving the world? He rubbed his shoulder and thought, *what a fool I've been. Yet here I am, with three more weeks to go. No sense in giving up my fantasies already. Save that for the third week.* One thing for sure, Jake was clearly in need of a few lessons on how Washington works, if there was to be any world saving going on. "The thing is, Jake, it probably doesn't matter which side gets in. Or who."

"Why do you say that?" Jake asked.

Pete recalled the argument he'd had with Keller back in Washington when he'd stood by the window and stared at the parade of SUVs and people with gadgets stuck to their ears. It seemed years ago. How had he put it? Joe and Jane Sixpack. "According to Keller, we can't go any faster than Joe and Jane Sixpack want to go." Washington seemed a million miles and years away now. Far below, the cry of the wolves drifted up from the dull black forest.

Jake said, "And you don't have much faith in the people?"

"Most of the time, I think if you give people the right information, they'll make the right decisions. But there's no way that can happen, any more."

"Why?"

Pete was surprised. Jake had never asked him – or anyone else – for information as far as he could remember. He'd given Keller's claim a lot of thought and he'd reluctantly concluded that he was right – Joe and Jane Sixpack weren't going to demand anything but more of the same. "Look, corporations spend half a trillion a year on advertising designed to turn people's wants into needs, and on creating new wants. Five years later those wants become needs. How much do we spend telling them what we're doing to the Earth in the process?" Jake didn't answer. He was staring out toward the horizon. "And the media – it's owned by corporations, so inconvenient truths don't get covered. Why do you think the media continued to cover the scientific 'debate' on global warming two decades after the debate ended?" He turned to the silhouette beside him and said, "Besides, in some ways, it's more dangerous to have the good guys in power than it was to have the last crowd."

"Why?" Jake sounded surprised.

"We'll pass some half-assed measure that's a compromise, invest in a few far-off silver-bullet techno-fixes, then we'll congratulate ourselves and meanwhile, we'll continue to spew out carbon for a few decades. And then we're really fucked."

"You think they'll do that, Pete?"

"You saw Keller's legislation. Sure there's lofty goals, but when it comes to real action, there's enough waivers and offsets that it'll be business as usual. They settled on a mileage standard for vehicles of thirty-five mpg by 2020 for god's sake – something we were capable of meeting two decades ago. There's a few good people with serious ideas, but at the end of the day, elections are bought and K-Street does the buying. Either way, the best we'll end up with is a Congress that'll pay lip service, do some PR and spread some BS."

"We'll have to do something about that."

"There's something else."

"What?"

"With global warming, we're going to have to convince people to act before the problem is acute. Humans have never done that."

"Then we'll do something about that, too."

"And if we can't?"

"If we fail, then it is the twilight of man. You were always just an experiment anyway. A noble one to be sure, but an experiment."

"An experiment?"

"If I were speaking in the language of science, I would say you were an evolutionary experiment, like size in the dinosaur. Nature has posited numerous such strategies."

The night closed in and the sweat from the climb was evaporating, chilling Pete. He let his eyes adjust, and looked around; the peak was dotted with broad patches of snow and rough granite boulders. Far below the camp stood out as a tiny orange glow and beyond it the lake gleamed pearl-like in the gathering night. To the west, blue-black mountains, shrouded in darkness, marched off in the distance for an eternity.

Jake stood up and surveyed the area slowly, sweeping it carefully, piercing the gloom, it seemed to Pete, with the force of will. "A grizzly passed by here very recently." He continued to scan the area. Pete thought he could hear him sniffing the wind. "This is where I was attacked. Do you know, I didn't even try to fight back? It's a helpless feeling to be attacked by something so powerful, isn't it Peter?"

Pete felt the words like a probe – something painful, invasive, and frightening, but he said nothing.

"I expected to be afraid of this place, but I am not. When I was very afraid, I had to avoid it. When I was a little less afraid, I had to come here. Now I can choose. Do you understand what I'm saying Peter?"

Pete nodded, scrambling to figure out whether Jake somehow knew and was just toying with him. But of course, he couldn't. It had to be another of his parables.

"I intended to move towards Spatsizi, but perhaps we should stay. What do you think?"

Pete decided that his only recourse was to treat this conversation on its face value. To quit conjuring up ghosts in every exchange. If Jake knew anything, he would have said so when Pete had confronted him about playing games earlier.

"How about it, Pete?"

Yeah. Face value. "I say we stay. There's game. Fish. I think it must be the most beautiful spot on earth."

"And the grizzly?"

"It doesn't much matter. There's always a grizzly of one kind or another wherever you go."

"Yes. A curious mixture of bravery and cowardice."

Pete reached across the darkness and grabbed Jake by the arm, "Whatever you think you know about my past, I'm no coward. I've known fear, but I'm no longer a coward. A coward will not act in the face of fear. I will."

"Really? We shall see, Peter. We shall see. Now, where was I? Oh yes. Evolutionary experiments. Did you know there were bear-sized Beaver in the Pleistocene? A failure. They consumed themselves out of existence. To your scientists, reason, intelligence, is just one more stab at evolutionary success. Perhaps also doomed to consume itself to death. But in the end, to scientists, all of these experiments are just one more scheme to carry DNA forward. No better than breeding prowess – the strategy used by bacteria and insects, and the single most successful one since the dawn of life."

"And you would disagree with their assessment?"

"I have learned other ways of knowing the universe. Their theories are true as far as they go. But there was always a much more ...divine ... capacity for humanity. What happens here and in the time after you get back will determine whether that capacity is realized."

"Jake. I want to make myself very clear. I am a moral man. An ethical man. I even consider myself spiritual. And I have devoted my life to protecting the environment. But I do not buy into mystical mumbo-jumbo and pantheistic dogma."

"We want the same thing."

"I was trained as a scientist. We will only get where we need to go through science, technology and policy," Pete said.

"Science can tell us how to reach our destination, but it cannot tell us what our destination must be."

"And you know that?"

"I know your ways of knowledge. I have a degree in physics, remember. But I've learned other, older, ways of knowing."

"I don't get how a physicist can believe in such bull ..."

"They're different, but not inconsistent. C'mon, Pete. I know your way. See if you can learn a bit about mine." Here Jake laughed. "It won't hurt you."

Jake's laughter was disarming. In fact, there had been something almost spellbinding in the way he talked, in the rhythms of his speech. And there was something reassuring in his admission that he was out to save the world. What the hell, he might even be good at it, Pete thought. Ben was right. They certainly weren't making much progress the old fashioned way. So he wasn't surprised to hear himself answer, "Only a coward would refuse."

The fire was picking up, and Pete caught a glimpse of Jake's smile in the flickering orange glow. After a few moments, he began to speak again, his disembodied voice quieter, but even more mesmerizing. "The Dunnez-za believe that all places and all people have magic in them. Lynx thought this mountain was one of the most sacred places on earth."

His voice seemed to come from all directions at once, from the forest below, the heavens above, from the Earth itself. "Listen. I will tell you how I came to know Saya, and how I learned to commune with the

Earth. Listen closely, with your heart open, and this place will take over, and tell you the story as it really happened, not simply as I would tell it. Listen with your mind open and you will learn your magic, and see your destiny."

Jake began. He described his preparation for his vision quest, after studying with Lynx for two and a half years. Pete watched the fire dance, and let the words and the voice wash over him, and waited for something to happen. Jake told how Lynx taught him to still his mind and open his heart; how to shut off his senses, then turn them on, one-by-one, so that he could perceive the world through the feel of the air on his skin, the touch of the earth on his feet and legs and buttocks; through ancient odors that were obscured when one's eyes were open; through sounds long subdued by the babble of voices and machines; and finally through sights now all the more vivid because they appeared in harmony with these other senses, rather than drowning them out with its intensity. Only when he could feel, smell, and touch with the exquisite sensitivity of a blind man, would Lynx allow him go on his quest.

"Try it, Peter," he said, "Close your eyes and let the Earth speak to you through her touch. I know you can do it. You've been listening with your heart for decades, now you need only to feel her with your body ... to let her tell you her story ..."

The voice went on, but the individual words disappeared, leaving only their meanings, and as Jake's story unfolded, Pete no longer simply heard it, but saw it as if it were a movie filmed from Jake's point of view and then finally, after listening for an indeterminate amount of time he lost sense of himself and came to know the story from a time and place that was beyond words ...

For the second time, the old warrior has come to this remotest of places seeking Death. His name is Lynx.

A younger man, Jake, sits across the campfire trying to read his face. He peers into the old man's eyes – two slits carved into leathered skin, crisscrossed by fine lines and furrows – hoping to see in them, answers to questions he's not sure he even knows how to ask.

But Lynx sits with his back to the setting sun, and for the most part his face is hidden in shadow. Now and then the fire ignites a bit of pitch and flares to life and Jake can see him; yet even then his expression is, as it always has been, unfathomable. Except his eyes. On this evening they glisten. And when the fire flickers Jake sees dampness in crevices of the weathered cheeks.

"Are you afraid?" the old man asks.

"No," Jake answers. "Are you?"

"A little."

"Is that why you cry?"

"No."

"Then why?"

"For you. For my people. For the Mother."

"Why for me?"

Lynx says nothing and the darkness creeps up the mountain towards them. After a time, he reaches across the fire and places his hand on Jake's shoulder. Already Jake feels, in the delicacy of the old man's touch, the life force draining from him.

"I have taught you all that I know, my son. The rest is in you; you have but to learn to See," Lynx says.

"I'd sooner learn it from you."

"This, only Saya, and the Mother Herself can teach." Lynx is silent after that, and both men stare into the fire. Finally, when the shadows are as long as they will be, Lynx raises his head and says, "I would spare you this last trial if I could. But those who have been chosen must pass through it. It has always been so." With that, the ancient Warrior stands, steadies himself a moment, then hobbles down the mountain into the gathering pall to find Death.

Just before he passes over the crest, he turns. His voice thunders out, filling the space between them. "When Saya sent you, I thought Him wrong. But I was wrong. The clay has been shaped. Now it must be fire cured. Learn well, my son. You are among the last to offer hope."

Pete sits on the mountain alone now, waiting. Far off to the West, a purple-hewed ridge slips into darkness, and a cold wind begins to rise up the mountain face, gently at first, then quickening until it roars past, whipping his hair back from his brow. Soon, the wind slices through him and despite all he has endured the cold penetrates in a way he has never felt before, chilling him from the inside out. But he waits, immobile.

Night settles in, the wind still rages, and still he waits. At some point it begins to rain, soaking his hair and flowing across his face like a thousand tears, and he thinks of the tear-tracks on Lynx's face and wonders. But this is his quest, and he must leave his mind and his soul open, and so he sits, immobile, and still the wind comes.

He loses all sense of time, as days pass into nights, and the wind continues to wash over him. He knows the passage of days not so much by the light, for he sees little, but by the sounds around and within him. By the howl of wolves as the days die, and the scream of the eagle as mornings break, and by the beginnings of the voice Jake told him to listen for.

One day, after he has been there for a long time, he smells the musky odor of a big boar bear, then hears it shuffling around below him and waits for the familiar fear. But it doesn't come. He is beyond fright, now. Beyond hunger, thirst, pain or cold. Very soon he will join with the Elders. Very soon he will learn to See.

The wind begins to change, and it feels at once more substantial and less so. No longer is the air rushing past him and over him; rather it feels as if time itself is passing through him. Yes, this is what Jake spoke of; this begins the journey he must take.

It starts in the eons long before man, when the sun was still young, the earth lifeless save for small pockets of the simplest creatures. He feels a moment's doubt as the story unravels, for it is told in the language of his own people, the language of science. Then he hears Lynx's words: "Each learns the Story in their own way, yet it is the same Story; each knows the Mother in their own way yet She is the same Mother."

And so he watches as time's phantoms pass by and through him, an endless parade, growing, blossoming, becoming more complex, covering the Earth with an impermeable skin of life, filling the sea, the land and even the sky. He listens, too, and he learns that over eons the Earth and this living membrane have become one; the life creating the Earth, even as the Earth creates life. He sees, in this parade of phantoms, that all is harmony.

The very essence of life – its secret code – changes but little as it slips easily from one species to the next. He sees that each is but an ex-

periment, each but a humble carrier for this sacred thing, none above the other, none able to survive without the whole.

As the winds sweep over him, he sees some of these experiments fail – trilobites, dinosaurs, bear-sized beavers. Those that don't fit must be discarded, but without malice. He knows this in his cells, at an almost chemical level. He has always known it. And it is good. The Mother prospers, and all life rejoices.

But as the winds bring him closer to now, he feels a faint discord, then a jarring, and he knows something has happened. Another experiment has gone wrong. But this time, the experiment has stepped outside the crucible. The Mother is in danger.

On the fortieth day, the winds subside, and the morning breaks in one of the first days of Spring – warm and fine and still – and Pete arises, and walks down the mountain. And he Knows.

"Peter?"

The voice sounds as if it comes from somewhere far off, and he tries to ignore it so that he might stay in this place for a while longer, but it doesn't let him.

"Peter. It grows late."

Slowly, the other world went dark, and gradually, his surroundings coalesced. When he had his wits back, he saw that he was on the mountain top again. Jake was talking to him, his voice insistent. "Peter, come back."

"How long ..."

"Just a couple of hours."

"But that can't be ..."

"It can be. As the man said, time is bendable."

"What did you do? I mean one minute I was seeing things through your eyes, then it was me there. Feeling those things. Talking to ...Oh Jesus, what the fuck did you just do?"

"I didn't do anything. You did. You let Saya take you. You discovered your magic. And that is to See. I knew you would. I knew it."

Pete rubbed his eyes and stared out at the mountains across the lake, then at the campfire, a twinkling orange speck far below them. He could still feel the presence of time within him, mingling a curious mix of fear and tranquility.

"What just happened here?"

"You learned to See as the Mother Sees."

"I need to understand ..."

"You can't analyze it. It just is. You will only understand when you let it be. Now, about Keller. You were afraid to fight him just now. A little more courage, and you will be unable to stop yourself from fighting him. Only when you have mastered your fears, will you be able to choose not to fight him. You must do so, Peter."

"I'm not sure I can do that."

"You will. I promised you that this trip would transform you. You more than anyone, Peter. It started tonight, and before we're done, you will do things you didn't believe possible."

CHAPTER 25

The following morning Pete was sitting by the lake, and Ben approached. "So, what did Bwana Jake have to say last night?" he asked.

Pete didn't answer. He stared out at the mist rising from the ice on the opposite side of the lake, studying the way it curled into the valleys then rose up the slopes like liquid pouring in reverse, and as he watched it he felt again, for just a moment, that sense of walking through time with the Earth. He didn't trust this feeling, yet he was reluctant to let go of it.

"Well?" Ben asked.

"I'm trying to figure out how to tell you."

"Pete Andersen stumped for words? I can't believe it."

"Don't patronize me Pops. You'll get your turn, I'm sure."

"Don't call me Pops, whippersnapper."

Being with Ben felt good. Normal. Pete had been sitting by the Lake for what remained of the night reliving the events on the mountain. Had he really been up there for millennia? Of course not. And yet, he had. On some level, he knew he should be worried, but he wasn't. It was as Jake had said. As if the Earth had spoken to him, and he'd seen the march of time as She'd seen it. It was a knowledge not contradictory to the facts, figures, mathematics, chemistry and physics that had formed the basis for his degrees in Geology, but certainly different, and in some ways more complete. It came with a sense of pathos and passion those disciplines stripped out of the knowing, and with it a greater sense of purpose and place. But there was no way to share these things with Ben. He'd think me crazy, Pete thought. And then he felt a chill. Perhaps I am again, after all these years.

"So you gonna tell me or not?"

Pete decided to level with Ben on the vision quest stuff, but he struggled to focus on Ben's immediate question. "Spilled the beans," He said, after a moment.

"And?"

"Well, Karen was right. He's a man with a plan."

Ben sat down on a rock beside Pete. It was early, and the others weren't up yet. The sky was cloudy with just a few patches of blue scattered around, and it was cold. To the east – behind them and to their left – a pale sun was just poking over the ranges and an icy silver caste spread across the sky staining the water below a dull pewter. A flock of Canada Geese flew over in a perfect V, their honks discordant, almost comical. The two men watched them pass, then Ben asked, "And that plan is?"

"It's more complicated than that."

"How so?"

"Well, the guy's a megalomaniac, for one thing. And quite brilliant. And a bit of a Shaman, I think."

"Well he's brilliant enough alright. Got a perfect four-o in physics at Cornell. But a Shaman?"

Pete pushed a rock around with the toe of his boot, trying to figure out how to tell Ben about his experience. "You ever notice how he always talks about the human race in the second person? *You* believe this; *you* do that?"

Ben nodded.

"It's like he thinks he's a race apart."

Raising his eyebrows, Ben asked, "So, tell me the plan."

"We turn Keller and his crowd into selfless eco-freaks, for one."

Ben laughed. "Good luck with that."

"At first that was my reaction. But if he can make others see what I've seen, we're on our way." Pete felt Ben eying him, and tried to explain. "He talked about going back to the Garden of Eden, and 'of other ways of knowing things' as he put it. He seems to want me to learn them. And that's where things get a little weird. Took me on what the Dunne-za call a vision quest."

"A vision quest?"

"Yeah. Played out like the real deal. Like a time trip or something."

"Really. Time trips and vision quests?"

"That's the weird thing. On the one hand, he scared the shit out of me. It was like he was looking inside me. I mean, he knew things about me no one else does. Like that stuff you and I talked about the other day? Or he seemed to. But on the other hand I feel better about him – about this whole thing – than I have since that class where he talked about death. He's being straight with me, now. And like you said, we all want to get to the same place. But I have to tell you, this guy's different. Thinking he could take on K Street and turn Keller and Congress into eco-freaks."

"Wouldn't it be nice if he could?"

"Yeah. And at the moment, crazy as it seems, I think he may be able to pull it off."

Ben reached down and picked up a small piece of rounded quartz, and began to rub it between his fingers. His eyebrows furrowed together and he looked at Pete as he worked the rock. Before the silence got uncomfortable he said, "What about that look when he killed the caribou?"

"Ohhh Jesus. Did you see that?"

"Still, I expect that's what it takes to kill an animal with your bare hands ..."

"Wait. Ben. I meant to tell you about this. While we were getting ready to start driving the caribou I saw that wolf again – I guess I should say he saw me. He was sitting behind me on a little rise, just watching."

"But if he was behind you, how'd you see him?"

"You'd think I was losing it if I told you."

"Can't be any worse than going on a vision quest."

Pete smiled. "OK. Maybe I've crossed that line."

"Maybe?"

"All right. All right. Do you want to hear this or not?"

"Please."

"It was like I felt him."

"That's not so weird. I've felt people, even dogs, staring at me."

"Yeah ... well ... here's where it gets weird. I felt him staring at me so I turned around, and it was like he's talking to me."

"Talking, you say?"

"Not really talking, but as I looked at him, it's like he was saying what you just said."

"What I just said?"

"Yeah, about what it takes ... and what it means ... to kill." Pete felt the older man scrutinizing him. Checking to see if I'm cracking, he thought.

"You OK, Pete?"

"Yeah. I think so."

"Ben?" It was Jake, his voice easily covering the hundred and fifty yards from the camp, shattering the morning air and ending their conversation.

"Yeah?"

"I'm going to take a little walk. Care to join me?"

Ben winked at Pete and said, "Watch this." He turned to Jake and called back, "I'm all booked up this morning. I can pencil you in this afternoon ..."

Jake covered the slope between them in what seemed like three leaps, and stopped just short of Ben. He spoke quietly, in a barely controlled voice, "I know you're only making a joke, Ben, but this is an appointment you can't afford to miss."

"Right. I understand," Ben said.

Pete had not seen the older man caught off guard until that moment, but as quickly as the tension mounted, it subsided.

Jake smiled, nodded politely to Pete, turned back to Ben and said, "Good. Let's go then shall we?" They started off, but then he turned back to Pete, and said, "We'll be going on another hunt day after tomorrow. Food'll be getting low by then, and Thom and Eunice need some waterproof pants. You and Keller will make the kill, so I want the two of you to flake some spearheads. And we're getting low on firewood. Have a few of the others gather some. Tell the them if they want to build better shelters, they can."

"Are you sure?"

"We have that choice, now, Peter. Understand?"

"Yes." Pete watched them walk off, heading east to the far end of the lake. He knew that by making him the bearer of such news, Jake was trying to bestow power on him. He wasn't sure he wanted it. As the two picked their way through the trees and disappeared from view, he recalled Jake's comment to him on their walk, "... I promised you that this trip would transform you. You more than anyone, Peter. You will do things you didn't believe possible before we leave." Working side by side with Keller on weapons certainly fit the bill, he thought. He turned to check out the camp. Nearly everyone was up, including Keller. Thom was sucking desperately on the stump of a cigarette – his last judging from the looks of it.

Pete walked up the hill to the camp, and sat by the fire next to Thom, warming himself.

"I want some coffee. I want a whole cigarette, I want a shower, I want a god damn Bloody Mary," Thom said.

"I'd settle for toilette paper. And shampoo. My head feels like one big scab."

"I don't need toilet paper. I haven't taken a shit in three days. And if I don't get some fiber, I may not take one for the whole fuckin' month."

"Thank you for sharing Thom. I'm not sure any of us could have made it through the morning without knowing the state of your bowels," Sarah said. Thom ignored her and carefully put his cigarette butt out, preserving as much as possible for another time.

Ruth wandered over to the fire. Pete studied her. She pulled at some knots in her hair, and he noted that she had dark circles under her eyes. She sat down next to him. "Jesus. I can't imagine spending another twenty five days out here," she said.

"Jake says you and he have become quite close."

"Yeah. You could say that. Jesus, I smell."

"We all do. It's part of the experience."

"Let me tell you something. When this is over, I am going to my houseboat, and never leaving the city again. For anything."

"Not even for tall blue-eyed hunks?"

"Especially not for blue-eyed hunks."

"Well, it's time for a little announcement," he said. He uncoiled stiffly and stood for a moment. "Can I have your attention, please. Come on, gather round." As they came Pete thought the speed and style of their approach said a lot about who they were. It occurred to him that aside from Ruth, Keller, Ben, and Clio he really didn't know these people. He was beginning to get a sense of Bill, Sarah and Thom. He liked what he saw of Bill. Both in the restaurant back in Washington and on the hunt, he'd exhibited a quiet confidence, and a certain resoluteness. He appeared to be someone you could count on.

Sarah and Thom. Like bookends. Sarah, with her swimmer's shoulders – young, confident, optimistic, idealistic, naive. Thom, slump-shouldered and pot-bellied – cynical, curmudgeonly, but for all that, delicate, shaken and bruised. Perhaps the real difference was age, he thought. Age and early success. He knew Thom well enough to know that like most cynics, he was a disillusioned idealist. But he thought there were probably a few patches of pristine snow left in his psyche – places where the dog of life had yet to lift its leg on.

Then there was Joan Du Mont – the quintessential Senate staffer. She approached the fire quickly, her face a curious mix of subservience and arrogance, her swan's neck and pale skin making her look like a marble statue once she arrived. Still, she was holding up better than he'd expected. Being on the staff of Congress apparently prepared you for a life mean, nasty and brutish, he thought. Eunice McGrath, on the other hand, held back, radiating discomfort, displeasure, and defeat. Some sort of rash was developing around her neck line, and her nose was red and runny. Her red hair was a knotted clot of tangles. She was in definite need of shoring up. He would have to mention this to Jake. McGrath would obviously be a key part of the plan.

Rita came up slowly, examining the others once she arrived, her eyes darting from one to another, running an internal calculator as she took each one in and assessed their condition, as if even out here she was looking for an internal weakness or edge of some kind. She looked strong; there was obviously more to her than the shallow vamp she liked to play. He remembered how skillfully she'd disarmed Jim that first day. Yeah, quite a reader of men. No wonder the oil industry paid her so well. In the last few months, she'd sized up Keller as a suitable mate, and closed in on him like a black widow spider – a match made in hell, he thought.

Then there was Jim. Jim, who spoke to no one – a dark brooding presence in an outsized body. He stood within earshot but made no attempt to move closer.

And finally, Dan Keller. The would be Alpha. What happens in a wolf pack when there's two Alphas? They rarely fought to the death. Usually, one or the other gave ground. When they couldn't or wouldn't, one left. This would be Jake's biggest challenge. And mine I guess. Keller was the last to approach the fire, and he hung back eyeing Pete suspiciously.

"OK, let me have your attention. I've got good news. Jake says we're going to stay put – at least for a while."

They stared back dumbly, except for Keller, who was a good enough politician to understand what it meant that Pete got to make the announcement, and it seemed to Pete, he ratcheted up his animosity another notch.

"And this is good because?" Joan asked.

"Because we don't have to cross those mountains," Pete pointed to a range of snow covered peaks due west of their camp, "and because we can make ourselves a little more comfortable here. We might as well get started. Sarah, Thom, Joan, would you guys gather some more wood? We're low. Dan? You and I are going to make some arrowheads. Jake says we're doing another hunt soon."

"What about me?" Ruth asked.

"Tell you what. I want to try to make some soup ... something with fiber in it. Can you figure out a way we can boil water?"

"I know a way," Clio volunteered.

"Great. And of course, there's fish jerky for breakfast."

They all groaned as one. Pete had an inspiration. "Eunice, take Bill and Rita to gather some arctic lichen and miner's lettuce. I saw some up on the wolf path you and I took the first day here."

"I'll go with them," Clio said. She took Eunice's hand and lifted her off the rock she sat upon. Pete watched – Clio's manic cheerfulness could cure a catatonic, he thought. And Bill's calm confidence should smooth things out for her, too. Rita was trading glances with Keller.

Pete walked over to Keller. "Looks like it's you and me boss."

"Jake's orders, right?"

"Yeah."

"So what's his game?"

"Game?"

"His angle. What's he after?"

"Why does he have to have a game?"

"Every body has a game, Petey. Everybody but you."

"OK, Keller. He wants us to save the world – or humanity, actually."

"Bullshit. Even you're not dumb enough to believe that."

"Maybe sometimes you just have to take people at face value."

"*You* may have to. But I don't. Now, let me tell you something. Destiny only knocks once. You only get one shot. Dan Keller is going to be President – with or without this guy's help. You coulda come along Pete. But the door's closed now ... and it won't open up again. Ever."

"Dan, you need someone like me to protect you from yourself..."

"That's what he wants me to believe. You know why?"

"Why?"

"Cause you're his way in. And that's his game. Same as all the rest of us. Power. I've got it. He wants it. And you know what? I'd hate to be you, right now."

"What are you talking about?"

"I'm talking about your great friend, Jake. And what he's going to do to you when you can't deliver." Keller pushed a strand of greasy hair out of his eyes, then looked at Pete intently before continuing. "I'll tell you something. He scares me. I'm not afraid of anybody, but he straight up scares me. And I'd hate to see what he does to someone who lets him down. Way out here? In the middle of grizzly country? No tellin' what could happen." Keller laughed.

CHAPTER 26

As Karen was returning from her interview with Dawkins, she'd gotten a cell phone call from the Deputy Administrator, EPA's second in command, summoning her back to Washington. She'd flown back, cursing the DA, one of those political appointees who'd been parked in the Agency because he was too stupid to be put in charge of anything, but who'd delivered enough money to the campaign that he couldn't be ignored. The morning after arriving, she went up to the eighth floor suites and noticed that he'd already changed the sign outside his office to read "Acting Administrator." She briefly considered adding in magic marker 'for the next twenty-four days.' Idiot, she thought as she entered his office. He sat behind his desk, looking smug.

When she was seated, he opened up the discussion by accusing her of leaking stories to the press, and then, incongruously, he insisted that she stay and fulfill her duties as Acting General Counsel.

"So, on the one hand, you think I'm a traitor, and on the other you're insisting I stay here and do my job?" she'd asked.

He tried to stammer out an answer, but she'd interrupted him. "You're an idiot, and I quit."

Now, two days after seeing Dawkins, she was arriving back at Chas' just in time for dinner. Rose Barnett answered the door and escorted her back to the deck. She was, Karen thought, the perfect compliment to Chas. A handsome woman nearly the same age as Chas, she had the same slim build, the same taste for casual elegance that he displayed, and if anything, she was even more garrulous. "Come in, my dear, come in. I'm Rose Barnett. Call me Rose." She took Karen's hand and pulled her in, continuing, "Chas has been telling me all about you, and I must say, he didn't do you justice. You're adorable. And you're in love? You must tell me all about him ... of course Ben's spoken very highly of him, and that's all I need to know... do you have a picture? Oh no, there I go, I'm embarrassing you. Well, come on back, darling, you mustn't let me bother you. In fact pay no attention to me. I'm turning into one of those nosy old broads we all vow never to become ..." They'd reached the deck by this time, and she stood aside and gestured for Karen to pass through. " Here's Chas, I'll get the wine and give Maria a hand."

"Has she let you talk yet?" Chas asked.

She smiled and shook her head.

"She's a rare one."

Since her last meal there, the deck had been transformed. The table was covered with a white linen table cloth, hurricane lamps flickered in the light breeze and a tall kerosene heater cast a circle of warmth over them. There was a salmon pate with cut vegetables on the table and it was set for four. Even in the breeze, she could smell the aromas from the kitchen, savory and a bit pungent. She could hear the busy clink of glasses, pots, pans and silverware, and above it all the steady stream of Rose's commentary punctuated by laughter from both Maria and Rose.

"Anything I can do to help?"

"No, we're excused. You're our guest, and they still insist on treating me as an invalid."

"So what did you find out about Jake's history?"

Barnett's jaw tightened for just a moment, then he said, "We'll talk about it after dinner."

"What's wrong with now?"

"House rule. No talking business over dinner. Let's save it for coffee." She started to protest, but he gestured to the kitchen and said, "Save it. Or you'll have to take it up with the boss ... and believe me, you really don't want to do that."

He walked over to the edge of the deck. "Come here. Look at my mountains." Across the sound, the Olympians, backlit from the setting sun, stood purple in the fading light of a May evening. Just above the mountains, the sun was a large red giant, its intensity gone, now gentle and soft. He was quiet for a moment, then said "You see the big one? Just to the left of the sun? That's Mt. Olympus. Home of the gods."

"It is beautiful."

"So, did you manage to keep your job?"

Karen smiled. "They gave me an ultimatum. Stay there, or quit. I quit."

Maria and Rose brought in dinner – a spicy vegetable stir-fry with chicken served on brown rice. Maria joined them, although she hopped up and down the whole time, refilling glasses, getting seconds, taking plates out. The meal was a slow, satisfying affair, and the Barnett's were warm and interested, and Karen was astounded to find that by the end of it she'd told them her whole life story. Right up to the present, and her fears about Pete.

Rose placed her hand on Karen's arm and said, "Don't worry. If he's with Ben, he'll be fine."

When dinner was done, Maria served coffee and Chas produced a sheaf of papers and turned all business. "I sent one of our investigators back to Jake's home town. This is what he came up with." He thumbed through the contents of one of the folders and said, "Where to begin?" He tossed the folder on to the table and started, "Jake's had a hard life. Very hard. He was the son of a Pentecostal minister in rural West Virginia. Do you know what that means?"

Karen shrugged. She knew a bit about some of the more extreme beliefs that thrived in the rural south, but she wasn't sure what Chas was driving at.

"The Pentecostal Church is a loosely aggregated set of fundamentalist Christians. Under the best of circumstances they are as strict and serious a bunch of bible thumpers as you're likely to find. Some of the rural sects have kind of splintered off into their own thing. Jake's father's church belonged to a group that tested their faith by handling snakes, inviting death into their services. Presumably it was to show that the Lord protected the righteous. Are you following this?"

"Yes."

"Good. Because at some level, I think you have to have grown up in a Southern holler to get this ... to really understand the craziness here. Anyway, Jake's father apparently got it into his head that Jake was chosen for special things. And he tested the child relentlessly from a very early age to prove it." Here Chas' voice tightened, and he shook his head.

"Tested?" Karen asked. "What does that mean?"

"Means some pretty horrible things. Like withstanding severe beatings to drive the devil out of him whenever he strayed from the straight and narrow. Like holding his forearm over a burning candle until his flesh burned without flinching, and doing it again if he showed pain. It meant fasting, and deprivation, and marathon praying. It meant a father who gave no love. No hugging. No laughter. Worst thing? It meant being crucified for three days on Easter, once he turned thirteen. Hung up in front of the church, roped to a cross from Good Friday until Easter Sunday with no food, no water."

"What's amazing is they all report him to have been a well-adjusted kid. Must have been because of his mother, and his kid sister. His mother had been a bright and pretty woman, kind and devout, but fun-loving. She was a no-nonsense Christian, but without the hard edges of the Church. And he was devoted to his little sister. She followed him everywhere. The two of them spent a lot of time in the forests and hills, according to neighbors. His mother and sister died when Jake was fifteen. In a car accident. Right before Easter. By that time Jake'd been through more than most prisoners of war. That Friday – Good Friday – the day after they died, his father set up the crucifix just as he had the year before. When Jake refused to get up on it, the old man started to beat him, but this time Jake fought back. Put him in the hospital. Nearly killed him.

"There was a trial. It was supposed to be sealed, but in a small community like that, there's no secrets. According to neighbors, when the judge heard Jake's story, he wept. The court took him away from his father and put him in a foster home. Jake's luck seems to have started to change there. By all accounts, it was a very loving family, and they welcomed him. They even formally adopted him after a year."

Chas took a sip of wine. "From here on, Jake grew up pretty normal. No. Better than normal. His teachers remember him as an outstanding student, a popular, athletic boy who mixed well with the kids from both the hollers and the townies. He was class President in his senior year, and graduated at the top of his class. After the incident with his father, the only sign of scandal is rumors that he got a girl pregnant and took her for an abortion."

"So what does it all mean?"

"Well ... you have to wonder how a kid comes from an environment like that and ends up so damn good."

Rose said, "It happens. But it does make you wonder."

"What about his stint in the psychiatric ward?"

"My guy is still trying to get the records. But we do know that Jake ran into trouble with the law up in British Columbia. He represented himself, and somehow he convinced them that he needed psychiatric care. So they ordered him into an institution. And after a few months he got them to check him out."

"That could be good thing, right?" Karen asked.

"Depends."

"Of course it is," Rose said. "Poor dear. It's no wonder he had a breakdown. No shame in that. Acknowledging that you need help is healthy, if you ask me. In fact, I'm sure he came out healthier than most of us."

Chas took his wife's hand and smiled at her. "That's my Rose. Always defending the underdog."

"There's something you guys need to understand, here," Karen said. "He may have had a hard life. But he's no underdog."

"That which does not kill me makes me stronger, eh Karen?"

"Yeah. I'd say he's closer to an Ubermensch than an underdog."

Chas nodded, then said, "Ubermensch or underdog – I figure we'll have all we need on Mr. Christianson by Friday. You'll stay here with us, of course."

Rose cut in. "Yes, Karen. We've plenty of room. And you can help with the investigation. You're so obviously a natural. You got Dawkins to open up. No one's done that."

"For all the good it did," Karen said. "Poor guy's obviously a little batty." She felt pleased to get Rose's approval, and grateful for the invitation; something about the Barnett's made her feel safe and cared for. But, the mention of Dawkins raised an alarm. Seemed like everyone involved with Jake had a history of mental illness of one kind or another. It was as if the whole world was going insane. Maybe even Pete.

CHAPTER 27

After Keller's warning, Pete had worked side by side with him for most of the day in silence, chipping arrowheads out of chert. The knapping had gone well. Pete enjoyed the work; it required concentration, and thus absorbed him completely. They roughed out six spear points, using a pair of rounded four inch quartz rocks to pound the chert into a crude shape consisting of the sharpened stone points with a narrow post at the base which would be used to fasten them into the spear shafts. Then they chipped out an initial edge on each side. Next came the finishing work. Using fire-hardened billets made from Alder, they removed the final flakes, sharpened the edges, and trued up the center line on the stones. Finally, they polished the edges using sand and water and a large flat block of sandstone. When they'd finished, their hands were stiff and sore, but they'd managed to make four good spear points out of the six rough hunks of chert they'd started with, each with an edge that could slice a blade of grass.

Just before dinner they worked with Jake down by the fish camp, fixing the spearheads into notches they'd cut into the spear shafts. Then, using pitch, which Jake and Ben had gathered, and sinew from the caribou, they bonded them into the shafts permanently. The spears would be ready to kill by morning.

While Jake worked with them on the spears, Pete could feel his eyes on them, watching with disapproval the way he and Keller worked together in silence. Pete had managed to keep Keller's warning at bay for most of the day, but it played over again as Jake studied them.

As night fell, the wind picked up and swept the skies totally clear for the first time since they'd arrived, and the temperature plummeted.

They stoked the cooking fire up and the whole group gathered round it, feeling the cold on one side and the heat on the other, beneath a sky with more stars than Pete believed possible. He rubbed his hands in front of the fire, soaking up its warmth in his fingers, now growing stiff from the flintknapping he and Keller had done. They were waiting for dinner, which Ruth, Eunice, Bill and Jim were preparing. Hunger had dwelled in Pete's belly like a chronic ache for a week now, but tonight the smell of food set off an appetite so acute that his stomach roiled and his saliva flowed, and he was forced to wipe the corners of his mouth.

While dinner simmered Ruth stood up with her back to the stream and the yurts and Bill stood by her. "We have an announcement to make," she said. "Bill, Jim, Eunice would you care to say a word?" All three demurred and Ruth continued. "We have, by popular demand, a three course meal tonight."

There were mock gasps around the fire, and some laughter. Pete studied Ben. He was quiet, and he seemed almost oblivious of the others. He and Jake had been gone a good part of the day, and Ben had been moody and standoffish since they'd returned. Several times Pete had tried to get him aside to talk about Keller's warning, but Ben had avoided being alone with him. But by dinner, Pete was feeling better. Sure, Jake was different; but he was ready to believe that maybe Ruth had been right back in Washington. Maybe a dangerous man was just what humanity needed right now

Ruth continued, "That's right, we have the last of chef Andersen's ever popular fish jerky," here there were boos, "and we've managed to make it tasteless by boiling it with reindeer moss, turning it into a gruel," more groans but Ruth went on, louder, now, "which I'm told has a very high fiber content and certain laxative properties." They cheered loudly, amidst much laughter. "Next we have the last of the caribou, and finally, fresh miner's lettuce, which we've chilled in the stream."

Dinner was good. Ruth had overseen the preparation, managing to boil the stew by placing a series of extremely hot rocks taken directly from the fire into a hole they'd dug and lined with rawhide and then filled with water. Now as they ate, they ripped and cut hunks of meat from the spit and shared the stew from a single bowl Bill had carved laboriously from a dead willow. Only Eunice declined, but a word from

Jake convinced her to eat. It was the most communal meal Pete had ever had, and as he looked around the fire he was struck at how quickly the trappings of civilization slipped away. Except for the clothes, it was a scene right out of the Neolithic. Nearly everyone was eating with gusto, ripping and tearing flesh, and sharing the two crude spoons Bill had made out of mussel shells and straight sticks. Their faces and hands, smeared with animal fat, glistened in the firelight, the women's hair was getting stringy, and each of the men had the beginnings of a beard. Definitely have to make soap, Pete thought. No need to go completely native. Soap and more bowls.

As he watched her preside happily over this strange meal, Pete wondered what had made Ruth open up, and drop her formidable defenses. More magic from Jake?

After dinner Jake led them up to camp, holding a torch made of strips of willow bark rubbed in caribou fat and wrapped around a thick branch. The torch flickered, giving the forest an eerie orange strobe-like glow, and the group was accompanied by twelve shadows doing a macabre dance against the tree trunks a few feet from where they walked. A delicious thrill passed over the back of Pete's neck hairs as he watched their shadows appear and disappear. When they arrived at the camp, Jake set the campfire going with the torch, throwing logs onto it until it licked the sky and danced in the wind. When it was roaring, he tossed the torch into the fire, and stood downwind from the flames. His face shifted in and out of eclipse; now crimson, now dark and phantom-like with only his eyes visible, glowing orange-yellow in the reflected firelight. "I suppose you're wondering why I've called this meeting."

They laughed, and Jake went on, "We have come to a unique moment in time and history. A time when the survival of the species is in question. Let me recite a quote to you ...

> *I am a member of a fragile species, still new to the Earth, the youngest creatures of any scale, here only a few moments as evolutionary time is measured, a juvenile species, a child of a species. We are only tentatively set in place, error-prone, at risk*

*of fumbling, in real danger at the moment
of leaving behind only a thin layer of our
fossils ...*

"Lewis Thomas, *The Lives of a Cell*," Clio shouted out.

Jake smiled at her. "Yes. Very good, Clio. Very good. It doesn't surprise me that *you* would have read it. "Now, Doctor Thomas was talking about nuclear weapons. But his point is just as valid for global warming. As far as nature's concerned there's little difference between a massive thermo-nuclear detonation and what we're doing to our planet now..."

"Bullshit, Christianson. That's taking things a bit too far. There's a hell of a difference ... between ..."

"Be quiet and listen Dan," Jake said. Uncharacteristically, Keller's voice faded off into uncertainty. Pete watched in shock. Perhaps it was the fire and the grisly effect it had on Jake's appearance, perhaps it was what they'd seen on the hunt, but if Jake had been dominant back at All Souls he was now something beyond dominant. Something Pete couldn't name. Jake turned to him and said, "Pete, you're our resident geologist, right?"

"By degrees. But it's been a while."

"Well let's see how good your memory is. How much energy is locked in fossil fuels?"

Pete did a quick, back-of-the envelope calculation, based on total global reserves of coal, oil and gas. "Several quintillions of BTUs, I'd say."

"Close enough. Now, as your resident physicist, I can tell you that's roughly equivalent to the energy contained in all the nuclear weapons on hand."

"How long will it take us to burn all those fossil fuels, Pete?"

"Let's see. We have about sixty years left, maybe a hundred if we count the dirtiest coal. We started burning the stuff in earnest in the nineteenth century. So I'd say ... oh, about two hundred and fifty – maybe three hundred years. But the vast majority of it in the last two decades."

"Right. And what is that in geologic time?"

"I'm not sure I understand."

"Come on, Pete. In the scale of mountain building, climate creation, evolution of life and life supporting systems, that kind of thing, what is two or three hundred years?"

"Oh. A blink – not even that. Basically, we're using several hundred million years worth of stored and concentrated solar energy in a matter of a few hundred years."

"Right. So, from the perspective of an individual looking at his physical surroundings – your buildings, your shopping malls, even these mountains – what do you see from your three hundred year burn? Very little. But nature sculpts the world at a more leisurely pace. To her, what you're doing is in many ways indistinguishable from a massive thermonuclear explosion – one that is virtually unprecedented in natural history. And all the balances, all the accommodations, all the painstakingly wrought physical, chemical, and biological systems that have evolved over epochs, what some call Gaia, will be tipped. She will survive. But She will be diminished. And in the end, She will take what measures She must to rid herself of the organism causing the imbalance. Then She will fashion new balances, new accommodations. But you may not be a part of that new Gaia.

"The survival that we must learn out here together is not just individual survival, but the measures and means we – and others who will help us – must take to avoid a mass extinction unlike anything the Earth has known. We will spend our days learning how to survive as individuals, our evenings learning what we must do to survive as a species. You are each here because you can contribute to that effort."

And there it was. Out in the open, Pete thought, and not a blink from the people surrounding the fire. Except Eunice, sullen as usual. And Keller. Pete could see that he was steeling himself for another go at Jake. Got to hand it to him. Not sure I'd try confronting him.

"You remember the story of the boy who cried Wolf?" Keller asked. "We've listened to cries of doom for decades and nothing's happened yet ..."

"Yes, decades," Jake thundered. "Measured by Gaia, that means these so-called doomsayers might be off in their predictions by milliseconds."

"I think we all do a disservice to environmental causes when we cry wolf."

Thom interrupted, "Oh, the wait-and-see crowd. Whoops, we've destroyed our children's life support systems ... darn ... what shall we do now?"

Jake held up his hand, silencing Thom. Then he turned to Keller. "You know why you want to wait and see? Because your kind owns everything. Because you are wringing out the essence of our planet for your own and you're using the clever sophistry of neoclassical economics to convince the rest it's good for them."

As Jake spoke, Keller stood up directly across the fire from him, and leaned toward him, lighting his face in that same flashlight-under-the-chin spookiness. Physically confronting Jake seemed to make him grow in stature, and feed his courage. "And you know why you want to stop it?" he interrupted, "Because you don't own everything, and you want to."

Jake stepped directly through the fire and stood inches from Keller. The air between them was charged, ready to explode. Pete marveled at Keller's courage. He stood face to face with Jake, ready to take him on. And Pete saw, in Jake's face, the same look he'd seen with the caribou, and he remembered Keller's warning, and fear flowed through him like liquid ice.

The voice came from the side away from the two men standing in that ancient embrace, ready to vie for power. It was quiet, but insistent and it cut through the tension with surgical precision, "The real lesson in that story may be that the wolves did come." All eyes turned to Thom.

"What did you say?" Ruth asked.

"The wolves. In the end they showed up."

"That's brilliant," she said. "That's exactly what we all forget."

"I have my moments," Thom smiled.

Jake had backed off of Keller, the rage intact, but he looked very conflicted, as if he were engaged in some inner struggle. He took a few steps toward the lake, then turned and said, "I do not like to talk of wolves in this way. Lynx taught that they were sent by Saya to teach you, to watch over you, and to protect you from that all-consuming compulsion within you. But did you listen? Did you learn? Did you see? No. Instead, you've slaughtered the wolves in order to silence their rebuke." With that, he stalked off to the lake.

CHAPTER 28

When Pete woke up the next day, Jake was still down by the lake staring across the water. Keller was up, presiding over the fire, and if such a thing were possible, he seemed even more cocky to Pete. Eunice, Rita, Joan and Bill sat around the fire with him, and they laughed periodically. Pete couldn't take it. He got up, stretched his legs and arched his back. The pine bough bed he'd constructed wasn't making the ground any softer and he was waking up stiff and sore. Besides, the wolves had returned in full force, and spent most of the night howling, so he'd not slept well. While he'd waited for the dawn to banish the night, he'd held the medallion Karen had given him and tried to relive the times they'd shared. He'd even let himself imagine a future with her.

Now, he searched for Ben and when he didn't see him, he walked down the hill and sat on the rock next to Jake without saying a word. After a moment, Jake spoke.

"I misjudged him."

"You're not going to recruit him. He's a selfish asshole, obsessed with power."

"I misjudged the extent of his single-mindedness, the total simplicity and purity of his ambition." Jake turned to face Pete. "But you knew."

Pete nodded. "What do we do now?" He asked.

"With most people, even very strong ones, there are keys that you can find if you probe. But some are so simple, so straightforward, that there is no subtlety, no keys and no place to put them. I encountered one like this before, a scientist like yourself. It gives them a peculiar kind of strength. But in the end, it is also their weakness."

"How did you handle him?"

"There are certain things you can do, but I'm not sure you would believe them. They invoke that other way of knowing things we spoke of yesterday."

"I'm not sure I want to know, then."

Jake sighed, and studied Pete for a moment. "Had I known what Lynx was asking of me, I might have refused. Such knowledge can make you a very lonely man."

"Why?"

Jake laughed, "It's always been this way. Throughout the millennia, prophets and saints have come in many guises under many banners, but they have all sprung from the same source – in fact they have all been one and the same – and they have all been reviled by those in power and killed by those they would serve. Just as you've done with the wolves."

Pete had no idea what to say to this. Did Jake believe the teachings of a dying Shaman from a disappearing people qualified him as a prophet? Damn. Him or Keller. Lose Lose. It occurred to Pete that in his effort to get to know people, he'd made significant headway with everyone but Jake. He remained an enigma. And Jim.

"I'm sending you and Keller out to hunt tomorrow. Will you do that?"

Pete nodded, "But what if he refuses?"

"He will. But I've found at least one key I can use." He stood up and offered Pete a hand, "Come on, let's join the others." He yanked Pete up with a force that could have launched him, had it not been controlled.

"Just a second," Pete said.

Jake turned, "Yes?"

"Last night ... Keller. You could have crushed him, but you didn't. Why?"

"Still trying to put old ghosts to rest, eh? Remember Pete, only a truly strong man can choose to run or choose to stay. Besides, I need him." They started up the hill, but Jake turned and stopped Pete. "It is easy to defeat someone. The challenge is to own him. You will begin to know what I mean before we are through."

As they approached the circle of the fire Keller broke off in mid-sentence and the group fell silent. Everyone was there but Ruth. "Someone wake Ruth," Jake said as he approached them. Sarah went over to the lean-to and shook her awake. When she approached, Jake spoke. "Last night we had a confrontation. As I said in Washington, these things will happen. We may even have a few fights." He looked at Keller as he said this. "The main thing is that we get past them. We have important work to do here. I said yesterday we need another hunt. Pete and Dan will be the hunters, Bill, Clio, Sarah and Thom will drive the caribou."

Ruth interrupted, "I'd like to go along."

"Fine. You can drive."

"I'm not going with *him*," Keller said, pointing to Pete.

Jake didn't bat an eye, "Of course. If you're frightened, I can get someone else," he said, turning toward Ben.

"Dan Keller isn't afraid of anything ..."

"Except hunting with Pete, apparently. Ben ?"

"I said I wasn't afraid."

"Then you'll go," It was a simple statement of fact, leaving Keller no option.

Just like that, Pete thought. So easy.

"The caribou may be a little skittish. By now, our scent has penetrated the forest. I'll scout around and check out the area today. When I get back, we'll plan out our hunt for tomorrow morning. Pete, make sure we have enough wood – we'll need some more food of some kind, too. Get someone to set some snares for ground squirrels or ptarmigan." He turned and took Jim by his elbow. "I'd like you to come with me." Jim remained rooted in place.

Pete waited to see if Jim would cooperate. If those two go at it there'll be nothing left of the mountain Pete thought. But after a moment they headed up the slope a little east of where Pete and Eunice had explored on that first night ... what? A week ago? He couldn't say. He was beginning to keep the calendar in the same way he kept time; by the character of the days, not their sequence. There were wet days; cold days; days with light and heat; days with an empty aching belly and itching skin; days with a full belly after a fresh dip in the lake; days where fear seeped down out of the mountains and enveloped the group like a heavy cloud cover; days where even the itchy, gritty, hungry, grimy reality that surrounded them paled against the impact of a staggering beauty beyond anything he'd dared to imagine.

As soon as Jake took off, Pete cornered Ben. "What's bugging you?" he asked.

"Your friend," he gestured to Jake, now disappearing with Jim into the trees upslope.

"Jesus. I was just gettin' to feel good about him."

"Yeah, well your girlfriend may have been right after all."

"About what?"

"About Jake being dangerous."

"Why?"

"It's hard to say, exactly. I've been going over our conversation yesterday again and again." Ben stopped and just shrugged his shoulders. "I'm not sure it's anything specific."

"So what did you talk about?"

"Saving the world." Ben stopped, collecting himself.

"Like you said, what if he can?"

Ben smiled, and looked up at the slope where Jake had gone. Nervously, it seemed to Pete. "What he's talking about takes planning and execution on a massive scale."

"He's been at this a while, Ben. His trips have included Corporate CEOs, politicians, philanthropists..."

"Oh, he's a remarkable man. But at the end of the day, his plan seems to be nothing more than casting a net for people and converting them twelve at a time."

There was that number again, Pete thought. More mystical mumbo-jumbo. And yet there'd been that experience on the mountain. Had Ben been exposed to anything like it?

Ben said, "You told him it doesn't matter who gets elected – the world belongs to K Street?"

"Yeah. I said something like that."

"How did he react?"

"Said he'd change it."

Ben eyed Pete closely, looked toward the mountain Jake had taken Jim up then scanned the campground. "Let's go down by the lake."

When they got there, Ben patted a rock, inviting Pete to sit. "I'm worried, Pete."

"This where I get to say I told-you-so?"

Ben smiled, and Pete saw some of the weight the older man had been carrying around for the day lift. "I pretty much told him what you did. Keller, Congress – politicians in particular and the people in general – we're all pretty much driven by greed, ego, power or all three. So even if he managed to make Keller a greenie or get one of his men elected, things wouldn't change much. Didn't go over very well."

"How do you mean?"

"First he got angry." Ben wiped his hand across his face then clasped them in front of him wringing them until his knuckles whitened, and for the first time he appeared frail to Pete, but then he spoke again and he seemed more like Ben. "Jesus Pete. I've never seen anything like it. Cursed you and me both, for being weak. Said we didn't have time for pessimists, only prophets." His eyebrows furrowed, and he looked out over the lake, perhaps searching for words. Pete replayed Keller's warning. He wanted to ask Ben about it more than ever, but he could see the man needed to talk, and so he waited. Each time he felt the fear starting to rise, though, he'd recall the mountain top, and the intimacy he'd felt with the Earth, and Her urgency and knew it would all be OK. Of course, Jake was right. We didn't have time.

Ben started again. "Now this next part ... this next part is unbelievable."

"How do you mean?"

"Just the way it happened." Ben looked up and the smile he gave Pete looked like an apology. "Let's just say I'll never give you grief about time trips or vision quests again." He waited for Pete to acknowledge him, and continued after Pete nodded.

"I've been pitched by the best salesmen in the world. You get that when you get rich. When I was setting up to take my companies public, I had people coming at me so smooth they made a baby's cheek look like alligator hide. Men and women who get millions a deal just 'cause they're the best in the world at doing it. Jake was better than any of them. I wasn't being sold. I was being seduced. Like you said, it was hypnotic. I was losing control. Never felt anything like it. By the time he was through, I was ready to turn my whole fortune over to him. Still am."

"So what's your problem, then?"

Ben scratched at his beard, and his eyebrows nestled down over his eyes. "That anger. At some point Jake's going to figure out we're right. I hope to God this trip's over when it happens."

"And yet you'll sign on to his scheme. Why?"

"Because we don't have a choice. Because no one else can do what needs to be done. Because the son-of-a-bitch just might be able to pull this off."

"How?" Pete asked.

"It's a long shot, but it's not impossible. He's using an outside-in strategy. Think of it as a hostile takeover only instead of Wall Street, it happens on Pennsylvania Avenue."

"Sounds a little far-fetched to me," Pete said. "How's it work?"

"Jake's assembled a team here. We've got the money people, the politicians, the press and the policy wonks. Ruth's a shoe-in for the next oped editor at the Post. Clio's one of the best legal minds in environmental law, and Joan and Eunice will re-write whatever legislation we end up with on global warming. And make no mistake, with the hurricanes, droughts and forest fires, and yoyoing energy prices, there will be legislation. Rita's one of the best political operatives on K-street. If she were working for us, instead of against us – well, it might change the calculus. As for Thom Kline, he may be a burnt out cynic, but they're still talking about his books and he's got a cult following. A couple of more with the right backing, followed by movies and he could do it again. As for backing, between Bill, Sarah and me we've got nearly ten billion in assets."

Ben looked as if he'd gotten a transfusion. His voice quickened and his eyebrows danced across his forehead like two caterpillars on amphetamines. "Great." Pete said. But why Keller? Or me or Jim for that matter?"

"Keller's the administration's point man on climate and he's got political ambitions. Jake intends to have him in his pocket. Jim? Not sure what he's got to offer. In fact, I don't know anything about him, do you?"

"Just that he's a soldier of fortune, he worked for Blackguard and he's an ex-SEAL. But what I want to know is how I fit in this scheme."

"You? You're the key to it all."

Pete snorted. "Why me?"

"No accounting for taste," the older man said. Then he turned serious. "There has to be a focal point – a spokesperson. Someone with the vision to pull this stuff together. To change the way we think about values, economics, environment. Someone who understands. Who can speak for the Earth."

"That's me?"

"Yeah. We're supposed to help you set up a new organization. Sort of a sustainable development SWAT team. I'm the inside guy, you're the public face."

"Why me? Why doesn't Jake do it himself?"

"I asked him that. He said there were some things in his past that might keep him from having credibility...besides, he doesn't have the bona fides."

"And I do?"

"When I pressed him, he said we needed an inside-the beltway type. He'd read some of your stuff, seen you speak and you seemed to have potential. He said after he met you, he knew you were the right one, and after the other night on the mountain, he said Saya approved."

"This thing in his past. Got any idea what it might be?"

"I asked him, but he wouldn't elaborate."

Pete stood up rubbed his butt and sat back down. That was one of the things he was beginning to miss about civilization: cushioned chairs. "How's a skinny old coot like you sit on these damn rocks?"

"Tough hide. Very tough hide."

"Think he can pull it off?"

"Sitting here talking to you it sounds plausible. But when Jake and I had our talk, he was getting pretty radical. I asked him if the ends ever justified the means. He said only if the ends to be avoided included the destruction of Earth. It was a very well thought out response. When I challenged him on it, he said if the Earth is a prerequisite for existence, then preserving it was a moral imperative. He reminded me we're not the only inhabitants of this planet, and then he got mad."

"He's got a point. Global warming will wipe out seventy per cent of all species by 2100."

"Yeah, but when he got angry, I started thinking what a guy like Jake might be capable of ... if..." Ben's voice trailed off, and the he looked up.

"Well, it's about to get worse."

"Yeah? Why's that?"

"I can't lead his little SWAT team. I've got something in my past, too. Something the K-Street Corporatists could use to completely discredit me."

"Has this got anything to do with what we were talking about the other night?"

"Yeah. The hospital stay I mentioned? It was a psychiatric ward."

"Shit. Feel like talking about it?"

"No. Not yet."

"This isn't going to go over too well. He's got a lot riding on you."

"The weird thing is, I almost think he knows."

"No. If he knew that, he'd change plans. No offense Pete, but America isn't ready to follow anyone who's been in a mental hospital."

Pete said nothing, but he was remembering Keller's comment '*I'd hate to let him down, way out here ... no telling what he'd do*' or something like that. And he was remembering the way Jake looked at Keller.

"You said he had fallbacks. Does he have one for me?"

"Yeah. There's a former Mayor in Seattle – wants to be Governor. A Senator and a couple of congressman. And Clio could take your role. I'm real surprised he didn't know about this, though. It's not like him to have loose ends."

"It was a private hospital. Very discreet."

They stayed down by the lake in silence for a long time, Pete mulling over Ben's story. Now and then he looked up at the camp. Every time he did he saw Keller sitting on the rocks by the fire methodically grinding a spear point and staring at him.

Finally, Pete told Ben about Keller's warning. "So what do you think? Should I tell him?"

"Let it ride, for now. But sooner or later you'll have to."

"Yeah. Well, I'd just as soon it were later. If Keller's right, I'm definitely grizzly bait once he knows."

"I don't think so. Jake likes you. You two are a lot alike in some ways. I get the sense that you're what he thinks he could have been if things had been different. But there is something damaged about Jake. Something hard."

Later, as evening closed in, Jake and Jim came down the mountain after being out most of the day, and he gathered the hunters and drivers around him. "The good thing about being out here is that you know the cost of consumption, because *you* have to pay it. You can't outsource your greenhouse gasses to some third world sweat shop, or pillage someone else's rainforest while you spew out sanctimonious bullshit about developed nations being the only ones capable of protecting their environments."

Pete wasn't listening. He was remembering Ben's comment about Jake. Something damaged and then 'you're what Jake thinks he could have been.' Exactly the mirror image of what Pete had thought about Jake in that second class so long ago. Maybe we're all damaged, he thought. Just in different ways.

"Listen up, Pete." Jake's voice snapped him back to the fire ring. "The caribou are in the same meadow, about four miles upstream from where we last saw them. We'll do the same thing we did last time. The drivers get downwind, come up behind, then chase them to Pete and Dan. Got it?"

They all nodded.

"So what's for dinner?" he asked.

"We're down to day old caribou stew – and I think half our pot melted into it," Rita said. She handed out a set of makeshift spoons, fashioned from muscle shells wedged into split sticks held fast with sinew. "But the good news is, Clio and I found some wild onion – a lot."

"Maybe too damn much," Thom said, sniffing the brew.

As they sat around the fire, Ben leaned over to Pete. "Check him out," he whispered, gesturing toward Jim.

Pete studied him a moment across the fire and noted that he was quiet, and apparently exhausted. But there was something else, too. He appeared almost dazed.

"Lot to think about, huh?" Ben said.

"Yeah. Looks like he got the unabridged version."

After dinner, Ruth asked, "What about religion? What role does it have in your – our– save the world efforts?"

Perhaps it was just the flickering fire, but Pete thought Jake flinched at the word. Pete waited, as did the others. "Religion," Jake repeated. He wiped his hand across his forehead, "I have seen sides of it you cannot even imagine." He seemed engaged in some inner struggle, but finally he went on. "I have learned from Lynx that there are different ways of seeing the world. But they are all, in the end, the same, and they are all, therefore, in their own way, true. Each seeks to know that which is divine, and they all arrive at that same place – the point where man and nature come together. Except our westernized version of religion which has strayed far from this truth. Long ago, we confused dominion with stewardship and we have been drifting from the garden since."

"How can we get back?" Clio asked.

"Paul Tillich said, 'God created man and man returned the favor.' I believe that to be literally true. But you do not create the god you want; you create the god you need. You have one last chance to tap the accumulated wisdom of all life that resides within you – to know by reason that which all other life knows by code. If you fail, this is the time for a jealous god; an avenging old-testament god; an angry god. A god who will protect that which is divine; that which is his."

CHAPTER 29

Pete and Keller were huddled in a small clump of brush within a stand of black spruce. The herd of caribou, Pete counted five and two calves, were grazing in an open plain by a stream about one hundred and seventy five yards in front of them, or due east. A stiff breeze blew down the U-shaped valley from the north, setting the leaves rustling. Jake was leading the drivers through some birch at the tail end of the valley, about a hundred yards east of herd. When they were spread out opposite Pete and Dan, they'd drive the animals to the hunters, same as before.

"This is mine, Andersen. You just stay out of my way," Keller said.

"It'll take both of us."

"You deaf? Stay the fuck out of my way."

So much for being Keller's buddy, he thought. After about ten minutes, he spotted Jake, signaling from the stream valley. He nudged Keller and pointed to the valley. Keller understood at once, and got ready. The caribou had wandered closer to the stand of spruce. There were at least a hundred yards of open space between them and the drivers. That would give the caribou time to scatter before the drivers could close in on them. But the mothers would stay with their calves, making them vulnerable.

Pete had mixed feelings about the whole thing. On the one hand he was exhilarated: the sheer primitiveness of it struck some visceral chord within him, rendering him more alive than he'd felt in decades. On the other, he was nervous. These were big animals, capable of inflicting real damage on a man, even killing him. Besides, he knew that they were disappearing – and the presence of the calves brought home the finality of what they were about to do. And then there was Keller, who, predictably, was turning the whole thing into a contest. Asshole.

As Pete was steeling himself, Jake broke from the stream bed, screaming and waving his arms. The others joined in, forming a line about a hundred and sixty yards long. Keller instantly shot up, too soon Pete knew, and so he grabbed his belt and pulled him roughly back down. "Wait 'til they break for us," he hissed. Keller tried to free himself, but Pete jerked him down and said, "Wait, asshole," his eyes on the caribou the whole time. It took the animals a few seconds to decide what to do, and then they broke toward the forest, right at Keller and Pete. The way it was supposed to work was that Keller and Pete would go out together, one of them turning a caribou and the other attacking it from the side. But as the animals thundered toward them, Keller wriggled loose from Pete, shoved him off his haunches, and ran out ahead. While Pete lay sprawled in the brush, Keller sprinted straight for the biggest of them, a bull leading the cows and calves toward the forest's edge. By the time Pete got up, Keller was nearing the animal.

He nearly reached the bull before it saw him. It pulled up, eyed the chasing drivers behind and closing from each side, and decided to attack the lone man in front of him. An enraged caribou is a formidable animal. It can deliver blows with its broad flat hooves capable of caving in a grizzly's skull, or sending a wolf flying. Now, cornered, it reared up and kicked viciously at Keller, who stood his ground looking for an opportunity to plant his spear. Pete had recovered and was now racing toward the two and he heard Jake shouting frantically, "Not from the front. No Keller. No." Keller continued to parry with his spear but the bull landed a glancing kick, just missing Keller's shoulder, but knocking the spear out of his hand. In his effort to dodge the kick, Keller fell backwards, sprawling helplessly on his back. Enraged, the animal was about to trample the now defenseless Keller. Pete knew he had just seconds to close the distance before it killed him.

He raced across the scrub willow and grass faster than he'd ever moved, yet he saw everything unfold slowly in front of him, seeing for the second time through the eyes of a predator – and seeing it thus, he felt good and clear and right and free and yes, savage.

Pete closed on the caribou as it reared over Keller and he launched himself at its flank, spear pointed just in back of the shoulder. The impact was clean, and Pete could feel the spear slide into the beast's insides, sundering flesh, slipping through the ribs, and tearing through blood vessels and organs, finally striking its heart. The penetration was somehow sensuous, and Pete let go a cry, as if from orgasm, except even more primal, and he lost himself in a new kind of lust, the life ebbing out of the animal shared, intimate, passionate, ultimate.

The animal died before it delivered its death blow to Keller, but it came down on him in heap, nevertheless. Pete came to, as if he'd been unconscious, and felt the animal's warm flank against his hand where he'd pressed the spear up to its hilt and saw that his hand and forearm were covered with blood, and shaking.

He was dimly aware of Jake arriving, shouting orders, and the others gathering around and lifting the big bull off of the thrashing Keller. He wanted to tell them to be careful, to be gentle, to be respectful – to tell them that something noble and good had just been destroyed, but if they were careful and mindful, they could preserve it now, in these few minutes after it was extinguished, while it was still here among them. He wanted to, but he did not know how, and so he said nothing.

Suddenly, Keller was up and waving off Jake's concern. "I'm fine, God damn it. No thanks to him ..." and he vaguely recognized that Keller was enraged, that he was screaming at him, trying to get at him, and that Jake was holding him back, keeping between Keller and himself.

Pete wanted them all to shut up and just go away – to end this blasphemy in the face of something divine. Then for the first time in twenty-four years, he felt pure anger, divorced from fear and doubt. Without thinking, he threw Jake aside and grabbed Keller. The strength he felt came from somewhere inside, somewhere other than his muscles, and he tossed Keller onto the ground like a rag, grabbed his legs and twisting them, rolled him over onto his stomach, then he planted his knee in Keller's back and gripped him under the chin and wrenched him back so that his spine was arched and his ear was right next to Pete's mouth. He wanted to bite it; to tear it off and spit it out, but a measure of calm was returning now. Instead, he whispered into that ear, "I just saved your life you dumb fuck. Now, I want you to be quiet – to be absolutely still for the next five minutes. If you don't, I will kill you. Do you understand?"

Keller said nothing, and Pete pulled further, arching Keller's back at an impossible angle and shutting off what little air he was getting.

He repeated each word again, distinct, separate, "Do ... you ... understand?"

"Yes," Keller croaked, and Pete let him go. But the thing he'd wanted to capture was gone now, and with its departure, Pete felt the old fear return as Keller was up and coming at him again, relentless, fearless, possessed with the same purity of anger that Pete had felt moments before – no, not the same purity – just a mindless, self-centered rage. He saw out of the corner of his eye that Jake was going to let it go on, and his veins filled with the familiar panic, afraid now of what he might do, and even more afraid that he wouldn't, but he fought it down, and prepared himself for the assault. He sidestepped Keller's charge, and delivered an uppercut, landing it cleanly on Keller's chin, hard enough to hurt his hand, hard enough to straighten Keller up. Then he took Keller's arm and twisted it, spinning him around into a hammerlock, shoving Keller's arm up into his back, making him helpless. "You son of a bitch, you almost got me killed." Keller screamed in impotent rage.

Pete couldn't believe what he heard. "Almost got you killed?" He shoved Keller hard, sending him sprawling onto the ground. Then he walked over to the caribou, pulled his spear out, and returned to Keller, holding the spear point against his throat.

He stood like that for several minutes, until Jake said, "Back off, Pete."

Pete didn't move, and he felt the tip touch Keller's neck, and he remembered the feel of it slipping into the caribou's flank. So easy, he thought. So simple and it would all stop ...

"I said back off." It was Jake's voice but still Pete stood with the point just grazing Keller's neck, in the cavity where the collar bones met.

Without taking his eye off Keller, Pete said, "You know what this asshole did? He knocked me over so he could come out and bag the kill on his own." After a moment, he moved the spear point aside and said, "If you ever come after me again, I'll kill you. Do you understand, Keller? I will kill you." Then he spun on his heels and crossed the grassy meadow to the stream to wash the blood off his hands and arms and face, oblivious now of the others.

When he reached the stream, he hopped down into the shallow ravine and got on his knees near a pool, cupping his hands and splashing the icy glacial water over his face and arms, watching the blood dissipate into the water and get carried away in pale crimson eddies. After taking a long drink he sat down, out of view of the others, and rubbed his eyes and face. The stream wasn't very deep, and within the broad ravine, it meandered through the plain in several strands that wrapped and twisted into each other, leaving fine gravel beds and larger terrace gravel shelves in between the strands. Pete leaned against the near bank, sitting on one of the gravel bars. He was reliving the kill, replaying it, trying to experience that feeling of raw power he'd felt throbbing through his veins, felt in his very cells. And that other thing. That inexplicable feeling that emerged not from his brain, but from some other place – deeper, archaic, communal. But he couldn't get it back completely. It was overlain now with another feeling; a sadness, a trembling almost at what he'd done and what he'd become. And then it struck him. Keller. He had an enemy out here, now, maybe two if Keller'd been right about Jake. "Fuck him. Fuck the both of them."

He stretched out a bit. The sun had emerged, and it was near seventy degrees. A few flies buzzed around, harbingers of a much worse time ahead. A time when they would swarm in such numbers that they could literally drive a person insane. He looked at his clothes – caked with mud and blood and grime – felt the massive, nappy, itchy mass that was his hair and scalp, stroked his beard – itchy, too – and he suddenly felt incalculably dirty. What the hell was he doing here? What did any of this have to do with the environment; with saving the world? How does killing endangered species make us somehow better able to do that which must be done?

Jake hopped into the gravel bed, landing just a few feet to Pete's left. He spun quickly, then crouched down on his feet in front of Pete. "You felt it, didn't you?" he asked.

Pete did not want to talk, so he didn't answer. And he was still unsure how Jake would react to his fight with Keller.

"Yes. You did. I wanted you to know it. To feel it. Because that is what we miss in the confines of your cities and the hallways of your office buildings. Seeking it is a big part of why you rape the earth; why you take everything with no thought, no care, no limit. It is there on Wall Street; it is there in the corridors of political power; in the corner office; in the insatiable desire for more stuff, bigger stuff. But they are all such poor substitutes for what you now know that you have to keep taking. That is what you shared with the wolf that day."

Pete was startled. How could Jake have known about that?

"Do you understand?"

"Yes," Pete answered. Then he added, "I'm sorry about Keller."

"Yes. So am I. But it was unavoidable."

"I hate that man."

"When wolves have a disagreement, it is almost always settled without a real fight. But sometimes a wolf who will not know his place comes along. He must be fought or driven off. You saved me the trouble. If we're lucky, you took his mojo, and he will join us. If not ...." He stopped and said nothing.

Pete was about to ask about the wolf, when he saw Jake arch his neck and sniff the air, while staring intently upstream. "Trouble," was all he said.

Pete followed his gaze, but saw nothing. "What?" he asked.

Jake pointed upstream, into the wind. "Grizzly. Male. Big one." But still, Pete saw nothing. Jake got up. "Come on."

"But ..."

"Now. He's almost here."

Pete got up slowly, his eyes fixed on the bank ahead where the stream curved. Jake tried to move him, but he stood, transfixed. After nearly half a minute, a huge grizzly rounded the corner and came into view less than a hundred yards away. It was lumbering down the ravine, its massive head up, moving back and forth, sniffing the air and it clearly had the scent of the caribou, but it hadn't yet pinpointed its location because of the wind. Pete had seen grizzly before. In Glacier, in Denali, and around Yellowstone. But never one as big as this. It sent an immediate electric thrill throughout his body, at once exciting and dreadful and nearly disabling in its intensity.

Jake whispered, "We have to get back to the others. Follow me. Walk backwards facing him. And don't run." He slipped up the bank, and the grizzly spotted the movement. Pete followed, scrambling up the bank as best he could with his back to the ridge, while facing the huge creature. His legs felt like useless weights hung from his hips, without strength, and the signals he sent to move them seemed to be blocked by the electric fear pulsing through him. The bear moved a little quicker toward them, now, not running yet but kind of loping, its huge head swaying back and forth like a pendulum. Once they'd reached the top of the bank, the bear was out of sight briefly, and Jake began to shout, "Ho grizzly. Ho, big fella." Suddenly it came back into view, as it stood up in the ravine, now not fifty yards away.

Pete began to shout, too, but the animal ignored them both, continuing to sniff the air, searching. The wind was still confusing him, but he definitely had the scent.

"Big grizzly in the ravine," Jake called to the others.

Pete realized he had his spear, still; he'd picked it up when they'd retreated. "I'll hold him off while you get the others to safety."

Jake laughed. "Very noble of you Pete, but we're better off together. Remember Herrero's book? Bears rarely attack groups greater than three."

The bear was coming over the bank of the ravine as they reached the others. Clio and Bill, who had been dressing the caribou, were covered in blood. Jake looked at them and groaned. He picked up a spear and tossed it to Bill, then picked up the third and took it himself. Keller still held the fourth one, but he was standing back, almost in a daze. "Bill, Clio. I want you to retreat into the forest. Once you're out of sight, run. The rest of us will try to stall him."

Jake eyed the bear and moved out a few yards in front of the others brandishing his spear. Pete moved out to join him. The bear was more than three quarters of the way across the plain, maybe seventy feet off. He'd located the scent now that he was downwind and he picked up his pace to a trot. Strings of spittle hung from his mouth and swayed from his slick dark lips in long slippery strands, breaking off as he ran, filling the air around him with a foul mist. "Everybody shout," Jake ordered. Then, "Go you two. Go." They began to scream and wave their arms as Clio and Bill slipped into the woods. Keller followed them. The monster stopped, stood up on his hind legs and began to sway back and forth, eyeing the carcass. He was huge. Jake studied the behemoth more carefully and he said quietly, to himself, "It's you."

It was maybe fifty feet off now, and Pete could smell him. Jake started out to meet the beast, and Pete took his arm. "No." Jake looked at him as if from a trance. "We're better off together, remember?"

Jake turned to the bear and said, "I know this bear – he didn't read Herrero's book."

"Let him have it, Jake." Thom said from behind. "Come on."

"Get out of here Thom. Go," Pete said as he took Jake's arm and tried to pull him back, to within a few feet of the kill. The bear dropped to all fours and lumbered forward. The others were retreating into the cover of the trees. It was clear to Pete that it didn't want a fight. It just wanted the caribou. What wasn't clear was what it'd do to get it. And Jake wasn't budging. When it was about forty feet from the carcass, the bear exploded, moving in with astonishing speed. It started out as a charge, but the bear came up short just five feet from where Jake and Pete held their ground, a few feet in front and to the right of the kill. It stopped, stood up, and roared. It was a sound as intense as any Pete had ever heard. It was almost physical, and he could feel the breath, smell its foulness fill the air.

The fear that had filled his veins and short-circuited him was gone now, replaced with an intensity that gave him a surreal focus in which he was able to slow down events, and see all that went on around him. He noticed that Jake was staring right into the behemoth's eyes, challenging it. "Look down. Look down, god dammit," he said. Jake did, reluctantly. "Now come on, move back." Pete took hold of Jake and started pulling him harder now.

"What're you trying to do, Pete. Save me from myself?"

"Yeah."

Jake gave way, and they were backing up, now, and he smiled. "Thanks."

Without stopping, Pete turned his head to check on the others, continuing to back away the whole time. The group was safe – well into the forest, and out of sight. Just a few more steps now and he and Jake would join them. The bear began to gorge on the carcass. It raised its head, its snout covered in blood, and snorted, then went back to feeding. As they passed into the forest, they could hear it ripping at organs, smacking and chewing contentedly.

After a few more steps, Pete turned them and they moved quickly toward the others. "What the hell were you doing, back there?" Pete asked.

Jake looked sheepish. "That bear and I have a history."

"What history?"

"He's the one that attacked me. And the one who killed two of my people."

"Drop it, Jake. We can't afford your personal vendettas."

Jake was smiling.

"What's so amusing?"

"You. Your challenge was to overcome fear. Looks like you've managed it."

"I hate to disappoint you but I was scared shitless back there."

"Yes, but not so afraid that you couldn't feel your anger and do the right thing – then and now."

"Now?"

"Most people don't get away with throwing me around the way you did." He smiled at Pete again, in that same paternal way he had several times before. "I just wish I'd done as well on my own challenge."

"You? What's yours?"

"Overcoming my anger – it can be just as debilitating as fear. It's a war I've fought for most of my life." They walked on in silence for a while, then Jake said, "Still, it might have been better to have faced that particular bear."

"Why?"

"I think he's developed a taste for humans."

CHAPTER 30

Clio, Thom and Pete talked the whole way back. Bill, Sarah and Ruth walked close by, content just to be with them. Keller stalked ahead, alone, and Jake trailed, checking the woods behind them as he went.

"You kept a cool head back there, Thom," Pete said.

"You weren't so bad yourself."

"When we get back, I want to tell Ben *this* is the definition of a dog-eat-dog world." Pete put in, and they laughed.

They arrived back at camp, hungry, dirty and bedraggled and learned from Ben that the snares had yielded only two ptarmigan and a ground squirrel. But Ben, Jim and Ruth had been busy collecting the inner layer of bark – the cambium – from birch trees which, when boiled made a kind of sweet dish with a spaghetti-like consistency. Ruth flavored it with the meager meat they'd been able to get, and added some of the wild onion. It was a passable meal, but they were still hungry when it was done. Pete noted that nearly every one of them had jockeyed to get a seat near Jake. Everyone except Keller, Rita, Joan, and Eunice.

Pete sat next to Ben, regaling him with tales of the hunt and the bear. Ben listened and laughed, but he seemed preoccupied. "Still worried about your talk?" Pete asked.

Ben looked surprised. "No. But I think we have trouble with those four," he nodded toward Keller, Rita, Joan, and Eunice. They sat off by themselves, whispering and glancing furtively in their direction periodically.

"Yeah, I noticed ..."

"Oh, I wouldn't worry too much about them. You probably put the fear of god in Keller." It was Thom who'd come over to sit with them.

Ben arched his eyebrows, "Oh really?"

"Yeah. He told Keller if he messed around with him again, he'd kill him. And after watching him toss Keller and Jake around and with that poor caribou ... not to mention the bear ... well ... He made a believer out of me."

"Nice career move, Pete."

"Yeah. I'm thinking he might bring it up on the mid-year review. But after that ... well, I think it's important to have clear communications with your boss."

"As my grandson would say, Livin' large, Pete. Livin' large."

After the meal they'd closed around the fire as the night chill moved in, Joan asked Jake, with a touch of belligerence, "The other night, just before you and Dan had your ...disagreement ... you mentioned something about neoclassical economic sophistry. Now, as an economist, I'd like to know exactly what you meant by that."

Jake launched into a devastating critique of the economic policies of the past thirty years that was sophisticated and dispassionate, made all the more compelling by the rigor of his intellect and the depth of his knowledge. But when he reached the present, he stood up and began circling the fire, his eyes dark, his voice intense and it seemed to Pete he transformed in much the same way he had when he confronted Keller back at All Souls that night, growing in stature like a threatening storm cloud. His voice thundered across the lake, "So now you are reaping the harvest of greed – you have allowed the rich and the elite to steal the rest of you blind. They have sold you debt and called it wealth; they have replaced production with consumption and called *it* wealth; they have replaced things of real value with mere money, and now your economy is crashing around your feet ..."

Keller said, "Hold on, Jake ..."

But Jake spoke right over him, and he stopped, "I wouldn't care if you were only screwing yourselves, but you are destroying a world that is not yours. It must stop and it is we who must stop it. No one else can; no one else will. It happens now, or it won't happen."

Joan was stunned into silence by the passion in Jake's voice, but Pete could see that Keller was struggling to make a reply. He finally gathered his wits, "We've been hearing these doom and gloom predictions for decades ..."

"And now they're here."

Keller interrupted. "Oh Jesus, Christianson. What's your fucking alternative? Economic stagnation? We had that in the thirties. It was called the Depression."

"All you're doing is liquidating the Earth's treasures and your children's future and calling it wealth."

"That may be, but you can't get in power by telling the people they're wrong," Keller said. He stood up and faced Jake across the fire. "I don't care how much money you can raise, Christianson. Doom and gloom won't sell."

Jake stepped around the fire and stood in front of Keller. "Great leaders lead. They take us where we need to go, not where we want to go. The real question is, are you willing to be a great leader?"

"Sorry. Not interested. Great leaders have to get elected first." He gestured at Rita, Joan and Eunice. "And they aren't either. We signed up for wilderness survival training, not dogma. We're leaving. Tomorrow."

Jake looked stunned. It was perhaps the first time Pete had ever seen him at a loss. "You can't ... we have a lot more time ... I needed that time to ..."

"We've already made up our minds. We'll call Duquoin tonight."

"I can't let you do that ..." The look turned at once toward anger – the kind of anger Pete had seen when Jake was ready to take on the Grizzly, but it quickly subsided.

"You can't stop us."

"Of course not, but you see, the radio isn't working ..."

"We thought you might try that."

"No. It really isn't. Duquoin forgot to put the battery in. I didn't mention it because I didn't want to alarm you all."

"It doesn't matter. We're prepared to hike to Cold Fish Lake. We'll call from there." Keller turned to the rest of them. "Anyone who wants to join us is welcome. We'll start early tomorrow morning."

Almost against his will, Pete jumped up in Keller's face, "God damn you, Keller. This is just like you to ignore reality ... to put your own petty career ..."

Jake intervened. "Whoa, Pete. This isn't a detention camp. If Dan and the others want to leave, of course they can. I'm only sorry that the radio isn't working."

He seemed to have adjusted already to Keller's announcement. A thing Pete found nearly unbelievable after what Ben had told him. But then Jake turned to Keller and said, "Dan, you'll need to know a few things about the trip to Cold Fish. And you'll need some stores. Walk with me and we'll sort it out."

Keller, confused at the sudden offer of good will, reluctantly agreed and the two started off toward the peak where Pete and Jake had sat several days earlier. Pete watched them disappear into the ebony, perplexed himself at Jake's acceptance, but sensing something less than benign in the exchange. The two had parried like sword fighters, and Jake, as always, seemed to come out on top, even when things were going against him.

CHAPTER 31

Pete had retreated to a rock at the edge of camp, overlooking the slope that led to the lake shore. As he sat there in the fading light, batting at the flies that had started to arrive, he looked up at the peak Keller and Jake had just climbed, and remembered his own talk with Jake. Keller didn't have a chance; Jake would convince him to stay. But he would never make a devotee out of him. Keller was just too damn self-absorbed, too damn ambitious.

Although Karen had never been far from his thoughts, for the first time since he'd arrived, Pete found himself thinking about Washington and EPA and the world back there. Clearly he would have to leave the Agency. That didn't bother him too much. Government was no longer capable of anything but stop-gap solutions – at least until the politicians freed themselves from K Street. But he wasn't sure that anything back there would make sense after this. He recalled the newspaper ad that had started this, what? Three months ago? Not for the faint hearted. Yeah. That's true enough. But the journey that had proven most difficult was the trip taken by the mind and soul, not the body. And yet as challenging as this whole fucking magnificent place has been, I can find my way out of it, he thought. But I'm not sure I can find my way back to Washington DC. Back to Pete Andersen. Maybe that's OK, too.

Now and then he looked up at the peak and tried to imagine the scene going on up there. Jake was one of the most persuasive men he'd ever encountered, but Keller was no doubt proving a challenge, he thought absently, and then he'd returned to his search for the missing Pete Andersen, whoever he was now.

After sitting by himself with his ghosts for about an hour, he thought he spotted something high up in the scree coming down the slope. He couldn't be sure in the gloom, but as he studied the mountain side he thought he saw occasional flashes – possibly from the reflective strips on Keller's parka. Finally, as the figure approached the edge of tree line, Pete could make out Keller, his orange parka unmistakable even in the light of the waxing moon. He was moving at an incredible pace, nearly running as he picked his way expertly among the talus, rushing headlong toward the camp. Pete watched the descent with dread. Finally the figure entered a forested area, and Pete lost him. Acting on instinct, he moved back to the fire and picked up one of the spears. Most of the others were in their shelters for the night. Only Clio was up, and she eyed Pete warily. They'd all been treating him differently since the kill and his run-in with Keller. Pete nodded reassuringly and settled down to wait for Keller to appear. He pitched another log onto the fire and stirred the coals a bit until it caught, the flames spraying the dark forest with a friendly orange cover.

The wolves had started up again after being quiet for a time, and Pete listened to them as he waited for Keller to show up. If he tried anything, Pete would be ready. Finally, he saw him break from the woods and sprint into camp. He went straight to the shelter that Joan and Eunice shared. Then he roused Rita. "Come on. We have to get out of here. Now."

"It's dark." Joan started to complain.

"If we don't leave now, we never will."

"What are you talking about?"

"Please. Please believe me. We must get out of here. Now."

Rita cut in, "Dan, it's the middle of the night, for god's sake."

"Alright, Alright. We'll leave tomorrow. But we've got to get away from here now."

"Where are we supposed to go?"

Keller looked over his shoulder. "I don't know. Down to the food camp."

"What about bears?" Joan asked.

"We'll keep a fire going. Come on. Let's go." Keller glanced at the forest again. Joan and Eunice began to get up.

Rita, who'd been studying Keller, turned to them and said, "Stay, go. But for god's sake let me get some sleep." She seemed disappointed.

Eunice and Joan gathered their things and the three of them started down to the food camp. Just before they were out of sight, Keller turned to Rita and said, "Don't tell him where we went."

Clio turned to Pete, "What was that all about?"

"Beats me," Pete lied. "I'm turning in. I suggest you do the same."

Just before he fell asleep, he heard Jake come into camp. He went to Ruth's shelter and they spoke in hushed tones, but Pete couldn't make out the words.

Pete woke before dawn the next morning feeling more tired than if he'd not slept. He'd been disturbed by a dream. In it he was falling into a lake, still asleep, and he felt his lungs fill with water and watched the light grow dim as he slipped beneath the surface and gasped for air. Still in the dream, he continued to drift down, twisted up in covers and sheets and unable to get loose. Someone was calling to him, begging for help, but he made no attempt to struggle free of the bedclothes – it was clear that he would be unable to. And so he just continued to drift into the cold blue water, the light growing steadily dimmer, the voice fainter, until he suddenly jerked himself awake in a panic. He got up immediately.

As he stood outside his shelter, stretching, and trying to shake off the dream, he spotted Ruth down by the lake sitting on the rocks and went to join her, still carrying the dream with him.

Approaching her, he noticed that she was wrapped tightly in her space blanket, almost in a fetal position, and she rocked back and forth rhythmically. When he reached her, she hid her face and said, "Go away, Pete. Go away."

"What is it?"

Still hiding her face she said, "Leave me alone."

He could hear the tears, her voice, nasal and moist. "What's wrong."

"Get away from me. It's not safe for you," she said. As she did she turned around. Her eyes were red-rimmed and tear-stained but more – they betrayed wounds inside, like his brother's eyes had as he lay crumpled at his feet so long ago. Her face was puffed up and swollen from crying.

"My god. What's wrong?"

She laughed. "He's trapped us here, Pete."

Pete was confused. "What do you mean, trapped?"

"I can't tell you." She rubbed her eyes, trying to hide the fear. Pete didn't know what to say. Then she looked up, her face the face of a child betrayed. "Why did he have to do it?"

"Do what?"

Ruth looked up at the campsite anxiously. "I can't say anything else."

"Why are you so afraid? He said he'd let them go."

"He has no intention of letting them leave."

"Come on, Ruth. You're being paranoid."

"You don't know him like I do. This thing with Keller. It's made him change."

"How?"

"Last night he came back from the walk with Keller and he was talking crazy." She stopped, checked the campsite, then said, "I really can't say any more."

Pete sat down beside her and put his arm around her. She leaned her head on his shoulder, and after a moment, she began to cry. When she stopped, he said, "You have to tell me what's going on here."

She lifted her head from his shoulder, "I'm afraid."

"I won't let him hurt you."

"It's not just me. It's all of us." She glanced up at the camp again then said, "Besides, there's nothing you could do to stop him."

Pete took her chin in his hand and gently raised her face until he was looking in her eyes "I won't let anything happen to you. Believe it, Ruth."

"I want to, but..."

"No buts. Now, if you think we're in danger, you have to tell me why."

She stole another look at the campground then began, "Last night when he came down from the mountain he came straight into the shelter without saying a word." She began to weep again and Pete waited for her to calm.

"I think it was Keller that set him off. He kept saying it was finished, he'd failed. He said over and over again that the experiment was done, it was time to return the garden to its rightful owners."

"Who can blame him. Keller's an asshole. If people like him stay in power the whole world is fucked." But then he recalled when he'd heard that phrase – return the garden to its rightful owners – and then Ben's warning.

Ruth spoke, interrupting his thoughts, "Yeah, but we're fucked right now, Pete."

"Why?"

"He took the battery out of the radio and threw it into the lake."

CHAPTER 32

When Karen woke, Maria guided her to the dining room and brought out coffee and a Dungeness crab omelet. "Chas went into work today," she said. "He told me to tell you he'd be back around dinner." Karen felt nauseous again, and much to Maria's irritation, she couldn't eat. The smells coming from the kitchen and the plate facing her made her stomach roil, and she was forced to dash to the bathroom and throw up. She heaved several times until she was vomiting thin strings of bile. Finally, she began to feel human again and she washed her face, ready to return to the table and face breakfast. When she came out, the omelet was gone, replaced by two slices of dry toast and skim milk. "So when are ju due?" Maria asked.

Suddenly, she knew. The tenderness in her breasts, the nausea, the bizarre food cravings – all of it made sense. Her first thought was for the baby. She did a quick inventory of her drinking. Half a glass of wine with Chas and one or two at dinner back in Washington. That would have to stop. Now. Next she calculated back to her last period. A couple of weeks before that first time she and Pete had made love in the office – they'd been careful after that. So she was about a month along. Then she remembered the last night they'd shared together, when Pete told her he couldn't be a father. Briefly, she thought about an abortion. Just end it and start over. But then she knew, whatever else might happen, she wanted this baby. Besides, this was a decision she couldn't make alone. It was his, too.

Karen used the day to set up a place for her and Pete to stay on Vancouver Island, a small town called Tofino on the Southwest side. She arranged to have her ship brought up and rented a berth there. Then she went shopping with Maria, picking up mussels, Halibut and fresh vegetables at Pike's Market, and helped her prepare dinner when they got home. The nausea returned several times as they'd shopped, but by afternoon, she felt better physically although she'd vacillated between joy and dread throughout the day.

When Chas and Rose got home, Chas seemed grim, but he didn't say anything until the after-dinner coffee arrived. He reached into an old leather briefcase at the foot of his chair and took a stack of papers, consulting some notes he'd made and placed on top of them. "That's the trouble with getting old. Ya gotta write everything down." He slipped his reading glasses on and said, "Let's see." Chas frowned as he read over the papers.

"What is it?" Karen asked.

"I don't know. With this guy, the more you know the less you know." He looked over his reading glasses at Karen, then glanced at Rose. She nodded, and he looked back down at his notes. "I talked to Jake's arresting officer – a Mountie named Baker." He took a sip of wine and continued to scan the notebook. Karen shifted in her seat and leaned forward.

"OK. Baker. Good guy. Straight arrow. Didn't say much at first, but when I told him Jake had a group up in Spatsizi, he opened up a bit. Anyway, a while back, Jake apparently stopped virtually all the logging operations north of Smithers, BC. Stopped it cold."

Karen interrupted, "Like a protest or strike or something?"

"No. According to Baker, it was Jake. All by himself."

"But how?"

"He wouldn't say. Apparently, everyone involved wanted to pretend Jake had nothing to do with it. His superiors asked Baker to rewrite his report and blame it on environmental groups and the First Nations. They seemed anxious to avoid a trial and publicity." Chas paused, and rubbed his eyes. His face was pale, and Rose looked on, worried. After a deep breath, he continued. "But Jake said no. Said if he'd been guilty, he wanted to be charged. At that point, someone came up with the idea of committing him and apparently, Jake went along.

"So instead of doing time, he checked into a mental health institution in Kamloops. Perhaps because of his history with his father, the shrinks there took it seriously and went along with the whole thing. After about three months, they checked him out. Then for the next year and a half he seems to have traveled around the world, stopping only at the wildest places left. Now here's the good part – all of this seems to have been an assignment from that Shaman. That Lynx character."

"How do you know all this?"

"The travel stuff I got from Baker. Seems Jake took a liking to Baker and sent him long letters periodically. As for the rest, it was all in his records. We even got the shrink's private notes." He held up the bundle of papers he'd been studying.

"How'd you manage that?" Karen asked.

"Confidentiality's become a commodity, just like everything else. And right now, the price is pretty low."

"What do they say?"

"Don't know. Our contact had to copy them and we didn't get them until five o'clock. I had a chance to skim the front part while Rose drove home. One thing for sure. Jake Christianson got a whole lot more attention than your average inmate. The attending psychiatrist, a Dr. Caesar, seems to have befriended him."

"You can understand that," Rose said. "He must have been considerably more interesting than your average patient."

"From what I've seen so far, that's putting it mildly." He took the psychiatrist's notes and split them up into three piles and distributed them. "Let's read it over and see what we come up with."

Karen received the initial history, the first evaluations and the test results. Nothing new here, she thought. IQ off the chart; a history that included one incident of extreme violence against the father with the word "Oedipal?" scribbled in the margin, then crossed out and replaced with "Justified", written in bold letters, and in a different hand. The conclusion to the admission report read, *Patient presents a classic unresolved oedipal conflict aggravated by the extreme and often cruel upbringing experienced by subject. Conflict is manifested in nearly psychotic delusions, centered, not surprisingly, on various religious fantasies involving perceptions of disciple/savior relationships. Indeed, patient says that his admission is an assignment from a Shaman named Lynx – designed to help him better know the "the source of the sublime and the evil that lies in the heart of the takers." Start course of Zyprexa, assign to individual and group therapy. Prognosis is favorable –subject is highly functional, despite delusions and devastating early environment, no doubt due to the intervention of loving and supportive foster care. Therapy should center on strengthening this pattern of identification with adopted father and family.'* She finished to find Chas and Rose looking at her.

"Well? Anything interesting?" Chas asked.

"No. Mostly just some old fashioned Freudian psycho-babble. And stuff we already knew. Other than religious delusions which he may have fabricated to get in, he tested fine."

"Rose? Anything?"

"There's a couple of fascinating observations by the doctor. Here, listen to this, *'Patient displays a remarkable empathy with other patients, and an ability to reach them that I frankly envy. In group, he has managed to pull Edwards and Kearns out of profound, nearly catatonic, states and they are making progress after years of stasis'* ... Yada, yada, yada ... *'I am at a loss to explain this, but patient displays what I can only call a charisma that is unprecedented in my experience ...'* More babble ...Oh, here. About five weeks in: *'Patient's influence over the others in group, while therapeutic, could be dangerous. Several are beginning to share in his delusions ... Subject is too powerful; for the good of patients, must terminate his participation in group."* Rose put her glasses down.

"Do you believe this? He's got catatonic patients talking and interacting and this asshole says he's dangerous. Christ. Anyway, let's see what else we got. Where was it? Here, at seven weeks, *Patient's mythopoetic visions of natural world scientifically informed and extremely compelling* ...Yada, yada. Now, listen to this ... *I feel myself coming under his influence. Reverse transference? MUST WATCH. Most powerful personality I have ever encountered."*

Chas spoke up, "That fits right in with my piece. Check this out – starts just after yours, Rose, at about eight weeks, *Jake has become my friend, and I now must ask myself, what if his delusions are real? What if there are other ways of knowing the cosmos? What if there is some force or process, be it blind watchmaker or celestial machine, that we* can tap into. *A force that strives to keep a harmonic balance? What if it sheds those life-forms that violate this balance? What if this is our last chance?"* Chas looked up. "Ok, that was eight weeks, into it. Here's one from nine weeks: *I now believe I was wrong to deprive the other patients of his compassion, his wisdom, his spirituality. I will petition Dr. Connor to have Jake rejoin group sessions ...* Now listen to this at eleven weeks, *After nearly three months of individual therapy, Dr. Caesar was removed from subject case. He lost objectivity and the therapeutic relationship was compromised. After several sessions with me, subject has suggested to me that he is cured – whatever that means. And I must say, in my observation, he presents no pathology that justifies keeping him here and certainly no sign of psychosis. A caution: I began to feel the same loss of objectivity as Dr. Caesar. There is a hypnotic aspect to subject. At some level, I feel as if he is toying with us. However, I can find no clinical reason for keeping him here, so I am clearing him for release. Nevertheless, it is my personal opinion that Jake Christianson is a very dangerous man."*

When he finished, Rose whistled, and Chas removed his glasses and looked up.

"Will the real Jake Christianson please stand up?" Rose said.

Chas peaked at her over his reading glasses. "Funny you should say that. That Mountie? The last thing he said to me was: 'I've spent the last fifteen years trying to figure out whether Jake was a god or a devil. And I still don't know.' "

"Maybe he's both," Rose said. "But what I want to know is what does this mean for Ben and those other people."

"I'll tell you what it means," Chas said, "It means there's a better than fifty-fifty chance our friend is roaming around the woods with a psychopath."

"We've got to do something." Rose said.

Karen remembered Lenny's advice. '... if things are like I think they are, you go on up there, wherever it is Pete's at, and bring him back.' Yeah, she thought, no standing idly on the widow's walk. Time to act. She stood up and announced, "I'm going up there and finding them," she said, "And then I'll bring them back."

"You can't do that," Chas said.

"Yeah, I can. I had the same training they had."

Rose interrupted, "Let the authorities handle it, Karen."

"And what would we tell them? That we *think* a crime might be committed sometime in the future?"

Chas slumped, and Rose's hands fluttered around, tidying the papers as she looked down at the table. They were quiet for several moments, then Chas said, "At least stop in Smithers and let that Mountie know what you're up to."

Karen agreed, and called Baker the next morning. When she told him what she was planning to do, he said, "I can't let you do that Ma'am."

"I'm going. And there's nothing you can do to stop me."

"There is. And I will."

"It's a free country, Mr. Baker."

"That may be, but you'll need to fly out of the Smithers airport and you'll need to get a back country pass. I can make sure that you won't do either."

"We'll see."

CHAPTER 33

Pete had Ruth wash her face in the frigid lake water. It seemed to help the puffiness. He took her up to camp but when she saw Jake asleep in her shelter, she stiffened in his arms, so he guided her to his own lean-to and put her to bed. He stroked her hair until she fell into a fitful sleep, but she jerked awake every time he stopped. Finally, she began a gentle snore, and Pete slipped away. He woke Ben and led him down to the rocks by the lake.

"We've got trouble."

Ben, still groggy said, "What?"

"Jake. I think he's gone off the deep end."

"Jesus, Pete. Make up your mind, will you?"

"No. Listen." He recounted how he'd found Ruth. How Jake had thrown the battery in the lake, what Jake had said to her.

Ben heard him out but didn't say anything.

For the first time since discovering her by the rock, Pete realized what a precarious position they were in, and fear started to replace the determination he'd felt. Protect her from Jake? What could he do? Jake was stronger, smarter, faster and he was in his element out here. Pete reached for Karen's medallion recalling the moment she'd given it to him. He made a silent promise to her to live. When he realized Ben hadn't reacted, he asked, "So what do we do now?"

Ben hesitated, then said, "For starters, I suggest you get a grip on yourself. Lovers have spats all the time. Frankly, I think it's a good sign that he's got a girl friend."

"Are you out of your fucking mind, Ben? This guy's thrown the battery in the lake for the only radio we have."

"All right, all right. Calm down."

"Calm down? We're stuck out here with a guy who seems to think humans are little more than ecological parasites and you're telling me to calm down? What'd you say the other day? 'At some point Jake's going to figure out we're right. I hope to god this trip's over when it happens. Well guess what? Keller just helped him figure it out."

"I had a chance to talk to Jake about all that. It's fine. He's fine."

"Jesus Christ. You get a grip, Ben. He's got you in some kind of spell."

"You're stressed out right now. Maybe you should get some rest." Pete recognized the tone at once. It was the same solicitous voice those doctors had used twenty four years ago when they were trying to reach an adolescent who'd retreated from this world.

"Wait here." Pete got up and went to the camp site. Jake was still asleep, but several others were stirring. He ignored them, and woke Ruth gently, and escorted her down to the lake. She was groggy, but she looked much better. The cold water had brought the puffiness down some and her eyes were no longer red, but they were still haunted, Pete thought.

"Tell him. Tell him what you told me."

"Pete. I'm afraid I was angry at Jake; he was very grumpy last night, and well, I just said some things to get even with him."

"What about the crying?" he said pointing to her eyes, but she said nothing.

Ben looked at her closely. "Pete says he threw away the battery to the radio."

She shrugged, and smiled a bit. "I was just being a bitch. I knew Pete would believe the worst – he's always been a bit paranoid." She looked Ben straight in the eye. "There never was a battery. Duquoin forgot to pack it."

Ben eyed Pete for a long time. "Look, Pete. You gotta get over this stuff, huh? He's different, but like you said, maybe he's exactly what we need. The more I reflect on my conversations with him, the more I'm coming to believe he's our last chance to get things right."

"Well, well, well. My three favorite people, down here plotting. About what, I wonder?"

Jake's voice startled Pete, and he whipped around to see him crouched down right behind them rocking on the balls of his feet. There was a flatness to his voice – a flatness and something more. Pete wondered how long he'd been there, what he'd heard. He could see from the panic in her eyes that Ruth wondered the same thing. Jake was working a smooth fist-sized stone in his hands, and Pete could feel his eyes, blue even in the dim morning light, probing them, and then he knew suddenly what that something else was he'd heard in Jake's voice – resignation. Not the kind of resignation Pete knew so well; the kind that wraps you up, paralyzing you. It was more the acceptance of a cornered beast, ready to explode and – if necessary – die.

How could Ben be so blind? How could he have been? Jesus. What a situation. He needed to say something quickly. The silence lingered in the air like a guilty verdict. "You can't let them go to Cold Fish Lake alone," he said, finally.

Jake had been staring at Ruth, and he turned slowly to Pete, "Damn them," he said.

"There's no way they'll make it without help."

"They've chosen to leave. I'm no longer responsible for them."

"You talked them into coming out here. You can't turn your responsibility off on a whim."

"WHIM?" Jake thundered, startling him. "This wasn't a god damn whim. This was your last chance."

He stood up, looming over Pete, menacing. "It doesn't matter what happens any more. Don't you understand? It really doesn't matter." He turned and walked up the hill.

"Now what do you think?" Pete asked.

"I think he's discouraged. We all should be. I'll go talk to him," Ben said. He walked after Jake, struggling to catch up.

Pete watched him a moment, then turned to Ruth, "Why are you protecting him?"

"It's not him I'm protecting."

"What's that supposed to mean?"

"You don't know what he's capable of."

"I can't help you if we're not straight with each other, Ruth."

She looked up. Tears were streaming down her cheek. "You can't help me anyway."

Pete put his arm around her shoulder. "Hey," he whispered, "Don't be afraid. We're going to get out of this."

"No. We're not."

She held her head in her hands and rocked, while Pete tried to think. On one level, he was sure that Jake was going mad. But then he remembered the night on the mountain, when he'd communed with the Earth, and he understood why. As long as men like Keller ran the world, the experiment *had* failed. And maybe Jake had concluded we were all Keller. That's enough to drive even a shaman mad. Maybe that's my one advantage over Jake, he thought. I've flirted with madness, and I know the way back – and I'm not ready to give up. He looked into Ruth's eyes and said, "Hey. I told you, we're going to get out of this. You've got a book to write, and I've got a date I don't intend to break." Ruth smiled up at him, but she was shaking her head.

She seemed about to say something when they heard Ben call out, "Good news." He scrambled down the rocks toward them, looking excited. When he reached them, he knelt down and spoke quietly. "Jake's going to have Jim help them get to Cold Fish Lake."

Pete mulled over Ben's statement. Typical Jake, he thought. Jim was the ideal guy to send. As a SEAL, he had wilderness experience and he was in good enough shape to make the trek there and back. And he'd gone to the mountain with Jake – something that seemed to put people under Jake's spell. No telling whether it had worked on Jim, though. Pete looked up and noticed Ben eyeing him.

"What else?" he asked.

"He wants to talk to you, Pete."

"Yeah? So why doesn't he?"

"Up there. He wants you to walk with him."

One of those silent alarms was going off in his head. And he decided it was long past time to start listening to them. "He can come down here, if he wants to talk."

Both of them looked at him, startled. "Don't Pete. Don't anger him," Ruth whispered, barely audible.

Ben added, "Don't give up on him."

They're both afraid of confronting him, he thought. But then so am I. Reluctantly, he rose and walked up the hill – he didn't know what else to do. As he approached, Jake was talking quietly to Jim, who was wrapped in his space blanket against the morning chill. Pete overheard the young man say, "I understand," then he watched him head for his shelter.

"Peter. I'm sorry I snapped at you. Come on, let's go up on the hill."

They'd spent more than an hour together up there. The talk had been disturbing. They'd sat in the same place, the cliff high above the lake overlooking the campsite. It was wrapped in the morning mists and the cascading hills marched westward into a shroud before ultimately disappearing. The sun was still hidden below the mountains behind them, but the first rays began glimmering on the lake far below as Jake spoke – quietly, persuasively, mesmerizingly about what was at stake. The sound was reasonable, but the words were alarming to Pete. He felt the tug on him, nearly overwhelming. "These are desperate times, Peter... You are the key...it is all up to you ... you must join me ... you must be willing to act on the things you believe in ... we must sweep away those who would stand in the way ... I can teach you things ... things beyond what you think you know ...you can become much more than you are ... you can transcend these flesh and blood bonds ... Just because we lost a few people, we can't stop ..."

The words, however circumspect, invited Pete to jump in, to say the unsaid, to buy explicitly into an epic struggle, the full dimensions of which, only Jake could see. In the end, Pete was able to resist the seductive pull of Jake's spiel only by focusing fiercely on the image of Karen's face, and the sound of her voice. He struggled to see the joy, to hear it in her speech, as Jake's words washed over him with the relentless force of a flowing river. After about an hour, it was all Pete could do to stare at the landscape in front of him and fight the pull he felt. He answered at the appropriate times and tried to be responsive without listening, but he no longer could focus on anything. He felt his head swimming like those times when you can feel yourself nodding off in a meeting or a lecture and everything in front of you spins into a blackness, and you know you have to stay in control but can't. Finally, he felt Jake's big hand clasp his shoulder.

"I know I can count on you, Pete. I've got to get down there now."

And he was up, leaving Pete to contemplate his next step. In the end, he decided they had to trust Jake. He was upset, but that was to be expected. He would adapt. He would recover. Then they could go on. Pete sat there on the mountain, listening to the wolves howling in the morning light, and he tried to lay out plans for getting them back to civilization in the event things deteriorated. But he found he was unable to focus. He would need Ben, but the old man seemed to have fallen under Jake's spell, too. They all had, except Ruth, and she was too frightened to act.

After a time, Pete got up and tried to clear his head. He looked at the sun, which had topped the mountains, and realized he'd been sitting there for several hours. He started down immediately, trying to sort out what he'd been thinking, trying to make sense out of the past few hours, but found instead, that his confusion spread to the past twenty four hours, since he'd started out on the hunt. For some reason it all seemed fragmented. He couldn't put it together in any coherent way; the events floated around independent of any sequence, defying the laws of physics. It was as if he could rearrange them at random, and he struggled to find the cause and effect that imposed sense and reason on experience, but couldn't. He remembered his fight with Keller, Ruth's confidence to him about Jake, the dream, the hunt – they all swirled about, dizzyingly. He stood up, and resolved to keep moving. Whatever else happened, he had to keep moving.

When he broke into camp, he searched for Ben. He spotted him at the edge of the site, looking out at the lake. As he approached him, they heard a scream from down by the food cache. Pete reacted instantly, racing toward it, dodging branches and skirting boulders and the screams got louder as he neared the site. The first thing he saw when he broke into the clearing was Sarah, her hands clutching her face, now ashen, as she screamed over and over while staring into the clearing. Ben reached them just seconds later, as Pete was following her gaze. When Pete saw them, he nearly threw up. He had to look away, and he took Sarah by the shoulders and turned her around. "Don't look," he said. She stopped screaming, but she fought to turn around to stare at the carnage.

The three bodies were strewn about the cooking fire like litter, their joints twisted and broken, jutting from their bodies in odd, unnatural angles; their clothes torn; their skin raked with deep gashes. Claw marks, Pete guessed. Keller's scalp was ripped from his skull and

Pete could see hints of the white bone beneath the raw wound. Pools of blood surrounded the bodies. Eunice's shirt was torn to tatters and her stomach had been gutted open and her innards had been dragged across the campsite in the direction of the forest. Joan still lay beneath her space blanket, a look of stark terror frozen on her face, her neck snapped neatly, and a row of four deep claw marks ripped right through her clothes and blanket.

Ben came up behind Pete and uttered a single word, "Jesus."

"Yeah," Pete answered. "Take her, will you? And keep the others away until we've cleaned this up a bit."

"OK."

Pete turned around and noticed now that nearly everyone was there. Only Ruth and Jim had not arrived yet. The group stood and stared, in a collective state of shock, the blood draining from their faces. Thom stood nearest to him. "I'll help," he said.

"Thanks," was all Pete could say. From behind, Pete heard someone retching and smelled the bile-tinged reek of vomit.

Jake moved to the front of the group and spoke quietly, "Alright, there's nothing you can do. Go back to camp. We'll take care of things here."

"Will we be OK?" Sarah asked, barely audible.

"For now. He's got what he wanted. Bill, can you take them up? Get a spear, crank up the fire and let Jim know what's happened." Bill nodded, and he and Ben escorted Sarah up the hill, with Clio and Rita following.

CHAPTER 34

"Start digging," Jake commanded, and he took one of the stone axes they'd fashioned and handed it to Pete. Then he took a thick spruce pole from the yurt and walked a little ways off from the bodies, near where the stream came into the lake and the ground was softer. He started pounding the pole into the ground, jimmying up thick clods of soft dirt, and Pete scraped it away with the flat side of the stone axe as it accumulated. They fell into a pattern without speaking, Jake loosening the earth, Pete scraping it out. Jake worked furiously, in silence, and Pete strained to keep up with him. He was like a human pile-driver, chewing through the packed earth with a relentless rhythm, showing no sign of fatigue. It was strenuous, but Pete was managing to keep pace. It felt good to be doing something. After about twenty minutes of steady work, his heart was beating heavy and fast in his chest as it did on a run, and the sweat started to pour off his brow, and under the familiar groove of steady rhythmic exercise, his head began to clear. After about three quarters of an hour, a broad flat hole was beginning to take shape, but Pete's arms began to feel weak and rubbery. "I've got to rest," he said, and went and sat on a log by the fire pit.

He examined the site again. Except for the pole Jake had taken, the yurt was intact, the bones and sinews lying by the fire were undisturbed, and there was no sign of struggle. Thom was crouched by Keller's body, studying it, and the ground around it. He looked up and caught Pete's eye and waived him over.

Pete got up slowly and walked over. Jake took the stone hatchet and started digging again, lost in a frenzy of work, obsessed now with the simple act of getting these bodies into the ground. He must realize that it was all over, Pete thought. All his grand schemes; even his career as a survival trainer. He listened as Jake pounded the earth continuously like some hydraulic device, relentless, tireless, mindless. Probably good for him, Pete thought. He knelt down by Thom, "What is it?"

"Look," he pointed to a long series of scratches across Keller's face and shoulder.

"Yeah?"

"There's only four claw marks."

"So?"

"A grizzly has five."

Pete nodded his head slowly. He felt his chest tightening and he sucked in air. He started to scramble over to Joan's body, but Thom put a hand on his arm and stopped him. "They're all like that. And there's something else."

"What?"

"There's no grizzly tracks."

Pete examined the area. It was scuffed up pretty good, but he couldn't see any tracks. Something nagged at Pete but he couldn't quite place it. He was scared now. As Thom talked, Pete heard Jake continue to dig, and he could feel the power in his strokes as the earth beneath them vibrated every time he struck it, each thunderous blow sending a shiver up Pete's spine.

"We gotta tell Jake." Thom said.

Pete grabbed his arm. "No. Don't mention this to anyone."

Thom looked at him, then took Pete's hand, the one clutching his arm, and pried it off of him. Pete watched Thom's face, as it went from puzzlement to shock. "Why not?"

"I ... I think we need to keep this quiet. Until we know what's going on," he said.

He felt Thom examining him, saw his expression change from confusion to something like shock. "Jesus. *You* did this."

"No," he answered immediately.

"Then why the secrecy?"

Pete managed to whisper back, "If it wasn't a grizzly and it wasn't me, it was Jake."

Thom looked at him, closely, "Why would he do this?"

Pete looked around at the bodies, "It's complicated. But Jake couldn't let them leave."

"Bullshit. You had it in for Keller." Thom blurted.

"Shhh. Not so loud." Pete listened, but the steady pounding continued.

Thom looked at Pete, waiting for an explanation, but Pete said nothing. How could he explain what he'd heard on the mountain – and if Ruth wouldn't repeat what she'd told him about the radio, the whole thing would sound crazy.

Thom turned and surveyed the carnage. Suddenly, his eyes fixed on Pete's windbreaker. "Look. There's dried blood all over you."

He looked down at the red-brown blotches caked all over his wind breaker. It was from the caribou, but he didn't have time for a lot of explaining. Jake would get curious in a minute or two.

"I'm telling Jake," Thom said.

Pete grabbed his arm again, squeezing it hard. "No." He had to stop Thom from talking to anyone – especially Jake – until he could get to Ruth. And Ben. He looked down at Joan. Her swan's neck was snapped and her head dangled at the end of it, a strand of blood-smeared hair obscuring the claw marks that raked across her cheek and onto her shoulder. Pete gently moved the hair aside and the pale face stared back at him, her eyes inanimate, a cold, almost blue pallor settling over her skin. No, not again. Not another failure to drag through life like Marley's chains. He leaned down, almost placing his lips on hers ... *Breath, compress, breath. Breath, compress, breath* ... No. Stop. Have to focus. Thom was looking at him skeptically, waiting. Pete whispered, "Jake's necklace. There's only four claws on it."

"What about that?" Thom asked, pointing to Keller's skull.

Pete looked down. "I don't know ... but he threw the battery ..."

"What's going on, over there?" Jake's voice cut through their conversation, drowning out Pete's warning.

"Nothing," Pete answered, quickly.

Thom said, "Yeah there is. There's something funny about this whole thing."

"What?" Jake thundered.

"Look. There's no tracks. And there's only four claw marks on all these bodies."

Jake hopped out of the hole and came over. "So?"

"What if it wasn't a bear?"

Pete interrupted him, "I was just telling him that's not all that unusual. This dirt's all packed down from us."

Jake shot a glance at Pete. Then he turned to Thom. "What's your point?"

"If it wasn't a grizzly, it was one of us." Thom was quiet for a moment, then added, "Pete threatened to kill Keller …"

Jake's look was like rolling thunder, and Pete trembled as he watched Thom cower before it. Jake held him immobile with his gaze for a long moment, then said, "You're letting your imagination run wild. A lot of bears lose claws. Happens all the time."

"What about the tracks?" Thom managed to say.

"Who knows? You'd be surprised at how lightly a Grizzly can step when he's stalking. Besides, like Pete said, we've packed the dirt down pretty good in the last week. Or maybe you wiped them out walking around, I don't know. But I do know if one of us did this, we'd be covered in blood. Look, the last thing we need right now is idle speculation. Let's not hear any more about this, huh?"

"But Jake, if it wasn't a grizzly …"

"Drop it, Thom. We got real problems here. We don't need to invent any."

"But what if it was one of us?" Thom persisted.

"I said, I didn't want to hear anymore of this." Something in Jake's voice cut through the conversation like a razor silencing Thom immediately.

Yeah, Pete thought. Of course you don't. Somehow I've got to get Ruth to tell the others what she'd told me. Until then, he knew he had a better shot of surviving this if the others continued to think a grizzly did this.

CHAPTER 35

They worked in near silence after Thom's outburst. Whenever Pete looked up, he'd catch Thom eying him with what? Fear? Suspicion? Maybe both. But he tried not to think, preferring the simple, sweat-filled act of digging to the confusion that overwhelmed him when he did try. But Thom's glances continued to land like a radar pings. Somehow he had to tell Thom what he suspected. His life might depend on it.

When they were satisfied that the hole was deep enough, they took the bodies, now stiff and rigid, and tossed them into the hole. Then they filled it over and when they were done, they patted the dirt down and covered the graves with rocks from the stream. It was futile, Pete knew, against the digging prowess of a bear, if there were a bear, and he said so. "This isn't going to protect them. In Denali I saw a grizzly dig out an entire hillside going after a marmot."

"You don't bury your dead to protect them," Jake answered.

"Then why did we do this?" Pete thought he knew the answer – to bury the evidence.

"Lynx says that the First People's burial ceremonies are about returning the soul of the dead to mother Earth. But the white man, he buries his dead and erects a monument because it is his last chance to lay claim to a part of the Earth – to own that which is not and never could be, his. To claim dominion, for perpetuity, even in death."

"But then why do it for *them*?" Thom asked.

"To keep them from stinking."

As they came over the rise to the main camp, Pete found the group sitting around, huddled by the fire despite the warmth of the day. They were silent.

"Hey. What's up here?" Jake called out.

"What do you mean, *what's up*?" Bill asked.

"There's things to do."

"Don't you get it, Jake? It's over," Bill said.

"It's not over until I say it's over. But either way, we've got to eat and we need fire wood."

Thom crested the hill, lagging a bit behind Pete and Jake, but apparently hearing the conversation. "Bill's right. Besides, I'm not even sure it was a bear that did this," he said.

"That's enough, Thom. We'll talk about this tonight, at dinner. Meanwhile, whether we go or stay, we're out of food, we need firewood, and we need to make some more spears ..."

"If you don't tell them, I will," Thom said.

Jake reached out and grabbed him by the collar, nearly lifting him. "I said we'll talk about this tonight, and that's the way it will be." He tossed Thom aside, sending him sprawling, and looked at the others.

No one moved. They sat in place, looking from Thom to Jake, wondering what Thom was driving at. Pete could see the fear and doubt in each of them. And in some, he saw anger. Bill and Clio, in particular stared back defiantly.

"Maybe we'd like to hear what Thom has to say." Bill said.

Jake walked over to him, and stood inches from his face. When he spoke, it was barely audible, yet each word landed like a blow, and Bill seemed to shrink in stature with each one. "I said we'd talk about it tonight. And unless you're prepared to join them, down there," Jake gestured at the graves below, "That's the way it will be."

"Are you threatening me?" Bill managed.

"No. I'm telling you what will happen to you," Jake turned and spoke louder, now, "to all of you, if you don't listen to me and do exactly as I say. We've got a man-eating grizzly out there somewhere, and whether we go or stay, we need food and fire and weapons." Jake then handed out assignments to each of them, and commanded, "Now get busy."

The afternoon passed slowly. Jake insisted that they set new snares, gather firewood and get miner's lettuce, onion, cattail shoots, and any other vegetables they could find. He also required them to go about in two's and threes, with one person in every group keeping watch and carrying a spear. As one of the best flintknappers, Jake had put Pete in charge of flaking enough stone arrowheads for everyone to have a spear, so he spent the afternoon on a rock overlooking the lake with his tools. Ben and Bill had gone off in search of suitable shafts, and the rest were gathering food or firewood. They had a stock of chert and flint ready, and Pete started immediately. He was left alone by the fire for most of two hours and he made good progress, once again finding solace and escape in the ancient skills he used, getting lost in the textures, warps and character of the stone, as he coaxed weapons out of the soul of the rock. Now and then a group would return to camp to drop off wood or foraged greens and Pete saw that Thom had been lobbying throughout the day. He chose his groups carefully, even as he avoided Jake's notice and as the day wore on, he'd managed to be out with everyone. By late afternoon, Pete could feel the doubt and suspicion – and the fear, swirling around the campsite.

Jake had gone off alone in the direction of the food camp for several hours. When he'd returned, he had a long straight staff, nine shorter ones, several long pieces of a fibrous material and nine smaller pieces of chert. He'd sat next to Pete for the rest of the afternoon knapping out nine perfect arrow heads, and fashioning a bow and arrow set. They said little to each other, but Pete had been fascinated with the skill and speed with which Jake worked.

The staff came from a birch sapling, and Jake had shaved and scraped it flat on each end, so that it was tapered and shaped into a passable bow. The fiber looked to be the inner bark of some tree, maybe willow, and it had been thoroughly soaked. He'd pounded it with a broad flat rock, then twisted it expertly, forming one long string, then strung it onto notches he'd carved into the tapered ends of the bow, measuring the tension carefully, and testing the pull. He shortened it several times, using a stone knife and twisting the ends and knotting them meticulously to keep them from fraying, before he was satisfied. Then he set it out in the sun and started in on the arrows. When he finished, he set them out near the bow, which had been lying on the hot dark rock for an hour and half in the sun. He picked it up and tested it again. The wet string had shrunk, and Pete could see the muscles on Jake's arms tighten as he pulled. He passed it to Pete, saying nothing.

Pete stood, and pulled back on the string. It was remarkably taut, and it took a great deal of his strength to retract the bowstring all the way back. "Don't snap it. Bring it back slow," was all Jake said.

"Will this stop a grizzly?" He asked.

"Piss him off more than likely. But it might make him run, if we're lucky."

"And you think there's really a grizzly?"

"I know there's a grizzly."

Then they'd fallen into silence again, leaving Pete to wonder whether to believe him or not. He wanted to. Desperately.

Later, as they sat around the fire in the gathering dusk, he could feel their eyes on him. Even Ben seemed to be looking at him. It was cold and they ordinarily would have sat tight around the fire, forming a close-knit ring, sharing the fellowship of the flames in a ritual as old as humanity. But tonight there was no fellowship and he found himself surrounded by fear and staring into haunted, suspicious eyes. Only Jake seemed at ease. And Jim.

Their meal, the first they'd had in over a day was simple but good – Ptarmigan and squirrel stew and they ate it in silence. When they were done, Jake stood up and turned to Thom. "Why don't you say out loud what you've been telling everybody throughout the day."

Thom seemed startled. "I ... I'm not sure ... What you're ..."

Jake walked over to him as he stammered, grabbed him by the collar and pulled him up so that once again he stood there at the end of Jake's arm, almost dangling in the air. His voice trailed off. Jake looked at him for a long moment, then said, "God I hate a sneak. Let's get it out." Then he let go of him and Thom crumbled. "Go ahead, say it."

Pete watched, helpless. He'd thought he'd overcome his old nemesis. He'd thought with his fight with Keller he'd found that thing he'd lacked for years, now; its absence always mocking him, always whispering to him, *Coward. You let him die. Come look. Come see what happened. See his eyes. See how he blames you ...*

He thought somehow, that he'd found the simple courage, the confidence that would enable him to trust himself and to stand up and confront the kind of intimidation Jake was dishing out and the accusations that were in everyone's eyes; that would give him certainty, and with it, the freedom to act. And maybe for a brief time, he had. But standing up to Keller wasn't in the same league as standing up to Jake. He knew that if he confronted Jake, it would be all or nothing ... besides, Jake might be the only person left who didn't think him responsible for killing the others.

And so he said nothing as Thom was thrown to the ground like a sack of flour, and the eyes that had been looking at him turned away, one by one.

He could see that the others were more than frightened; they were dazed, confused, and unable to focus. Just as Pete had been. But he could feel Clio and Sarah, still eyeing him, still waiting for him to step in; to tell them what he'd done. But now, as Thom lay at Jake's feet they issued a rebuke not a plea. Fuck, you, he thought. Fuck you all. It wasn't me. He looked over at Ben for support, but his eyebrows hung down, almost obscuring his eyes. No support there.

Jake walked over to an open area where he could confront them all, and he stood there eyeing each of them in turn. In the gathering darkness, Pete felt Jake's gaze pass over him like a beam from a lighthouse, at once illuminating, searching and signaling just as he had that first day of class. "Now I know many of you are scared. And some of you are mad." He turned to Thom, "And some of you are suspicious." He stepped in closer to the fire. "I have been here before. I have confronted this beast and won. And this time I will route him, and kill him, once and for all." He walked behind Pete, now, and continued. "The easiest thing in the world, would be for us to quit now. To pack it in, go home with our tails tucked in and our heads hanging." Jake raised his voice, startling them, "But I won't let you do that. I didn't pick you because you were quitters. We still have important things to accomplish, and we still have twenty days to go. We're going to stay. And we're going to triumph. And we're going to do great things when we get back. Because they must be done. Because you are the ones who can do them."

Pete studied their faces. They were staring up at Jake, flickering orange and black in the light from the fire. He tried to read them, to see whether Jake was working his magic. Sarah and Rita listened raptly. Ben looked troubled. Clio, dear Clio, was angry, and it showed clearly in her frown. Bill and Thom were, too. Ruth looked down, avoiding his glance, but she looked defeated, and ashamed. Jim was staring back at Pete, intently. Jake stalked around into Pete's field of vision and continued, "Ten years from now, you will measure yourself by what you choose to do here tonight. If you stay; if you confront this evil with me; you will walk in pride and confidence. If you run, you will never stop running. You will never hold your head up. You will never truly trust yourself again." He sat down on a rock a little ways off from the fire and studied them. The words struck at Pete with force. It was as if Jake looked right through him, and saw. Knew everything. But he didn't know the thought now forming now in his mind – that the beast that must be confronted was Jake, not the Grizzly. And that he had little hope of overcoming either. If only Ben were himself.

Clio stood up. "What if Thom's right? What if it wasn't a bear that killed them?"

"Do you really think a human could have done that?" Jake asked, pointing towards the cooking area. An answer formed immediately in Pete's mind, *no but you could.*

Bill said, "No tracks. Four claw marks. Just like your necklace."

Jake dismissed him. "That necklace has been missing since the fourth class. Now look. The real issue here is whether we stay and do what we set out to do, or whether we run like cowards."

Clio said, "We'll vote on it."

"There will be no vote." Jake said from the edge of darkness.

"But ..." Clio looked around, asking, almost begging for help, and Pete struggled to gather the courage to step in, but before he could, Jake continued.

"Don't look to the others, Clio," Jake said. "We have to stay here and stay together. If we split up, if we try to run from this, he will stalk us and kill us one-by-one. You will just have to trust me. And trust yourselves. And each other."

CHAPTER 36

Peter sat in the door of his shelter and tried to figure out his next step. He'd been there for two hours, now, ever since they'd broken up after dinner. They'd gone their separate ways, quietly, each to his own shelter, and except for some muffled voices from Ruth's lean-to that Pete tried not to listen to, it had been quiet. His shelter was off to the side of the fire pit, and he'd faced it out toward the lake, to give him some privacy and a view, so now he couldn't see the others, but he knew they were all awake, too.

They had to leave, that was clear. Whether his suspicions were right or wrong about the bear didn't matter any more. Bear or man, they had to leave. Jake had convinced half of them that it was a bear. The other half seemed to think it had been Pete. But the fact is, he thought, we're dying out here, and we seem powerless to stop it. We need to go.

Somehow he had to convince the others that if they stayed out here with Jake fighting some imaginary battle they'd die. And that meant confronting Jake. Jesus. How did this happen? What the hell was I thinking? Spend a month in the woods, and then what? But he knew. It was not just about cathedrals. It was a search for that part of him he'd found briefly after killing the caribou, and after beating Keller. The part of him that would still the voice. The one that would bring him at last the peace of a simple, quiet self-confidence, closely held and truly felt. And he knew, too, that the search for that would make him take up this last fight. This inevitable confrontation with Jake.

But how far would Jake go to stop them? And in the end, would the others support him if he tried to confront Jake? Clio, at least, was looking for anyone to stand up to Jake, but by the end, Jake had won them over. Or most of them. He did a mental tally. He could count on Clio to confront Jake. And maybe Thom, if he could get him alone and explain what he was thinking. But he needed Ben and Bill. Jim will be against anything I advocate. The rest would avoid the whole issue. Rita and Sarah seemed to be under Jake's spell, completely, and Bill drifted in and out. So do I for that matter, Pete thought. So do we all. Then there is the problem that most of them think I did it. He had to get Ben onside. He was the key.

He started to creep over to Ben's shelter, a neat wigwam, tight and warm, set on the hill across the fire circle from Pete's, also overlooking the lake so that the two shelters stood sentinel-like, facing outward on the far end of the campsite. As Pete made his way over, he looked back and noticed that no one was up, and the fire was dying. He put another log on the coals and stirred it up until it caught. Another alarm went off. Why the weapons, and the rest of all this, but no guard, no fire?

He found Ben awake, sitting in the doorway, staring. It was a dark night, the clouds hiding the stars and the moon. Still, this time of year in the far north, there was an almost perpetual dawn, and real darkness came only at the full depth of the night. Now, at about ten, the clouds still glowed with the remains of the day. "What do you think, old man?"

Ben jumped. "Jesus, what are you trying to do? Give me a heart attack?"

"Sorry."

"That's alright. Guess I'm a little jumpy."

"How about it? What should we do?"

Ben didn't answer. He kept his eyes fixed on the lake ahead, but Pete could see through the gloom that he was struggling. Finally he said, "We have to give him one more chance."

Pete slumped. "No, Ben. We've got to leave."

"I'm staying."

"I'm leaving. And I'm taking anyone who wants to go with me."

Ben looked startled. "Pete, don't. He'll ..." but his voice trailed off.

"He'll what, Ben? What'll he do?" But Ben said nothing. "Look, you must see that if you're afraid he'll do something to me for trying to leave, there's something wrong, here. Something terribly wrong." Pete studied Ben, but the older man continued to stare ahead in silence. "I know he gets inside you. I've felt it, too. But we're in trouble, here. Bear or man, we're in trouble. And I need you to be on my side." Pete spoke quietly, deliberately, trying to keep the rising fear he was feeling out of his voice.

"There's no sides. We're all in this together," Ben answered, still staring straight ahead.

"Yeah. And we're all going to die together if we stay out here."

"No offense, but if we are going to face a life and death situation, I'd sooner have Jake in my corner than you, Pete."

"Unless it's Jake we have to fear."

"Will you just give it up? For god's sake, give it up."

"No dammit. I don't know why she changed her story, but Jake threw the battery away ..."

"He's trying to save us. What about the weapons. And going around in threes?

"Answer me this. If there's a man-eating bear out there, why don't we have a person on watch?"

Ben seemed shaken, but he didn't speak.

"Why don't we have a fire blazing?"

Ben answered slowly, almost automatically, "Maybe he forgot. There's a lot going on ..."

"Bullshit. Jake doesn't forget."

Finally, Ben turned to face Pete, "Then why?"

"I'll tell you why. Thom's right. There is no bear."

Ben turned away. "Thom seems to think it might have been you, Pete."

"I don't have a bear claw necklace."

"Neither does Jake." Ben's eyes glazed. "Now leave me alone."

Pete grabbed him by the shoulder and whispered, "Listen to me Ben. Try to fight this thing. You know I'm right. Jake would post a guard ... he's just got you under some kind of spell."

"Listen to yourself. Do realize how crazy you sound? Go get some rest. Let me be."

He looked at Ben, and saw it was hopeless. What could he say? What could he do that would bring this man back. He could think of nothing. Not reason, not fear, not friendship. He was fighting a phantom. Something he couldn't touch or see, let alone understand.

Pete didn't sleep. He rolled around most of the night, his spruce bough bed feeling lumpy, and his thoughts twisted and confused. By morning, he'd almost convinced himself that Ben was right. He was just letting his suspicions cloud his thinking. Or worse. But then he remembered Ruth, and the battery and her eyes. Finally, just before dawn, as the sky turned a cold, pale, yellow, he fell asleep.

He woke feeling as if he were encased in cement. His whole body felt heavy, weak, immobile. Movement seemed almost impossible, and so did consciousness. But there was something insistent tugging him into it. Then he felt it, the hand shaking his foot, and then he heard it, the voice, anxious, scared, urgent.

"Pete. Wake up. Come on, dammit. *Wake up.*"

Pete sat up and saw Clio silhouetted in his entrance against the morning light. He could see that it was still early, so he hadn't slept long. "He's gone," she said.

Pete tried to shake off the sleep, but couldn't. He didn't want to hear this, whatever it was. He didn't want to fight any more dragons. He just wanted to sleep. He slumped back down. "Not now, Clio."

"*Peter.* Wake up. He's gone. Thom is gone."

Pete bolted up, awake at once. "What do you mean, gone?"

"I mean he's not here."

"How long has he been missing?"

"He was gone when I got up, maybe a half and hour ago. I went to talk to him about what he's been saying, and he wasn't there. I waited and when he didn't show up, I came here. I'm scared, Pete. Real scared."

"Me too. But it's gonna be alright. Go get the others up. And get the fire going. We're going to have a meeting."

Pete pulled his boots on and went immediately to Thom's shelter. It was set against a rock wall a little way off from the fire and the rest of the shelters. Thom had used an overhang to form his back wall and most of his roof, so he'd ended up with a nice tight little dwelling with a minimum of effort. All he'd done was to construct a front wall with an entrance. Pete noticed immediately that one of the branches he'd used to frame the door had been pulled out and was jutting from the frame. Like he'd been clutching it, Pete thought. He looked about for signs of bear, but saw none. The soil around the hut was thin and rocky, so he didn't expect to see tracks. But then, as a sliver of morning sun broke through the cloud cover, he saw it in the underbrush; the glint of sunlight in a dew-soaked gossamer web, refracted so that it appeared in rainbow hues. And then he saw another. One side clung to a spruce sapling that had sprung up in a fracture and the other was fixed to a boulder. The middle had been torn, and it was hanging in the light. He remembered one of Jake's lessons. "In the mornings, you can sometimes trace a trail over even the rockiest terrain by looking for things like tracks in the dew and ripped cobwebs."

Pete went to it and scanned the area for another damaged web, saw one several yards out, and moved toward it. Ahead, the earth was softer and he scanned for prints. He wanted very badly to find a bear print. But he saw only one set, a man's. He couldn't be sure, but the dirt and forest litter was churned up. Like something was dragged.

"Andersen. Get over here." It was Jake, and he sounded angry.

"Hang, on," Pete waived him off, trying to see where the trail led.

"Now, Andersen."

Pete looked back. The others were assembled and waiting.

"The next time you call a meeting and wake us all up, you better be here," Jake yelled.

Pete weighed his options. Then he remembered something. The time Jake had manipulated Keller into hunting with him. You just have to use the levers, Pete remembered Jake saying. Or something like that. And right now, Pete needed Jake gone. He started to return to the site, the plan barely formulated. It would all depend on Ruth, though. That, and his ability to make Jake leave camp, if only for an hour. Time to pull some levers.

CHAPTER 37

Two days after announcing to the Barnetts that she was going to save Pete and Ben, Karen was entering the Alpenhorn Restaurant in Smithers to have lunch with Baker. She spotted the Mountie off in a corner, dressed in his Reds. Except for the fact that he was on the short side, he had exactly the look she expected from a Mountie – square-jawed, straight-shouldered, wavy-haired. He stood as she approached and extended his hand, "Ms. Flannigan?"

"Call me Karen." She'd already decided to launch a major charm assault in hopes of getting him to lift his blockade.

"I go by Baker," he said.

They exchanged a few more pleasantries, ordered lunch, and within a few minutes Karen found herself looking at a picture of a pretty woman with full cheeks and chestnut hair, surrounded on either side by two clones aged seven and ten. When she'd handed the wallet back to Baker, he'd taken a moment to gaze at them before slipping it into an inner pocket in his blazer. "Sometimes I look at the three of them, and it's hard to believe I had anything to do with it," he said. As they'd talked, a procession of locals stopped by to say hi, or to ask after a friend or relative in some part of northern British Columbia. "I'm pretty much all the law there is between here and Dease Lake," he said. "I'm part police officer, part father confessor, occasional mailman, and full-time therapist. Not bad for a country boy."

As the lunch crowd thinned, he asked a few questions about why she was worried, and Karen explained about what Chas had found out, and about her own misgivings from the class. He asked a few more questions, and then a few more, always listening closely to her answers and commenting appropriately. His empathy was real, and she ended up shifting from what Chas had discovered in Jake's medical reports and about his messianic save-the-world lectures, to telling him about Pete and her, about quitting her job at EPA, and about the medallion she'd given Pete. Baker had an easy way about him and by the time the lunch crowd had disappeared, it dawned on Karen that she was the one being charmed.

"Why Mr. Baker, I do have the feeling you've been interviewing me this whole time. Should I be asking for an attorney?"

"Like I said, part therapist."

"Let's cut to the chase. I think they're in danger. And I think you do too, or you wouldn't be sitting here picking my brain."

Baker took a sip of his coffee, then studied the mountains through the window. He toyed with a sugar packet for a few moments then sighed heavily and stroked his chin with his palm and stared at Karen. "I can't say they're not in danger. Most probably they are. And when it comes to Jake ... well, I don't quite know what to think."

"So you understand why I want to get out there. At least check on them?"

"Understand? I guess. But I wouldn't be so quick to accept what that doctor said. Tell you what. Let me tell you a story, and when I'm done, you can decide for yourself if they're in danger."

She nodded, and Baker began. "Jake was my first case. I was just starting out. Nearly ruined me."

"How?"

"A bunch of people were sabotaging logging operations from here all the way to Prince Rupert. At least that's what the official report ended up saying. My initial version said something different. But they asked me to rewrite it."

"Why?"

The Mountie just raised his hand in a gesture that said, 'You'll see.' Then he went on, "Lumber companies agreed with me. Claimed it was Jake, acting alone. Claimed to see him popping up everywhere, sometimes appearing fifty kilometers apart within a single day. But of course, that couldn't be, could it?" He didn't wait for an answer.

"Here's what was happening. During the day, the choke setters would disappear. One minute they'd be settin' cable on the downed trees, next minute they'd disappear. People who went down to hunt for 'em would disappear too. Come the evening, they'd find most of a crew out there, gagged, blindfolded and wrapped in their own cables. Next day, same stuff would happen seventy-five kilometers off. Most of them saw nothing, but a few of them caught a glimpse of the guy before they were taken down and blind folded.

"Didn't matter how far apart the incidents were. Every time there was a witness they described Jake. Or his twin. One time I talked to a fella at Takla Landing who'd been assaulted on Tuesday noon, and another who'd been tied up that afternoon south of Fort Barbie – that's about forty miles away, with no roads connecting them. Both of them said it was Jake. "

"How could that stop logging?" Karen asked.

"You ever see a clear cut operation?" She shook her head.

"It's an amazing thing. They can take down an entire stand in a week. They'll cut some roads into high ground and set up a yarder – kind of a big crane with cables going out in all directions. Then they start leveling trees, bucking them up into lengths as they go. The choke setter, he carries around this cable – weighs maybe fifty pounds – he crawls through the brush and wraps the choker around the bucked up log, then attaches it to one of the cables overhead leading to the yarder, signals the operator and gets the hell out of the way 'cause the yarder yanks that log up across the cut to the top of the hill at the speed of light. Then they're trucked out. Choke setters are the grunts of the operation. They're either drunks or uneducated or shiftless or all three, but they have to be strong. Real strong. And they have to have stamina. They drag this cable around all day through brush, as the cutters rape the hillside. A forest that's been standing for a thousand years can be dropped in a week this way. But the choke setter is the key. Backbreaking work. Hardest job there ever was. Stop him, and you stop the operation."

"But how could you bring all logging to a halt just by getting a few at a time? There must be hundreds of these operations going on."

"There are. That's the part that's haunted me for ten years, now. These guys I interviewed? They weren't just beaten physically. In fact, most of them were unhurt. But they were all beaten spiritually. There's no other way to describe it. They were completely whipped. Some of the tribal people said it was Saya, come to take revenge. There was talk about the wolves coming round and acting threatening. Anyway, none of the Indians would work. As for the others? They were just plain scared. And these aren't the types who scare easy. They mentioned the wolves, too. Said they'd just stand there watching, like they were guarding something. Once these guys started talking, no one wanted to go out there anymore. It spread through the camps like a flu, and within a month, the companies couldn't field a crew."

"Beaten spiritually. What's that mean?"

Baker studied her for a moment before answering. "I'll tell you what it means. I've been all the law there is around here for fifteen years. There's some strange and scary things that go on out there. I've seen men beaten to a pulp by other men. I've seen women who've been raped and brutalized. I've seen people go stark raving mad just because they couldn't stand the isolation of winter living in some remote cabin. I've talked to people just after they've been mauled by a grizzly. You ever seen any thing like that?"

Karen shook her head.

"In about half the attacks, a grizzly'll pick a man up by the head and shake him. I've seen people holding their scalp over their skulls after an attack. I mean, I've seen the skull bone, itself. You learn pretty quick that you can see some of the terror these people have seen, by looking in their eyes. It lingers there, and plays back, kinda' like an echo. Now, in all my years, I've never seen what I saw in the eyes of those choke setters. Never. And that's what I mean by being beaten spiritually."

They were quiet for several minutes. Back in the kitchen, dishes were rattling, and someone had turned on a radio and a country-western song drifted out. Across the room, a waitress began filling the salt and pepper shakers.

Karen broke the silence. "So, he beat up some people, and scared the hell out of the others. Sounds like the shrink had it about right, to me."

"Jake never hurt anyone, unless they tried to fight him. Even then, he only did what he had to do to subdue them. But here's the thing. Those forests he was trying to save?"

Karen nodded.

"They're all but gone now. What's left is getting chewed up by pine-bark beetles. So you tell me, who's crazy. The lumber barons or Jake? An' now it's worse. Barbara – that's my wife – she tells me we're on the verge of heating up the planet to the point where it won't recover and you tell me Jake wants to save the world? Seems to me it needs a little saving."

"But there's ways to do this. There's laws and institutions ..."

"That why you quit EPA? 'Cause that stuff was workin' so well?"

"But isn't that your job? Upholding the law?"

"Do the ends ever justify the means? That's the question you're asking me. It's the same one Jake asked when I arrested him. I'm coming around to the notion that sometimes they do."

Some country boy, Karen thought. He's going to start quoting Kant to me any second now. But Baker surprised her again, and said, "What you're really afraid of is that Pete will come back different than he left. And that you'll lose him."

The comment landed with authority. Shit. Has my soul suddenly gone transparent she wondered. But then she thought, fuck him and his psychobabble. Fuck them all. "I'm going. And you can't stop me."

"I've already seen to it that no one takes you up there out of this town's airport. And there ain't no other towns. So, yeah, I can stop you."

"Why are you doing this?"

"I'm a fan of Jakes, but I've noticed folks who cross him don't fare too well."

"Why do you say that?"

"He had a trip go bad a while back. Lost two people. I interviewed a survivor, a scientist – Dawkins was his name, I think. Guy had been attacked by a bear. But something else happened too. Something involving Jake. And it wasn't good, whatever it was."

"I talked to him. I thought he was a little paranoid."

"Maybe he was. But he looked an awful lot like those choke setters."

Baker took a call on his cell, then stood up. "Gotta go. You best get yourself back down to Seattle. You're not getting anyone to take you North. Nothin' you could do up there anyway."

CHAPTER 38

After Jake yelled, Pete hesitated for just a moment, then he came back toward the fire a few steps – just enough that he could see and be seen by all of them. And more important, heard. "Thom could be hurt. I'm going to find him. Anyone want to help?" he said simply.

Clio answered immediately, "I will." Several others offered, too. Pete watched Jake carefully. He'd soon know whether he was being paranoid.

Jake eyed Pete, then stood up. "No." Jake said. "We can't have all of us traipsing around out there at once. That's how we wiped out the trail down there." He gestured at the fish camp.

Pete broke in immediately. "Right. Then I'm the one to go. I finished best in the tracking test."

"No. I'll go," Jake said.

Damn right you will, Pete thought. So far so good. Of course, even if he got Jake to leave, he would have to do the rest in front of Jim and he'd likely tell Jake. So once he committed, there was no turning back. He'd either convince them, or he'd end up like Keller. *But if I'm right, we're all destined for that anyway.* Jake lingered at the site, though, making no effort to join Pete on the trail.

Then Jake said, "We have some things we need to sort out here first, though."

"I better go then."

"I said I'd go, Andersen."

"No. You take care of whatever it is you need to do, and I'll get started."

"You're trying my patience ..."

"But you told us the most important thing is to get on a trail while it's still warm," Pete turned and started off in the direction he'd seen the trail take earlier. He moved deliberately. He could feel Jake's eyes on him, and as he moved into the forest, he tensed, waiting for him to make his move.

Jake got up and raced after him, grabbing his arm as he reached him and spinning him around, saying, "I said I'd do it."

Pete freed himself from Jake's grasp with difficulty, forced a smile, and said, "Alright, I'll leave you to it then," and walked quickly back to the fire, leaving Jake standing on the perimeter of the camp where the trail entered the woods. His arm ached from the pressure of Jake's grip, and his heart was kicking into overdrive, the adrenaline pouring into his system, but he was pleased. Jake would have virtually no choice but to go on, now.

Jake saw his dilemma and smiled. Pete thought he nodded just barely perceptively, in his direction. Then he turned to group and said, "We make no decisions until I get back."

Some of the group nodded, but Pete stepped in. "I called the meeting. I'll run it. We can talk when you return."

Jake glared at Pete and he felt as if he'd just been injected with a refrigerant. His muscles went numb with fear, and he was just able to stand, but he gave no sign of any of that to Jake. Instead, he looked directly back into his eyes, holding them defiantly. The stare went on for too long, and Pete finally said, "You better get going. Good luck."

Jake turned slowly and headed into the woods. Pete knew he wouldn't be gone long. He tried to choke back his fear, tried to convince himself that Jake was not pausing on the edge of the forest, watching, listening, taking names. Inexplicably, an old Christmas song came to mind ...You *better watch out ... He's makin' a list; Checkin' it twice; He's gonna find out who's naughty and nice ...*

Pete went and sat near the fire in the place normally occupied by Jake. It wasn't too late to just leave in the dead of night. To start running and keep going until he reached Cold Fish Lake and a radio. He had a chance of outrunning Jake now that he was acclimated to the elevation. And that chance was better if he were alone. But he'd already decided: no one gets left behind. It would be their death sentence. He looked around at the group, trying to gage their state of mind. Clio was still her own person, and intent on getting out of there. Rita and Sarah looked from Jim to Pete, confused. Jim stared at him, full of hate, but for some reason, despite the fact that he was, perhaps, even more physically powerful than Jake, he held no terror for Pete. He continued his scan. Ben and Bill waited, their expressions difficult to read, but he thought he saw some fire back in Ben's eyes. Then there was Ruth. She still held her head down, looking up at him almost furtively. She didn't look ready to step forward and take a risk, and Pete needed her to. She was the key.

He was nervous. Once he started there was a good chance he wouldn't survive the night unless he convinced them all to go, right now. Even if they bought into what he was about to say, and they went together, their lives would be in danger. But not as much as if they stayed. Here goes, he thought.

He tried to tell himself it was just another decision meeting – just like a thousand meetings he'd had before, back at EPA. But then he envisioned Eunice, her belly torn open and her guts dragged out into the forest. Did she live to see it happening to her? Was she forced to watch? And he saw Keller, his body twisted and broken. He saw them as he'd seen them that other morning, and he knew what he was about to do brought him closer to that same end, and he froze. No, this was not just like any other meeting. There was much more at stake here; he was fighting something more powerful than politics, ego, and faulty logic. There was something here he didn't understand; something he couldn't name, and it robbed him of his last bit of courage. The song danced through his head again: *He's makin a list; checkin it twice* ... His body began to shake and tremble, and he was afraid to speak, afraid it would come out in a high-pitched squeak, forced out between vocal chords screwed tight with fear, lips taught with terror. The scene went blurry before him, and he held his knees to keep from visibly shaking.

They sat around the fire and looked at him, waiting. He managed to look toward the forest. Jake was nowhere to be seen, but that didn't mean he wouldn't hear what was being said – and who was saying it. He glanced at Jim. Maybe it wasn't too late to back out and just sneak off. What did he owe these people anyway? But even as he asked, he knew. He owed them everything, for the simple reason he could never walk away from this and keep even a shred of dignity. Gus had taught him that much.

Yes, his only hope was Ruth. Somehow he had to get her to tell the truth – to tell the others what she'd told him. It wouldn't be easy. She hadn't backed him up so far. He understood now, why. She knew first hand what they were facing, what he was capable of, and what he intended to do to them. She knew the fear he was only just beginning to understand. But Pete would have to convince her that, while they were all in danger, they could act. They could at least try. He would have to make her see the inevitability of their fate if they stayed and did nothing. Their bodies broken and ripped, their lives snuffed out. He had to make her see and feel the terror of being stalked, then killed one-by-one by a predator more terrible than the bear. He would have to make her believe they had a chance; that he could save her and them, from Jake's wrath. But he wasn't even sure *he* believed that.

"Alright, there's been a lot of loose talk around here ..." Jim started.

He's like a jackal, Pete thought. He senses weakness and closes in. Pete inhaled and stood up, gathering every resource he had and focusing it on his voice. If I can just speak, he thought. But even as he trembled, he felt another emotion start to creep into him, as if from outside. It was the feeling he'd had when he'd stood over the caribou, its life ebbing out of it to some place Pete wanted to know. It was the feeling he'd had when he'd flung Jake aside and pitched Keller to the ground. A blazing white hot intensity that went beyond anger, welling up from the DNA of his soul, forging his emotions into a weapon, pointed, focused, precise.

Pete stepped forward. "Shut up, Jim." The strength of it surprised Pete, and it landed on Jim like a blow. Pete went on, "Last night we started on a vote ..."

"He said there would be no vote ..."

"I told you to shut up." Pete walked over to Jim and stood before him. Unaccountably, the bigger man seemed to cringe in his presence, "I say we're having one."

"Me too." It was Clio. Pete could have kissed her.

Bill rallied. "Count me in."

"I'm with Pete," Rita said.

Pete turned to Ben. If he had him the others would follow. "What about you, Ben?"

The older man looked at Pete, then Jim. "A vote can't hurt," he said, finally.

Pete turned to Jim. "That's it. We're having one. You can vote or not." Pete returned to the center of the fire ring, and addressed the rest of them, "But before we vote, I want you to hear something." This was it, he knew. This was the moment. No way out, once he started. Again, he thought briefly of dropping this burden and just running. He could leave tonight, and get enough of a lead that no one could catch him. Not even Jake. He could get to Cold Fish Lake, call the Mounties. Maybe they would even get here before Jake killed them all. And maybe I'm wrong. Maybe Jake had nothing to do with Keller's death. He *was* with Ruth ...

"What is it, Pete?" It was Ben, his voice gentle, but insistent.

"Huh?" Pete said. So much for great leadership. He still didn't have his mind back. It seemed very hard to concentrate. He looked about at the faces again, waiting expectantly, and struggled to remember what he'd started ... you have to hear something ... yes, that's it.

"You have to hear something that only I've heard. When you hear it, you'll know that our only hope is to get out of here. Now." He stepped around the outside of the ring and stopped behind Ruth, placing his hands on her shoulders reassuringly. "Tell them, Ruth." He could feel her shoulders stiffen, and then start to shake. He knelt down beside her and whispered in her ear, "Tell them. Tell them about the radio." She looked at him, then at Jim, then back at him. She began to whimper, quietly, but Pete could feel it in her shoulders.

"I ... can't," she whispered barely audible. "I can't."

"You have to. They deserve to know, Ruth."

"I'm scared."

The others watched, and Pete could see that Jim was steeling himself for another attempt. He leaned closer to Ruth. "We're going to die if we stay here, Ruth. It's time to return the garden to its rightful owner, remember?" But she would say nothing. She just sobbed.

Pete rose and stood, staring at Jim. The fear was coming back, now. He had to do something. "Thom thought it wasn't a bear, and when he had the nerve to say so, he turns up missing ... I believe he's dead."

Jim stood up directly across from Pete, "If Thom is dead, it's the bear that did it." Then he turned to Ruth. "Tell them where Jake was when Keller and the rest were killed."

Ruth began to weep, hysterically and irrationally, the sound of a frightened two year old. She started to rock back and forth, the way she had when Pete found her by the lake that morning. He wouldn't get anything out of her. And he knew Jake would be back very soon. Or maybe he'd been out there in the edge of the forest the whole time, listening. The thought chilled him, but he had to keep going, there was no choice now. No way out but forward, straight through it.

"If there's a man eating bear out there, why didn't Jake post guards last night? Why didn't we have a bonfire?"

Jim ignored the question, and faced Ruth. "Tell them. Tell them that Jake was with you last night. And the night before. He couldn't have done any of this."

Pete wasn't listening. Just a second ago he'd heard a branch break somewhere near the perimeter of the forest. It might as well have been his spinal chord breaking. Jake was out there. God, this is turning to shit, he thought. He had to get as many of them committed to getting out of there as he could. And save himself. "Nobody's saying Jake did this. What I'm saying is we have to get out of here."

"Why, Peter?" It was Jake, his voice even and measured. He was walking into the camp from the direction of Thom's trail.

"Because we're dying. Because we're getting killed. Because we didn't have guards last night. Because this whole thing has taken a terrible turn, and we aren't going to transcend anything. We're not going to pass Thoreau's test out here. Not this time."

"We won't if you run at the first sign of trouble, Peter."

"I don't call four people dead, the first sign."

"We'll talk later, Peter." He said it quietly, but it burned into Pete like a brand, silencing him. "What matters now is that we go on, until we're done. We have something to finish. And we're going to finish it."

"Where's Thom?" Clio asked.

"I couldn't find him. But I did see bear sign." Jake turned to the others. He gestured up the trail, "This beast we are facing is an old one. He is wise; he is malignant; he is malevolent. You know him in your soul.

You know him from a million nights spent huddling in terror in the back of some cave, waving torches in his face while you trembled, consumed in fear. He is one reason why you must build, create, dominate. Because you cannot stand that fear, even as you crave it. If we face it here, we will learn to silence it. And nothing will be safe until we do. But we must stand together as one ..."

Jake continued, but Pete lost the string of the individual words. What he heard was the voice, comfortable as a set of well-worn jeans, and there seemed an innate wisdom behind them. As Jake continued, his voice strong yet soft, Pete came to understand again why they were here. It seemed almost as if he were waking, the confusion from before just the nonsense of a bad dream. Of course they had to stay ...

CHAPTER 39

After Jake's speech, the rest of the day passed in a fog for Pete. It was as if he were drugged – his essence subsumed in a mist, and he moved around, a shell. Something was wrong, but he couldn't name it. The one thing he knew was that he was in danger and as the night drew closer, his dread intensified. He tried to avoid Jake, although he couldn't say why, and he kept his spear by him, but that was as much as he could do. Jake's last speech washed over him, again and again, and he thought, almost by reflex, *Of course we have to stay. Of course we have to face this ... running away won't work ... the Beast must be dealt with, killed, exterminated.* Yet he couldn't name the Beast. It was just some vague thing that threatened all of them – everything. But every once in a while that old Christmas song would play in his head again, *You better watch out ... He's makin' a list, checkin' it twice; gonna find out who's naughty or nice ...* It left him agitated, confused, but somehow it seemed to penetrate the mists he was walking through.

It wasn't until nightfall that the fog cleared completely. It happened when Pete was out looking for firewood. They'd let their stash run low, again. Stupid, Pete thought. Another oversight, especially since a brutal cold front had closed in. Most of the deadwood near the campsite had been picked clean, so he drifted up the peninsula to the mainland, then he headed north, toward the wolves' dens. It had been off-limits to everyone but Jake, so other than the first day, that one night with Ben, and twice with Jake, Pete had left the area alone.

The trees were thicker here, so that as Pete moved further into the woods, the light faded. He peered into the darkening forest and spotted an opening and a patch of light. Somewhere up ahead, it opens to a bluff overlooking the north end of the stream valley we hunted, he thought. He headed for it, following one of the wolf trails. It was difficult going because the trail was clear of branches and brush up to a height of only about three feet, and the slope was steep. Above three feet spruce branches formed a twisted web forcing him to alternately duck under and push aside tree limbs. It made the climb strenuous, but the exertion felt good.

About three-quarters of the way up, he saw a pile of leaves and brush forming a mound about six feet long and four feet wide, east of the trail. He'd spotted it as he'd ducked under a branch, and twisted his body to straighten up. As he'd turned, there it was. Partially hidden, but unmistakable.

It looked fresh. There were marks in the soft earth where the branches and forest litter had been scraped up to form the mound. Pete edged into the thicket to check it out. He knew that bears would frequently cache a kill in mounds such as this, but here? Among the wolves? As if on cue, they began to howl. They were near, so near their calls registered not just as sound, but as force. He could feel the vibrations of their opera, moving through the thin, frigid air and striking him, sending fear through him in spasms. In a series of chemical reactions forged in the mists of time, his body flushed with adrenaline, his muscles tensed, his heart began to thump, his hair stood on end and goose bumps formed on his flesh; at the same time, the ends of his nerves shed their dopamine and he prepared to act and think, mind and body as one. Everything was now focused on the simple task at hand: to survive. And with it there came a startling, chilling clarity. And with that, the knowledge of what was in that mound. And what ... who ... put it there.

He was certain the wolves were aware of his presence. They were no more than twenty five yards east of him, just down a narrow slope on the other side of the mound in a clearing. He couldn't see them because of the trees and brush, and the gathering darkness, but he knew they were there. He hesitated. Should he move forward? Uncover the mound? Risk agitating the wolves further? Or run – no, not run. Back out. Slowly, facing them. But then he would have his back to the real terror.

Involuntarily, he looked over his shoulder. What he saw should have multiplied his fear, but for some reason, it didn't. It was those same golden eyes, glowing in the fading light, framed by that same silver grey fur. It sat there on the trail Pete had left just moments before, not ten feet from where he now stood. As before, there was a kind of communion between them. He was certain this was the Alpha. As he looked into the eyes, he sensed no fear, and no hostility. Just curiosity. And an alertness; a wariness; a protectiveness for his kin.

Pete took a few steps toward the mound, then sat near it, keeping his eyes on the wolf the whole time. It didn't move, but Pete heard a low, grumbling growl from deep within its throat, just barely audible, but unmistakable in its power. "You don't want me near this?" Pete said softly. The wolf sat, immobile, the growl still reverberating in its throat, like the long rolling rumble of a distant thunder clap, his head forward now, ears back, the lips snarled up revealing the sharp canines. Pete knew he was being warned. He looked right into the yellow eyes and spoke, his voice as quiet and soothing as he could make it. "Do you work for him? No. You don't work for anyone." Then he said, "This is one of my people. I must know what happened to him."

The wolf seemed to relax some, and Pete continued to talk. "I am not like you. It is not in my genes to be the leader. But I must. Or my people will die. Just as this one has. Do you understand?" Questions seemed to distract the wolf. Perhaps it was something in the inflection that signaled submissiveness. But each time Pete started to pull the litter off the mound he would growl. No matter how carefully he moved, no matter how slowly, no matter how soothing his voice, it would growl, then glance down the trail toward the camp. Pete felt for his spear. It was there, lying near him. But he doubted that he could raise it in time if the wolf attacked. Besides, there were very likely others nearby, watching him. As a pack, wolves are the supreme predator. No single animal could withstand a coordinated attack by wolves. Their moves had been choreographed for five hundred thousand years, their dance of death a perfection of cooperation. Like us, Pete thought.

Once again, Pete looked into the wolf's eyes, and spoke. This time, in a firmer voice. Not threatening, but not soothing either. "I am going to do this thing, because I must. You do what you must." He gazed a moment longer at the wolf getting lost for a time in those glowing yellow eyes, then turned and began to strip off the brush from the mound.

He kept his back to the Alpha and pulled off a small spruce branch, then began to sweep away some leaves and spruce needles from near the top, working slowly and deliberately, waiting to feel the slam in his back, the fangs closing in around his neck. He spoke as he worked, in that same voice. "I have to do this. I must protect my people, just as you must protect your pack. Do you understand? Jake says that Saya put you here to show us how to live within the world; to teach us to care for that which we must take. I understand that, now. I've known it. But we must care for our own, too." His words formed frozen white puffs in the air and drifted away in the breeze.

Pete was silent a moment and he paused in his work, listening for the growl. He didn't hear it, and he turned around, slowly. It was gone. He searched up the path, and peered into the glooming forest, but he could not see him. Then he heard, from the top of the slope, near the clearing he'd been heading for when he'd first seen the mound, a loud howling, a calling to the others, and it was answered by at least seven wolves, their replies echoing from all around him: off in the clearing just over the small rise, from back down the slope between him and the camp, behind him on the opposite side of the trail, and again from the clearing atop the slope, ringing, resonating, echoing, and chilling in the way they filled the space around him. He is calling the others, Pete thought. Soon they will be here. He stayed calm; he had no choice. He was surrounded.

So he ignored them, and continued to clear the debris from the pile. The first thing he saw was Thom's face, partially torn and chewed, but remarkably free of blood; then the full head, then the shoulders. The head lay at an odd angle to the trunk, the neck twisted and limp. Pete continued to scrape away the cover, until he could see the stomach. The thin red lines, four of them, raked across Thom's abdomen, tearing deep into his flesh. And as with the face, very little blood. Then he knew, no bear did this. The mound was a good imitation of a bear stash, but no bear would cache it anywhere near a wolf den. And if this was faked, so were the others. Pete sat back. It was nearly dark, and extremely cold. He noticed with relief that the wolf calls had retreated off to the east and north. They were on a hunt. He pulled his knees up, more scared now than when he'd confronted the wolves. He had to keep this clarity. He had to avoid Jake. And he had to convince Ben they were in danger.

He was there a long time. A breeze shushed through the spruces, and he looked up past the swaying branches. The sky drifted in and out of view, and he saw stars so thick they nearly blotted out the blackness with a mother of pearl patina, turning the woods and everything in it a dim blue. Then he heard it, off behind him, on the wolf trail. The snap of a twig, and he turned.

He couldn't see well, but there was a figure squatting almost exactly where the wolf sat. He held in his hands a small branch, snapped in half. Pete froze.

The figure sat there, motionless, regarding him for a long time. As Pete stared into the murkiness, trying to divine who it was, he saw the eyes. They were the same as the wolf's but different. Different color. Same intensity; same wisdom; same sense of being in control. Same power. And he knew, without seeing anything else that it was Jake.

"We've been worried about you Peter." The voice was soft, soothing, the way Pete had talked to the wolf.

"You did this."

"You're upset, Peter."

"Stop. Don't say anything else. I'm not listening to you. But you'll listen to me. His neck is snapped. Just like Joan. And you know what? He hardly bled at all. That means those claw marks were put there after he was killed."

Jake was silent for a long time. "So you think you know, Peter. What now?"

Pete didn't say anything.

"Choose carefully, Peter. Much rides on it."

"You killed him," was all Pete could manage.

"I take responsibility, yes. But that's not important, Peter. What matters, is what you choose to do now. Choose incorrectly, and you and all that you love may be swept away. But there is more to the choice than just your life. The trial is over, Peter. The experiment is done, and the results are in. The Earth has spoken. You were to be my rock. You still can be. You can help me in this last chapter."

"You're mad."

"There is a strength in you, Peter, that even you don't know about. I have spent too much of my time and energy trying to reach you. Perhaps that's why the others were so ... independent minded." Jake smiled in the dark, showing his teeth.

"You're completely insane."

Jake sighed, stood up, and started toward Pete, "Labels such as this after all you have been through? I had hoped for more from you."

CHAPTER 40

After her talk with Baker, Karen had managed to track down the one person who might take her to Spatsizi. She was on her way to meet him, now. Turning off of the Yellowhead Highway she found herself rattling her kidneys as she crawled along a pot-hole studded dirt road for about four miles through a landscape that alternated between scrub willow, open fens dotted with small ponds, and aspen groves mixed with spruce in the uplands. After an eternity, the road dead-ended into a lake. There was still a thick evening mist hanging over it, stained a dim blue in the starlight. She could make out the De Haviland parked against a well-maintained dock. Duquoin was home. She got out of the rental car and walked down to the dock to check it out.

Almost at once, she felt it. Someone or something was studying her. She could feel the eyes upon her. Not hostile, not even intense, but they were there, alert and watchful. She looked around to where the gaze came from.

A trim cabin sat on a promontory overlooking the lake, set in a copse of aspen. In the failing light, the aspen and spruce combined to make the house appear almost an apparition – seen in outline only, but murky in its details. A path made of stones carefully set into the hill led from the mist-shrouded lake up to it. Karen surveyed the steps. There was an almost Zen-like precision about their design and placement. They followed a curved arc that cut neatly through the forest without disturbing it. A curl of smoke came from the chimney, and an old Suburu was just visible near the side of the house.

From somewhere far down the road, she heard the faint sound of a truck downshiftng, and then a silence fell over the place as the throaty backthrottle drifted into the mists surrounding the forest and bogs. She walked up the path, spotting a series of rock sculptures set off the trail in the gloom of the aspens. They were made of boulders improbably balanced one upon another with great care, so that they appeared to defy gravity. In the dimness they resembled an army of stone soldiers, frozen in mid-march. The effect was surreal, and a little unnerving, and Karen started to regret coming out here so late. Duquoin might take me for a prowler and shoot me, she thought. She was about to turn around and walk back to her car when she heard him.

"You've come this far. Don't be turnin' back now."

She couldn't pin-point where the voice came from, but she assumed it was Duquoin's. She peered up at the cabin, but the door was closed. Sitting on the stoop though, was the most beautiful dog she'd ever seen. It had one blue eye, and one golden-brown, and the sharp aquiline face of a wolf, with a thick, bushy coat of mottled sable, grey and white. It didn't bark or wag its tail. It seemed mainly indifferent to her, although it did track her movements carefully. Somehow she knew that it'd watched her from the moment she'd left the car.

"He won't hurt you."

Karen jumped. Duquoin had appeared at her side, silently. She backed up, and said, "A man could get hurt sneaking up like that."

"It's a good thing you aren't in Spatsizi. I could have been a bear. An that's why the answer is no."

"Doesn't that depend on the question?"

"We both know why you're here."

"Actually, I'm here for the coffee. I hear you make the best in BC."

Duquoin smiled, then nodded. "You have to drink it black," he said.

"Fine." She studied the dog, "Beautiful dog. Can I pet him?"

"He's not exactly a dog. He's a breed. Part wolf, part Siberian Husky. An it's not up to me, now is it? You should be askin' him."

Karen walked up to the stoop and got down on her haunches, holding her hand out. "What about it, boy? Can I pet you?"

The dog got up languidly, stretched, and came over to her, sniffing her hand. Moving slowly, Karen placed her hand on the back of the dog's thick neck fur and kneaded it gently. It cocked its head to facilitate the rubbing, half closing its eyes with pleasure as it did. After a few moments, it lay down in front of her. She was pleased to note that Duquoin watched, stunned.

"He doesn't take to most people like that."

"What's his name?"

"Lupus. Lu for short."

"Hey, Lu. Tell him you got good taste. Right boy?"

"Wait here. I'll get your coffee."

Karen got up from her knees and sat on the stoop. The dog settled down next to her, laying its chin on her lap. She continued to pet it absently as she waited, watching the mists curl off the lake, thinking what an incredible place this was, and wondering how she could get this man to change his mind. Duquoin emerged with the two mugs of coffee, and sat beside her. "Looks like you have a friend."

Karen smiled and rubbed the dog behind his ears.

"Now, the answer is still no."

"Why?"

"That place is no place for a woman to be roamin' around."

"I'm not going there to roam around. I'm going to get those people out."

"And just why do you wanta do something like that?"

"I think they're in danger."

"There's not a man alive that can take better care of them than Jake."

"Yeah. True enough. But there's no one who could hurt them as much, either, is there?"

Duquoin said nothing. "They've got a radio, right?"

"Yeah."

"You know the frequency they're using?"

Duquoin nodded.

"So give them a call. Ask if everything's alright."

Duquoin didn't answer. He rubbed his forehead in both hands then scratched the dog's back. Karen was becoming impatient, when Duquoin looked up as if he were going to say something, but he hesitated and stared out at the lake for a while. Finally, he said, "Already did."

A wave or relief swept over Karen, "And?"

"No answer."

She felt as if the wind had been knocked out of her, and whatever doubts she'd had about going up there evaporated. She put her hand on Duquoin's arm and when he looked up into her eyes she said, "Mr. Duquoin, we both know something bad happened on that last trip. And we both know it can happen again."

Duquoin started to pet the dog-wolf on its rump again, his eyes fixed on the lake.

"It's Jake, isn't it? You're afraid of him," she said.

"Maybe it's not me that should be afraid."

Karen bristled. "I can take care of myself."

"I'm sure you do all right in Washington. But this ain't Washington." Duquoin patted the steps near him and called, "Lu." The dog snapped its head up off Karen's lap, turned and wriggled his way over to Duquoin without getting up, laying his big head on the man's lap and turning its rump to Karen. Duquoin took the animal's snout in his hand and peeled back its lips, revealing a set of large canines. "You see this? This animal is not like other dogs. He can bite with more force than even the baddest Pit Bull. Why? 'Cause he's wild. He has the soul of a wolf in him. I love him, but I respect that part of him. Follow?"

Karen nodded.

"That's how I feel about Jake. An that's another reason why I won't take you."

Karen petted the dog's rump for a few minutes and sipped her coffee. Then she spoke. "I had lunch with Baker yesterday."

"Good man. He told me you'd be by."

"Do you remember what you said to him after Jake's last trip?"

Duquoin frowned, then stood up with his back to Karen. When he spoke, his voice was quiet. "Those were bad times. I was upset. I said a lot of things. Too many to remember."

"Let me refresh your memory. You said 'You whites. You give an Indian fire water and laugh because he can't handle it. Yet it is just so with the knowledge of the Shaman. The white man cannot handle it. He becomes intoxicated with it, and in the end, just as with all his passions, it consumes him.'"

"Jus talk, Miss. Nothin' but talk."

"I don't think so. I think you knew something. And I think you know it now."

Duquoin turned to face her. "Listen. If things has gone bad up there – an I'm not sayin' they have – then there's nothin' you can do. There's nothin' any one can do."

"I can get those people out of there," Karen said.

"Not if Jake don't want you to."

"I'm not afraid of him, Duquoin. And I don't know about this Shaman stuff. But I do know this: if people die up there again and we could have stopped it but we didn't, then none of us is going to sleep very well for a long time to come."

Duquoin, who was still standing, turned his back on Karen again. After a moment, she heard just one word, "Shiiit." Duquoin said it as if it had several syllables, as if it were a surrender. He turned around slowly, "There's nothin' you can do. Nothin."

"You just get me up there. Then we'll see."

"Like as not you'll end up dead."

"Maybe. But that's my problem, not yours."

He ran his hand through his hair and looked down at the dock and sighed. "Alright. I'll take you. But you'll have to sign a waiver and cover my fee. In advance."

"Fine. How soon can we leave?"

"Not for a couple of days."

"Why wait?"

"I'm booked. And I wouldn't be in such a hurry if I were you. While you waitin' you might want to say goodbye to your friends and loved ones and get your affairs in order."

CHAPTER 41

Pete watched Jake approach. In silhouette, the figure seemed to grow as it neared, and Pete braced himself for the inevitable. How would he do it? A broken neck? Pete imagined himself lying next to Thom, his head dangling from his body as if he were being disassembled. Just a few more steps. Pete decided then, that he would put up a fight. Make him pay. Leave a mark.

Jake had been speaking as he approached. "I am sorry, Peter, but you must see I have no choice." Jake felt his neck and hesitated.

"Forget your necklace, Jake? Too bad. Can't have me lying here with a broken neck and no claw marks. But then one look at Thom and the coroner will already know."

"You're very confused, Peter. I have to stop you from panicking the others. It'll be alright. Trust me."

He was coming very slowly, as if he were worried. And the talking, why? Then Pete felt the spear by his side, and he knew. Jake was unarmed. He'd been too confident. Pete raised his spear, but even in the dark, Jake saw it and kicked it out of his hand before Pete could position it. He moved cat-like, with speed and precision. Pete shouted and scrambled after it, and managed somehow to find it in the blackness, before the blow came. He lay in the dark, clutching the spear, his face buried in the leaves and needles covering the forest floor – its smell pungent, fetid, and fertile, the smell of life and death and in the seconds before the blow came, he felt a moment of hope. Because Jake couldn't kill him without the necklace.

He decided to lay there and wait. If he attacks my back, I'll spin over and spear him after he delivers the blow, as his arm arches over his shoulder and leaves his belly exposed. If he flips me over, I'll have a shot at planting it into his side. His plan formulated, he lay there ready, waiting for the inevitable.

But it didn't come. Why? Then he heard it. Jake had evidently heard it before him. The sound of people crashing through the brush, and voices, off about fifty feet down the trail.

"I heard a scream. Right up here." It was Bill.

"Hullooo." Ben.

Jake hollered down, "Up here. Careful, he seems a little distraught." He smiled at Pete and backed off silently onto the trail, as the two crashed through the forest toward them. "Watch it, he's sitting back there next to Thom's body brandishing his spear. Seems very anxious. I went in to have a look and he threatened me."

Ben had arrived at the trail and stood next to Jake. "Thank god you found him, Jake."

"Yeah, but he's upset. He trusts you. Have a talk with him, will you? But be careful."

Pete was still trying to sort through what had just happened. He was still prepared for the fight. Still locked in a chemical frenzy designed to make him act without thought, and he listened to Jake in disbelief. He sounded so reasonable, so compassionate. Pete knew he had to be just as calm; just as convincing, but he was afraid to speak, afraid the emotions would pour out making him sound … mad. So he said nothing.

Ben leaned in, peering through the dark. "Pete?"

"He's lying, Ben." It sounded desperate. He tried again. "He's not what he seems." But it wasn't much better.

"It's all right, Pete. It's going to be all right."

"It's Thom. He's here. They killed him."

Bill had come up trail and he stood with Jake, listening. Ben, asked gently, "They?"

Pete heard Jake whisper to Bill, "He's been like this since I found him. Shock I think."

Pete tried to think. Tried to fathom what he could say that would make him sound as reasonable as Jake. Ben was closer now, but he moved as you might around a mad dog. "It's going to be alright, Pete. I want you to get up and come with us. It's going to be alright."

But Pete didn't move. He sat by the mound, clutching his spear, trying desperately to make himself calm, and realizing that the harder he tried, the more difficult it was. How did Jake do it? He tried again, willing his voice to be measured and reasonable. "Ask him why a bear would stash his kill near the wolves' den. Ask him that, will you Ben?"

"Come on, Pete. Just let it go ..."

"Ask him," he screamed.

"Pete, it was Jake who insisted we put out a search party."

"Just ask him goddamnit. For the love of god ask him." He shouted as he spun on his old friend, holding his spear. Ben jumped back, and Pete knew he was in trouble. He'd blown it. He put the spear immediately down, and continued, his voice quieter, but each word came out as if strained through a filter – tight, distinct and flat. The sound of a madman Pete thought as he listened to himself. "The ...bear...wouldn't...bury... his...kill... here, Ben. Not...here. That means it was faked, and planted here so we wouldn't find it. And if this one was faked, Thom was right about the other ones. Don't you see that?" He was nearly crying and he could feel the desperation in his voice.

Hesitantly, Ben turned to Jake. "What about it, Jake?"

Jake just shrugged. "A bore the size of the one we're facing might've buried him here, wolves or no wolves."

Ben turned to Pete, "See? It's alright, Pete." He came in close, now, and put one hand on the spear, and the other on Pete's shoulder, "You have to let us take you back. It's freezing out her. We can talk when we get there. OK?"

Pete shoved his hand off his shoulder and stood up. "Ask him about the blood. There's not enough blood."

Ben turned to Jake. He sounded angry when he answered. "Look, we have to get out of here. If that bear comes back, we're in danger."

But Bill interrupted, "What about the blood, Jake."

In the dark, Pete could feel Jake's anger and for a moment he was afraid for Bill. After locking eyes for too long, Jake said, "How do I know? Maybe he licked it off, maybe the cold stopped the bleeding. Now come on. Let's get him back."

Ben gave Pete a reassuring pat and said, "Let's go," then escorted him out onto the trail. Through the dark, he thought he could see Jake smiling at him, and he forgot his fear. "Your arrogance is going to be your undoing, Christianson."

Jake put his hand on his shoulder, and smiled. He was the picture of compassion. "You've been through a lot, Pete. You have to let us help you. After supper we'll have a long talk. Just you and I."

"We don't have anything more to say to each other, Christianson. I'm through listening to you." Pete thought briefly about putting his spear right through Jake, and ending it there and then. But of course, the others wouldn't understand. They wouldn't know. And they had to know. So he didn't.

On the way back, Pete walked near Ben. They said little, but at one point, Pete leaned close to him and said, "Don't let him be alone with me."

"Pete."

"*Promise* me that. As my friend."

"Don't worry, Pete."

Pete's mind raced as they walked back. He had to figure a way to make them believe him. Funny after all these years, here he was again – trying desperately to convince people that he was OK. He remembered pleading with the doctors – telling them that he was fine. And before that, with his father. *Nothing I could do*. But he'd answered with the same skepticism as Ben was showing now. Even the doctors, who spoke with soothing voices, seemed not to really listen to him. 'What happened was terrible, Pete. But it doesn't have to ruin your life. You can go on. But you won't get better until you accept it...." He'd tried to. But he couldn't. Terrible? They didn't know the meaning of the word. And now, here he was again, trying to convince people that he was sane, not sure himself that he was. But they had to leave. That was what he had to remember; that was what he had to convince them of.

Clio was ready. So was Bill. He might even convince Ben. Although by now Ben no doubt thinks me a madman. But even if he convinced them, they didn't understand the danger they faced. They didn't know that even if they chose to walk out, they confronted much more than a bear. But in the end, he decided he had to get them to leave. Once they were free of Jake's influence, maybe he could convince them. And until then, he'd just have to protect them somehow. Because he knew now, that Jake would come after them.

Pete ate in silence. The others had eaten already, but they gathered around the fire hoping for news of the bear. They'd snagged a hare and a marmot, and someone had gathered some young cattail shoots, still green and tender this early in the spring. It was the first food they'd had in a day, and Pete knew the others had fought off their growing hunger to save him some, but he just toyed with it. Ben, true to his word, stayed close, but they didn't talk. Several times Jake spoke to the group, but Pete shut him out entirely. It was easy. He just thought of Thom, and that neck, and the velvet voice seemed to take on a sharpness he hadn't noticed before. But the others were listening. They didn't hear the edges that Pete heard. He could see them slipping. He watched as they silently nodded their accord; he watched as they slipped beneath the spell.

Pete knew he had to stop him. He got up and took a step toward the fire, turned and faced outward and spread his arms out like wings. He knew what he had to do. Slowly, the others turned their heads from Jake's siren song and watched as Pete stood there in the firelight, his arms outstretched as if he were on a cross, waiting, silently. Finally, when all attention had turned to Pete, Jake stopped. "What is it Andersen?" he snapped.

"You interrupted a vote. It's time we finished it. But before we do I have something to say."

"Not now, Andersen, I'm speaking."

"If I waited for you to finish talking, the trip would be over." Jake looked shocked, and Clio laughed. A few others chuckled, but then they looked at Pete strangely. "And we'd be dead." Their faces turned serious. "So I *am* going to have my say. And you *are* going to listen, for a change." Pete continued quickly, before Jake could recover. "Tomorrow, I'm leaving. Regardless of the vote. And if the trend continues, that means I'll be killed tonight."

"That's enough, Andersen."

"No. It's not. Are you afraid to let them hear me, Jake? What is it you are so afraid of? I think I know." Pete turned to the group. He had to just dance to the edge of accusing Jake, without doing it. They would have to do that for themselves. "You see, this is a very selective bear. He only kills people who say they're going to leave. Have you noticed that? He is a very selective and intelligent bear. It's almost like he's listening to us ... So when I say I am leaving tomorrow, I'm taking a big risk. Do you know why I'm willing to do that?"

Jake had come to his feet and was walking toward Pete. "I *said* that's enough, Andersen." He stood before him now, seeming to tower over him, menacing.

Pete stared back at him, defiant. "Why is it enough, Jake? Is there something you don't want them to hear? Like how the others died?"

"Silence," Jake thundered.

"Or maybe how it's time to return the garden to its rightful owners ..."

"I said shut up." Jake raised his arm and was ready to hit Pete, to sweep him away like a fly, but he stopped. As he looked around, the others were staring at him. He turned back to Pete, dropped his arm and brought his face right up to Pete's so that it was all that Pete could see, then whispered, "Very good, Peter. Very good. But you know what this means, don't you?"

"We'll see. We'll see."

"It's not too late, Peter. You can still join me."

"Hey. What are you two whispering about?" It was Clio.

"Never."

"Never is a very long time, Peter. We shall see, indeed."

"Hey. Knock it off. Let us hear."

Jake stood aside, "I believe you have the floor, Mr. Andersen."

Pete knew his only chance was to shake their confidence in Jake, without accusing him of anything. Otherwise Jake would have no choice but to intercede. If he caused a confrontation now, it would be Jim and Jake against the rest of them. Sarah and Rita might even side with Jake. Either way, it would likely go badly. Pete knew that Jake intended to kill them, but if he didn't accuse Jake of murder, they might buy some time. At least then he had a chance of getting them out. If he could convince them to leave. He walked outside the group, into the shadows and began.

"Last night we slept with no fire and no guard. And we are told there is a man-eating bear out there. A man died as a result. A man who said he wanted to leave, just as the others did before they died, just as I have said tonight. Thom was convinced there was foul play. That there was no bear. That something has gone horribly wrong. I say it doesn't matter. Foul play or not, we are dying. We have no radio. Our leader seems powerless to stop it – indeed he stands accused of disabling the radio to keep us on some Quixotic quest, long after it has ceased to make sense. This trip *has* gone horribly wrong. There is no shame in ending it. Only wisdom."

"Now, I know you are walking in a fog. You are struggling to regain that sense of self that makes you, you. I have felt it too. But there is a voice within each of you saying 'Wait. Something is wrong here. Something is terribly, terribly wrong.' " Now Pete's voice lowered to a whisper, yet he could be heard by all of them, "Listen to that voice. Fight that fog. Find your anger, find your passion. And fight it." Pete turned now and walked near to Jake and pointing to him said, "Because it is him. He controls us somehow." Then he stopped short. Jake was smiling at him, beaming in that same proud paternal way he had on the airplane. And as he looked at Jake, he saw his own fire lit image reflected in the man's eyes, and he saw the dreadful truth.

But he had to go on anyway. "So before you vote, look within you to that place no one else can touch. Then ask yourself what you are doing out here. Ask yourself what you want to do. Once you know, do what *you* want to do, not what *he* wants you to do."

Jake put his hand on Pete's shoulder and whispered, "You've learned well. Very well. I'm pleased."

Pete locked eyes with him, trying to read him, trying to understand whether it was true. Then he took his hand off his shoulder and said, "I'm through with your games, Christianson." Turning to the others he said, "Let's vote. Anyone who wants to go with me, raise your hand."

"Just a moment, Peter. I let you have your say, now let me have mine. I know we've already talked about this, but what we're deciding here is important. More important than you could possibly understand. Eleven weeks ago, you all answered an ad. You were in search of something. You didn't know what it was then, but you do now. It was something of the divine. It dwells in each of you. You are nearly ready to take it for your own. Don't squander this opportunity to find it. Such moments are not offered to all."

Jake turned to Pete and continued speaking, "Before you decide to follow my good friend Peter, there are some things you should know about him. Did you know that twenty-four years ago, he stood by and watched his brother get beaten to death? Or that he spent months in an institution? Did you know they strapped him down and zapped his brain with five hundred volts in an attempt to get him right? Do you know that he still hears the screams? Still shudders at the silence? Do you know that he still wakes sweating in the middle of the night?"

Jake draped his arm over Pete's shoulder affectionately, then said, "Is this the man you want to lead you out of here? The man who's been running from his past all his adult life? Running out on things is his specialty. Hiding is his specialty. He needs to stay here and face this more than any of you. But you all do. Each of you do, for your own reason. That is why you are here. That is why you must stay."

Pete's head was reeling. Before he could recover, he screamed, "It wasn't my fault. There was nothing I could do."

"Come now, Pete. You know you will never get better until you accept what you've done. Isn't that what the doctors told you?"

Pete said nothing. He saw the others staring at him, accusingly, just as they had in school. Expunged records? No, this would never be expunged. Not until he could face it. Maybe Jake was right. Maybe he needed to be here.

Jake continued to talk, his voice wafting over them like a tide, and Pete felt the pull again. There was a part of him that watched even as he slipped slowly, inevitably under Jake's spell, but he could hear Gus's moans again, and he feel the knife piercing his clothes, the steel cold and hard against his back, feel the fear again, rising like bile through his soul. But another part of him felt rage, white hot and primitive, and Pete struggled to hold onto it.

The others were looking now from Jake to Pete. He saw hope in some of their eyes, fear in others, suspicion in some. And he saw that they were slipping into Jake's world as he continued to seduce them with this Eden; this place where they could transcend.

He remembered Keller, racing down the mountainside, hurtling through the camp, desperate, afraid, and Pete imagined him, knowing that he was literally drowning in the massive ego that was Jake, running headlong from it with all the frenzied, thrashing, flailing urgency of a drowning man. Keller'd known he couldn't hold out. And if a man like Keller couldn't, what hope did he have. What hope did little Petey have, still hiding from the shadows, all these years later. And then he understood. In a way, Jake was right. He did have a shot at redemption. But it lay in fighting this feeling. It lay in getting these others out. It lay in facing Jake.

"What Jake is telling you isn't the whole truth. We all have our own devils, our own ghosts that we run from. I've only just begun to understand that you can't run from them. The only way you can escape them is to run *to* something, not *from* something." Pete touched Karen's medallion unconsciously, then continued, "Jake uses our weaknesses like handles. He picks us up and shakes us by them. But in the end it doesn't matter what you are running from – it only matters what you are running toward." He turned to Clio, "Do your boys need you to be risking your life out here?" Then to Bill, "Will you erase the scars you saw inflicted on your father by staying out here? Will you erase the shame you feel because you've been able to carry your blackness with pride, and that pride came at the price of his anger, his pain, his dignity?" Then to Ben, "Will your grandchildren's world be somehow better because you died out here facing a bear that may not exist? Will you somehow escape the fact that you missed your own children's youth, or that you feel like you killed your wife because you were chasing money?" He continued to address each of them, seeing the hidden places in their souls, and exposing them.

Pete walked around the circle, placing himself in the glow of the fire as he looked at each of them in turn. Then he spoke again, marveling at the power of his own voice. "Each of us have secrets, each of us have things we are ashamed of, things we regret." Again, he swept the circle with his gaze, like a lighthouse piercing a storm-ravaged sea, then he said, "Staying out here and getting picked off one-by-one isn't going to ease that shame or wipe away those regrets." Pete looked the group over one last time, then said, "I leave tomorrow. I know what I'm going toward. Anyone who wants to can join me."

CHAPTER 42

After Pete's speech at the fire, he'd gone to his shelter. Several of them had looked at him as he'd spoken with – what? Curiosity? No. Confusion. Skepticism. And something else. Something like pity, almost. But pity mingled with fear. Something like the way you would regard a madman, he realized. He did sound mad, he knew. And the terrible aspect of this was that he couldn't say for sure that he wasn't. What if all this was just another descent into that pit? What if, once again, he could no longer trust his thoughts? He sat there, trying desperately to tease out the truth; to know the real.

He reviewed the past week with growing dread. The moments of cloudiness, when he couldn't think. Periods he couldn't remember. And times that stood out clearly, but which rang false, like an off key note – flat, and dissonant. There was the wolf. Communing with him. That couldn't be. And the increasingly paranoid thoughts about Jake. And the looks. From Ben and the others. Only Ruth seemed to regard him as reliable. As sane. Perhaps it started with the wolf that first time, on the hunt, when he'd stared at it and ... what ... talked to it? Absurd, obviously. Now, as he sat here, he wasn't even sure he could say for certain that there had been a wolf there. All the while, Jake's voice played over and over again, *He needs to stay out here ...*

"Pete?" He felt a hand on his shoulder. "Pete. Are you all right?"

He turned slowly to see Ben looking at him, the bushy eyebrows hovering somewhere between doubt and concern. He realized dimly that his friend had been there for some time, trying to talk to him, before he'd resorted to shaking his shoulder. Another sign. But no. There was Ruth. The radio. And Thom. And the things Jake had said to him back there at the mound. No. I am OK. He almost managed to convince himself. He would have, but for what Ben would tell him.

"Pete. Answer me. Are you OK?"

Pete struggled to sound sane. "I'm fine, Ben. He's the one that's mad."

"Pete, stop."

"Why else would he keep us here?"

"He's not."

"What?" Pete struggled again. What Ben was saying made no sense.

"He's not keeping us here. That's what I was trying to tell you last night. He wants us to stay, sure. And he'll continue to try to convince us. That's who he is. But while you were missing, he told me he would go to Cold Fish and call Duquoin if that's what we want. He just told me he's leaving tomorrow."

"Why is he going. If there's a bear why doesn't he stay and send you and me."

"I asked him that. He says he can cover the ground in less than three days. And he thinks the bear will follow him."

Pete thought about his speech. Thought about Jake telling the others of his secret. Thought about the looks he was getting and then he knew. If Jake were going to help, then none of this made sense. Nothing. "If you all knew, how could you let me go on like that?"

"Only Jim and I knew. Jake wanted to try to convince the others to stay one more time."

"He's just conning you."

"No. He's already made all the necessary preparations."

There is perhaps no more explicitly sane moment than that instant when you realize you are insane. For embodied in that time is a clear image of what sanity is, and the measure of the gulf between it and your current state. With the clarity comes the inescapably horrible knowledge that you cannot trust what you see, what you know, what you are. It was a moment Pete had faced once before – one he thought he'd left behind. But now he knew he'd never be shut if it. He said nothing, but he felt tears running down his cheeks as he gazed out toward the lake, a prisoner of his own madness.

After a moment Ben said, "Pete, I know this is hard. My sister married a man who had PTS. You can be helped. There's medication.

And therapy. But you can't trust yourself right now, and that's very up-setting."

Ben's hand was on his shoulder. It was comforting, and Pete was grateful that he was there. He was flooded with a mix of other emotions. Embarrassment; a sense of relief that he didn't have to take on the burden of saving them from – but he didn't want to go there again. But mostly, he felt an overwhelming fear that he would never be able to trust himself. And he could never let Karen marry him. But from somewhere in his core a voice spoke to him, soft, seductive. "He's in on it," it said. "Don't trust him." Pete shook his head, "No," he mumbled. "No more."

Ben stared at him, confused for a moment, then he said, "Yes. They can."

"What?" Pete asked.

Ben looked at him strangely, and in the reflection of his look Pete saw himself, and it frightened him. "They can help you. I promise."

And Pete wanted that help. Wanted it now, as he had never wanted anything. Wanted to stop that swirling dizzying doubt permeating his mind, draining his soul.

The next morning, Jake came by Pete's shelter early and woke him. Pete had found his madness liberating, and he'd slept well, free of that sense of responsibility that had been hounding him for the past week. Free of the dreams. He'd felt someone shaking his ankle gently, and he woke fighting the sleep that draped his consciousness. When he sat up, Jake spoke quietly.

"I'm sorry it has to end this way, Peter."

Pete tried to wipe the sleep away. There seemed to be genuine re-morse in Jake's eyes and in his voice. Pete looked out at the lake, saw the mists rising off it and creeping up the valleys onto the hillsides, against the growing greenness of spring. It was going to be a beautiful day. "So am I, Jake. But it's for the best."

"Are you sure about that, Peter? Because I need to be sure. It is such a drastic step, I need to be sure."

What's he talking about? Leaving here isn't the end of the world. And where was this doubt coming from? Jake never had doubt. Well, whatever he was looking for, Pete didn't have it. He was out of the hero business. He was out of the confrontation business. Redemption lay in acceptance. Accepting madness with grace and optimism. That was the best he could do. Yet he looked at this man before him, so powerful, so sure, who a day ago he believed to be a murderer – no, not a murderer exactly, but an executioner of his own codes – and saw an inner doubt and a pain and a plea for approval that he'd never betrayed before. Was this what Ruth had seen? Jake crouched before him as a child, seeking what? Absolution? Pete didn't know. Whatever it was, he didn't have it anymore. If he ever had.

"I'm not sure of anything, Jake."

Jake looked surprised. "Really, Peter? Doubt at last. Too late, it seems. And at too high a cost with the others. They do believe you're mad, Peter. But you have been persuasive even in your madness." Jake sat down at the entrance to Pete's shelter and looked out at the mist-covered lake, which lay before them like a cloud descended from heaven, thick and white and puffy. "Beautiful, isn't it?"

"Mmmm," Pete mumbled in reply.

"Do you have any idea how intricate, how complex, how delicate this all is?" He didn't wait for an answer. "But of course you do. That's why I picked you. Humanity was to have been the crowning achievement. Such a curious race you proved to be. Such poor stewards, destroying it all even as you began to uncover the truth about its exquisite delicacy."

He sat quietly for a time, then said, "I did try, Peter. God knows I tried. I started with the scientists. Keepers of the knowledge – the rightful high priests of this age. But instead of sounding an alarm, they turned the grail over to politicians and economists and spoke in hushed tones about scientific uncertainty, and the need to be 'economically responsible.' Fools. Like the Captain of the Titanic waiting for the ship to sound before announcing there might be trouble. Fools and wimps. They've known for decades that we're altering our climate and that every living system is in decline. But they were afraid of being branded as 'alarmist'. And as they cringed in their labs, waiting for conclusive proof, your people drifted into the range of the irrevocable.

"And the environmentalists," Jake continued. "God knows what they were doing. 'I'm sorry Mr. Christianson, but we must avoid doom and gloom. We can't be seen as negative ... We need to talk in terms of solutions and good news stories. We can't turn people off...' Fools. As if people would flock to solutions for problems they didn't see. It was as if they stood in a theater, saw a fire, and refused to yell a warning until they knew where all the fire extinguishers were, because they didn't want to ruin the show. And we know what the show was, don't we Peter?"

Pete didn't answer. A single phrase was ringing over and over in his head ... '*It's such a drastic step.*' What could it mean?

"Tell me what the show was, Peter. It would help me very much to do what I must do to hear you say it. Say it. Please?"

Hearing the plea in Jake's voice brought Pete back. It sounded almost foreign coming from him. Pete flipped through Jake's meanderings the way a reader goes over pages he's already read, finding his place, then answered, "The show? That we could have an infinitely growing economy in a finite world."

Jake smiled. "Yes. It's so simple, really. So very simple. So simple that you could only have ignored it because you'd been blinded by greed." He looked out over the lake again, letting the silence between them expand, before saying, 'I did try. We tried, Peter. Government was the last resort. Big, ponderous, lurching bureaucracies. I thought we'd made it. Even after squandering eight years, I thought we had a chance to undo all the evil they'd done. But I've come to understand there is within you a fundamental flaw. A species destined for insanity. The very thing which makes you nearly divine, is that which makes you dangerous. Intelligence enabled you to step outside of the evolutionary crucible – to override the wisdom hardwired into all other life. In the end, allowing you to approach divinity without obtaining it was an evolutionary mistake. One that will be righted."

Jake seemed lighter in spirit to Pete. He stood up and stretched. "Thank you Peter. And now I am off to do what I must. I am truly sorry it's turned out this way. You and I could have been friends." Jake stared out at the lake for a while, then said, "I've never really had a friend. I think it would've been nice."

PART THREE:

SURVIVE

There will come a time when a terrible beast emerges among you: pale, lean, cunning; but soulless, insatiable and all consuming. You will look to Saya to save you and He will be gone.

The Last Words of Lynx to the Real People

CHAPTER 43

Ben seemed to be in a race against the night, Pete thought. As darkness closed, he set about a frenzy of activity, getting folks started on scrounging up a dinner of some sort, setting up a guard schedule, assuring there was enough wood to last the night, distributing the spears. He left Pete out of just about everything, and for the most part, Pete didn't care. But he kept his spear when Ben came for it. Now, as the evening closed in, Pete wandered down to the lake. He was feeling much better. Or more precisely, he was not feeling, which was much better. The others had avoided him throughout the day. Even Ruth, who'd passed his shelter several times earlier, was unwilling – or unable – to so much as glance at him.

Not thinking, just giving in to that nearly blissful state of lassitude that his madness afforded him was almost pleasant. If you can't tell the difference between what is real and what isn't, then nothing can be demanded of you. And you can't demand anything of your self. Now, he could finally put down the weight of responsibility that he'd carried for the past week, dragging it around as if he were pulling it upstream, against a rip current. And in less than a week, Duquoin would touch down on the lake, and this whole thing would be over. And he could get some help. And yet as he looked out across the lake, golden now in the last minutes of daylight, he realized that a part of him would miss this. But Jake had been right: nature was both sublime and terrible. He would miss her sublimity. And somehow, he knew he would have to do something to save these sacred places so that others might also know her in this intimate way, and knowing her, work to save her. It is what Lynx would want. It is what Saya would want.

He tried to imagine being back in that other world. That world of cellulose, and plastic and metal and arbitrary deadlines: deadlines made for no other reason than that we needed them. What would he do? Certainly EPA was out of the question. He would never again be able to sit in a meeting listening to a policy wonk spew out one of those lopsided arguments about the costs and benefits of stopping global warming, explaining why the models said we couldn't afford to halt it, as a bevy of senior managers nodded sagely; grateful for the excuse of avoiding action and the simultaneous release from responsibility. Just like madness, Pete thought. After all, if the economists and their models said it cost too much, then what were they to do? Their hands were tied. No. There was no way he could endure one of those self -serving scenes of collective sophistry. He'd have to jump up and throttle the wonk. Literally knock some sense into him, and into those who listened to him. That wouldn't look too good to his therapist.

And then there was Karen. He clutched the medallion, and shook his head.

As he sat there, trying to adjust to his new status – the status of the madman – the one that left him outside of the world he'd known, unable to trust it and untrusted by it, he heard a noise in back of him. He grabbed his spear and whirled to face it, surprised at his speed and agility and more by his clarity of purpose.

As he turned, he expected to see Jake, necklace off and wrapped tightly around his fist, ready to ... But it wasn't Jake, and even before he saw her, he was telling himself that he had to stop, that it was all a delusion. And yet as he stood there facing a very frightened Rita, he half remembered that phrase Jake had used earlier. It played there at the edges of his consciousness, a silent warning, telling him he was all right. But he couldn't trust these things.

"I'm sorry, I'll leave," she said, retreating quickly, her eyes averted, but still betraying that look; the one that diagnosed him, certified him as dangerous, scary, mad. A look that told him he was one with those poor wandering muttering people with shopping carts.

Pete dropped the spear. He wanted her to stay. To see that he wasn't dangerous, and in seeing it, convince him of it also. "No. Wait. It's all right. You just startled me." He gestured to the other rock, the one he'd shared with Ben on that first night. It seemed so long ago now. "Please."

She came forward reluctantly, and sat, but she seemed jumpy.

When she was seated, Pete sat down and turned to her. "You wanted to talk to me?"

"Yes."

"What is it?"

"Never mind. It doesn't really matter." Pete could tell she was trying to figure a graceful, and safe, way to get back up that hill, away from him.

"Rita, you wanted something from me when you came down here. If I can give it to you, I will. And stop looking so worried. I may be crazy, but I'm not dangerous." And then for the first time in what seemed a very long time, he smiled, not some forced social nicety, but a real, soul-inspired smile and he could see as she smiled back, that it tempered her fears.

She adjusted herself on the rock, making herself more comfortable. She hesitated a moment, then plunged in, "Last night when you spoke? You were like him."

He looked at her blankly, not understanding.

"You did that same thing he does."

He struggled to remember what it was she was talking about. Could it have been his little speech at the end; the one where they'd looked at him in that way? "I'm not sure what you mean."

"You made me see through your eyes. You ... I don't know. It was like you were taking me over."

"Look, Rita. We've been thrown into a very intense experience. We're hungry, we're sleep deprived. We're dirty and smelly and I, for one, itch all over. I suspect we're all a little vulnerable to suggestions right now." He reached out and put a reassuring hand on her shoulder and looked straight into her eyes before continuing, "We're going to get out of here. But you're going to make some changes when you get back. Right?"

She nodded and looked down. "Yeah. I've been thinking a lot about getting a new line of work."

"No. Don't. You're one of the best. In a Darth Vader kind of way. Keep your job, but get a new client."

"Who?"

"How about the Earth? I understand she's looking for a good lobbyist."

"How's it pay?" she asked.

"Pretty good. Sleep-filled nights. Clean conscience," Pete gestured at the vista before them. Across the lake, a loon called, lonely and haunting and it drifted through the mists to where they sat. Pete watched as she stared out toward the call. "And a thousand moments like this."

"Funny. A couple of weeks ago, I would have laughed at you for saying something like that." She chucked a rock into the lake, and watched the rings disappear into the night. When the lake was still again, she turned and said, "Now it makes sense."

"It's this place. It kind of works on you. Makes you see what's real, and what's BS."

"Except poor Dan. He never did get what Jake was trying to do," she said.

And now he's dead, he thought. Again, the alarms went off, and the phrase that Jake had used, the one that had been bobbing around at some subliminal level, popped into his head. *'It's such a drastic step, I need to be sure.'* And he knew then, what Jake had been seeking absolution from. And he knew, too, that he couldn't hide here in the seductive velvet safety of madness, even if he were mad. He had to act. Besides, there was one person who could confirm everything. Or deny it. Then he'd know for sure. He stood up abruptly. "There's something I need to do up there." He reached out his hand to her and she took it. He pulled her to her feet but held her hand a moment more and said, "If you really want to change teams if we get back, I can help."

"If we get back?"

"Yeah. I don't want to talk about it right now. But whether you think I'm crazy or not, I need your help if we're going to get out of here."

"You're sane, Peter. Those fogs you talked about? I felt them, too. So have the others."

"If only sanity were a vote."

"Out here, it just might be."

OK, he thought, maybe it's time to tell her what he was thinking, "Jake's not going to let us leave."

She withdrew her hand and stepped back. He didn't blame her. In two minutes he'd gone from a spear-wielding paranoid to their savior. Probably am crazy he thought, but who gives a fuck. I'm going to get us out of here. He took her hand again, and stepped closer, looking into her eyes until he saw measure of calmness in them. "I need you to trust me. We can't rely on Jake. We've got to get out of here on our own." She looked away, but he took her chin, and gently raised her face. "It'll be OK, Rita, but we have to take charge." He could see her wavering. "You know I'm right. Do I have your vote?" They stood like that for several moments, and finally she nodded. "Good. Don't say anything to anyone about this. Especially Jim. OK?"

"Yeah."

Now he had to get the others on board. He went straight to Ruth's shelter. He ducked inside and was surprised to see Ben there. The two stopped talking as soon as they saw him. He could just barely see their faces in the faint glow the fire cast on the interior of her shelter, but he couldn't make out their expressions.

"I need to talk to you, Ruth. Now."

She looked to Ben, then answered hesitantly, "Sure, Peter. Go ahead."

"Out here, where I can see your face." His voice was calm, but commanding and she got up immediately.

Ben put a hand on her arm and said to Pete, "She's upset. She doesn't need this."

"None of us do, Ben. But here we are. You come too. I want you to hear this."

"Just hang on Peter. You can't go around ordering ..."

"Shut up and listen."

He started to object, but Pete shot him a glance and he stopped. Pete took Ruth's arm and escorted her to his shelter and Ben followed. He sat her down in front of it, so that she faced the lake, her back to the fire, then directed Ben to sit beside her. He sat down opposite her, silhouetted against the last of the evening's light, his eyes drinking in the flames and reflecting them back, much the way Lynx must have looked on that last night, he thought. When they were comfortable he took Ruth's hand in his, and peered into her eyes. She looked down, averting her gaze, but he called her name softly, and waited until she looked straight into his eyes.

"Tell us about the battery."

Her mouth began to quiver, and her eyes filled with tears, but she didn't answer

Ben made a move to intervene, but Pete froze him with a glance. "Tell us." He said it gently this time, almost whispering. Then he put his forehead against hers and held her behind her head and said softly, "People will die if they don't know the truth, Ruth. You know that."

"They'll die anyway," she said, barely audible.

But Ben heard. "What do you mean?"

Ruth said nothing, and Ben pressed her. "Why will they die anyway?"

When she didn't answer, Ben turned from her to Pete and back again. "You mean it's true?"

Ruth nodded. Ben turned to Pete and said, "Then ... you're not ..."

"Crazy? Maybe. But I may be our only hope, anyway."

Ben put his hand on Pete's arm and said, "I'm sorry."

"It's OK."

"No. It's not. I should have listened to you."

"Don't worry about it. On the whole, I think I preferred insanity."

"What do we do now?"

"How long has Jake been gone?"

"Close to a day, now."

"We've got to get the hell out of here. And we can't raise Jim's suspicions."

"Jim?"

"I think he's a part of this."

"Where do we go?"

"Cold Fish."

"But that's where Jake's going."

Pete just shook his head.

"What about Duquoin?"

Ruth looked up. "Duquoin's not coming, Ben. And I don't think Jake's going to Cold Fish. He's out there now, somewhere. He probably knows I've told you." She stopped. Pete could see that she was shuddering.

He put his arm around her and said, "I won't let him hurt you. Believe that."

"I want to Peter, but ..."

"Believe it. OK?"

She nodded yes.

He turned to Ben. "I take it he left you in charge."

"Sort of. Habits of an old CEO. I took charge."

"Can you get Jim out of here for a while on some pretext? The longer the better."

"Hang on. Just because Jake pitched the battery doesn't mean he's killed anyone. And what's all this about Jim?"

Pete cut him off, "You've handled uncertainty in business, Ben. If I'm wrong, we take a long, unnecessary trip. If you're wrong we all die. You want to hang around and see who's right?"

Ben thought a moment. "If we stoke up the fire real good, we can say we don't have enough wood to last through the night."

"Good. Can you do that Ruth?"

She nodded and hustled off to the fire. Within seconds, they heard her pitching logs into it.

"What's your plan?" Ben asked.

"The way I see it, we have two choices. Wait here and get picked off one by one, or head toward Cold Fish and get picked off one by one."

"I like the second."

"Yeah. Me, too. If it gets bad, there is one other option."

"What is it?"

"Let's just let that one be for now. I'm not ready to play god. Yet."

CHAPTER 44

The fire was shooting up into the night, its flames seemingly licking the stars. Smoke billowed out and the heat drove everyone back. As Ben and Pete approached, Jim and Bill were shouting at Ruth, who was cringing convincingly. Ben stepped forward, "What's going on here?"

Bill turned. "This fool's put all of the wood on the fire at once."

"I told her to keep it high once dark closed in."

Bill snorted. "High is one thing, but this is ridiculous ..."

"All right. All right. Jim? Can you get some more wood?"

Jim looked back sullenly. Pete held his breath. If he went, he'd be gone for well over an hour – the whole area was picked clean for at least a quarter mile. That should be enough time for a head start, he thought. But two things could screw it up. If he's smart, he's going to ask for company. Pete was banking that his sense of machismo wouldn't let him. But then that same macho bullshit might make him refuse to take orders from Ben.

Finally, he said, "Sure. Give me a spear."

Pete didn't want him to take a spear, but he couldn't think of a reason he shouldn't. Partial victory, he thought. Then a third element came in to play and screwed things up. Bill stepped forward and said, "I'll go with him. We shouldn't let anyone go out there alone."

Pete looked to Ben, but he just shrugged. There was no way to stop him.

"Uh, that's fine, Bill," he said.

As the two disappeared into the night, Ben turned and whispered to Pete, "What now?"

"Obviously we have to wait. We can't leave Bill. I'll just have to deal with Jim when they get back."

"There's no way you can take him, Bud."

"I know. I'm counting on you to help me if it comes to that."

"An old man like me?"

"You're only old when it suits you."

"Hey. You know I'll be there. But even with the two of us, I'm not sure we can take him."

"We can if we have to. But there may be another way."

"You going to explain that?"

"No. You'll see. Call the others around the fire. I want to be ready to leave as soon as they get back."

When they were assembled, Pete looked them over. Sarah, Clio, Rita and Ruth. And Ben. It seemed a small and vulnerable group compared to the even dozen that started out so confidently a week or so ago. Pete readied himself. He knew he'd be working against Jake, even though he'd been gone the day. His presence was still there in each of them. In me, too, he thought. In me more than anyone.

He eyed the fire, noting its dance carefully and moved to where the light would be right, then he stood there quietly. Ben stood next to him, and Pete gently seated him, guiding him wordlessly to a spot to his right. Then he waited. He could feel the flames dancing on his face, alternately flickering it into shadow, and casting it in an eerie orange. Yes, this was it. When all eyes were upon him, he started, stalking back and forth within the area he'd staked out. "I know some of you think me mad," here he smiled, "And you may be right. I think we may all be a little mad at the moment. But it's important that you listen to me. And believe me. It is time to end this trip. If we don't, we are all in danger. We are in danger anyway, but if we can get to Cold Fish, we may get help."

Sarah looked up, "You're not making any sense." Ben stood up, ready to refute her, but Pete put out his hand and stopped him.

"Go ahead, Sarah."

"I suppose you're still going on about Jake. Well, he's headed for Cold Fish. If we're supposed to be afraid of him, then why go there after him?"

"She's right." It was Clio. Pete was nonplused for a moment. He'd expected Clio to support him.

Then Ruth broke in, "No. She's wrong. He's come unhinged. And he's here." Something in her voice chilled each of them.

Pete walked over and put a hand on her shoulder, "No Ruth. He's not unhinged. Dangerous, yes. But it may be us that's unhinged." But then he stopped. Sarah and Clio needed logic and reason, not shades of grey. "Sarah, if you're right, and Jake poses no danger, then following him will be safe. If I'm right, then Jake isn't heading for Cold Fish. He's out there somewhere. Waiting." Pete gestured to the blackness of the forest, beyond the thin wall of light that penetrated feebly into the infinity of darkness, limitless and terrible, now. And he *knew* now that Jake was out there, and since his vision quest he thought he understood why. But enough of this. I must save these people. And even as Pete set about doing that, knowing how to appeal to each one of them, and knowing in some uncanny way what their levers were, a thought plagued him. What if all this were just a part of the madness?

But he ignored that nagging voice and turned to Clio, "So the only dangerous course is staying here. You see that don't you?" He placed his hand on her forearm gently as he spoke, and she nodded, mutely. Then he approached Sarah, squatting down on his haunches in front of her, so they were eye-to-eye. He took both her hands in his and said, "I know you're frightened. Leaving here, going out there on your own without *him* is scary. But don't you see? This is the test you asked for back in February, when you said it all came easy. And I'll help you. I'll make sure you make it. OK?"

Sarah chewed on her lower lip, "Can you do that?" She asked.

Pete responded, believing it at last, "Absolutely."

Ben was staring at him in silent amazement.

"Aren't you forgetting something?" It was Rita.

They all turned to her as one. "What?" Ben asked.

"The bear."

"There is no bear," Ruth snapped back.

But Pete wasn't sure about that. He couldn't see past that forest; he couldn't know what forces were at work. But bear or no bear, he knew their best bet was to move. The sooner the better. "If there's a bear, he may be territorial. Getting out of here is the best thing we can do."

There was no more discussion. He'd convinced them. He gave tasks out. Collecting food. Filling the skins with water. Gathering up the tools and weapons. Rigging up a rawhide kindling bag so they wouldn't have to use one of those damn fire bows. Within minutes they were all at work, preparing to leave as soon as Jim and Bill got back. Pete tried to think what he could do about Jim. There were levers there, too. There had to be, but none came to mind. Within the hour, they were ready. Pete sat and waited. And then he heard it. A scream that rang out of the darkness of the forest and across the ages; a scream of terror and anger and pain. It lasted but a few seconds, but it filled the night and the group sat huddled together, frozen. The wolves heard it, and answered. Without thinking, Pete raced into the darkness, straight toward the sound.

CHAPTER 45

He dashed and dodged through the spruce limbs and brush, swatting them out of his way as he ran, nearly tripping several times over the boulders and brush that covered the forest floor. The screams had stopped after a few seconds, but he still had a fix on where they came from and as he hurtled over rocks and debris, shrugging off the scratches from the overhanging branches, he prayed that he was wrong about its source. As he entered the thick blackness of the forest, he heard the wolves howling in a frenzy. They sounded closer than usual. He was nearing the spot where he thought the screams came from, and he slowed down and began to scan the area. In the dark, he listened carefully, but all he heard were the wolves, and the crashing sound of someone following him through the dense growth. He was hoping it was Ben.

He stopped and tried to hold his breath to hear better. There. Off to the left. A low moaning sound and ragged breathing. He peered into the gloom but he couldn't see anything. Cautiously, he approached the sound until he spotted Bill crumpled on the ground, clutching at his chest. When the wounded man saw him he clawed frantically at the air, beckoning him closer. The crashing sound behind him was louder but Pete squatted down and leaned into Bill, trying to ignore it. He did a silent prayer that it was Ben, and began to attend to Bill. His chest rattled and gurgled with each raspy breath and pink foam was leaking out of the gaping wound. As he inspected it, Bill grabbed him and pulled him nearer, groaning with the pain of the movement, but desperate to say something. Pete leaned in. "It ... was ... Him. He ... did ... this." Behind him, the crashing was about to arrive and Pete readied himself, even as he ripped off Bill's shirt to get to his t-shirt. He would use it to staunch the blood and maybe plug the hole in his lung. But Bill would not stop. "It ... was ... Himm."

"Who?" Ben asked from behind as he arrived. Pete hadn't asked. He knew. "The bear?" Ben asked hopefully.

Bill struggled to answer, but he only made gurgling sounds now. Pete noticed, as he wiped the blood off his chest and tried to patch his lung with his t-shirt, that there was another wound on his neck. It had been ripped out by a powerful swipe, leaving four deep claw marks furrowed into his throat. Pete took the shirt and tried to wrap it around the neck wound, but he could feel the life ebbing from Bill, and he knew there was nothing he could do. As he worked, he was assaulted with Bill's thoughts, felt them as if they entered him from the dying man through his hands as he tended him. He felt the fear, but more the confusion, the profound sense that this had to be some mistake – that they had to step back and see that this could not be. And finally, he felt Bill's cold realization that there was no reprieve, and the deeper, ultimately dreadful question: Why? What had this life been about? And what now?

He had to say something to staunch this profound existential angst, even if he could not stop the blood, but all he could think to say was, "You'll be fine, Bill. Just rest." And he felt the man's life slip away, wondering with Bill as he felt it ebb, where it went.

"Who? Who did this?" It was Ben. The others had arrived and crowded behind him.

At the back of the group, Ruth was crying and moaning, saying over and over, "You said you could protect us."

Pete ignored them, as he tried to stem the onslaught of death he could feel in Bill pour through his hands. When the last of Bill's life force was gone, Pete removed the shirt from the wound, stood up, and faced them. "Be quiet Ruth. Bill died because he made a mistake. From now on, we stay together. Let's get back to the camp. We start for Cold Fish now."

"Was it the bear? Did he say it was the bear?"

"He didn't say. But I don't think so. There's four claw marks."

"We've got to find Jim," Sarah said.

"Who do you think did this?" Pete asked.

Both Clio and Sarah were looking at him with that same skeptical stare they'd used before, but Pete was beyond caring what anyone thought. He no longer had time for doubts about what was happening or who was doing it. He knew only that they had to move. "You can trust me or not. But if you stay, you'll die."

Ben said, "Pete, you sure Jim's involved?"

"Yeah." He continued without waiting for an answer, "We have to get to Cold Fish, and we have to start now." He spun on his heels without saying anything more and headed back toward the camp and the howling wolves. The others hesitated only a few seconds, then followed. Ben caught up and walked by his side for a moment. Pete could feel him studying him, and he anticipated the question. "I'm not sure I can tell you what's going on, Ben. But when we see Jim again – and I'm afraid we will – you'll see he's injured. Bill's right fist was bloody and one of his knuckles was broken."

"I want to believe you."

"You've got to believe me. 'Cause Jim is the least of our problems."

"But what if ..."

"If I'm crazy?"

Ben said nothing.

"If it helps you, go back and look for bear tracks. My guess is you won't find any. Just a big size thirteen shoe print. And there's only two people out here who wear that size."

They walked on as quietly as they could, but it was difficult to be silent in the dark with all the trees and brush. Pete couldn't be sure, but several times he thought he heard something off to their left and slightly behind them – the crackle of dry leaves or the swish of a branch being pushed out of the way. It tracked them, neither gaining nor losing ground. He put them in single file, with Ben at the front, and he took up the back. He did it wordlessly, through gestures, and kept them moving as they formed up. Ruth took up the last slot ahead of him, and he whispered to her, quietly, "Keep going. Stay close. I'll be back here a ways."

In back, he crouched behind some brush and listened as closely as he could. It was hard to hear over the howling of the wolves and the noise from the group but as they pulled away, Pete held his breath and listened. At first he heard nothing, but then he heard the follower, falling into place and padding nearly silently behind Ruth, and he moved as fast as he could through the underbrush to catch up. At about twenty yards away, a dim figure began to take form in the darkness. Creeping closer, he was able to just make out the massive shape of Jim. Whatever injury Bill had inflicted must have been slight; he seemed to be moving well. Too well. And he was carrying a spear. He realized with a start that he'd left his behind.

Pete bent over and felt for a rock, not taking his eye off Jim. He found a good one, a little larger than a baseball, and well-rounded. It fit his hand perfectly. He hurried to close the gap, doing his best to step silently and duck the branches that blocked his passage. His bobbing and weaving took on the elements of a dance, and he was in its rhythm. He'd expected to be afraid, but instead, he felt a power and a strength and an uncanny concentration not unlike what he'd felt after the hunt. He stalked nearer, now closing in on his prey, and soon he could see Ruth and the rest just ahead of Jim. Pete guessed there were ten yards separating the two, and fifteen or so separating him from Jim. Jim was moving in on her steadily, intent in his own stalking, and Pete closed the distance to ten yards. Jim was raising his arm, and Pete readied himself to deliver the pitch that would stop him.

Snap. The sound came from behind and to his left. Pete froze, terror icing his veins. It was Jake. He waited, holding his breath, straining to hear the next footfall, but afraid to look. When it came, it sounded close. Ahead, he thought Jim was pulling something over his head, but he couldn't be sure. Pete remained anchored, frozen in doubt. Now Jim was closing on Ruth. Pete tried to yell, but couldn't find his voice. He gauged the distance between them. He couldn't close it in time. Besides, he felt as if he were being held here. He watched Jim's arm reach up and back. Ready to deliver a blow? Pete said aloud, "Fuck you Jake," then wound up and threw his best fastball, aiming for the spot just above where Jim's skull met his neck. Jim's arm came down as Pete released the rock, and he managed to yell, "RUN" as he let it fly. It landed true, and Jim collapsed.

CHAPTER 46

Karen looked out the window of the DeHaviland at an endless montage of forest and mountain. "This here is amazing country. God's country," Duquoin said above the din of the old rotary engine.

"Is that why you left Haiti?" Karen asked.

Duquoin laughed. "No. I left Haiti because I had to. And because I wanted to. Do you know there's not a tree left there? And now Haiti is washing into the sea, leaving only the spines of the mountains behind. My people, they say you can see the Earth's bones. But you know? Now I'm older, there's not a day goes by I'm not freezin. I dream of goin' back there. Specially now that the same thing's happening up here. Maybe someday soon."

Duquoin was following highway 37, and it rolled out beneath them in a patchwork of forest, clear cut, and a silent stalking death of some kind that left vast expanses of grey and brown, where the trees stood like dead phantoms, as if some huge war was being waged. The trees were losing, Karen thought.

"Stumpage fees," Duquoin said.

"What?"

"It's all about stumpage fees. The government builds roads and gives the cutters access to the forest. Then they charge the cutters a fee on the trees they cut to pay for it. They call it the stumpage fee. Now, some people, they say the stumpage fee is too low. They say we're cuttin too much and gettin too little for it. Others, they say it means jobs and money for the economy."

An old argument, one Karen had seen play out a hundred times in Washington, and always, those advocating jobs and economic growth won. "What do you think?" she asked.

Duquoin banked the plane east, leaving the road behind. Beneath them, the land turned more rugged, and took on a red hue – the color of blood, Karen thought. The immense isolation of the place frightened her and she forgot for a moment that Duquoin hadn't answered. After he'd straightened the plane, he cleared his throat. "I think stumpage is a good word. It's what you end up with, when you think you own this," Here he waived his arm in a gesture encompassing the vast forest below.

"In Haiti, we share the island. Our side is stripped of trees. It is bare naked an' we're among the poorest people on Earth. If cuttin' trees was good for the economy, we would be the kings of the world. Don't matter much now, though. All this is pretty much gone anyway, what with the Earth heatin' up." He reached up and throttled back a bit then pointed out at what looked like one of the last of the vast dead zones. "See those trees? Pine and spruce bark beetles. As the place gets warmer, the trees get weaker an' the bugs get stronger. Jake says they'll be gone south of here within a decade."

At the mention of Jake's name, Karen's stomach flipped and her fear ratcheted up a notch. She imagined the headline, "Ditz Dies on Solo Safari. World Yawns." I could tell him to turn around, she thought. Nobody would blame me. All this damn wilderness, and a psycho-superman. What the fuck was I thinking? Baker was right. Rose and Chas, too. She thought about having Duquoin try the radio one last time – he'd been calling since her visit – but decided it wouldn't make a difference. Suppose they got him. Could she trust anything Jake said? Another shiver ran through her, and she tried to think of a way she didn't have to go through with this.

She thought of Peter, and remembered poor Dawkins, and she knew there was no one else who would go up there; no one who would believe her vague suspicions. It was up to her. She clamped her jaw down to keep it from quivering and set her gaze straight ahead. They were quiet for a long time after that. Finally Duqoin said, "Here, look. We're comin' up to the Lake."

As Duquoin banked the plane Karen saw Cold Fish nestled in among snow covered peaks, their bases plunging right into the water. The eastern and northern shores were covered with ice. On the south facing side up by the near end, there was a break in the mountains where the land flattened some, and she saw the Tommy Walker Cabins, their red roofs sticking out from among the spruce and willow where the land met the water. Behind them a meadow crept up a small hill, and behind that, the mountains started up again, marching north for as far as she could see. She looked for signs of life. Smoke curling up, a boat on the lake, but she saw none.

Duquoin read her look. "It's a bit early for anyone to be here. Might be someone comin' along in a week or two, though." He studied the lake, and said to himself, "More ice than I'd like here." He'd been taking the plane down into the basin formed by the mountains, but he pulled back up, abruptly. "Need another look." He climbed, circled, and Karen caught a glimpse of the land to the east beyond the ranges. For as far as she could see, there was nothing but trees, meadows, streams, bogs and mountains. No buildings, no roads, no fences. Just an infinite stretch of wilderness. Duquoin pointed to a stream bed that cut through the mountains south and east of their heading. "That's the way to the Spatsizi River. Tatlatui an' Kitchener are on the other side of those ranges. Likely they'll be somewhere between here and there by now."

He brought the plane around in a full circle and lined it up with the open water, then came down sharply. "This could be a bit rough," he said, "Not as much room as I'd like." He throttled back hard, and the plane plummeted out of the sky, kissed the water, skipped off the surface, and came down again, hard, but it stayed. As he taxied, the De Haviland's staccato shattered the silence and bounced off the mountains, and Duquoin struggled to slow it, relying on the flaps to push it down into the water and hold it there. They slowed quickly. When he was satisfied with their speed, he angled over to a dock near the cabins and came to a stop.

He turned the engine off, plunging them into silence. Karen climbed down onto the dock and stretched. It was sunny, much colder than she'd expected, but she hardly noticed. She was, at that moment, transfixed. Although she'd been to most of the National Parks back home, she'd never been anywhere as remote as this – or as beautiful. The sky was incandescent, the hills a brilliant mix of umber soils, emerald grasses, olive and lime colored trees, and the lake reflected it all back through air so clear and crisp and dry that it seemed to crackle with the colors. "Jesus," was all she could say.

Duquoin had joined her on the dock, and he was emptying her pack and food from the plane. He let her take the scene in for a few minutes, then said, "Let's check out the cabins."

As they walked, Karen noticed a length of rope coiled neatly lying near the center of the dock. A rowboat was flipped over bottoms up and lay on the grassy shore. She followed Duquoin past it to the nearest cabin, a short squat thing made of logs and topped with a tin roof. An antenna marked it as the main building. Duquoin, who was up ahead of her, got to the cabin first, and said, "Shiit."

"What?"

"Bear." Duquoin pointed to the door. It was hanging on one hinge, and the planks were splintered along one edge. He searched around the entrance and saw several prints in the soft earth, then pushed the door open and stepped in. Karen was still outside studying the prints– they were huge – when she heard Duquoin, again, "Damn. We got trouble."

She entered the cabin, and when her eyes adjusted, she walked over to Duquoin. On the floor in front of him was the radio; every dial had been smashed, and the olive green case was cracked, exposing its guts. "No big deal. I've got this." She pulled the satellite phone out of her pack.

"I think you should come back with me."

"No. I'm not leaving until I know those people are OK."

Duquoin looked at the radio, then went to the kitchen area, where the cans of food remained untouched. "Those people are not OK."

"Then I really have to stay, don't I?"

Duquoin looked at her sadly. "You could get some help."

"You think Baker's going to come up here because bears wrecked the radio?"

Duquoin inspected an intact sugar tin. "I'm not sure this was a bear."

"Fine. You convince him to come up, then. But I'm not leaving."

Duquoin shrugged and walked to the door. He turned back and said, "Listen. Jake isn't a bad man. In fact, he's a good man in a bad world. But that can make a man do bad things, sometimes."

"Yeah. Well, tell that to Baker. Meantime, where can I find him?"

"More likely, he's gonna find you. But if you're gonna stay, that's where I'd go." Duquoin pointed to a single peak, jutting above all the others across the lake. "Nation Peak. It's the highest point around here. If you want to find Jake, camp up there. If they're around, you'll see 'em before they see you. Look for smoke in the mornings and evenings. And take the Glock. Now I got to go. Call me if you need me. Good luck."

She followed Duquoin out the door, watched him walk down to the dock, climb into the Otter, rev it up and then, giving her a wave, watched him taxi the plane out to the middle of the open patch on the lake and accelerate. Watched it take off, followed it until it was just a speck against the mountains, watched it disappear around a peak, listened as the thrumming whine faded. She heard it for a long time, but finally, it was gone, and she was alone.

CHAPTER 47

Pete looked back at the figure that had been following them for the last five hours.

"You should have killed him," Ruth said.

"Perhaps. But then we'd be no different than him," Ben said.

"At least we'd have a shot at coming out of this alive."

Pete turned to her. "I told you, we're going to make it."

They were on a high ridge, totally spent after a night and full day on the move. Pete sent them down the west side of the slope with Ben to pick out a good campsite, and stayed up on the ridge for a few moments more to study the weather. And to look for more tracks. For most of the afternoon, they'd watched as a massive set of anvil-shaped cumulonimbus clouds formed up to their north. Now, as evening came on, the clouds were mushrooming up and out, filling the whole northern sky, threatening to blot out the horizon, and peppering the ranges with lightning strikes and heavy rains. He could see it fall, even at this distance, like some thick steel-grey curtain suspended across the sky. It would be on them in a little better than an hour, and Pete had instructed them to build a shelter down below tree line. Too bad. They needed to put more distance between them and Jim. Twice within the last two hours, as they'd crested a peak, Pete had looked behind them and seen the hulking figure of Jim, following relentlessly. Pete wasn't sure how he could be keeping up, let alone closing the gap.

When he'd flipped him over last night after pegging the stone, he'd seen what Bill had managed to do. Several gashes covered Jim's face, his left eye was swollen closed, and blood crusted his nostrils. And Pete's throw had been deadly accurate, striking Jim right at the base of his skull and raising a monster of a bump, leaving him unconscious. He had to have at least a concussion. And yet here he was just twenty hours later pursuing them, even closing ground.

He scanned the small group down the hill in front of him. Ben could keep going. But the rest were done in. No way they could trudge through this storm anyway. They'd have to camp, eat, and rest a bit, Jim be damned. Besides, for Pete there was another, far more immediate threat. Twice today, he'd seen prints of Jake's big boot, and they looked fresh. The first time, around noon, as he'd pushed and cajoled the small band over one more hill, eking out a few more miles from their fatigued bodies with a combination of threats and encouragement, he'd see the tracks as he'd stood alone in the valley for a moment checking behind them, unable to shake the feeling someone was near. The prints – size thirteen with Jake's tread – came from the west, in front of them, and circled back behind them, the way a predator stalks it's victims.

The group had been well ahead, and none of them seemed to have noticed.

He'd seen the second set just fifteen minutes ago as he'd stood on the ridge waiting for the others to catch up, checking behind them for Jim. Once again, a size thirteen. Jake's tread. Coming in from the north this time. So he *was* out here somewhere, circling them.

Now, he looked down to where the tired little band was building a shelter. They were spent; this was a race they would never win. Time for plan B. Time to play God. When it was dark, prey would become predator. He would stalk Jim, and kill him – before he kills us all. Then he'd deal with Jake. He knew now what he had to do. They had to separate. He'd have Ben take the others to the old abandoned railway right-of-way south of Spatsizi. From there it would be a long, but relatively easy hike to the town of Iskut and Route Thirty Seven.

Meanwhile, he'd continue northeast to Cold Fish. *Jake will have no choice but to let the others go and chase me down before I get to the radio and contact the authorities.* But first, Pete would have to stop Jim. He couldn't send Ben and the others off while he was still alive. They couldn't out run him; the son-of-bitch was still gaining on them.

He rejoined the others and took Ben aside. Sarah, Ruth, Rita and Clio were busy gathering spruce and pine boughs and shoring up the walls of the shelter. "I think Jake's nearby."

Ben eyed him skeptically. It was clear to Pete that the older man was not entirely ready to trust him yet. "Why do you say that?"

"I've seen his prints. He's tracking us."

Ben pointed to a thin plume of smoke that was rising from a tall ridge line way off to their west. "I rather thought that might be him."

Pete stared westward. At first he missed it. It was barely visible; but for the setting sun's rays staining it salmon, he would never have seen it. If it were Jake, he'd made damn good time. He'd only left a day before them, and he was near Cold Fish already. On the other hand, it was unlikely that there was a back packer in Spatsizi in mid-May.

"Come on. Follow me." He led Ben back up to the ridgeline to where he'd seen Jake's tracks. At first he couldn't find the soil-filled depression, but then he spotted it. He led Ben over and showed it to him, then went to look for others. There were only a few nearby, but the area was rocky and the snow cover spotty at best so that didn't surprise him. He returned to Ben. "Well?"

"It's Jake alright. Thing is, it could be a day old."

"Looks fresh to me. See how that edges are still distinct?"

"It's hard to tell in this mud, Pete. Why're you so sure?"

"I saw some earlier. Came in from the west and circled behind us." He eyed Ben a moment, trying to read whether the old man believed him. "I think we should split up."

"What happened to 'nobody gets out of my sight'?"

"If we split up, Jake will follow me."

"What if he doesn't?" Ben sighed and looked at the smoke curling up from the west. "What if he's not even here?"

"He's here. And if I leave, he doesn't have a choice. You guys go to the old right-of-way south of here. You'll make Iskut in a less than a week. I can make Cold Fish in three days."

"And what about Jim back there? There's strength in numbers, Pete."

"Yeah. That's the tough part. I'll have to take him out."

"I'm not going to be a party to that."

"You don't have to. I'll take care of it."

Ben stared at him. He seemed to be weighing his response carefully. "You're willing to kill a man on the basis of a few footprints? Are you so sure about what you're seeing?"

"I know what I know, Ben."

"Yeah. And I know what I know. You've been paranoid about Jake since the first class. We don't even know it's not a bear that's done all this."

"What about Jim?"

"What about him? All we know is that poor Bill was killed and Jim was injured at the same time. You knocked him out and hustled us off before we could get anything out of him."

"And Ruth?"

"Oh, come on Pete. She's fried. And so are you. I've gone along with you so far because it seemed like the right thing to do regardless of what was happening. But not this."

"You still think I'm crazy?"

"I think you're under a lot of stress. You've been carrying a big load. Maybe it's time to put it down."

"I tried that already. And another man died."

"Do me a favor. As a friend?"

"What?"

"Don't do anything rash. We'll start early tomorrow. We'll stay ahead of him."

"You and I could. And Sarah, maybe. But not the others. I'm not leaving anyone behind." Pete stared out at the storm bearing down on them, as he tried to formulate his next statement. "Jake is around here somewhere. I know it."

Ben nodded to the ridge behind them. "Jim's stopped."

Pete looked east across the broad valley separating them, and saw smoke spiraling up from the side of the mountains a little less than half way down. About time he thought. Son-of-a bitch must be exhausted. "What about Jake?"

Ben nodded to the plume of smoke to their west. "I'm still bettin' that's him."

"He'd have to have covered one hundred and eighty miles in less than three days."

"Jesus, Pete. All I'm asking is that you not kill anyone for a day. Can you manage it?"

Pete felt foolish. What Ben was saying seemed reasonable enough. But he knew it was the wrong thing to do. He knew they were in danger. But in the end, he decided they had nothing to lose by waiting. "You make it sound like I want to kill him – we're in real danger, here, Ben. And he's part of it."

"One more day Pete. We'll post guards throughout the night, and see how it looks in the morning. Whatya say?"

Pete studied the northern horizon again. They were done in, and the storm would hit them pretty soon anyway, so reluctantly, he agreed.

By the time they had the camp set up, the wind was picking up and a wall of rain was rolling across the valley toward them like a tsunami. They'd eaten some fish jerky and drank down most of the remaining water, and now they huddled inside the shelter waiting for it to hit.

Pete risked another trip to the summit to check on Jim. He was still hunkered down just below tree-line on the ridge to their east. He could no longer see Jake's fire – the storm was shrouding the mountains. On the peak, he watched the lightning strike at the rocks north and west of them again and again, igniting the whole valley between them like a blue tinted black and white photo. He tried counting the seconds till the thunder clapped, but it rolled and reverberated continuously up and down the valley, so he couldn't. Somewhere, wolves had begun to howl, but even their calls were drowned out. Now, as he stood there, he could feel the hair rising on the back of his neck, and he knew he had to get down, quick.

He scrambled over rocks and debris and as the first drops fell, big as pearls and stinging against his skin, a bolt ripped through the air, striking a rock on the ridge near where he'd been standing seconds before. In the flash, he thought he'd seen Jake on the top, lit for just a moment, as if in a strobe light, frozen in the act of movement, staring down right at him, the rain drenching him already, running down in small rivulets across his face, leaving his hair stringy and plastered against his cheeks. His eyes bulged, manic, and he seemed to be laughing. The flash lasted just a second, but the image of Jake lingered, like a photo, and he looked impervious to everything – the rain, the wind, the cold, even the lightning. The crash sounded immediately after the flash, and Pete could feel it and smell the ozone from the burnt air, but none of that mattered. He was struggling to locate Jake, but he couldn't find him. Yet he couldn't erase that image; the grinning figure leering down at him, caught in the spotlight. That he could still see.

His heart raced, and his stomach iced up as his eyes darted around desperately. He tried to tell himself that Jake couldn't see him either. But he couldn't believe it. He could feel his eyes on him. He could feel him watching and waiting calmly among the thunderbolts.

Then there was another flash and Pete searched the blue black light for Jake, but he was gone. He scrambled down the mountain quickly and found the shelter. When he got there, their fire was hissing out as raindrops pelted down on it. Ben greeted him, warmly. Pete was glad. He thought their earlier exchange might have soured things between them. "We've got the watch set up. Hour and a half each. You pull last, so you might as well do your best to sack out now."

"If it's all the same to you, I'll take first. If something's going to happen, it's likely to be in the next hour or so."

Sarah was scheduled for the first watch, but she was exhausted. "That's fine with me."

The shelter worked reasonably well. It was a lean to, built against a rock overhang, and the dirt floor sloped away from the rock wall that formed the back, so for the most part, they stayed dry, although when the wind was wrong it blew the rain against the network of spruce branches that made up the outer wall and it would leak in a few places. The overhang was high enough so that you could stand if you stooped over, and it was easy to sit. Pete took a spot by the door, and sat up watching the lightning flash and listening to the thunder. He took a steady dose of spray from the shifting rains, and without the fire, he started to get chilled. He wrapped his gortex parka closely around his neck, and pulled the hood over his head, but he removed the hood after a few moments because it interfered with his hearing. Not that he could hear all that much between the thunder and the wolves and the pounding rain.

"Do you think he'll stay put?"

He turned from the door. It was Sarah. She was laying next to where he sat. "Who, Jim?"

"Yeah."

"He's not going anywhere tonight. He's got to be tired. Besides, he'd be a fool to cross the ridges in this."

"Good." She turned onto her side and stretched out as best she could. Within a few minutes, the shelter was filled with the steady breathing of five exhausted people.

He tried to stay alert, and each time the lightning flashed he expected to see Jake, staring into the shelter, rain dripping down his face, his shirt soaked and his hair bedraggled, that look – the one he'd first seen on the hunt – his lips pulled back, teeth barred, his eyes predatory, ready to carry out his sentence. For the hundredth time that day, Pete wished he had his spear. That's another thing for Ben to ponder, he thought. If Jim were knocked out and Jake long gone, who'd taken them from the camp last night? But eventually the flashes came less often, and Pete could feel himself giving in to sleep. It was getting warmer in the shelter now, the six bodies filling the space, and when he figured his hour and a half was up, Pete managed to convince himself that he wouldn't come tonight. Even Jake needed to sleep. He woke Clio and took her spot, gratefully.

CHAPTER 48

Pete woke quickly, shedding sleep in a rush of adrenaline. Something was wrong. He jumped up. The sun was already over the peaks to their east, and the day was warming. He saw with satisfaction – and a little surprise – a curl of smoke rising over the crest from the direction of Jim's camp. Must be boiling water. Of all of us, he'd been the most careful about giardia, refusing to drink unless it were filtered or boiled. But Pete's internal radar was still sounding. He looked around, then looked into the shelter. Clio was stirring, but the rest were still asleep. Then he knew. Sarah. She should be up. He searched among them for her, angry that she would have fallen asleep, leaving them unguarded. He would have to have a word with her in private. Impress upon her the importance of a little discipline, a little courtesy ... but as he scanned the sleeping figures, he could not find her.

He counted them, adrenaline kicking up a notch now, replacing the caffeine he still missed. Four. Jesus. She's gone. He shifted from alertness to fear, to dread, to anger. Anger fueled by the sure knowledge of what had befallen her, and by the guilt that came from knowing that if he'd listened to himself, trusted his feelings, it would not have happened.

He leaned across the sleeping form of Clio, and grabbed Ben, and shook him awake, "Are you happy you sanctimonious old bastard?" he shouted, "He's killed her."

Ben put his arm across his face, protecting himself from Pete's onslaught while he struggled to wake up. "What the hell are you talking about?"

"Sarah. She's gone. Jesus, I wish I'd just taken him out." But even as he said it he knew, Jim didn't do this.

"Hang on. Have you searched?"

"I don't need to search. I know what's happened."

"The rest of us might not be so prescient. I suggest we organize a search."

The others had woken with the ruckus, and they eyed the two anxiously. "What is it?" Clio asked, rubbing sleep from here eyes.

"Sarah," was all Pete said.

"Is she ...?"

"Yeah." Pete knew what they would find. "Come on. We have to locate her."

They got up quickly, none of them speaking. Ben wanted them to spread out, but Pete refused and made them pair up. Clio and Ruth went down slope, Ben and Rita circled the camp, and Pete went up slope. From the top of the ridge, he saw two plumes of smoke – One west of them and one to the east. *Was Ben right? Were they staying put?*

Within a few minutes, Pete heard a shriek from Ruth, and Clio shouted, "We found her." Pete didn't need to see – he knew what they'd found, but he ran down anyway, arriving last. Sarah was lying on her back, stretched across a boulder, drenched in a mixture of rain and blood. Her neck was snapped, and she'd been disemboweled. Four claw marks streaked her face and her shoulder. The place reeked of death. The corpses Pete had seen in funeral parlors were swathed in silk, dressed in finery, and covered with makeup, and even so, they'd always looked dead enough to him, but looking at the body before him, he knew they'd been death disguised. Here, the blood-stained, rain-soaked figure of Sarah, white and waxy-skinned with blue-black circles under her eyes, sprawling limp and lifeless across the rock, here was the real face of death. And yet she had a kind of surprised look frozen on her face, as if she were shocked that this could be happening. It felt to Pete like an accusation. He'd told her she'd be all right. Perhaps her last thoughts were that he lied. Pete checked her hands. Sarah was a powerful woman and he expected she'd put up more than token resistance, but there was no sign of blood or fur – or hair – under her fingernails. He held the hand a minute more, cold and slack and shapeless in his now, little more than a slab of meat, and he muttered, "I'm sorry. God, I'm sorry. But no more. No more." Then he turned to Ben, "We do this my way, now. We start with Jim. If I can stop him without killing him, I will, but I'll kill him if I have to."

"But Pete. Don't you see? Jake and Jim stayed put. This must have been the bear."

"See any prints?"

Ben looked around quickly, and shook his head. The others did, too, and they came up blank. "The rain wiped them out," he said. "We might see some by the shelter." Ben scrambled up the hill to where they were camped. The others followed. When they arrived, they found him searching outside the entrance. When he was finished, he looked up and said, "It must have been the rain. If it had been one of them, why wouldn't they have killed us all?"

Pete shrugged. "Maybe he didn't think he could."

Ruth interrupted, "It's Jake isn't it?"

Pete nodded.

"He could," she said, "He's just toying with us."

Pete didn't know what to say. She was probably right. But it was time to change the game. Time to make him guess. He put an arm around Ruth's shoulder, but she threw it off. Then he beckoned for the others to gather around, and they sat on some rocks dry already from the morning sun.

"I don't think we can take Jake. But if we split up, he'll follow me. And I might be able to outrun him."

"What about Jim?" Clio asked.

"I'll disable him."

"Let's call a spade a spade, Pete. You're going to have to kill him," Ben said.

"If I have to."

Ruth approached them, "Jake's out there. He's listening to everything you say. He's going to kill us all." Her voice rose an octave with each sentence, ending in high-pitched panic.

Clio got up and stood in front of Ruth, "Maybe. But I, for one, plan to make it hard for him." Then she turned to Ben. "You two big men have been conducting a running debate about what to do. Well, it's not up to just you. We have a say, too. I understand what you're feeling Ben. Out here, disabling Jim is the same as killing him. And we're supposed to be civilized people; the kind that don't kill. But in case you haven't noticed, we left civilization back there. And we're dealing with wild animals out here, bear or man. They're not honoring your code now and they won't start. So get this: I plan on seeing my children and my husband again, and I'll do whatever it takes to make that happen. I'm with Pete. We take out Jim then split up." She walked over and stood by Pete. "You'll need some help."

"Can you do it?" Ruth looked scared.

"We don't have much of a choice. You have some books to write, remember?"

Ruth smiled, doubtfully, but nodded.

"Rita?" Pete asked.

She nodded her head and walked beside him.

"What about it, Ben? If you got another idea, I'm willing to listen. But getting killed one-by-one isn't on my list of options."

"No. I guess I'm all out of ideas."

"OK, then. The problem is, Jim's got a spear."

"That and he's twice your size and strength," Ben said.

"That, too. But I think he's still hurting – otherwise he'd be on the move by now."

Ben interrupted, "What if we all went after him?"

"Wouldn't work. He'd see us coming a mile off and get ready. Even if we got him, we'd lose too much time and maybe a few of us in the process. We need to surprise him."

"What if I went straight up there in plain sight and you doubled back behind him?" Ruth asked.

Pete looked over and smiled. She was stronger than he'd given her credit for. "No. He'd suspect you." Pete looked at Rita. "Our decoy has to be an unknown quantity."

Rita looked straight back, "I guess that would be me?"

"Yeah."

"OK. What do we do?"

The plan was simple. Pete would circle around behind Jim, moving under cover of a stream bed about a half mile south of them. Rita would start approaching about ten minutes after Pete left. She would come up over the ridge line and head down into the broad valley that separated them from Jim, moving as much as possible in plain sight, distracting him.

There were flaws in the plan, Pete knew. Not the least of which, Jim would likely take up his spear at the first sign of anyone. And then there was Jake. Ruth was probably right. He was likely out there, aware of everything they were planning, and just toying with them. But the only way around that was to act, and act fast.

Pete drifted off toward the streambed, pretending to look for firewood. He found himself surrounded by dense thickets of willow growing like clumps of grass, and soon he was surrounded by a wall of willow shoots standing about seven to eight feet high. Several times as he scrambled down the narrow ravine toward the valley, he thought he heard something rattling in the thick scrub. When he reached the valley, the stream spread out and meandered across it, forming bogs and pools in a kind of random pattern, and the wall of vegetation surrounding him cut his field of vision to about four feet in any direction. He was forced to stop and take bearings on the mountains in front of him to keep from becoming hopelessly lost in the vast thicket. Every time he did, he would hear the rustles from the willows. The sound would stop just after he stopped, and start as he started. He became convinced that he was being stalked but he couldn't be bothered with that now. From here until it ended – however that might be – Pete's survival, and that of the others, depended on his ability to keep moving, to keep ahead of the thing that was after him. He had about two and a half miles more to cross. Rita would be about half a mile north of him, walking back the way they'd come yesterday – over a slightly raised and well-drained meadow of sedges and wild flowers.

By following one or another of the shallow streambeds, Pete was able to keep up a steady jog. After about an hour, he emerged from the thicket, coming out on the southern end of the base of the mountain where Jim had set up his camp. He fought his way up some scree, the loose rock acting like an escalator stuck on down, but he finally managed to reach a granite knoll where the spruce forest started, several hundred feet above the plain. He searched for Rita and spotted her immediately. She was nearly at the base of the mountain, and it looked as if Jim might have seen her; she was gesticulating and, although he couldn't make out the words, he thought he could hear her shouting. He checked briefly to see if he could spot whatever it was in the brush below that had been following him, but saw nothing. Then he turned and headed up the hill, breathing hard now, but not from the exertion. By the time he made the crest, Rita was halfway up the hill. In a few more strides she'd be out of his sight.

Pete worried briefly about Jake. If he were around, he would almost certainly guess their plan by now and Rita would be in danger. That might explain why he wasn't hearing whatever had been tracking him anymore. He ran across the face of the ridge just where the trees thinned into krumholtz, confident that Jim would be facing down slope. Smelling the smoke from Jim's fire, he headed down toward a grove of trees, and spotted his campsite just a little more than two hundred yards into the woods below him. Jim was standing near the fire, his back to Pete, looking down at Rita. He was hunched over, carrying himself as if he were hurting. Pete scanned the area, looking for the spear, and saw it near the fire, just a few feet from where Jim stood. He hesitated, catching his breath and steeling his nerves. He would let Rita get a little closer then make his move. He couldn't see her, but he could hear them talking, and Jim sounded suspicious.

Now that it came down to it, Pete had no idea what he would do. He was no match for Jim physically, injured or not. And even if he managed to get the spear, then what? He knew Jim would not simply fold. He'd force Pete to use it. And Pete thought about the act of plunging the spear into another man – remembering as he did the almost sensuous feel of the point slipping into the soul of the caribou. And he knew that he would not be able to do it. Not to a human. But he also knew that Jim would.

Rita would be nearing the top, now. Very soon she would be in danger. It was time for him to move, but he couldn't. His heart thundered in his ribcage, and his limbs trembled, leaden with fear, and he heard again those thuds and then the screams, echoing across the decades, finding him here still afraid, hunkering in the brush unable to move, unable to act.

Something behind him dislodged a boulder, and it rolled down toward him, setting off a small cascade. He jerked around, a thousand volts of fear surging through his body, jacking up his terror to new levels, making him tremble then freezing him, stopping even his breath. Jake? But where? And how? He swiveled around, unable to see him, but certain he was there.

Pete looked down at Jim, expecting him to be looking for the source of the noise, just as he was. But he seemed unaware of it. Wherever Jake was, he was close enough to see everything but hidden well enough not to be seen.

But Pete stopped caring. *Move and keep moving. No matter what.* He crept down the slope toward Jim. Rita was getting close. When there was less than a hundred feet separating her from Jim, he launched himself. As he hurtled down, crashing through brush and bounding over rocks, he saw Jim start to turn his head, stiffly. Once again, it seemed to Pete that while he sped across the distance between them, the rest of the world paused, then moved ahead in slow motion. He took in every detail, knew the meaning of every nuance. He saw Jim start to wheel around to face him, then turn toward Rita, thinking to use her as a hostage, then saw him turn back and begin to bend over to pick up the spear, just as Pete closed on him. Now Jim had it in his grasp; now he was straightening up, now he was raising it ... but Pete catapulted himself from about five yards out, a human projectile, watching the spear head come up and twisting to avoid it even as he flew through the air. He hit Jim full in the chest, knocking the air from his lungs, and they both went down. Pete was up first. Jim was on all fours, struggling to catch his breath, and Pete kicked him square in the chest, and the bigger man collapsed, the rush of air audible, as his lungs emptied. Pete leaned over to pick up the spear, which was lying now just to Jim's left.

As Pete grabbed it, Jim shot his hand out and clamped an iron grip around Pete's forearm. Even as Jim gasped, trying desperately to get air, Pete felt the strength in that grip – a strength forged by hours spent each day in weight rooms under the tutelage of some of the best trainers in the world, working until they had coaxed out every scrap of strength permitted by human genes. Jim's hand closed vice-like around Pete's arm, crushing it, even as he struggled to fill his lungs.

Pete knew what to do from his karate training: twist his arm down in the direction of the thumb, thus pitting the entire strength of his arm and shoulder against Jim's thumb. It was a move that had never failed him in any of the classes he'd taken, in any of the thousand wrestling matches he'd had with his brother. But it failed now. At first, he managed to twist Jim's arm and he felt the man's grip loosen just a bit, but then he felt Jim's clasp tighten and gradually, he managed to fight Pete to a standstill, though Pete was now leaning his whole body and using his legs as leverage in an attempt to free his arm. Using just his hand, Jim reversed the movement and began to twist Pete's arm now, and Pete knew he would not be able to hold on to the spear. He could almost feel his bones beginning to reach their limit, on the verge of snapping. He heard Jim's breathing even out, felt his strength increasing, saw him start to push himself back up, holding Peter the whole time, and he knew he had to do something – anything.

He let go of the spear, then planted his foot behind Jim's elbow, as he took the bigger man's forearm in his other hand. It was a move he'd practiced a thousand times with Gus, and Pete was able to leverage the pressure against the back of Jim's elbow. But Jim didn't let go his death grip, and the two stayed locked like that for a full minute as Pete stepped harder and harder against Jim's joint. Finally, he pulled his foot back and jumped, stamping on the back of Jim's elbow, applying all his strength and his full weight, literally leaping on his arm. He didn't know what would happen, but then he heard the sound of bone splintering; he was not sure at first whether it was his or Jim's, then he heard Jim scream in agony and felt his grip slacken and finally let go altogether. He kicked him once more, full on the face, and Jim rolled over, and passed out.

Pete picked up the spear and felt his own arm to see if it were broken. It seemed OK. Jim's finger's were etched on his skin, red indentations, and it ached, but other than that Pete felt fine. Jim was not fine. His arm dangled unnaturally, bending backward from the elbow, a bone poked out where the forearm had shattered, and he was bleeding.

Pete walked to the edge of the level where Jim had put his camp, just above a small rise. Time to pull the next lever, and he shouted, his voice amplified through the haze of fear and anger and triumph he felt. "Jake." His voice boomed across the valley, and came back in an echo, frightening in its power even to Pete. "It's over. I'm going to Cold Fish. You can't stop me."

Below, Rita, who'd scrambled up to the crest, froze, her face overtaken by a primitive fear, and something else. She stood there looking up at him, waiting for some sign that it was OK to keep coming.

Pete looked down, read her fear and his expression changed easily from savage to the old Pete. "It's alright Rita. Come on up. Quickly now. I want to stabilize him, and then we have to move." He looked down onto the plain and saw Ben and Clio and Ruth nearly at the base of the mountain. It was important that Jake not catch them together. Then he noticed that Rita had not moved. "Come on. We have to get going."

"But your voice. It sounded ..."

"Come on. I need your help."

She hustled up the last of the hill, and stood near him, breathing hard, eying him warily. He took her hand. "It's OK, Rita. Really." Then he smiled. She smiled back tentatively. They went to work trying to set Jim's arm. It was too shattered to set, so in the end they simply tried to stop the bleeding and splint it. It didn't appear that any arteries or veins had been punctured, and he came to as they were finishing. He tried to get up but Pete put a hand on his chest. "Stay here. I'll leave you some water and send a helicopter as soon as I can."

"You can't leave me out here like this."

"Yeah, I can. Meanwhile if you try to follow us, know this: next time I will kill you. Understand?"

"But why?" Jim asked. Pete ignored him, and he and Rita took off down the hill to meet up with Ben and the others.

CHAPTER 49

By noon, Pete was jogging over the valley toward the continental divide. He was moving well, and apart from a nasty bruise on his forearm, he felt good. He was confident that Jake was after him, and for some reason that didn't hold the terror he thought it would.

He ran a steady, even pace, and his breath came in deep, strong pulls. It had been almost two weeks since his last training run, and it was good to be at it again. He moved easily over a mix of sedges and willow scrub, picking his way among the rocks deftly now that he was on flat ground. The run up to the pass where they'd camped the night before and the descent to this plain had been tough. Now, the sun was over his head and the day was warming quickly. In the dry air his sweat evaporated off his skin as quickly as it formed, leaving it salty. The footing was a little bumpy, and in places where the water pooled, a little slippery, but it was soft and forgiving – an acceptable running surface for the distances he had in front of him. He made good time. After about an hour and a half, he'd covered maybe twelve miles despite the mountains and the footing. But ahead, he faced the high peaks of the continental divide.

He turned around looking for Jake. No sign. But he knew he was back there. No matter. There was no way Jake would keep up with him now that he'd acclimated to the altitude; he could go all day. After another mile, he reached the base of the slope, and he entered the spruce forest that started on the hillsides. It hit him about halfway up the mountain face, headed for a pass between Tauton Peak and Mount Umbach. His breathing deepened, and his legs started to feel the strain of this second climb. He saw the crest of the pass about three and a half miles up slope where the trees gave way to krumholtz, and angled toward it.

He would stop there for a few minutes and drink some water and catch his breath. He backed off the pace just a bit as he climbed. Even at this slower pace, the slope and the altitude began to take their toll. Despite his conditioning, his breath was getting short, and his legs were starting to burn.

Still, he knew he could run through pain; if there was one thing he could do it was to keep going no matter what his body was telling him; to take one more step even when it seemed impossible, and then do it again, a thousand, ten thousand times if it was necessary; to reach down and find reserves where there were none. So he pressed on, confident. But when he crested a rise, he saw that he'd been victim of one of those cruel tricks that mountain ranges play on people. What he'd assumed to be Tauton and the divide was a smaller peak that obscured the real mountains and the continental divide some thirteen miles off, and several thousand feet higher than the ridge he was climbing. He kept up the pace, even though now his legs started to burn in earnest, and his steady breathing gave way to deep, fast pulls, in a desperate attempt to keep his body supplied with the oxygen it was consuming. But he kept the pace.

Pete knew that distance races were won by the most determined, not by the fastest or even the strongest. And he knew you could melt an opponent's determination by appearing stronger than you were. He'd seen people collapse in a marathon for no other reason than they sensed that the person ahead was prepared to take more pain than they were.

Even Jake would be hurting trying to match this pace. So he kept going through the pain he felt in his legs, through the screaming agony of his lungs, though the jelly-like weakness he began to feel all over as he passed out of the last of the spruce and headed above tree line. When your body gives out, you run with your mind, he told himself. And now, as the trees started thinning out and getting smaller, and the footing became more treacherous as the spruce-carpeted floor gave way to rocks and boulders, he allowed himself a little rest, and he backed off the pace a bit more.

By the time he reached the crest, though, he was panting. He stood there, bent over, his hands on his knees and pulled in air with long deep breaths. His legs quivered, and his eyes burned from sweat too copious to evaporate. He searched the area around him. Nothing but red rocks, red dirt, and a few patches of snow here and there. He scanned the peaks before him. The pass over the continental divide looked to be about eight miles away, across a series of lower peaks punctuated by a network of lakes and snow. He would have to cross the valley, climb the divide, then head a little north to meet up with Buckinghorse Creek, following it to the Spatsizi River valley and then to Cold Fish. At least it would be relatively flat, once he cleared those peaks ahead. But right now, he had to stop.

He looked behind him to his east, scanning it carefully for any sign of Jake. In the valley several miles back and a little south from the base of the pass he stood upon, he thought he saw a figure moving within the willow thickets. Jake. His pace had slowed considerably, and Pete allowed himself to relax. *The son-of-a-bitch is tired.*

The sun was sitting lower in the west now and Pete guessed it was four, maybe five o'clock. The air was crystalline after last night's storm, and it was still warm – near seventy degrees. He pulled out the skin and drank greedily, almost draining it, then sat down and leaned against a rock, allowing himself a few minutes of rest. He stretched out, laying his head on a large tuft of sedge. Don't sleep, he admonished himself. *Don't sleep.*

The trees shushed in the afternoon breezes, and he listened again to the sounds of the wilderness – the raven's harsh call; a warbler's more melodic response; a scurrying shuffle as some small critter hustled through the sedges – all interspersed with moments of pure silence. The sounds and the silences blended into a steady stream. A conversation. And it was at once mesmerizing and restoring. The pale sun warmed his face, the soft grasses cushioned his body and the soft winds caressed his skin. He remained there for some time, watching the sun's arc as the clouds traversed the sky above. He felt the Earth beneath him as an embrace, until he was no longer lying upon her, separate, but an intimate part of her. All was well. All was good. The breeze quickened as the afternoon wore on.

You've done well, Peter. You grow stronger in spirit everyday. It was the same voice he'd heard on the vision quest. Initially Jake's, but then more – disembodied, coming from everywhere, from the Earth itself. He knew he should be startled, but he wasn't. There was a moment of silence. No birdcalls, no scurrying, just the murmur of the winds. Then it continued. *But did you really think you could outrun me? Ah, and now that you know what I am capable of, you worry about the others? Splitting up was a clever plan, Peter. But you are not fast enough. I could have reached them, then come back for you. But there is another out here who must be dealt with. She could cause trouble. So now you have some time Peter. You can consider whether you should join me, while I go and take care of her.*

He tried to will himself to get up, but he couldn't break the embrace. After another moment, the voice continued with the same surreal resonance.

You know you should. Your people are an evolutionary abomination. They'll perish anyway, victims of their own greed and hubris. The voice was still for a moment, and when he heard it again, it seemed further away. *You don't understand yet, do you, Peter? You still don't know who I am. Let's have a little test, then, shall we? I will go do what I must, and return. The only way you can stop me is to get to Cold Fish before I can do it. But be fast, Peter. Be fast. I travel on the wind. Then laughter, mocking and knowing, and Pete felt fear.*

He jumped up. The sun had moved – maybe an hour had passed. He searched the valley for signs of Jake, panic overcoming the pain and weakness in his legs. *No sign of him.* He immediately scanned the slope and the area around him, fighting the growing sense that Jake was upon him. Even as he looked, the feeling of oneness lingered, swirling like a shadowy whirlpool, refusing to dissolve into incoherence the way his dreams did.

Another? She could cause trouble? Who could he mean? But Pete knew who the mutual friends were. He thought of Rita and Ben and Clio and Ruth. And he remembered promising to protect them. 'Can you do that?' Ruth had asked.

He walked to the edge of the crest, ignoring the aches in his legs and screamed, "Christianson. If you hurt them, I will find you, and I will kill you. Do you understand? I will kill you." He was stunned by his voice. It seemed to fill the air and carry forever, as loud on the divide as here, rolling, thunder-like, and undiminished in all directions. Far to the west some wolves heard him and answered, their howls swept by the winds to where he stood, sounding like a rebuke.

CHAPTER 50

Eight miles further, Pete reached the high pass that marked the continental divide and collapsed. He lay panting, his face on a patch of snow, looking out at the peaks and rivers and lakes below, bathed in shadows now as the last of the sun disappeared into the mists of mountains that went on forever to his west. He was parched and exhausted, and his legs began to lock up as he lay there in the night's chill. His calf muscles cramped again, and he balled up his fist and beat them, then kneaded them, pushing the muscles in the direction of the heart, as he'd been taught, but it did little good. He'd been going for more than eight hours now, covering nearly fifty miles, most of it uphill, and he'd been exhausted when he'd started. He'd raced the wind, and lost. He knew the signs.

It was no longer simply a case of setting his mind against the pain. This was physical. His glycogen stores were gone, his muscles starved for glucose and choked in a soup of lactic acid. They simply wouldn't work. Soon, he would lose control of his bowels and then he would become delirious and begin to hallucinate as he used up the last of his electrolytes. The mind wouldn't – couldn't – work without them. Finally his heart would go haywire, beating frantically, its electric circuits literally blown.

He had some jerky, but it was mostly protein. He needed minerals and carbs, and he needed them quick. And a little rest. But he couldn't. Somewhere south of here, Ben and the others were counting on him. Now they were being chased down. He was certain of that. Somewhere between here and there Jake was still going; relentless, vengeful, intent on destroying them and everything else. And Jake had spoken of another – one who could cause trouble. He touched the medallion Karen had given him, and he knew then who it was. And he knew he had to keep moving now no matter what. He ate some snow, knowing he was inviting hypothermia, but he'd run out of water a half hour before.

He tried to plan through his exhaustion. He would struggle to his feet. It was downhill from here for a while. Different muscles. Perhaps they still held some glycogen. Do they do that, he wondered. Do they store it in specific muscles, or does your body sop it up from all over? Didn't matter. It would have to be in specific muscles. Perhaps if he believed that, he could keep going. Then, if he could find a birch tree down there somewhere, he could get at the cambium layer under the bark – it would have the sugars, minerals and carbs he needed. Then maybe he could rest a little. Meanwhile he would use gravity to keep himself moving as fast as he was able for as long as he could.

He struggled to his feet, his calves threatening to ball up again, but holding off. Then he lurched down the hill, surprised to find that it felt almost good. His legs seemed lighter and he threw them out in front almost effortlessly. But after going a few yards he tripped, fell and rolled into a rock, then lay there stunned, and dizzy. He was unhurt, but he knew now he was losing control of his muscles. He would have to be very deliberate; he would have to make each move a conscious choreograph of what needed to be done. And so he got up, and thought his way down the mountain, planning each footfall; making each step an act of cognition and volition.

He moved this way for two and a half more hours, using the light from the nearly full moon to navigate. Mercifully, most of it was down hill or flat, but now, about ten miles out, he hit a small hill. He'd found a birch tree at the base of the divide about an hour and a half back and eaten as much of the sweet cambium as he could stomach. He'd lain back against the trunk, using his stone knife to carve off long thin strips of the inner bark, wet and slick and rich in sugars with the first of the rising sap, then forced them down. He'd also found a stream and drank greedily, not bothering to boil it. Lying there against the tree, he allowed himself to think he was beginning to feel better, even though he knew it would take hours to replace the glycogen and hours more to strip out the lactic acid.

Now, as he prepared to head up the grade, he stretched continuously, imagining he could feel the stuff being transported out. But as he tried the small hill, he knew he was fooling himself. He simply could not move up it. Several times he tried and his legs collapsed. Finally, he began to crawl. The rocks and debris dug into his knees, sending messages of sharp pain up his legs, but he was able to move forward, pulling with his arms as much as his legs, so that it was almost as if he were swimming up the hill. Even in the chill that had settled in with the night, his face was covered with sweat, but that was good, he knew. At least he wasn't dehydrated. About three quarters of the way up, he began to hear grunts and a curious whimpering sound. He heard them first as if they came from somewhere else, and he wondered for a moment what pathetic creature could be making such a noise, and then he realized it was him. With each movement, he would issue a guttural plea or a whine, and pull himself forward a bit. He stopped now, frightened that he might lose his mind, and continue blindly on, no longer knowing why or where.

"OK Pete. You are going to Cold Fish. Just get over this rise and it's downhill to the Spatsizi River. Follow it. Save them." He repeated this several times, then went on self-consciously, monitoring himself for signs that his brain, starved of the metals and salts it needed, had stopped functioning and had slipped into insanity. He'd read about runners who'd done that – stripped of their electrolytes they'd gone mad. He seemed lucid, yet. But then, what was lucidity, if not the ability to question whether one were lucid? Of course you always thought yourself lucid, even when quite mad. Perhaps it was the opinion of others – your being reflected off of them, and thus defined – that constituted sanity. But no. The others had been ready to declare me insane – just as the doctors had. And they were wrong, weren't they? He continued on for what seemed an eternity, locked in this existential debate, until he'd crawled to the top of the small hill, his left knee bleeding now where he'd scraped it across rock and dirt and brush. He lay there, half sleeping, but the debate spinning in his head, the cold penetrating his body, the sense of urgency palpable. Finally, he fell into a deeper sleep filled with more bizarre dreams.

When he woke, he saw the smoke from a campfire about halfway down the mountain. Had to be Jake. Finally he'd stopped. He was tired. He needed rest. Pete felt a moment of exaltation. He'd done it. He'd raced the wind and won. The others were safe.

CHAPTER 51

Rest. The word sounded like a symphony to Pete. Jake needed rest. His first instinct was to hunt him down as he slept, and kill him. But in the end, he knew his best bet was to get to Cold Fish. He would keep Jake after him to protect the others.

He got up and tested his legs. They were wobbly and sore. As if they'd been beaten with baseball bats. But they had enough strength in them to allow him to move. Better than yesterday. Much better. He studied the route before him. He could see the map in his mind clearly now. Buckinghorse Creek stretched out below him and carved a valley on its way to the Spatsizi River. It would be all down hill until he came to Mink Creek, and then it would just be about a five or six mile hike up a reasonably gentle grade to Cold Fish. There was even a trail right to the cabins. Incredibly, he'd covered better than sixty miles yesterday, ninety in the last two days. Thirty-five or so more to go. It hurt to think about it.

It was going to be warmer. There was a hint of it even now, as the early sun hit his back. Pete stretched out his legs, feeling surprisingly light. Yesterday seemed almost a nightmare. It unfolded in a haze of pain and confusion. He thought of himself crawling up the mountain face whimpering, and for some reason, it made him laugh. Tearing off a hunk of jerky, he ate it, nearly gagging on its pitchy taste. He'd learned a lot since that first night when he and Clio had sat by the fire in the fish camp and smoked this vile stuff. A real journey of the mind and soul. He was a different man, but he wasn't sure whether he'd passed Thoreau's test. Not yet anyway. And he had a much sterner test ahead of him.

He spread his legs as far apart as he could, then rocked from side to side in long fluid motions, shifting his weight gently from one leg to the other, testing the limits before the pain got too bad to move any further. Then he bent forward from his waist, legs still spread, and tried to lay his palms flat on the ground before him. He wasn't able to, but then he never could. He seemed to have pretty near his full range of motion. Next, he carefully stretched out his calves and his quads; nothing ballistic, just slow, easy pulls held for the count of twenty. His legs were better after the stretching. He could almost feel the muscles squeeze out the lactic acid, and some of the soreness and stiffness went with it. He hoisted his water skin and his knife and the spear he'd taken from Jim and set off.

He saw that if he angled across the slope to his north he would hit the Spatsizi about ten miles below where it was joined by the Buckinghorse, cutting off a few miles in the bargain and he took off, heading across the small slope to a point north of the confluence. Although he was stronger than yesterday, hiking proved tough going. His legs still ached and several times he stumbled.

He made good progress at first, but soon the pain and fatigue caught up with him. Even though it was mostly down hill, by the time he reached the Spatsizi his legs had begun to cramp up again, and he was having that internal dialogue common to all endurance tests: the body begging the mind for an out, trying to trick it with pains and twitches and balled up muscles. Soon, he knew, the mind would join in and nothing but will – whatever seat of the soul that might come from – would urge him on, then finally the end of physical capacity when nothing – no will; no motivation of any kind – could keep him going. It was a terrifying place. Terrifying because of the pain you would endure to get to it. Terrifying because you could stop it at any time simply by sitting down and it tested you, told you what you were made of, and you would always in the end come up wanting. It was as if you treated yourself as a prisoner of war, enduring self-inflicted ignominies of unimagined cruelty for a reason that evaporated with the pain and the exhaustion and the abject weakness of spirit they brought.

The difference between champions and others in these contests was their ability to reach this place and continue anyway. And Pete had always had a measure of this doggedness. In marathons, he would refuse to think of the finish line. And as a result, he could run strong without the wilting effect of knowing there were ten more miles, even when his body was screaming enough. He'd always taken himself to some other place and so the finish line seemed to come as a surprise when it came. But now, there was no finish line. The miles stretched on for an infinity, the terrain was punishing, he'd already run the equivalent of more than four marathons, and his body was giving out. Having met such a test yesterday, he had no reserves – physical, psychic or spiritual. He would very soon be literally on empty.

Again, he found a birch, cut out some strips of inner bark and choked it down, then lay on a rock, dipped his head in the river and drank it in, greedily. Fuck giardai. When he'd drunk his fill, he lay flat on the rock and felt sleep taking him. As he began to doze, he watched a log caught in an eddy across the river trace slow circles in the quiet water. Three others were pinned against the bank. He thought about Jake. Would he be rested, now? Yes. He struggled up, determined to continue. In his exhaustion he hit on a plan. If he still had the nylon twine he'd used to smoke the fish, he could make a raft and float down to where Mink Creek joined the river. He reached into his cargo pocket and felt it there.

He stepped out into the river and the water swirled up until it reached his waist, and he felt its power and struggled to stay upright. Even before he reached the middle, it felt as though icy fingers were clawing at his legs, and his breath came in quick, shocked gasps. The cold was slamming his body and turning his blood into a thick, torpid sludge, and he moved through a slow motion world, his strength ebbing as the river strengthened. By the time he reached the middle, his legs were cramping and he dimly understood he was in danger of hypothermia. He recalled the first survival class – convection, conduction, respiration, radiation – and then the full folly of his actions hit him as the river swept him off his feet and he rocketed downstream. He managed to swim to the opposite bank and lay on a broad flat rock in the sun.

He was spent. There was no more strength in him. If only he could rest a few hours and let the glycogen from the birch fill his muscles, he might be able to go on. But he didn't have hours. He was sure the wind he'd been racing had swept over him, and he lay there almost crying from the pain and the indignity of yet another failure. For a moment, he heard his brother's screams. And now he would have to live with the knowledge that it was his weakness alone that killed Karen and Ben and Clio and all of them. Another set of screams to haunt him throughout time. But, no. He would not have to live long with this horrible reality. Because now Jake was coming for him. He was almost relieved, and for several minutes he lay there waiting for this bearer of death willingly, almost eagerly.

But as the rock warmed him, a measure of hope returned. He would not give up. He had only to beat Jake to Cold Fish. It was that simple. He got up immediately, moving Frankenstein-like in his stiffness upstream to the bank where the logs were trapped, trying to remember whether there were any serious rapids between here and Mink Creek. As best as he could recall, with one exception, the contour lines on the map showed a gradual fall, with nothing more than a Class II rapid the entire length. The exception was about a mile downstream from here where the river cut its way through a high basalt dike and tumbled into the Spatsizi Plateau. He'd have to pull over and check that out before heading into it. A couple of miles past the chasm, the river spread out and meandered across the plateau, lined with oxbow lakes and a few bogs. He knew between here and the cataract it was fast and deep and it seemed relatively free of rocks. He reached into his pocket, hoping he still had the nylon twine. Yes. It was there. He had to work fast, the night was closing in, and with it the cold.

He waded into the quiet water in the backflow and pulled the circling log he'd seen earlier toward the others. The cold was numbing, and he worked quickly, wrapping the twine over and under the logs then pulling it as tight as he could. He was able to taper it to a point on both ends by putting the longer logs in the center. By the time he had the front end done though, his legs and hands were numb and his left calf was seizing up, but he kept going. He was muttering to himself as he set to work. "Come on Pete. Just ten more minutes. Come on. You can do this Pete. He's tired, too. Yes, he's tired." After what seemed an eternity in the frigid water, he had a crude raft, about eight feet long and nearly four feet wide. He climbed on in the calm water, and tested it. It floated nicely, even with his added weight, and the logs, averaging nearly two feet in diameter, were thick enough that they rode high in the water. He might even get dry. As he prepared to push off, a full moon rose in the east, bathing the area in an eerie light.

The arrow was the first sign that Jake was near. It passed by his ear with a low rushing sound then thwacked into the raft, striking the log near where Pete held it.

"So this is your answer, Peter? Wrong answer, I'm afraid." Pete turned toward the voice and saw Jake silhouetted against the moon about a hundred yards upstream. He was pulling another arrow out of a quiver and notching it. Pete grabbed his spear off the rock and dragged the raft out into the current. He alternately pulled and pushed the thing out to the center, the cold hitting him now, making every move an effort. He kept an eye on Jake as he moved. He had the arrow notched now and was aiming at a point well over Pete's head. The string pulled back, rocketed forward and he saw the arrow start its arc, saw it peak, then watched it come down right at him, its point barreling unerringly toward him, but it struck the raft a foot to his right.

As the raft slipped into the fast water, Pete centered himself and he shot down the river.

Jake's voice resonated above the river, "You can't escape Peter." He pulled another arrow out and took aim. By the time he released it, Pete was a hundred and fifty yards off. Again, it struck a lazy, but deadly arc that seemed destined for him, but Pete couldn't follow it. He knew the arrow was true, knew it was heading for him, knew he had to watch it and move, but he could not take his eyes off Jake. They stared at one another, held frozen in some dance choreographed a million years ago as the arrow whizzed down from the sky at him, a missile of death. But once again, he heard the arrow thwack into the raft inches from the other arrow. He centered himself, yanked the arrows out and stared back at Jake, who was now over two hundred yards back and disappearing rapidly as the raft hurdled downstream. Pete let himself relax, but Jake called out: "You won't get away, Peter."

Then Jake began running along the bank after him. Pete was stunned at the man's speed. They'd jogged together on hunts, but he'd never seen him go flat out before. Despite the rough terrain he was beginning to close ground. And he showed no sign of tiring.

Pete tried polling the raft with his spear, but it did little good. He was already moving downstream on the back of the swift swollen river. The problem was not that he was going too slow, but that Jake was going too fast. As Pete watched him close the distance, he saw Jake's teeth glint in the moonlight and he thought he saw a sneer crease his face. At least Jake couldn't stop and let another arrow fly. But unless the river quickened, he'd soon be on him. Pete turned and surveyed the landscape in front of him. The gorge was about a half-mile downstream. He heard the roar of the water as it cinched and then fell, rumbling, and tumbling into the plateau beyond. The banks shot up on either side about fifty feet high, enough to cast the gorge in shadow. He had to choose now, between Jake and the cataract. But there was no choice. He would have to face the rapids. He had to enter them before Jake was on him. If he could make it through them, he'd be home free.

Behind him Jake continued to close the gap, slowly, but relentlessly. In the moonlight he looked like a steel grey machine, efficient, tireless, the pace unwavering. Pete was reminded of the Olympic sprinters, their legs churning in a blur, their arms reaching out and grasping huge hunks of air, almost pulling themselves through it in an explosion of power. Except Jake's explosion didn't stop. It kept on as he got steadily nearer. Pete tried to do the mental calculus of the chase, and found it too close to call. He knew from his training that humans were capable of sprinting at more than twenty-six miles per hour, and doing longer distances at about fifteen miles per hour. Sprints were all muscle; distances were all heart. But it looked to Pete that Jake was moving at close to twenty miles an hour – a phenomenal pace for any distance over a quarter mile – and the river was going at something under fifteen. He was maybe five hundred yards from the cataract now, but Jake had closed the two-hundred yard gap to less than seventy yards. It seemed to Pete he'd picked up the pace some, as they neared the granite wall. Fifty yards. Forty. The man was streaming over the rocks and logs and detritus that lined the stream as if it were an asphalt track. Thirty yards. The gorge beckoned. Twenty. As he neared, Pete could see him measuring, waiting for the opportunity to pitch himself out onto the raft. Fifteen yards. Pete couldn't take his eyes off Jake. He hunkered down clutching his spear, ready. Then, without warning, Jake pulled up, and Pete slipped into the cut, the palisades shooting up on either side of him, giving Jake nowhere to go.

"We're not finished Peter."

Pete shuddered as the raft tumbled into the torrent; the swift water, compressed between the rock faces, its power concentrated now into a space no more than fifteen yards across. It grabbed his little raft and jerked it into the moonless shadows. He sat up and began to push it from the walls and did his best to keep it centered and headed downstream, but it was difficult and several times the little craft spun in a circle and careened into one or the other of the walls and Pete half expected the nylon ties to give way, pitching him into this cauldron. He was having an increasingly hard time staying atop the thing as it was tossed around over rapids and against the rock walls. And so he readied himself for a plunge into this raging flood, remembering his white water lessons: feet downstream, knees lose and flexed, head up. Don't know which is worse, Jake or this he thought. But he knew. At least this was mindless. Jake was anything but that.

But now he had to ready himself. He couldn't see in the gloom, but he heard a deafening roar from up ahead. He pointed his bow downstream, grabbed the nylon chord and searched for downstream Vs, ready to steer into them as best he could, hoping that the thundering he heard was not a waterfall.

CHAPTER 52

Karen was about to spend her second night on Nation Mountain. She'd been studying the horizon to the east through hi-powered binoculars, looking for signs of the plumes of smoke she'd seen the night before, before the storm arrived. They'd been spread out about ten or so miles apart, and Karen knew it had to be them. No campers would be up here this early. Duquoin had been right; they'd left Kitchener and were heading this way. At least they were coming to her.

She didn't know what to make of the fact that they'd split up, but she remembered Duquoin's counsel, "If there's trouble, he'll come here," so there was trouble. Where was Pete? Which fire had been his? Then for some reason, she thought of Dawkins, and she shuddered. Was Pete being chased? But no one could catch Pete. Not even Jake. So he must have been at the nearest fire, and he must be headed this way. She considered going out to meet him, then thought better of it, and decided to stay on the peak for at lest another day to be sure they were headed to Cold Fish.

She'd been scanning the area over and over again since the morning and there'd been no sign of any campfires. As she'd searched, the sun had set behind her, and the hills and peaks before her shifted from purple to indigo before finally fading into the dark blue night. She allowed herself to drop the binoculars when she could no longer see. Her arms ached and she tried to rub the stiffness from her neck, but the cold was bighting at her fingers and making her clumsy and she fumbled with the draw string on her parka. She fought the stiffness and raised the binoculars again. Perhaps she'd be able to see a fire through the gloom.

As she continued to scan, the moon, nearly full, rose to the east lighting the entire area below. She put down the binoculars and watched in awe as the universe got recreated in a silver blue light. God, it's like standing on top of the world she thought. Far below and to her left, Cold Fish Lake shimmered with shattered moonlight, and all around her, the snow-capped peaks vibrated blue-white, and even the valleys glowed faintly blue.

It was getting colder now, and her breath left white clouds lingering in the air before her. She'd have to crank her fire up soon. She scanned the area one more time. She'd been focusing on the western horizon, but when she looked off south and west of her target area she was pretty sure there was a curl of smoke rising in the moonlight. If it were one of them, they'd changed directions. The map showed an old abandoned right-of-way off to the south. Maybe they were headed toward it. Tomorrow, maybe she'd strike out and see, but for now, she had to prepare for the night. She tossed some wood on the fire, put on her headlamp and took out a packet of freeze-dried chicken stew. As she ripped it open she noticed it was marked "Gourmet," and she allowed herself a smile. "I'll bet," she said. She thought about moving away from camp to cook, but decided she'd be alright. Her food container was air-tight and bear proof, and when she was done, she'd put the wrapper and cooking gear in it and stow it a little ways off from the camp. In a few minutes, the stew began to steam, and it did smell like a gourmet meal. But then right now Alpo would have. The package said it would take twelve to fifteen minutes of boiling to rehydrate at this altitude, so she sat back, wishing now she'd set up a separate cooking fire, as the smell penetrated the forest below. She was glad she brought the Glock. Shooting something, even a bear, had seemed impossible back in Smithers, but it made a whole lot more sense now, as the odors announced her presence to everything within miles.

But dinner passed without incident. She packed up the cooking gear, got into her tent, closed the bag around her, then slipped out of her parka and pants. Inside the bag, her longjohns and wool socks kept her warm enough. Keeping the headlamp turned on, she spread out the map and examined it. Odd that they'd headed for the right-of-way. It added two, maybe three days to their trek. Sure, it was the right thing to do, now that the radio at Cold Fish was broken, but they couldn't have known about that. Maybe someone was injured, and they were trying to go around the worst of the mountains.

She was getting drowsy when she heard the wolves howling. She'd heard them the night before, but they'd been a ways off. Now, it sounded as if they were right outside. Karen wrapped the cowl of her bag a little tighter around her head but their calls continued, so loud now they nearly shook the tent. She tried to think of something else, anything, but the wolves didn't let up, and after several minutes she could hear what sounded like paws treading in the snow just beyond the thin tent wall. She pressed the side gingerly; the six-mil rip-stop nylon felt insubstantial and she began to nibble that certain spot on the inside of her cheek, the one she'd chewed raw after her mother died, and repeated over and over to herself, "There hasn't been a fatal wolf attack in more than a century ..." It didn't help. She knew she shouldn't be afraid – or she hoped she shouldn't – but then how many women alone in the middle of a wilderness like Spatsizi were captured in those comforting statistics? None, probably. Besides, actuarial numbers didn't silence the howls, or the panting she thought she heard. Once, after lying still for what seemed an eternity, she felt what she thought must be a nose press against the tent wall poking her in the back of her head, and she heard a snuffle followed by the sound of several wolves padding around the tent, panting heavily. They know I'm in here, was all she could think. She lay there still for what seemed an hour, too frightened to move, so scared it was physically painful, all the while asking herself what the hell she thought she was doing sitting up here at the top of the world. Did she really think she was going to save Pete? From *Jake* no less. As if.

Sometime after she began to tremble, she decided that if she survived this night, she'd call Duquoin, tell him to pick her up, and take her back to Smithers. She'd also pay Lenny a visit and slap him across the face. *You love him, you got to do somethin'.* Yeah, easy for you to say, asshole. Maybe she could even get her job back. Christ. What the fuck are you doing, girl?

At some point she realized the howls had stopped, and she could no longer hear them stalking about. Not knowing where they were was scarier than knowing. She had to get up and locate them, or she'd never sleep, might even possibly die of fright. Moving as silently as possible, she slipped her pants on, then her shirt and parka and boots. When she was dressed, she took a deep breath, pulled out the Glock and unzipped the tent flap. The zipper sounded like a large industrial machine of some kind, but there was no turning back. She slithered out, her ears straining to catch any sound of their presence, as she breathed in slow, measured pulls so that they wouldn't hear her. Once out of the tent, she walked over to the ledge she'd stood upon earlier, seeing their paw prints in the snow circling around her campsite. The moon was higher, now, and the night was neon.

She saw them as soon as she reached the ledge. They were cavorting in a snow field right below her on the eastern side of the mountain in a shallow depression. In the moonlight, they appeared to be a living pewter sculpture set in motion. There were seven in all, but three stood out: a big black and tan, a slightly smaller charcoal colored female, and a large silver grey one that seemed to run the pack. The other four looked to be about two years old, full grown, but not yet aware of their power, not yet able to handle their bodies with the grace and skill that the three exhibited.

The big silver-grey one dominated the play. He set himself at the top of the snow field, and dared any to take him down. Adept at using his paws, time after time he'd knock the back legs out from beneath one or another of the others, sending them caterwauling down the slope. They would get up resolutely and scamper up the hill, but none were able to take his place. After about fifteen minutes of this play, their breath was coming out in large glowing moon-silvered plumes that froze in the air, hanging there suspended for a time before disappearing, and the leader stopped abruptly. He loped to an overlook just twenty five yards below Karen and surveyed the area intently, paying no attention to the human above him, but rather focusing on some point to the east off in the distance. Presently, he howled again, and Karen grabbed the Glock from her belt. The others gathered round the silver one and joined in. After a moment, he turned and stared at her. From this range, she could see its eyes, molten gold against the thick silver grey fur and the night behind him, and she took her hand off the pistol, marveling at such perfection.

She'd stopped trembling. Watching them play together had made the wolves seem less threatening. Clearly they weren't interested in her, at any rate. Except the Alpha. That exchange between her and the silver grey one, was – she searched for the right word, but all she could come up with was: intimate. No sleeping now, she thought. She returned to the tent, and noticed the fire was dying down, and her wood pile was depleted. She'd have to get more.

Her camp was just at tree line, so she was forced to head downslope to gather up firewood. She went to the south side of the peak, away from the wolves. It was darker among the trees, and the wolves had started another round of howls as she collected wood. At least she knew where they were. When the howls stopped, she hustled back to the tent, feeling the same cold clamp of fear around her chest as she'd felt when Duquoin'd showed her the bear track back at the cabins. But by the time she got back, the wolves had settled down again. They were huddled up in a tight wad on the snow field below her camp. Now that she was over her initial fright, there was something comforting in their presence. She steeled up her nerve and shouted, "Hey. You. What's your game?" Her voice echoed down the valley, but the wolves ignored her. "You heard me. What do you want?" The silver grey one yawned and stretched, creating a fury of supplication from the lower ranked wolves, who got up, walked around, their hindquarters wiggling, their heads low, before repositioning themselves. Presently, the big grey wandered over to the ledge and howled and the others joined in. Once again, at this range she found the resonance of their calls stunning. It sounded at once powerful and plaintive and it drove out any remaining fear she felt, leaving only awe. Awe and a sense of a shared pathos, as if both of them had been driven up here to this highest peak in this last refuge by the hundred fates and furies that filled the world down there, leaving nothing – no room for the wild things in life, be they passion or person – save the scripted conformity of humanity.

Then, as her eyes met the golden gaze of the grey once more, she thought she knew for just an instant, what Duquoin had been trying to tell her about Jake when he'd shown her Lu's fangs. What it was he sought, and what he would be capable of doing if he didn't get it.

CHAPTER 53

As he barreled down the funnel formed by the basalt walls, Pete saw the source of the roar. A large rock stood directly in the center of the river at its narrowest point, just before it flowed over a small ledge and shot down a long chute. The water was hitting the boulder and curling up and around it, forming a standing wave of some six feet and generating a sound like liquid thunder. The froth glowed in the moonlight, and Pete was fairly sure he could make out a hydraulic on the front side, left of the ledge, waiting to suck him under. He studied the water, trying to divine the safest route. Once he'd chosen which side of the rock he wanted to try, he'd use his spear to push off the rock in order to get there. As he hurtled toward the big boulder he got a good look at his choices. Neither was good, but it appeared as if the right was a little easier. The current would take him left. He wasn't sure he could get enough power to push himself off the rock in any case, and right now he was careening straight toward it. As he got his spear ready, something crashed into the water from above, just left of his head, startling him. He looked up and saw Jake standing on the edge of a precipice, maybe thirty feet above. He was looking down and shaking his fist. That settled it. Pete would have to go left and try to put the rock between him and Jake, hydraulic be damned. But Jesus. How did the son-of-a-bitch get up there so fast?

As he hurtled straight at the big boulder, he took his spear and shoved it out, trying to get it on the left face. It struck, and Pete leaned into it as hard as he could, spear in one hand, the other twisted into the nylon twine in the front of the raft. It slowed for just a second, and then the spear shattered, and the raft slammed into the rock, bounced back then hit it again, turned broadside and remained pinned there by the current.

Jake hurled another rock down on him, and it splashed into the water less than foot to the right of the raft while the water held him there, helpless, in the center of the river. The raft was jammed against the boulder, and the front edge started to go under as hundreds of thousands of gallons began to push it from the front. Pete rolled over to the left, trying to stabilize it with his weight and at the same time, put his foot against the rock, the nylon chord digging into his hand now, and he shoved with all his strength. He knew enough not to push against the current; instead he pushed at ninety degrees to it, hoping it would be enough to kick it off the rock. Slowly, the back end started to come around, then suddenly the current caught it and whipped it off the rock, spinning it to the left and nearly swallowing the raft under the water. It hesitated at the standing wave for a moment, tilting crazily, then popped over it and Pete went spinning down the chute holding on desperately, one eye on Jake, the other on the rapids ahead, unable to do anything about either one.

Once past the rock wall, the Spatsizi went down a long chute carved into the softer rock. It was deep enough to carry the raft, and Pete's main challenge was to hold on. He did this by laying flat on its surface, and digging his foot under the nylon chord on the bottom, and his hands under the one on top, although the exact meaning of top and bottom was dubious in the spinning, twirling trip Pete was being taken on. There were a few rocks in the chute, and a downed aspen blocked a good part of the river at one point, but the craft stayed with the water and other than bouncing off several rocks, it passed through pretty well. Pete didn't mind. It put more distance between him and Jake, although distances didn't seem relevant where Jake was concerned. After several more miles of fast water, the river reached the plateau and spread out, running shallower and more slowly, meandering across the soft glacial soils. Its banks were shallow, and bogs lined either side and here and there an oxbow was left stranded. As slow as it was, Pete could take some solace in the fact that Jake would be forced to backtrack and detour around the swamps and shallows that lined the river for the rest of his trip.

He guessed he had ten or less miles until he got to the Cold Fish Lake and the Trail. That would put him there well after midnight. He weighed leaving the raft, and striking out on foot, but decided against it. He was fairly sure Jake would catch him either way, but at least he'd be fresh if he rode. And besides, if Jake got tired, who knows? Just before he'd come out of the chute onto the high plain, he'd spotted Jake climbing down the rock face. Although it was only about hundred or so feet higher than the plateau on this side, it appeared to Pete to be a technical climb, requiring rope and carbines and hardware, but Jake was doing it freehand. Crazy son of a bitch.

As he flowed easy across the flat, he tried to figure out what had happened here. Clearly, Jake had wigged out. Some kind of God complex. But then, maybe he had, too. Could this all be part of the "training"? Would he arrive at Cold Fish and find Keller and Eunice and Joan and Bill and Sarah and Thom waiting for him, big grins on their faces? God if only it were so. If only he weren't being chased by some psychotic superman intent on ... on what?

But he knew. Cleansing the Earth. Somewhere on this trip, he'd become convinced we couldn't be anything other than mindless agents of consumption, unchecked by evolution. And now he was a one man environmental vigilante. There was another possibility, but Pete wasn't ready for that yet. He wasn't ready because at some level, it was the only thing that made sense, and it violated much of what he believed. And then there was the fact the he basically agreed with Jake, even if he didn't come to the same conclusions about methods and means.

He took stock of himself and his situation. No weapons. But his strength was coming back. He was able to rest, now, and much of the stiffness and soreness was gone, maybe from his plunge in the icy river. He'd been taking in water and jerky and birch strips. He'd slept some last night and this afternoon. As far as he knew, Jake had only had a few hours sleep in the past several days. But it didn't matter. He knew now he was no match for Jake. No one was. But it didn't frighten him. Instead, he started to plan; to use his head, instead of locking himself into some macho proving ground. And the more he thought, the more obvious the solution became. Once again, he would have to become the hunter. He noticed that he'd wedged the arrows Jake had fired between two of the logs and he wrenched one out. For a moment, he wondered how Jake had missed him. The man had consistently hit knot holes at fifty yards when he was testing the bow. Maybe he'd missed on purpose. Maybe it was a warning of some kind, he thought hopefully. Then he studied the point and said aloud, "Fool."

The moonlight was intense, and Pete searched south and east for signs of Jake. He thought he saw him way off, detouring around a large bog that lined the river, but in the fading light, he couldn't be sure whether it was Jake or a caribou or even a bear. He just knew it moved. Next he scanned the river in front of him. There looked to be a stream coming in from the west about three miles downriver. If so, it would be the Mink. He'd be coming to the trail soon. That's where he'd spring his trap. He'd read of cougars, who when hunted, would come around behind the hunter and stalk him. That would be his tactic. He'd lead Jake up the Cold Spring Trail, right to the cabins, then circle back down the trail a mile or so. Jake would drop his guard then, and sprint to the cabins to prevent him from getting to the radio. Pete thought about trying to reason with Jake, but he realized that as they got near the cabins and the radio, Jake would become increasingly desperate. No, he would have to disable him, or if necessary, kill him. And to do that he would have to take him by surprise.

The next three miles were critical. He had to beat Jake to the Mink and the trail head. He searched the wide flat valley repeatedly as his raft drifted slowly toward Mink Creek. Several times he thought he saw a figure, dim in the moonlight, far to the east, but keeping up with him, running an easy lope along the higher, firmer ground nearer the mountains. Periodically he'd disappear, and Pete would double his vigilance, fearing that Jake would appear out of nowhere, or fearing that he'd hear that voice – close, yet coming from everywhere, ubiquitous, like thunder echoing around in a valley. But the figure stayed to the high ground. It was the right thing to do, Pete knew. Earlier, he'd come out of the chute wet and even in the gortex, he'd come dangerously close to hypothermia. And yet Jake's willingness to put miles between them for the sake of staying dry was disturbing to Pete. It meant he wasn't desperate. It meant he had strength. But it wouldn't matter. Not this time.

Pete pulled past Mink Creek, the full moon at its peak. Perfect timing he thought. Only six more miles. Somewhere east, way off in the mountains on the other side of Cold Fish, he heard some wolves begin their nightly howl, and he smiled, confident in what he was about to do.

CHAPTER 54

Karen sat before her open tent flap. By now, the wolves had become familiar – almost companions. Periodically, she fixed her binoculars on the cabins and the trail leading to them to see if any one were arriving. It was past midnight, and the moon had come up high, lighting the area below her. It was almost as good as daylight. Her fire was dying again, and she pulled on her parka and headed downslope to get some more wood. She came to an old lightning-gnarled spruce nestled beneath a cliff face, its dead limbs looking something like an enormous scarecrow in the blue-black light of a moon shadow. As she was bending over to pick up a fair sized branch at the base of it, she looked up and saw the silver wolf standing on the ledge above, staring at her. At least she thought it was. In the moonlight, its silver coloring made it almost invisible, and its eyes, although possessed with the same passion, seemed to have turned an intense blue . When she shook her head and tried to focus in on the spot again, it was gone. After that, she hustled back to the tent and fed the fire.

She warmed her hands before it, then scanned the area carefully again with her binoculars. Nothing. It was a calm, transparent night, and the wolves still sat on the rise below her huddled close again, but seemingly sharing in her vigilance.

"So, what're you after?" She called to the big grey. But again, it ignored her. The others stood and shifted around in the snow, their pelts luminescent. It looked to her like some staged production of a black and white film, the figures moving about like silver specters against a backdrop of opalescent pearl. She watched, surprised to find that she wanted to join them – to take her place in the preordained order that was the pack, and never have to question again, just go by that other script, the first one, the one that had no choices.

The wolves were becoming individuals to her now. There was the alpha female, with a thick charcoal coat; the beta male, a big black and tan, only slightly less regal than the alphas. Then there was the omega – a handsome physical specimen that nevertheless earned the scorn of every member of the pack. Shunned, excluded from eating, destined to fawn and grovel beneath the barred teeth of every other wolf, yet somehow satisfied with its place. Then there were the other two year olds. Probably a new pack. It could be that they have never seen humans. That might account for their interest. But, no. When she and the alpha stared into each other's eyes, there was a knowledge there. Intimate, knowing, it seemed to stare through and into her, seeing that which no one else saw, and not judging.

But of course that could not be. She stood up and stretched her legs, then walked to the edge of the cliff face and took in the area one more time, before going to bed. She saw nothing, and returned to the tent. Tomorrow she would pack up and head back down. Perhaps hike out to where she'd seen that fire and see if she could pick up a trail. But for now, she needed to sleep. She chucked a few logs onto the fire, stripped off her parka and pants, then crawled into the tent and back into her bag. She put her clothes in with her, to keep them warm. In just a few moments her body heat filled the down bag and she felt drowsy and good. The last thing she saw before falling off to sleep were the strange shapes of shadows from the fire silhouetted against the tent. Sleep came easy.

Sometime after she'd fallen asleep, she heard them. They were howling again, from somewhere very far away. There was desperation in their calls. She rushed out of the tent, afraid for them and listened, trying to pinpoint the direction of the howling. Finally, she did, and she put her binoculars on them. The moon was at her back, now, and she saw everything clearly.

CHAPTER 55

Pete hunkered down in the shadow of a small grove of spruce, just off the trail behind a thicket of willow. It was an ideal spot, just inside the moon shadow, so that he was very near the trail, but out of sight. He'd gone into the center of the Tom Walker Cabins, and circled out behind the trail to get here, so there would be no sign to tip Jake off. He was just within sight of the cabins, and the moon, now sitting above the large peak across the lake, lit up the path in front of him brilliantly. He was scared, but ready. His breath was coming fast, and his heart was pumping hard, as if he'd been running, but he sat frozen still, his eyes glued to the trail, waiting for Jake. He had a good vantage point; although he was in shadow, the trail passed through a meadow for better than a hundred yards on its way to him after coming up over a small rise. With the moon light, he'd be able to see Jake coming as soon as he cleared the hill. And this close to the cabins, Jake would be intent on tracing Pete's trail and getting to him before he reached the radio, so he wouldn't be looking for an ambush. Now, all Pete had to do was keep from freezing while he waited. In the last few hours, the temperature had plummeted.

The rock he held in his hand was about the same size as the one he'd hurled at Jim. He wouldn't throw it, though. He wasn't about to risk missing and confronting Jake unarmed. He'd jump out and knock him out from behind, tie him up with the nylon twine he'd salvaged from the raft, then bring him to, lead him into the camp and radio the authorities. After that, he would be their problem. But now that it was coming down to it, he was having regrets. There was that other side to Jake. The side that represented hope. The side that offered an answer.

The side that seemed to exhibit so much compassion, so much wisdom, albeit in the midst of brutality. Pete had the sense that he'd witnessed some struggle within the man, between forces unknown and unknowable to him. The one that won, however, had to be brought to justice for what he'd done.

"Seeking justice, Peter?"

It was as if every part of Pete's corporeal body had suddenly turned to liquid, and then been flash frozen. He went weak, then went still as a block of ice. The son-of-a-bitch was behind him.

"Did you ever notice how the moisture in your breath freezes on nights like this? And how the moon lights it up? You can see those puffs floating like clouds of silver from quite a ways. Quite beautiful, actually."

Pete turned just his head, and saw Jake about twenty yards behind him, standing on a rock, an arrow notched and drawn, pointing straight at him.

"Don't move, Peter. We're in danger."

There was an urgency in his voice. Why was Jake being so cautious? He remembered Thom's burial mound by the wolves' den and how careful Jake had been then. What is it about me that does this, he wondered.

"What's the matter, Jake? Scared of me?"

He laughed; the sound was mocking. "Bravery? Well, Peter, you've certainly overcome your little weakness, haven't you?"

"And I guess you still haven't."

"What do you mean?"

"Anger. You said it was something you've been working on for a long time."

"You've no idea how long." Again, Jake laughed, but it sounded hollow.

Pete tried to think what to do. He needed to keep him talking, but other than that, he was fresh out of plans. Perhaps he'd have a chance to heave the rock.

"It's over, Peter."

"Let's talk about justice, Jake. Even if you kill me, they will find you. They will bring you in and make you pay for what you've done."

Jake shot back, "Kill you? I'm trying to save you from killing your-selves."

"You're mad, you know."

"Me, mad? That's rich, coming from you. All I've ever done is to try to save you from the bear. You? You've concocted some story about me being the bear. Jesus, Peter, don't you know? Don't you know yet? Do you believe this choice has been easy? You were the last hope. And in the end you turned on me. You denied me."

"Quit speaking in riddles, Jake. There is no bear. And you know it."

"No. You are wrong. He's been stalking us. He still is."

No more listening to his bullshit. Pete stood, whirled, and pitched the stone in one smooth motion. A strike. He knew it as soon as it left his hand. It hurtled at eighty miles an hour straight for Jake's forehead, dead center. In the instant that it took to travel the twenty yards, Pete was readying his next move. It would knock Jake out, and he could tie him up, just as he planned. Even if it didn't, it would knock him down and daze him, and he could finish the job before he recovered. But even as these thoughts flashed across his mind, he watched in horror as Jake dropped the bow, ducked and shielded his face with his left arm. He heard the rock smack into Jake's arm and heard a muffled cry of pain.

He watched Jake clutch his arm. What happened during the next ...what? ... It could have been a few minutes, or several hours. He could remember parts of it, but it would never be completely clear to Pete what happened or how long it took. Or, perhaps he did remember it, but couldn't accept it.

He took off immediately. He had no real hope of out running Jake, but he had to try. He sprinted in the direction of the cabins, hoping he might get there in time to barricade himself in and maybe get a call out. Or find a weapon. He was moving as fast as he had ever run, chewing up the ground in powerful, fluid strides, but he could feel Jake behind him, closing. The nearest cabin was perched on a hill just off the trail and it stood maybe a half mile off, now. Pete could feel himself tiring, and he heard Jake's breathing behind him, getting closer with each stride. He wouldn't make the cabins. He looked for a place where he could make a stand, maybe duck out of sight or find something to use as a weapon, anything. About a hundred yards ahead there was a stand of aspen off to the right and uphill a bit, the trunks leaden in the moonlight. He ran for it. Maybe he could use the trees to his advantage. With Jake's footfalls getting closer, he dug into a place he'd never touched and quickened his pace. Incredibly, it sounded like Jake was falling behind. But then he heard a grunt or maybe a gasp and Jake began to close again. But it didn't matter. Pete would make the aspen.

He dodged his way through the trunks, taking branches in his face as he went and headed for a rock in the center of the stand. He hurdled onto it and spun around to face Jake, assuming a crouch, his side to the attacker, holding his arms out, and standing on the balls of his feet just as he'd been taught in karate.

Jake pulled up about five yards out and seemed to be studying him, looking for a way in. "You need help Peter."

But he stopped, and seemed to be staring over Pete's shoulder with something like horror. At least as close as Jake could come to horror. Pete assumed it was a trick, and refused to turn, even when Jake said, "I want you to get down from the rock and stand behind me."

"What do you take me for?" But Peter stopped. Because now he smelled it – the same dank death smell he'd encountered back at the stream after the hunt, and he knew. And then he was flying through the air. He hit a trunk and crumpled against it. The bear came into view, big and silvery-black in the moonlight. Jake was trying to raise the bow, but his left arm wasn't working.

Pete wasn't sure whether he'd been thrown by Jake or the bear, but Jake was between him and the monster now, repeating calmly over and over again, as he circled in an arc just out of reach of the bear, but keeping himself between it and Pete, "Get to the cabins, Peter. Move now. You've got to go."

But Pete couldn't move. He lay against the trunk, stunned, wanting to help this man. As he started to rise, Jake, using his right hand, pulled his stone knife out and waved him back. "Go," he said.

"No, Jake. Come on. We'll go together."

The bear looked at him a moment then fixed his black-eyed glare on Jake. Jake spoke in a monotone, without taking his eyes off it. "Go now Pete. This isn't an ordinary bear – he'll come for you after he gets through me. One of us must live. I hope you've learned, Peter. I hope you know what I was trying to do. Trust what you believe ..."

But Jake never finished. The behemoth drew back its right paw and swiped it across Jake's chest ripping his shirt and leaving claw marks across his shoulder. As Pete watched in the pale blue lunar light, the blood oozed purple-black from the wounds across Jake's chest and over his shoulder and Pete counted, in horror, only four bloody tracks. Jake plunged the knife into the bear's shoulder, but it barely noticed, and took another swipe at Jake, this time raking him across the face, leaving four purple trails over his left cheek. Pete watched Jake crumple to the ground, his head striking a rock, his neck snapping with an audible crack.

Suddenly, Pete was back in that alley. He heard Gus screaming; heard the sickening thuds, felt the knife pressing into his back; felt the white hot rage but felt no fear. He heard the bear snort and was back here in the moonlight, and Jake lay at his feet.

He counted the claw marks on Jake's face again. Four. And despite the fact that the bear was turning, now, to him, he could not stop counting, could not stop mumbling over and over to himself, "It couldn't be. No, it couldn't be." And then he knew he was next, and it didn't matter. He grabbed the knife from Jake's hand and managed to stand up, his back against an aspen. The bear was coming now, but Pete felt no fear.

CHAPTER 56

As Karen focused down the binoculars, they came into view. The Alpha was out in front. He tore across an open stretch of meadow a little less than a half mile east of the cabins, his body coiling and uncoiling as the earth sped by beneath him. Grace. It was the only word that would do, and Karen groped for it, couldn't find it, but knew it in that place beneath words, that place of essences. The female was just behind, followed by the Beta and then the others. They were racing toward a small copse of aspen, still leafless this early in the spring. Karen moved her binoculars to the aspen and saw the bear first. It was a big bruiser, and she worried immediately that the wolves might get hurt – if that's where they were headed. But then she saw the figure of a man, leaning against the trunk of an aspen, holding something in his hand, trying to ward off the bear with it. Even in the pearl moonlight, she recognized Pete. She pulled her clothes on, grabbed the Glock and started running.

Pete kept the knife pointed at the bear as it circled him. It seemed to be agitated, and it sniffed the air nervously, but it continued to study Pete, its small black eyes on the knife. After sniffing the air one more time, it stood on its hind legs and made a few clumsy steps forward, then dropped onto all fours The smell was overwhelming and he remembered the sound it made as it crunched the caribou's skull between its jaws, crushing it as if it were an eggshell. It could reach him now, and Pete readied himself. He knew what to expect, having just watched the attack on Jake. It will use its right paw, it will go for my trunk first, then my head once I'm wounded. Sure enough, he saw the right paw come back, then shoot out, lightening quick, putting even Ali's jab to shame. But Pete was ready, and he knew what was coming – and so, just as the bear started his swipe, he dropped and brought the knife up hard under its chin, plunging it into its neck as the paw brushed over him. It roared, then dropped back a few steps and studied Pete and rolled its head back and forth as if it were saying no. A long string of red-tinged spittle drooled out the left side of its mouth. Again, it sniffed the air, seemed disturbed, and it rose up on its hind legs, towering above Pete swaying back and forth as it studied the forest in the direction of the cabins. It dropped down and cocked a paw back and Pete readied himself, but this time it struck him a glancing blow with the right paw. The claws raked across his shoulder, creased his scalp and sent him flying. He landed about eight feet away, his shoulder aching, his head foggy. He waited for death. But the bear stood back up on its hind legs and sniffed, looking to the east. Pete tried to clear his head, tried to wriggle away, but the bear spied him moving and it dropped to all fours again, and started to saunter over to him. Now it was over, he knew. Now, Death was coming.

The Alpha launched himself at the bear from seven yards away. It hit him right at the neck and clamped its jaws down tight, as the black and tan came in from behind and ripped at the bear's hindquarters. With a shake of its neck, the bear flung the alpha off, but he took a mouthful of flesh with him. The bear turned on the beta, but the wolf sprang back, and the alpha female darted in and tore at the bear's hindquarters from its backside. The alpha male was up again, and it moved in, its head down, its teeth barred, a low rumbling roar issuing from deep within its throat. The others rushed in now, positioning themselves between Pete and the bear.

Can't be happening. Can't. But though his head was still spinning, and his shoulder was throbbing, and he was losing consciousness, he knew it was, and he knew he had to help the wolves. He fought to stay awake. The bear pivoted to face the Alpha, exposing its back to Pete, and he lurched forward, slicing at the beast's hamstring with the knife. He heard it roar, watched it hobble as it sought to turn on him, saw the wolves circling and closing in as it turned. The bear was backing away, into the forest. Safe now, he thought. Safe. Then as the whole fantastic scene before him faded into a growing wall of black, he caught the molten-eyed glance of the Alpha, a benediction he would carry with him to the grave.

Karen found him lying against a boulder. As she squatted down to examine the extent of his injuries, she said over and over again, "No. Please. No." His left eye was swollen closed and his windbreaker and shirt were ripped open. Four deep claw marks ran across his shoulder and his face, and five more creased his back, but the bleeding was light, and he was breathing. He held a stone knife in his right hand, and his left clutched her medallion, and Karen struggled to keep from crying.

She cut his windbreaker off then cut through his shirt. Using the remains of the tattered shirt, she wiped the wounds, and then she examined them. Each of the four gashes was a serious injury in itself. She cleaned them out with water from her canteen, then she ripped several strips from the shirt and used them to apply pressure to the lacerations. When she was satisfied they were as tight as she could get them, she tied them off and turned to Pete's face and scalp. She took what was left of the shirt and soaked it then held it against his face. She kissed him gently on his forehead. Pete started to come to. He looked up and saw Karen, confused at first, but then recognized her and smiled. "So is this heaven?" he asked.

"It is if you're OK."

"Yeah ... yeah, I think I am."

She hugged him, and he tried to hug her back with his good arm. After a second he stiffened, then struggled to get up and said, "The bear?"

Karen supported him, "Gone."

"Jake. Is he ...?" Then he remembered. "I want to bury him."

"Jake?" Karen asked.

Pete looked over to where Jake had fallen. There was nothing there.

EPILOGUE

Pete opened his eyes to find a man studying the wounds on his shoulder. He seemed to be in some kind of hospital, but he couldn't remember getting here. The doctor – if that's what he was – looked to be about fifty years old, but his face was weathered, thick-skinned and wrinkled, and permanently tanned. Pete shifted a bit as the man examined one of the claw marks.

"Welcome to the land of the living."

"Where am I?"

"Dease Lake. I'm Doc Benson. How are you feeling?"

He lay back into the pillow and took inventory. His arm hurt a bit, and his face felt tight, as if the skin had been stretched, but other than that he felt good. "Not bad," he replied.

"Not surprising. You've been asleep for over sixteen hours ..."

"The others?" Pete asked.

"They're fine. Helicopter picked them up yesterday." Doc Benson replaced the bandage on Pete's face and stood up. "Your girlfriend said I was to get her as soon as you woke up."

He reached for the medallion and felt the embracing figures. He remembered the wolves, the bear, Jake and then her image hovering above him. "She's alright?"

"Yeah. But I sent her out about a half hour ago. Hadn't left your bedside since you got here." He checked the saline solution and the intravenous line and added, "There's a Mountie out there who needs to talk to you about what happened ..."

"Not sure I can tell him much." Then he asked, "Doc, is it possible to get cut up like this and not bleed much?"

He looked at him for a moment, then said, "Why do you ask?"

"Just curious."

"Well. Ordinarily, a person with wounds like yours would've lost a lot of blood. But when it's real cold that'll slow it up sometimes."

Pete frowned. That would explain Thom. But he had to let all that go. He knew that now.

"You don't remember the attack?" Benson asked.

Pete looked at him, the image of the bear and Jake and the wolves swirling before him. "Yeah. Some. The attack's clear enough. It's what happened before."

"Look, Pete. You've been through a lot. It's natural for you to bury this. When you're ready you'll remember. Meanwhile, you just tell the Mountie what you can. And if you get tired, call me. I'll get him out of here." Then he hustled out.

Pete lay there, remembering how similar the words from another doctor were, nearly twenty-five years ago. Then he was back in that kitchen, and he heard his father saying ... *He didn't even try* ... and he said out loud, "Yes I did, you son-of-a-bitch."

As he waited for the Mountie, trying to reconstruct the past two weeks, he came to understand something. In a sense, Jake was only doing – had only tried to do – the thing Pete couldn't do twenty-five years ago. Protect what he loved.

The room seemed quiet, and the bed extravagantly comfortable. There was the steady hiss of an old, ornate radiator, parked just beneath the window. Like most hospitals it was too warm, the windows were kept closed and the air was stuffy. Trying to keep the germs in, his mother used to say. He felt drowsy, and he let himself drift off for a moment. Cool lips kissing his forehead woke him and he stretched, then opened his eyes. When he saw Karen, he smiled and took her hand. "You OK?"

She smiled back. "Yeah." Then she stammered out, "I was afraid I'd lost you."

"I told you I'd be back."

"You said we'd check in when the trip was over? See where we are?"

Pete looked down for a moment. How could he tell her what he barely understood himself? "I've got some things I have to do, Karen."

He saw the sadness in her eyes, then watched as she gathered herself. "Somehow I knew you were going to say that." They held hands for what seemed to Pete a long time. "I think he was a very lonely man," she said.

"He was."

She took his hand to her lips, and kissed it. "We could do these things together."

"Are you sure? If you stay with me, your life will never be easy."

"Yeah. I thought you might say that, too." She squeezed his hand and blinked back some tears before she stood up and leaned over him, and kissed him. "But here's the thing. It's never going to be easy if I don't."

She lay down beside him, and they held each other until Doc Benson came back in. "You ready for your visitor?"

"Tell 'em to come back later."

"Already tried that. He's got a lot of territory to cover and he wants to wrap this up. "

Benson went to the door and called out, "Baker? He's ready."

Karen stood up and smiled broadly as the Mountie walked in. "Canada's finest."

Baker shook her hand and smiled back. Then he turned to Pete and said, "I hear you had a rough time out there."

Pete nodded, and Baker turned to Karen, "You might as well stay. Got some questions about your statement."

"I wasn't planning on going anywhere."

Baker pulled up the one chair in the room, but didn't sit. Karen sat back down on the bed and she and Pete held hands. "Well, there's some lose ends," he began. "Like Jake's body's missing, and Jim looks like he was beat up pretty good before his death."

"Jim's dead?" Pete asked.

"Yeah," Baker answered. "Just got the coroner's report. A real mess. Bear got him. But he'd been in a fight before the bear."

"How many claw marks?" Pete asked.

"What?"

"How many claw marks did the bear leave?"

Baker flipped through his notebook. "Report says four."

Pete nodded. Baker turned to Karen and said, "And you have no idea about what happened to Jake?"

"Told you. He was gone before I got there."

Baker turned to Pete. "What about you?"

"From what I saw, the bear must've killed him."

"And the bear. What happened to him?" Before either one could answer, he answered himself, "Oh yeah. According to Ms. Flannigan, you told her you and the wolves chased him away." He sat down in the chair and sighed. "Disappearing bodies. Invisible bears. Friendly wolves. Sounds like a godamm Disney movie. What am I supposed to tell my chief?" He put his pen away and folded his pad, then leaned back in the chair. They were quiet for a long time, listening to the sounds of the clinic. The hissing of the radiator, ringing phones, pages, the thrum of motors, all muffled by walls and halls and doors. Finally, Baker leaned in close and said, "Here's the crazy thing. I believe you. I've been tryin' to figure out this guy for going on two decades, and every time I try, it gets crazier. So help me, Peter. Who *was* this guy?"

Pete looked up, studying Baker for a long time, then said, "Who's asking? Baker the man, or Baker the Mountie?"

"It's gone way beyond the job."

"OK. The way I see it, there's three possibilities."

"I'm listening."

"Well, it could be a bear ran amok. That's the easiest one. It's the one I'm trying to believe."

"It's happened before. Over in Quebec one time a big black bear got a taste for campers. Killed seven before they bagged him."

"Yeah. Could be that's it. There's just some things that don't add up."

"Like what?"

"Like a bear leaves tracks."

"So does a man."

"Yeah. A man would, too, I guess."

"So what's number two?"

"Number two? Number two is Jake ran amok. Lost his mind."

"Jake seemed pretty sane to me."

"Yeah. But he cared too much. Maybe he just couldn't stand to see another forest mowed down. Or maybe he got tired of watching us fuck up his world with oil and greed." Pete stretched and adjusted his pillows. "You know Baker, the whole time he was in Washington, I had the sense that he was almost stunned by what he saw around him. SUVs and trophy homes. Every square acre built up or blacktopped. Every hand holding PDAs, cell phones or Ipods. Every destination a box store, a mall or some trendy gotta-be-there palace of plastic gew-gaws or designer food. Everywhere stuff. Stuff we want, but nothing we need." Pete was still fiddling with his pillows, and Karen adjusted them, leaning into him as she did. As he felt her press lightly against him he thought about their nights together – two weeks ago, or was it two years – and he felt a rush of desire.

Baker coughed and said, "You were saying?"

Pete looked at Baker blankly, and Karen said, "I think you were go-ing into your Nieman Marcus rap."

He laughed and started again. "Did you know that in 2006 for the first time in the history of humanity, more than half of all people lived in urban areas?"

Baker shook his head no, and shrugged, then Pete continued. "Imagine yourself as Jake and look forward, Baker. What do you see?"

"I can't imagine what Jake sees," he answered.

"I'll tell you. Generation follows generation, each one more es-tranged from nature than the one before. No connection to the thing which shaped our essence, or any knowledge of the crucible which formed us. The natural world he loved so much becoming more like an alien landscape to rest of us with each passing decade. Already, most of us see nature only through televisions or on desk calendars. You can't love what you don't know, Baker. And you won't preserve and protect what you don't love."

Karen squeezed his hand and said, "Hey, you're getting good at this. Much better than that cathedrals in the forest crap. "

Pete grabbed her and pulled her down, chucking her hair and they laughed.

Baker smiled at the two, then checked his watch. "I'm still not sure what your point is."

Karen sat up, and examined his dressings, then got him a glass of water from the plastic pitcher on his night stand. "Maybe when he took us out there and he couldn't reach us, maybe he just cracked. Or maybe it's us that's cracked. I mean which is more insane. Chewing up every last stick of lumber and spewing shit out of smokestacks and tailpipes until you're baking the earth, or trying to stop it?"

Karen remembered her conversation with Baker about the choke setters and asked, "Sound familiar?"

Baker nodded, then asked, "How about the third explanation?"

"The third. It makes the least sense, but as I lay here, I keep coming back to it. "

"What is it?"

"You a religious man, Baker?"

"Not especially."

"Me neither." He took a pull of water then continued.

"But what if all this Shaman stuff was real. What if Jake were connected to the Earth in some way we just can't fathom? What if he could feel its insults and its injuries? Every balance tipped, every forest raped, every ecosystem pillaged, every species extinguished piercing his soul?"

"I'm afraid that's a bit too far out for me."

"Yeah. Of course. And yet as I lay here, I imagine what he must have felt – I can even feel it myself in some way I can't explain."

"What do you mean?"

"I'm really not sure I could articulate it yet."

"Try me."

"OK. Here goes. You think of yourselves as the watchers – the seekers and keepers of knowledge. And yet you've only been around for a scant fifty thousand years. And it's only in the past thirty thousand years that you've been pecking about for information, recording it, then pecking about for some more. You've kept it in myths and legends; you've written it down in tablets and books; you've inscribed it on disks and hard drives. You believe yourselves to be the compilers of the accumulated wisdom of the ages – but what you are is intellectual pack rats, hoarding billions of bits of information randomly scattered across your society. It is not wisdom. It is merely information. You with me?"

"I think so."

"Know anything about the human genome project?"

"Just what I read in the news. And what my wife tells me."

"OK. You see, the whole story resides within you. You have your history – the history of all life for that matter – 3.8 billion years worth of wisdom hardwired into you, inscribed with A's and G's and C's and T's. Everything that has ever happened. It's the true source of what we call wisdom. But somehow – perhaps when that first hominid glanced at his image in a pool of water and thought, 'Behold: it is me, and I am man' – you stepped outside this crucible that made you and you lost access to that wisdom. And somehow, I think Lynx and then Jake were the last threads of that link. But in the end, DNA, demigod or demon, it doesn't really matter. What matters is the truth of what he said."

"I'm afraid I'm not following you."

"How much time you got Baker?"

"I got all the time you want. Like I said, I've been chasing down the answer to this question for a long time."

"Might as well make yourself comfortable. I'm only just beginning to put this together. Let's just say that Jake has been able to touch that thing we have within us – that river of time that is our collective wisdom. How would someone who could do that see you? How would he measure your march over time? As progress? Suppose he looks over your fifty thousand year journey checking in every hundred years. He watches you utter your first words; watches you make your first tools. Watches you build your first structures, plant your first gardens, assemble your first cities, scribble down your first letters. It is exquisitely slow, this progress, but endlessly fascinating to him.

"Four thousand years ago, you write up rules and laws. Two thousand years ago you temper these laws with wisdom and love and empathy. I imagine him seeing the fruits of your efforts every hundred years with increasing interest, now. By the year 599, Rome has fallen, and he sees the dark ages overtaking Europe but he has hope because there are seeds of wisdom sprouting in Abbeys and Castles. And across the world, in China, in America, other cultures are living and growing in different ways. And you prosper – there are two hundred and fifty million of you now.

"Over the next five hundred years he sees knowledge and values and wisdom begin to flourish and expand outward like rings from the stones you have thrown into the intellectual firmament. Buddhism,

Confucianism, Mohammedism, Judaism, Christianity, Hinduism, the beautiful earth-centered religions in Africa and the Americas. Surely they will grow and join. Oh yes, he sees the greed, the violence, the lust for power, the folly and atrocities committed in the name of the churches, synagogues, mosques and organized religions, but surely this gift of reason will join and defeat these forces, rooted as they are in the basest, most primitive part of your being. So he sees you growing and prospering, becoming ever more complex, ever more like the ideal. Every hundred years, a steady march of progress. The Magna Carta, the Renaissance, the Enlightenment, The Declaration of Independence. Copernicus, Da Vinci, Bacon, Newton, Darwin, Jefferson. He sees humanity prospering. The experiment is working – it might even be some crowning achievement: life, aware of itself, charting its own course.

"By 1800, you number less than a billion, but you are thriving, and beginning to unlock the secrets of the universe. And by 1900 you surpass a billion – your people, growing wise, transcending the boundaries of space and time. The automobile, the train, and in three years, the airplane.

"But a mere hundred years later when he looks again, there's more than six billion of you, and something has gone horribly awry. There is precious little left of this world – your heritage. And no recognition that it is going. You scramble over it, consuming it like blind maggots on a corpse.

"You need help. Something must be done. What tools would he use to manipulate this far more complex world? In times past, Shamans and Saviors used miracles. But they happen every day now. No, he would have tried to tap into the political system of the world's most powerful nation. And what anger would he feel when it failed? When you had come to be more powerful than he? Could it be enough to drive even a deity mad? Perhaps. Or perhaps the madness is your own and he has, in the end, just chosen to go away, sensing your indifference to your own survival. Certainly he must feel your indifference to anything he would consider holy or sacrosanct. I keep going back to something Jake said, *You were an experiment.* Sometimes experiments get out of hand. Sometimes they blow up the lab and you just have to walk away and start over."

Baker was quiet. His eyes seemed glazed and now and then he nodded in agreement as Pete spoke. Pete had almost forgotten he was there as he talked. For a long time, no one spoke. Pete was half expecting Baker to say something like, *you're crazy*, and for one of the first times in a long time, he wouldn't have to actively consider the truth of it.

The radiator hissed on, and finally Baker said, "I don't know what my report's going to say, Pete, but there won't be any charges, and I don't see a trial."

"Oh, there will be a trial, Baker. There will be a trial."

Baker walked out, and Karen brushed the hair back from Pete's forehead. She lay down with her back to him, and he put his arm around her. She had something to say, and she was afraid to see his face when she said it. Even though she'd thought of several clever ways to broach it, in the end she blurted it out. "I'm pregnant."

The silence seemed to go on for too long, then he said, "Guess we better get busy, then. Got some whales to save. And a planet. Can't have our baby growing up in a world without Cathedrals."

She snuggled against him, and smiled. Yes, he was the one.

ACKNOWLEDGEMENTS

As with most first novels, many people provided advice, criticism, encouragement and support as I wrote it. Thank you all. In particular, I would like to thank Bill Adair, Kay Jackson, Joseph Romm and Brian Castelli, who were kind enough to read the earliest versions of this novel, and Joe for his continued advice and support throughout the process. To Marie Justice, who convinced me this story needed to be told, my sincere appreciation. My incredible writing group, Cindy Pon, Janice Coy, Kirsten Kinney, Tudy Woolfe, and Mark McDonough gave me the gift of honesty when I needed it, praise when I deserved it, and their unflagging support always. Thanks to my agent, Jill Marsal for her encouragement, persistence and wisdom. Finally, thanks to my family. My son Will believed in me when I didn't; my daughter, Megan, was as unstinting with her encouragement as she was with her advice; and my wife, Linda, was my sternest critic, my staunchest ally, and my partner in this as in all things.

Made in the USA
Lexington, KY
08 April 2013